In a Heartbeat

Donna Richards

A Samhain Publishing, Ltd. publication.

Samhain Publishing, Ltd.
512 Forest Lake Drive
Warner Robins, GA 31093
www.samhainpublishing.com

In A Heartbeat
Copyright © 2006 by AUTHOR
Print ISBN: 1-59998-636-1
Digital ISBN: 1-59998-493-3

Editing by Jessica Bimberg
Cover by Scott Carpenter

This book is a work of fiction. The names, characters, places, and incidents are products of the writer's imagination or have been used fictitiously and are not to be construed as real. Any resemblance to persons, living or dead, actual events, locale or organizations is entirely coincidental.

All Rights Are Reserved. No part of this book may be used or reproduced in any manner whatsoever without written permission, except in the case of brief quotations embodied in critical articles and reviews.

First Samhain Publishing, Ltd. electronic publication: March 2007
First Samhain Publishing, Ltd. print publication: January 2008

Prologue

"Perfect."

He slipped his hand over his freshly shaved chin. Smooth. Pure. Clean. Not a scar, not a nick. Tilting his head for a better view, he noted the reflection of a plastic bag stuffed with a blood-soaked blouse, lacy panties slit to ribbons, and a denim mini-skirt tucked away in the corner. A smile tugged at his lips. He'd always been good with a razor.

Behind him, a television in the cheap motel room blasted some early morning talk show. The loud volume masked the sound of his movements through the thin motel walls. No one would know he was gone until housekeeping checked the room. By then he'd have crossed the state line, long before anyone discovered a naked woman with her throat slit, slowly decomposing in the middle of a soybean field. Perfect.

He carefully dressed, then checked the room to make certain nothing incriminating remained behind. His hand lingered on the doorknob when the word "transplant" stopped his egress and pulled his attention to the television.

"Dr. Lewis, are you suggesting that memories are embedded in our vital organs?" A woman in a beige suit looked skeptical. "Like words on paper?"

"Well, I'm not sure about your analogy, but yes. There are documented cases." A young man in a white lab coat stiffened in his chair, adjusting his glasses.

"Can you give us some examples?"

"I know personally of one man who, after receiving a new heart, began dreaming of a young woman named Martha."

"Surely, there's nothing unusual about a man dreaming about a woman." The woman eased back in her chair, chuckling at her own wit.

"Yes, but this man didn't know any woman named Martha." The doctor leaned forward, a smile played about the outer corners of his mouth. "Martha, you see, was the fiancée of the heart donor. The recipient had no knowledge of the donor. The memories came from his new heart."

"But that's incredible," the woman said, clearly astonished. "Does that happen all the time?"

"No," sniffed the doctor. "But it happens enough to defy coincidence."

"And does this happen with other organs?"

The doctor's response was lost in the screaming of his brain. Other organs were of no concern. A cold fury built in his chest. The implication that a heart, a donated heart from a dead lifeless body, could remember the man responsible for its demise chased all other thoughts from his mind.

"Miranda, you, bitch!" With a swing of his arm, he threw the plastic bag of clothes across the room, toppling a lamp and a glass of water.

"How can you do this to me?" he ranted. "Do you have any idea how long I planned your murder? Down to the most minuscule detail." He pressed his thumb and forefinger together as if lecturing her ghost. "It was unparalleled. Perfect."

He paced the small room, stabbing his fingers through his hair. "You should have died faster. No one would want your dead cold heart then. You'd be dead and buried and that would be that." He stopped in front of the long mirror of the bureau and screamed at his reflection. "You should have died faster!"

He sunk onto the bed, cradling his head in his hands. Rocking slowly back and forth, he whispered to himself, calming the violent shaking in his body, quieting the laughter he heard ringing in his ears.

"It's okay. Ssh... She won't talk from the grave. I can fix it. I'll fix everything." The rocking ceased, and he glanced up at the mirror. "I'll fix it. Just like always."

Chapter One

"Seriously, it's not a problem." Angela raised her voice for the car phone as she jammed a few stray tendrils up under her gray chauffeur's cap. She guided her brother's sleek white limousine under the portico of the downtown Hyatt. "I'm already here."

"I really appreciate this, Angie." The dispatcher's voice filled the car. "I didn't know who else to call with your brother out of town. Annie's little girl was sick and I told her—"

"It's okay, Ed," Angie said. "A sick little girl needs her mother."

"That's right. You would know... I forgot you had a heart transplant."

Angie grimaced behind the steering wheel. How could she ever expect to experience life like a normal person if everyone knew of her condition? Her family already treated her like a piece of delicate spun glass.

"What's it like almost dying? Were you scared?"

Angie stared at the car phone, surprised at the intimate question. In truth, she knew too many patients who died waiting for a donor organ. She'd come to terms with death. But life...

"Gotta go, Ed. The client's name is H.P. Renard the third, right? Rhymes with hard?"

She heard something like "yup" before she pushed the button to end the call. Showtime.

"Angel-face." A grinning bellhop, several years her junior, hustled to her door. "Long time, no see. Where's Stephen?"

5

She stepped out of the car, returning Brian's wide smile. "He's driving Mom down to Florida. I'm filling in."

"As you do so well." Brian said with an appreciative once-over.

Angie felt the blush blossoming on her cheeks, mentally cursing the pale complexion that exposed each and every emotion.

The sudden swirl of the revolving door halted their conversation. Brian whistled low under his breath. Angela numbly nodded her head in agreement. She had thumbed through enough magazines during her convalescence to recognize a high fashion model when she saw one, even if the model was shoving her way through a revolving door.

"How can you expect me to move to this cow town?" The model whined as soon as her escort emerged from the whirling doors. "There's no parties, no clubs. What am I supposed to do?"

"Quiet, Liz. You just got here," the man lightly scolded. "You haven't given Columbus much of a chance."

"Philip dear, can't you just commute from New York? Just take one of those little planes and come home for the weekends."

Angela held the passenger door open, awed by the famous Elizabeth Everett. Stephen had often regaled the family with stories about the famous people who had ridden in one of his cars, but this was her first celebrity.

The model's full-length mink coat flapped open, revealing a tall, willowy body wrapped in sensuous black silk. She towered over Angela, casting her a brief, bored appraisal before slipping elegantly into the dark interior of the limo. It happened so quickly, Angie forgot for a moment that the car was ordered for Renard, not Everett.

"I'm sorry, Mr.—" She began, unsure how to politely insist the man remove his date from the car.

"Renard," the man supplied. Angela glanced up, surprised by eyes the color of slate warmed by the afternoon sun. He radiated the self-confidence and calm control of a man well used to the lush leather interior and darkened privacy of a limousine. Impeccably dressed in a tuxedo, he stood quietly assessing her. "You must forgive Elizabeth's urban attitude. She's not good with change."

"Of course," Angie mumbled, resisting the urge to moisten her suddenly dry lips. How had she missed noticing this drop-dead gorgeous man earlier? "Sir," she added quickly. His air of authority demanded it even if he looked to be only a few years her senior.

He chuckled deep in this throat. A quiver flashed about her ribcage in response.

"Philip, come on. You're letting the cold air in," the model grumbled from inside the limo. Angela's short statue, together with her position behind the opened door, enabled her to look in at her passenger. The woman bent over a powdery substance sprinkled generously on the length of her raised finger. A moment later the substance was gone. Shocked, Angela quickly closed the door, barring Renard entrance.

"You and your date will have to find another ride, sir." Disgust tinged her voice. "We don't allow that kind of thing here."

"What kind of thing?" His brows lifted, a dimple flashed briefly before his gaze shifted to the closed door. "What are you talking about?"

"Drugs," Angela hissed, keeping her voice low. "This may not be New York, but we have our standards." She nodded towards Brian standing just inside the Hyatt entrance. "Brian can call you a cab."

The man's eyes narrowed, two dark slits that chilled her more than the cool September wind. He stepped around her and yanked the limo door open. "What the hell are you talking about?" His bulk filled the tiny doorway. "There are no drugs in here." Straightening, he turned and faced Angela. "I don't know what your game is, lady, but there are no drugs in that car. We're running late for a dinner engagement. So if you don't mind—"

"I do mind." She stretched out all of her five foot four inches. "I know what I saw."

The man's glare worked like a battering ram. She braced against the solid support of the limo door, wishing some of the steel would magically osmose into her trembling legs.

"You know I could have your job for this," he said.

"Yes, sir," she squeezed out between tightly clenched teeth. No need to tell him this wasn't her regular job.

Their gazes locked. Her knees weakened. If the issue was anything but drug use she wasn't sure she could hold her ground.

"Elizabeth," he shouted, not breaking eye contact with Angela. "There's been a change in plans. We're taking a cab."

"But Philip—"

"Don't talk to me, Elizabeth. Just come."

He turned and stormed back to the hotel entrance. The man's tone made it clear he expected to be obeyed.

"So much for my big tip," Angela murmured to the breeze slapping at her cheeks. She held the rear door as her famous passenger bolted from the backseat and chased after her date. Alone at the curb, she slumped against the car, bewildered and exhausted from the unexpected confrontation.

"Are you all right?" Brian walked briskly to the curb, casting a worried glance at her chest. "Should I call someone? Stephen?"

Angela rolled her eyes to the heavens. "I'm fine, Brian. Just fine." She slammed the door shut. "It'll take more than threats from a pompous, New York, third-generation jackass to bother this heart of mine." She yanked the chauffeur's cap off her head, freeing the mass of pale blonde hair.

Brian smiled wanly and signaled for a cab. Slipping back into the driver's seat, Angela reached for the car phone. Better Stephen heard the news from her than a disgruntled client.

CR♥80

The next morning, she walked through the double doors of Falstaff and Watterson, Certified Public Accountants, knowing full well her face broadcast her sleepless night. She blamed that man, the third something or other, for the weariness about her eyes. Every time she'd drifted to sleep, steely gray eyes would haunt her, reducing her once again to the vulnerable, powerless invalid she had been before her transplant. She'd awaken with a start, reassured by the fierce pounding of her heart. As long as it maintained that steady, consistent thump, she was alive. She was strong. Then she'd close her eyes, and he'd be back. Intimidating. Powerful. She shivered.

"Angie, did you get the word?" Max, one of the junior auditors, greeted shortly after she dropped off her purse and audit bag in her cubicle. "Falstaff is looking for you."

"Shoot." An anticipatory tremor slipped down her spine. The grapevine had buzzed all day yesterday about one firing resulting from the weak economy. Angie wasn't immune to the whispers. A surprise summons from the firm's partner rarely meant good news.

Angie paused outside Falstaff's office and sent a quick prayer skyward. *Please, don't let him fire me. I need this job.* She pressed her hand to her chest, reassured by the steady beat of a stranger's healthy heart. Truth be told, she'd work for the medical benefits alone.

She lifted a fist to knock on the oak doorframe, then noticed a few stray dog hairs on her jacket sleeve. "Oreo," she grumbled, hastily brushing her sleeve before peeking around the portal. "Mr. Falstaff? You wanted to see me?"

"Um-hmm," he spoke into the phone receiver pressed tight to one ear. With his bifocals pushed up on his wide, balding head, he had the appearance of some mutant insect sporting four eyes. He gestured her in, then swiveled his chair toward one of the windows.

Angie slipped silently into one of the stiff-backed padded chairs immediately in front of his desk. She'd been in this office before, of course. No staff accountant managed to completely avoid this gut-wrenching experience. She glanced at the volumes of accounting and business texts lining the floor-to-ceiling bookcases and began to count. She'd already estimated the number of ceiling tiles on earlier visits.

"I see." Falstaff drummed his fingers on a manila folder on his desk. "We were planning to begin our interim work out there tomorrow. Is that still on?"

Her eyes followed Falstaff's repetitive tapping to the folder beneath, a folder with her name typed boldly on the tab. Her personnel file? She gulped, her pulse quickened. *What did I do?*

"How about we meet first thing tomorrow morning? Good. My team will be there." Falstaff's chair straightened with a noisy squeal before he spun back to the desk. "I'll look forward to meeting him. Take care, Jim"

He hung up the receiver, then slid his glasses down from their perch to rest properly on his nose. "That was Jim Owens, owner of Hayden Distributing. Sounds like they finally hired a new Chief Executive Officer."

"A new CEO," Angie said, nodding absently, her eyes locked on the folder. "I thought they would promote Tom Wilson. He's been there forever." *Why am I here?*

"I guess John wants to shake things up a bit. You were planning to start out there tomorrow, weren't you?" She nodded, her throat too constricted to speak. "I thought so. Looks like I'll see you there, but that's not why I called you in."

He hunched forward, rounding his back like a man who had spent most of his fifty-plus years studying workpapers. "Jim Stevens turned in his resignation today."

"He wasn't fired?" Angela gasped, letting relief wash through her. Resigned sounded much less threatening. Falstaff glanced at her quizzically, then opened the folder.

"According to your personnel file, you've got the technical qualifications to move into his old position." Falstaff smiled across the desk. "You're a very good accountant but we have several good accountants. You have limited management experience and virtually no marketing presence."

"The Audit Manager position requires marketing abilities?" Still numb from his unsolicited compliment, she struggled to focus on his words.

"It does if you plan to be promoted beyond the manager position." Falstaff frowned. "These are hard times and if this firm hopes to survive, we need to attract new clients."

He stood and paced behind the desk. "We need to look professional, act professional, and be on the lookout for extended service opportunities. We want to help the client expand his bottom line," he smiled over at her, "and ours, of course. Take this new CEO, for example. You should be thinking how you can make the best impression on him. This, after all, is the man who'll decide if we'll perform the audit next year."

Angie shifted uncomfortably, feeling the promotion opportunity drift away before it was ever really hers. She knew how to push the numbers, but salesmanship was something else entirely.

"Tell you what." Falstaff braced both arms on his desk and leaned toward her. "Let's make this Hayden job something of a test. If you can bring in the job, within budget and without compromising quality, *and* you make a good impression on this new CEO...I'll personally recommend you for the Audit Manager's position."

A promotion? Her mouth numbed. Her lips refused to move. Not only wasn't she to be fired, but maybe she'd even be promoted. Tears stung the corners of her eyes. The increased money couldn't come at a better time. She'd be able to move out of her mother's house and finally live independently like a normal twenty-six year old.

"Thank you, Mr. Falstaff," she gushed as she accepted his outstretched hand. She vigorously pumped it up and down. "I won't disappoint you. I promise."

"I'm sure you won't."

Chapter Two

By the time she arrived at Hayden Distributing, Max had already set up shop in the conference room. Stacks of manila folders, a nondescript audit briefcase, and a network of power cables to feed their laptop computers covered a long oak table.

"Have you seen Falstaff?" she asked with a little trepidation. She draped her trench coat over the back of an adjacent chair.

"I think we're the first," Max replied, "I haven't been here long myself, but Beth said..."

"Beth?"

"The receptionist." Max smiled. "You probably waved to her on the way in here." He tugged on the bottom of his striped tie. "I just spent a few minutes checking to see what's new."

Angela sighed. When Max turned on the power of those long lashes, few girls stood a chance. The receptionist would just be another in a long line of conquests.

"Hayden Distributing hired us to audit their financials, Max, not to flirt with their personnel." She unpacked her own briefcase and added a stack of papers to the items on the table. "Just be careful you don't get caught. You know the rules."

"Relax." Max leaned back with a lazy smile. "I'm just being friendly. Besides, I doubt a receptionist makes key financial decisions. Even "fuddy-duddy" Falstaff can't believe Beth is a breech of independence."

"Independence is an important ethical principal among accounting firms," she lectured, crossing to the opposite side of the room. "If it even looks like you might have a reason not to be objective on the job, or that someone connected to the company could be influencing your decisions, you could be reassigned or fired."

"Or both?" Max teased.

She smiled, mentally stepping down from the soapbox. "Just be careful." She stooped, mindful of her short skirt, to rifle through the boxy audit bag on the floor. "Have you seen that folder with—"

The conference room door flew open, sending loose documents sailing on the sudden air current.

"Let me introduce our audit team," Falstaff announced. Angela stood hastily, tugging discreetly at the back of her skirt.

"Angela, come over here," Falstaff beckoned. "I want you to meet—"

"You!" The masculine voice sent a shudder of expectancy down her spine.

She looked up to familiar steel gray eyes. Shock lodged in her throat.

"Is this some kind of joke?" Her disgruntled passenger from two nights ago looked her up and down. "I thought you said your people were well-qualified," he snarled to Falstaff.

"Angela is a wizard at analyzing data," Falstaff said. "Very competent. She's—"

"So grateful to be assigned to Hayden," Angela supplied, extending her hand for the ritual handshake. She forced a smile on her face. "Pleased to meet you, sir."

The memory of stumbling over the address two evenings ago warmed her cheeks.

His hand enclosed hers in a firm grip. *Please, please,* she tried to telepath. *Don't say you've met me before.* His gaze bore into her, but she held her own, enthusiastically pumping his hand.

His brow rose. "Angela?"

"Angela Blake, the auditor in-charge," Falstaff droned. "I assure you, her experience makes her uniquely qualified for this engagement. Max Keller over here is one of our newest hires."

Renard's hand squeezed hers. "We'll discuss your 'unique qualifications' another time." Smiling tightly, he dropped the handshake. A shiver tripped down her spine. She hadn't left the frying pan yet.

"What exactly constitutes interim testing?" he asked.

Falstaff jumped in to answer. "We need to test our understanding of your accounting systems to make sure our year-end procedures will be effective."

He addressed his question to Angela. "So you'll be—?"

"Flowcharting your systems, interviewing your personnel. Once we've documented how paperwork flows through the company, we'll run a few checks to see if our understanding is correct."

"I see." He stepped back and considered her. Angela felt the familiar wavering in her knees. The man made the very air ripple with authority. "I need to acquaint myself with the systems as well. No need to make unnecessary demands on the department heads by doing two interviews. I'm meeting with Tom Wilson in his office at ten o'clock. Be there."

"But I've already scheduled an appointment for –"

Falstaff interrupted. "Excellent idea, Henry. Angela will be happy to accompany you."

Her mouth hung open. Henry? Didn't that woman call him Phillip before? Renard raised an eyebrow in her direction.

"Are we through here, Bill?" Renard asked. "I want to talk with Jim Owens before he leaves for the airport."

"Mr. Owens is here?" Angie asked. She knew he owned the company, but she had never so much as seen the man.

Falstaff clapped Renard on the back as if they were old friends and not recent acquaintances. "He came in to introduce his new CEO." He turned to Renard. "I'll walk you down the hall. I need to head back to the office myself."

Renard nodded curtly to each of them. "Ms. Blake. Max. It's been a pleasure." They were gone as quickly as they had arrived. The conference door closed quietly behind them. Angela leaned on the table for support, expelling her captive breath in an audible sigh.

"What was that all about?" Max asked.

"What do you mean?" She took a deep breath, catching the lingering traces of a deep woodsy scent, *his* scent.

"That Renard guy looked at you like he wanted to tie you to the rack."

A fit description, she thought. "I've met Mr. Renard and his date before under unflattering circumstances."

"Unflattering for who? You, or the avenging warrior?"

Avenging warrior, how apropos. She closed her eyes. That Brooks Brothers suit was a thin layer of civilization over a more primitive individual determined to mete out punishment.

Punishment! Her eyes flew open. That squeeze before he ended the handshake. Those steely eyes that broadcast his disapproval of her to everyone in the room. Punishment was exactly what he had in mind, and ten o'clock was the time for execution.

Renard waited till the door to the conference room closed before allowing himself the slightest suggestion of a smile. So the little minx was moonlighting as a limo driver. No wonder she stood her ground so courageously. He had to admire her for that. In fact, he'd backed down out of appreciation of the elfin chauffeur's stalwart principles and the knowledge that Elizabeth might have had drugs, even though she swore to him she'd abandoned the practice. That disturbing thought pulled the smile from his face. He'd have to deal with that possibility later; he had more immediate concerns at the moment.

Falstaff, who had been talking nonstop about the weather, the town, and who knows what else, extended his arm for the obligatory handshake. Renard brought his thoughts back to the present and responded accordingly. He had just a few minutes to catch Owens before his interview with Wilson. *Our interview*, he amended with a tiny burst of anticipation and a quick glance down the hall towards the conference room.

After cramming an hour's worth of review in the fifteen allotted minutes before their "shared" interview, Angie sat on the edge of a padded office chair utilizing a tiny corner of the controller's desk for her notepad. Renard, she noticed, had no qualms about taking up vast quantities of space. He leaned back next to her in a similar chair, resting one ankle on the opposite knee. His highly polished wingtip nearly brushed her kneecap.

"Sorry to keep you waiting." Tom Wilson, a distinguished, gray-haired gentleman with a faint southern accent, appeared at the doorway with a full coffee mug in hand. "My meeting with Purchasing ran a little long." He exchanged handshakes with Renard, passed completely by Angela and took up position behind his desk.

"Did you catch the game last Saturday?" he asked Renard, referring to the local university football game. Without a professional team to call its own, Columbus sports fans followed the college circuit with a passion.

Renard shook his head, "Although, now that I'm taking up residence here, I guess I'm going to get reacquainted with the Buckeyes."

"You went to Ohio State, didn't you?" Wilson asked Angela.

The question surprised her as she was beginning to feel ignored. "Yes, but I—"

"Heck of a team, those Buckeyes. Now, what exactly are we here to discuss?"

The acute dismissal lodged in her gut and rendered her speechless. Renard cleared his throat. "Basically, we'd like you to walk through the accounting systems and reports so we can get an overall view of the system."

Although Wilson acknowledged Angela's presence with an occasional nod, the meeting was clearly staged for Renard. Angela seethed as she took notes. How could Renard regard her as a peer, if she was already reduced to the role of secretary? Tom finished his exposition on how product was shipped from the vendor to the warehouse with a flurry of statistics no doubt gleaned from the stacks of computer printouts on his desk.

"Excuse me," Angie interrupted.

"Yes, ma'm?" Tom smiled with a patronizing glint to his eye. "Am I going too fast? Would you like me to repeat that last ratio?"

"I was wondering if everything flowed through the warehouse?"

Tom pulled forward and picked up a pen on the desk. "I'm not sure I know what you mean...?"

"I believe I saw mention in the workpapers about something called a direct ship."

If Renard hadn't been sitting so close, she might have missed his slight shift in her direction. As it was, she welcomed his attention. Now she could show the arrogant bastard that she knew her stuff.

"Oh, direct ships." Tom relaxed, a wide grin on his face. "For a moment there, I thought maybe you were suggesting we were diverting merchandise." He chuckled, glancing over at Renard. "I was going to have to see about gaining my fair share."

Again, Angela fumed over the joke made at her expense. Tom Wilson leaned back in his chair. "Honey, direct ships happen when the merchandise goes directly from the vendor to the customer. It's shipped direct, you see."

She could feel the tips of her ears heat. "So the answer is yes, some of the merchandise bypasses the warehouse."

"I suppose you could put it that way." He smiled a sort of half-smile at Renard.

Angela felt her self-esteem oozing away like coffee out of an upended mug. She had to do something to staunch the flow. A printout on Wilson's desk titled Vendor Masterfile caught her attention.

"One other question," she added. "When someone makes a change to the vendor masterfile, is a report printed out?" Tom nodded his head, his patronizing smile still in place. "And do you initial it to designate your approval?"

"Ms. Blake," Renard interrupted, "I'd like to see you in my office for a moment."

"I have a few more questions for Mr. Wilson," she protested.

"Now," he insisted.

She rose and silently followed him out of the office and down the hall. He closed the door behind her and leaned in close. Too close. The scent of his woodsy cologne transported her back to their previous confrontation at the Hyatt. Only this time, she didn't have the support of a limo door to reinforce her shaky knees.

"These questions of yours are a waste of time," Renard stated without preamble.

"What are you talking about?" She bristled. "I'm following the standard audit questionnaires to determine internal control strengths and weaknesses." There. He had to respect that she had established procedures on her side.

"Then your standard questionnaires are asinine. Who cares if some printout is initialed or not."

That hurt. His lack of appreciation drained some of the wind from her sails, but she still rallied. "It's visible proof that someone did their job. How else do you know that someone checked the report for improper changes?"

"You trust them to do their job." His tone, low and cold, held more command than if he had shouted. "All initials prove is someone has an ego problem."

Takes one to recognize one. She clenched her jaw to keep from repeating the childish refrain.

"You'll cease asking these useless questions immediately."

"I'm not your employee," she reminded him.

"Thank God for that." He glared. "I would hate my first official act as the new CEO to be to fire the auditors."

She felt the blood drain from her face. He could do that. He could fire the whole firm of Falstaff and Watterson if he wanted. She swallowed, backing up a step. One call and she'd lose her promotion and most likely her job.

"I'm sorry," he said, avoiding her gaze. He raised a hand to his forehead and stepped around the desk. "I shouldn't have said that."

"I'm only doing my job," she said around the lump in her throat. "I can have Max ask these questions if you prefer, but I need to have the answers to document any internal control weaknesses."

"Internal control weaknesses?" He raised his gaze to hers. His eyes narrowed slightly. "Do you really think not initialing some report is an internal control weakness?" She nodded, though without enthusiasm. He braced his arms on his desk. "Or maybe you're looking for things that aren't there, like drugs in a limousine."

"Is that what this is about?" Her spine stiffened. This reprimand wasn't about business after all. "You're still upset about the other night?"

In a Heartbeat

An awkward pause hung in the air. Renard sighed and his shoulders sagged a bit. Angela noted dark shadows under his eyes that she hadn't noticed earlier. "Look," he said. "I'm just suggesting that some of your questions are targeted at the wrong things. This company is losing money and that's not because someone forgot to initial a report."

"Well, thank you for your observations of my professional prowess, Mr. Renard. I'll take your observations under consideration." *Like hell I will.* She turned to storm out of the office.

"One more thing," he shuffled papers around on his desk, "when you are interviewing or working with my people, you will wear pants or a longer skirt."

She stopped abruptly, and turned. Heat flared from her face. "You think my skirt is too short?"

"How you dress on your time is your business. But I'm trying to do a job here and I can't do it if my male executives are drooling over your legs." He glanced up at her. "You can go now."

Clutching her legal pad to her chest as if it were a shield, she backed out of Renard's office. She was still swearing under her breath when she returned to the conference room.

"Hey, boss lady," Max greeted her. "Your mother call—Whoa, are you all right?"

"What do you mean?" Angie asked, catching her breath after her stormy retreat down the hall.

"Your face is bright red." He pushed back the chair and stood by her elbow. "Do you need your pills? Maybe you should sit down."

Now that he mentioned it, she did feel flushed and her heart... Well, her heart reminded her that there were worse things in life than Renard, although at the moment she couldn't think of one. Still she didn't need Max fawning over her like an invalid.

"I'm fine, Max." She took a deep breath. "Just give me some air. I had another run-in with the arrogant egomaniac."

"Renard," Max supplied with a knowing glance. "You know, Angie, all the secretaries and clerks like him. A lot. You're the only female in this building who can't seem to get along with the guy."

"That's because the rest of the women don't have to work closely with him." She pushed herself away from the wall and walked over to the pink pile of phone messages left by her computer. "If they did, they'd know better." She picked up the top note. "My mother called?"

"Yeah, about ten minutes ago. She said it wasn't important but to call her when you can. So what did he say this time?"

"He said I was wasting his staff's time and, Max, can I ask you a question?" She shifted uncomfortably. "I need your honest opinion."

"Sure, Angie, what's up?"

"Do you think this suit is professional and appropriate for work?" She worried her lip, hoping he'd give her the answer she wanted.

"I'm not the fashion police but I think you look great."

His wide smile gave her the confidence to narrow his response. "And the skirt, you don't think my skirt is too short?"

"I'm not complaining."

"Max." A bit of doubt dampened her sense of righteousness. "Be serious."

"I am serious. You've got the best set of legs in the office." He gave her a thumbs up.

Her heart sank. His overzealous response revealed what his words didn't. How was she supposed to get through the rest of the afternoon when all she wanted was to hide under the conference room table? She lifted her trench coat from the back of the chair and slipped her arms in the sleeves.

"Now you're cold?" He frowned. "Are you sure you're feeling all right? Maybe I should call your brother."

"My brother?" She narrowed her eyes. "How do you know my brother?"

"From the company picnic last July, remember? He played right field." Max visibly withered under her glare. "He just happened to mention that if ever you needed help or anything, you know, due to your condition, he said I should call him."

"He did, did he." A weight heavier than that of the khaki trench settled on her shoulders.

"He also said you'd be pretty ticked if I mentioned it to you." Max's voice dropped. "Sorry about that."

She buried her face in her hands. Her eyes burned. She might as well be back in that hospital bed with absolutely no privacy and unable to do the simplest thing for herself.

"Angie?"

Still, her heartbeat pounded in her ears, reminding her of the foolishness of that feeling. If only the others could hear the strength of that beat.

She pulled her hands away from her face and clasped them together in front of her. "You don't have to call Stephen." She chose her words carefully, not wanting to lash out at Max. "He sometimes forgets I'm not the little invalid I once was."

"Angie, I didn't mean to—"

She held up her hand to silence him. "I know, I know. If ever I feel I'm in need of medical assistance, I'll let you know. But I promise you, this isn't one of them." Max looked so mournful she didn't know whether to laugh or cry.

She picked up the stack of telephone messages. The one from her mother probably was to make sure that she was dressed warm enough, or that she had taken her meds, or that she had gas in the car. Angie sighed. She thought a thousand miles between them would have eliminated this daily game of twenty questions. Apparently not.

She picked up the next pink sheet. Panic spiked through her. "The office called?"

"Yeah, Falstaff wants you to stop by tomorrow morning."

She recalled Renard's threat. A tremor sped down her spine. He couldn't have. Not this fast.

"How'd the interview go?" Max asked.

"Hmm... The interview?" She glanced up. "Not so well. And," she frowned at her watch, "I have a whole twenty minutes till the next one." She slumped in her chair. "I may not survive." Her fingers slipped to her chest, lightly sliding up and down the scar beneath her blouse, while she pondered alternatives. "Max?"

"Yeah?"

"What do you think would happen if I asked Falstaff to transfer me to another job?"

"I think it would be rotten timing, looking for work right before the holidays," he said, half-in-jest.

"I'm serious, Max." Maybe she could prove her marketing skills on a job without the insufferable Mr. Renard.

Max leaned back in his chair. "One of the secretaries told me that Bennett did that once."

"Bennett? Why, he's been in the same position since Falstaff was a manager."

Max nodded. "That's what I heard. He asked for a transfer and they transferred him right off the promotion track."

Ouch. If that were true, she'd have to tough out this assignment. A promotion was more than a financial brass ring. It would prove to her family that she was independent, capable of handling everything that came her way, including the Renards of the world. That thought pulled at the corners of her mouth.

She picked up the phone handset and punched in the numbers to the office. All too quickly Falstaff's voice rang in her ear.

"Angela, how are things progressing?"

"Fine, sir. Max and I are right on budget."

He sighed in her ear. "I'm not talking about the budget. I was a little concerned about Renard's reaction when he met you earlier. Is everything going smoothly?"

"Smoothly, yes, sir." Her stomach tightened with the lie.

"I don't need to remind you how important Hayden is to this firm, Angela. I'd like to impress Renard with a good strong letter of recommendations. Keep your eyes open."

"Yes, sir." She replaced the receiver after cursory goodbyes.

"What's up?" Max asked.

"Falstaff wanted to remind us to document points for the rec letter." She scrambled around for prior year's files. "I want to track my notes against the documentation from last year. No one initials the vendor masterfile report for changes, and I didn't see any signoffs on the bank reconciliation."

"The ol' lack of documentation review point." Max shook his head. "Those always seemed so lame to me."

Angie stopped her shuffling and looked hard at Max. She would have choked him if she could reach him. "It's still important."

"Maybe, but it sure isn't sexy."

Chapter Three

The brisk chill winds of the workweek gave way to a warm weekend, uncharacteristic of early October. Only a fool would not take advantage of nature's early gift, and Angela was no fool. After her stress-laden week, a walk in the flame-splashed woods that bordered the reservoir seemed therapeutic. She even knew the perfect spot, a secluded section a short walk from an isolated parking lot. For years this had been her refuge, her sanctuary away from an over-protective family and her own struggle to be normal.

She steered the car into a deserted parking lot. Oreo jumped back and forth over the front car seat in fevered anticipation of a romp through the woods. "I suppose there's no harm in letting you off the leash." Angela looked about, verifying there were no strangers around to object. "Looks like we're all alone."

She opened the car door, escaping only seconds before twenty pounds of black and white fur. Oreo raced on ahead, stopping a few feet away to sniff at the innocuous ground. Angela retrieved the dog leash from the front seat, just in case, before closing the car door.

They walked together through the woods bordering the reservoir, Angela lost in her thoughts over the past week, Oreo lost in the titillating smells of leaf mold and wild animal. The dog trotted ahead of her, sniffing at rotting logs and upturning piles of brown leaves with her nose before chasing a surprised chipmunk or squirrel. Accustomed to her forays, Angela paid little attention until Oreo's mad dash through a low clump of bushes generated a very human, and very male, cry of alarm. She ran after Oreo through the bushes.

"What in the— Oreo!"

Angela's foot caught in the low branch of a bush, propelling her forward, head first into a blur of flannel.

She landed face down in a strange man's crotch.

"Don't move!" A strained voice, forced and breathless, warned. Taut denim brushed the humiliating heat of her cheeks. She breathed the deep, musky scent of the man's most intimate parts. Oreo would be proud, she thought with a shudder.

If only her limp body could somehow dissolve into the ground, she wouldn't have to eventually see this poor man's face.

"I'm so sorry," she said, but the words were lost in the stream of obscenities overhead. The man took a deep breath, inadvertently causing her head to sink deeper into the warm nest of his thighs.

"Jesus." His voice regained some control and depth, and for an instant, seemed vaguely familiar. "Are you all right?"

Soothing fingers gently pulled at her hair, exposing an ear and part of her cheek to the air and the searching thrust of Oreo's cold, wet nose. "Shoo." He pushed the dog away. "Did you hurt anything?"

My pride, she wanted to scream.

She turned her head, acutely aware that her chin dragged up the inside of a very muscular thigh. Pushing her hand against the ground, she struggled to sit up until a sharp pain slammed up her leg.

"My ankle," she groaned.

"Don't move," he commanded again. She froze as his thighs jostled beneath her. A steady hand cradled her chin briefly. "Here, rest your head on this." The synthetic lining of a jacket replaced his hand. He slipped out from under her.

First, she saw retreating denim, then the muddy bank of the reservoir, then his shadow stretching over her onto the bank beyond. She gulped. It must be a trick of the light that his shoulders spanned that impressive width. The shadow doubled over, hands on knees.

"Are you okay?" she asked.

"Catching my breath." His voice still sounded a bit shaky.

He dropped to one knee. "For a little bit of a thing, you sure pack a wallop." She turned her head from side to side, but he was too far back for her to see.

"Which ankle?"

"The right." He worked the laces of her hiking boot and gently tugged it free. Oreo pressed her furry body tight against her side, worming her dog head under her arm.

"Stop that," Angela scolded. "You're going to be a mess, scooting along the bank like that." Oreo responded by inching up higher.

"What kind of dog is that?" the man asked, peeling back her sock.

"A mutt," she answered, trying to keep her lips clear of the advancing dog nose.

"Well, that mutt scared the hell out of me." Strong fingers gingerly touched her ankle. She stiffened in reflex. "It's pretty swollen," he said. "Could be broken, or maybe a bad sprain. Can you wiggle your toes?"

She complied, but hissed as pain radiated though her ankle.

"I think I'd better take you to have this checked." He laid the injured foot back down. "The problem is I'm new in town. You'll have to tell me where to take you."

The voice clicked. She rolled to her back and pushed up on her elbows, ignoring the throbbing pain. The friendly gray eyes, the dimple in the right cheek. She gasped.

"Heavens no, not you!" Her head dropped back onto his jacket. "Tell me this isn't happening."

"Angela?" The name stumbled out. Recognition drained the warmth from his smile. "What are you doing here?"

"What do you think?" She pushed Oreo away from doing a happy dance on her chest. "I should ask what you're doing here. You shouldn't even know this place exists."

"Fishing." He stood and walked toward the water's edge. "At least I was until your dog jumped me." Bending, he picked up the remnants of a fishing pole from the bank.

"In October?" she asked, bewildered.

"It helps me think," he snarled, examining the broken halves of his pole. Slapping the two skinny sticks against his open palm, he marched back to her. "Look, is someone paying you to make my life miserable, or am I just lucky where you're concerned?"

Angela rolled to her knees, wincing from the pain in her ankle. "If you'll just hand me Oreo's leash, I think it flew out of my hand over there." She pointed with her chin. "We'll leave you to think in peace."

"I doubt that," he muttered, stooping to collect the leash. "How are you going to walk with your ankle swollen?"

She retrieved her boot from the ground and pushed herself up, balancing awkwardly on her left foot. "Perhaps you could find me a stout stick?" she asked hopefully.

He mumbled something she couldn't quite catch, but the damning tilt of his brows translated for her. Tossing his broken pole under a tree, he marched toward her. Her breath caught, her pulse pounding in time to the throbbing of her ankle.

"Don't you think you've done enough damage?" With alarming ease, he swooped her off the ground and into his arms. "You need a stick to finish me off?"

"I didn't mean—" She wasn't sure what to do with her hands. At first they fluttered up to his shoulders by instinct, her boot almost whacking him in the head in the process. She opted to keep very still.

He continued down the bank, the dog trotting merrily behind. "I said I'd take you someplace to have that ankle checked and I meant it."

"But we're going the wrong way," she protested. "My car is in the lot on the other side of the woods."

"My car is closer. You can have someone come back later to get your car."

"I can't." She pushed away from him slightly to make her point. "My purse is in the car. My medicine—"

"You're sick?" He stopped and studied her face. "You don't look sick."

"It's personal." She buried her head back in his shoulder so he couldn't see her face. "I have to keep my medicine with me. It's important."

"All right. We'll drive over to your car and collect your purse and your medicine before going to have that ankle x-rayed. Any more objections?"

She shook her head, relieved to see a car parked nearby. Perhaps with a little distance between them, she could regain some semblance of control.

⋘⋙

Severe sprain, the doctor said. Keep it elevated, put ice on the swelling, and don't walk on it for at least 24 hours. On Monday, after the swelling went down, she was to see an orthopedic doctor. With those words of wisdom, a pair of crutches and an elastic stocking to control the swelling, she was discharged from the clinic.

Renard had only raised an eyebrow when the nurses had recognized her on sight. And if he thought it strange that they had listened to her chest and took her blood pressure before looking at her foot, he didn't comment. He chuckled with the rest of them when the doctor pronounced this "a common injury". His absence of questions made the ride home a bit awkward but now as they sat in his car across from her house, the silence became downright annoying.

"You live here all alone?" he asked, assessing the old two-story brick building.

"I live with my mother." She reached behind the bucket seat, trying to grasp the crutches in the back, but Oreo kept interfering. "But she's in Florida right now with my sick aunt." She pushed the furry head back, "Stop that."

"And your father?"

The question drew her up short. She stopped fishing for the crutches and glanced up into Renard's eyes. "He died about ten years ago. Heart failure."

"I'm sorry," he said, a bit awkwardly. He glanced about, at everything but her. Eventually, his gaze found the house.

"How do you plan to get up the porch steps?" He turned back toward her, one brow raised.

"I'll manage," she answered tersely, though in truth, she wondered the same thing.

"Isn't there someone who could help you, a neighbor, a significant other?"

She laughed at the suggestion of a boyfriend. "No, just Oreo and me." She scratched between the dog's floppy ears. "Right, girl?"

"And the dog?" He petted the furry white head as it extended further and further between the seats. Oreo's tail thumped out a rhythm against the back seat. "You'll be able to manage this terror on paws all alone while on crutches?"

That one stumped her for a moment. She supposed she could call Stephen. He should be back by now, but she dreaded the smothering attention that plea would bring. Wasn't she the one who had demanded independence? The one who had asked her family to stop interfering in her life as if she were still an invalid, too weak to do anything but ask for help?

"Is she housebroken?"

Indignity on behalf of her pet flooded her. "Of course she is," she snapped, "not that it should matter to—"

"Give me your keys."

"Excuse me?" Indignity on her own behalf made her twist sideways so she could face him. She scooted her back to the door to maintain distance. "Why do you want my keys?"

"The company provided me with a fully furnished ranch-style house to use until I find a place of my own." He spoke more to the windshield than to her face. "There are four bedrooms, no stairs to hobble up and down, and plenty of room for Fido here."

"Oreo," she corrected, "and the answer is no."

"Look, I'm not interested in anything but giving you an alternative to doing permanent damage to your ankle." He turned toward her. "The house is too big for one person." His lips turned up in a faint smile. "We wouldn't even have to see each other, if you like."

"Mr. Renard…"

"Hank," he interjected. She glanced up. "My friends call me Hank. And after our chance meeting this afternoon, you know parts of me better than my best friend."

She lowered her gaze, her memory of that meeting burning bright on her cheeks. "Okay, Hank. It's not that I don't appreciate your offer, but I can't afford to lose my job."

"Who said anything about losing your job?"

She looked up at him askance. "You did. Twice."

He dismissed her response with a wave of his hand. "I wasn't serious. You just...managed to catch me at a bad time."

Skeptical, she wondered if he ever had a *good* time. She took a breath. "If Falstaff and Watterson found out I was staying at your house, they'd fire me for certain."

"We're not meeting for some clandestine affair." He looked incredulous, as if the thought of her as a sexual partner was beneath consideration. The dismissal stabbed at her. "I'm only offering a spare bedroom. Why should that jeopardize your job?"

"Because of appearances." She fumbled with a button on her coat, afraid he might recognize her disappointment if he saw her face. "Even if it appears that we're not involved, then Falstaff and Watterson could question my objectivity. They might not trust my judgment when auditing your books."

"Let me get this straight." She heard laughter in his voice. "If you exercise some common sense and accept my offer, you get fired. But practically emasculating me, that's okay?" He hesitated. "And I pay you for this?"

She yanked on the door handle, wanting to run from his laughter.

"Wait." His hand grasped her thigh, stopping her exit. She froze. The heavy denim of her jeans felt almost sheer beneath his touch, especially as his fingers drew tiny circles on her leg.

"I'm sorry. I didn't mean to upset you." His voice, so gentle and apologetic, lured her acceptance, but she kept her face turned to the window so he couldn't see her hurt. "The truth is," he said, "the house I'm in is extremely private. More people have probably seen you sitting in my car here than will see you at my place."

That pulled her around. She hadn't considered how this innocent discussion might appear to someone driving by.

"I guarantee I won't say anything to Falstaff and Watterson." He raised his hand as if taking an oath. "Unless you tell them, I don't think your job is in jeopardy." His dimple deepened as his lips lifted in a smile. "After all, we both know your objectivity is uncompromised, at least as far as I'm concerned."

She looked into his eyes and for the first time wondered if that were true. Warmth spread from the base of her spine. The same protected, secure warmth that she had felt in his arms as he carried her effortlessly along the bank of the reservoir.

Oreo whimpered from the back seat. Angie slid out from under his hand. "We've got to go." She tugged Oreo forward. Using the toes of her injured foot for balance, she staggered out of the car.

"Wait a minute, let me help you," Hank called, his door already creaking open.

"No, I need to do this myself." Angela opened the back door, retrieved the crutches then braced herself for the hobble across the street.

"Will you at least turn a light on, or wave from your window, or something, so I know you got inside all right?"

She nodded her head and closed the car door.

He watched her step-swing-step across the street, Oreo trotting by her side. She managed to scale the porch steps and unlock the front door. She paused, then gave him a little wave. The late afternoon sun broke through the clouds, highlighting her pale blond hair as she disappeared into the dark forbidding house.

The memory of that silken hair flowing across his thighs on the muddy bank made his groin tighten. And her eyes, those clear, expressive blue eyes that in unguarded moments spoke of vulnerability and frailty. He glanced up at the dark windows. Frail. That's hardly the word he would have used when she plowed into him earlier. He chuckled. The last thing he had expected when he decided to sort his life out over the arch of a fishing pole was to play nursemaid to an elfin chauffeur/accountant. Damn. He meant to ask her about that. He glanced at the windows.

Still dark. Of course, the way things were going their paths had to cross again. The thought pleased him. It should scare him to death, he modified. First thing Monday he would check the provisions of his health insurance.

Health insurance. He frowned at the still dark windows. Medicine. What was all that about? She didn't look sick. She certainly hadn't felt sick when he held her in his arms. She felt good, too damn good. He gripped the steering wheel tighter. What was she trying to hide? He reached for the door handle. And why wasn't that damn light on?

He found her a few minutes later, sitting midway up a flight of steps, crying her eyes out.

Chapter Four

"Earth to Reggie, earth to Reggie." A young woman in a white lab coat smiled down on the dark-haired man seated at the reception counter.

"Excuse me?" He glanced up from his stack of papers, forgetting for a moment that his nametag said "Reggie", the alias he'd adopted for this position at the Organ Transplant Clinic.

"Aren't you the industrious one?" She leaned on the counter, flashing her cleavage his way. "Where is everybody? This place is like a tomb."

"One of girls is pregnant and the rest took her out to lunch to celebrate. I'm holding down the fort." *And doing a bit of investigation when you nosey bitches aren't around.*

"Well," she said with a sniff. "You must take this data entry job seriously. I've been standing here for five minutes already." She pouted. "Or are you ignoring me on purpose?"

"Never," he protested, searching his memory for the woman's name. Manipulation of fools could be so tiring. "You must be exaggerating. I could never ignore such an attractive woman." She practically purred at the praise. It never failed to amaze him how women fell for those insipid compliments.

"I must have been concentrating too hard on these numbers." His finger tapped the computer monitor. "I key these long chains of numbers all day and get to wondering if there's any rhyme or reason for them."

"Oh, I can tell you that, silly." She slipped around the counter and leaned over, almost buffeting his nose with her breast. "See, these numbers tell you what hospital the organ came from." She pointed to the first block of digits in a thirteen-digit case identification number. "This series tells you what was transported." She glanced to her side. "One donor can provide organs and tissue for more than two hundred people, did you know that?"

"Wow, that many." Pretending to care, he leaned back a bit in his chair. "It's a wonder that anyone would have a problem getting a transplant with that kind of efficiency."

"Well, not everyone agrees to donating. And then there's the timing factor."

"Timing factor?" he prodded.

She nodded. "Certain organs have a limited life span. Hearts, for instance, have to be implanted within six hours from the time they're harvested. Even then there's no guarantee the recipient's body won't reject the new heart."

He smiled, silently thanking Miss Whoever-You-Are for providing this important piece of information. Knowing that his search would be limited to within six hours of Miranda's death should narrow the field considerably. He tapped his finger on the billing form in question. "Do any of the numbers tell you who the organ went to?"

"Not who, like an individual or anything. That information would be confidential, you know, like adoptions." She beamed at her analogy.

"So if I wanted to find out who received," he waved a hand in the air, "oh, say a heart transplant, I couldn't do it?"

"Not from here. The closest you could get is the hospital it went to. That's all we need for billing purposes anyway. That's this group of numbers"

"For billing purposes," he repeated softly. "Isn't it amazing how entire lives are reduced to a bunch of numbers for billing purposes?" He paused, already planning the next segment of his search. Computers made it so easy.

"Yeah, sure," she looked at him intently, as if she hadn't seen him before. He had the uncomfortable feeling that she might suspect his real purpose for his questions.

"Listen," she said, returning to the opposite side of the counter. "I'm free for dinner tonight if you'd want to make a night of it."

"Can't do, sweetheart." He gave his full attention to the computer screen. "Maybe some other time."

Her eyes narrowed and lower lip protruded. "But you said—"

"Didn't you hear me?" he growled. "I said I was busy."

"Well, excuse me for living," she said in a huff before stomping down the hall.

The alternative could be arranged, he thought with a smile. But his current mission left no time to indulge in Miss Pouty Puss's petty fantasies. He waited till the sound of her footsteps faded down the hall. Opening one of the drawers, he removed a listing of hospital codes that he had confiscated from his supervisor. Now that he knew what block of numbers signified the supplier hospital he could begin his search in earnest.

Miranda had been rushed to Euclid General Hospital when her parents had discovered her with the back of her head bashed in. That much he remembered from the newspapers. "Served her right, stupid bitch," he muttered under his breath. She should never have laughed at him, or called him a freak. "Well, she's not laughing now."

Get a grip, he cautioned himself. *Now's not the time to relive the memory. Save it for later.*

He flipped through the thick stack of computer printouts until he found an alphabetic listing of hospitals. He dragged his finger down the pages until he found the line he sought. After scribbling the code for Euclid General in a small pocket notebook, he quickly returned the listing to the drawer.

He checked around the office, verifying that everyone had left. Using a pilfered credit card, he opened the manager's office and turned on the computer. He lifted the computer keyboard and removed the slip of paper he discovered on an earlier search that held the manager's password. With a few deft strokes, he accessed the clinic's invoicing database. Perfect.

Initiating Hospital? The cursor blinked waiting for a response. He pulled out the notepad and entered the scribbled numbers.

Organ code? The cursor waited.

Damn. He looked in the desk drawers for a list of codes but didn't find anything that remotely resembled an organ list. He stood, nervously running his fingers through his hair. Think! He looked around the office. Where would she keep... He spotted it on her bulletin board. He quickly entered the required code for a heart.

Range? (Optional) He entered the date of Miranda's death for a start and the day after for an end.

Five data lines appeared on the screen.

Laughter from the hall announced the return of the billing department.

Print? The cursor blinked at the bottom of the screen. He typed in a "Y" and the printer sprung to life. "Come on, come on," he urged the grunting machine. The voices intensified in the hall. They'd be here any minute.

The printer spit out the requested document. He flipped the switch on the terminal reducing the lines of information to a fading green dot. Slipping the purloined document into his pocket, he quickly vacated the office.

"Reggie." The manager greeted him as he crossed the department floor. "Thanks so much for staying behind. Any problems?"

"Nothing I couldn't handle," he replied smoothly.

"Great. Why don't you take your lunch then, and don't worry about hurrying back. We owe you one for letting us celebrate."

"Thanks, I appreciate that." He stopped at his desk and grabbed the listing of hospital codes and headed out the door with no intention of ever returning.

◊◊◊

Oreo worked her furry, white head beneath Angela's elbow, looking up with huge remorseful eyes.

"I know you didn't do it on purpose." Angie sniffed between sobs. Once the tears started, she just couldn't get them to stop. Thanks to a stumble on the steps, her ankle throbbed painfully in its restraining bandage. Her favorite pale blue sweater looked as if it had been dragged through the mud, which, as she recalled her embarrassing "slide into home", it had. The shrill irritating beep of the answering machine meant her mother had called with another round of questions. And to top it all off, come Monday, Renard would probably insist on a more professional auditor for his company, causing her undue embarrassment and most likely costing her that promotion. All things considered, it had been a god-awful day.

Oreo licked her chin in sympathy, then cocked her head and looked at the front door.

Renard peered through the tiny windows flanking the door. Darn, she thought he would have left by now. *Go Away!* she telepathed, swiping her damp cheeks with her hand, blinking furiously to keep the fresh ones at bay.

The doorknob turned and within moments he rushed to her side, leaving the front door wide open in the process.

"What's wrong? What happened?" He sat down beside her on the step, pulling her into the curve of his arm. The concern in his voice, combined with the security of his surrounding warmth melted her initial resistance. Oreo, tail thumping madly against the step risers, perked up at the sound of his voice and practically jumped into Angie's lap.

"I'm okay." She took a deep breath. "I was going upstairs to change." A tear escaped, sliding quickly down her cheek. She pressed her face against Hank's side, hoping his jacket would absorb the fresh evidence of her lack of control. "And Oreo bumped me from behind. I tripped and banged my ankle." He swore something under his breath. "It stung like anything, but I'm fine now."

"Like hell, you are." His glare sent Oreo sulking down the steps, her ears flattened close to her head. "I knew this would happen," he said. "What kind of person keeps a dog in such a tiny house?"

"She was a gift." Indignation burst through her humiliation.

"Some gift." He snorted.

"My brother gave her to me after he moved out." She pushed herself free of his arm, and rummaged in her purse for a tissue. "For protection."

"Protection, hah." He glowered at Oreo and the dog's tail drooped another inch. "Your brother is an idiot."

"He is not." The crumpled napkin at the bottom of her purse would have to do. One good blow and hopefully the nasal whininess of her voice would dissipate. She saw Hank wince at the honk worthy of an elk in heat. "Stephen's not an idiot, he's just con—"

Oreo's intimidating growl halted her rebuttal. A man not much older than herself stood on the front porch, separated from them by the screen door. His stiff posture at odds with his casual attire, her neighbor always made her uncomfortable.

"I heard noises," he said, making no attempt to move closer. His uneasy glance rose from the low-growling dog up to Angela. "Do you need assistance?"

She smiled politely. The poor man looked like he would run in the opposite direction if she were to open the screen door. "I'm fine, Mr. Thomas. But thank you for your concern."

"Walter," he said. "Please, call me Walter." He frowned briefly at Hank. He probably disapproved of Hank's rumpled shirt, Angie thought. Of course Hank's unfriendly glare didn't help. Walter cleared his throat. "Then I needn't call your brother?"

"My brother?" Her eyes narrowed. "How do you know my brother?"

"He stopped by a week ago and left his card. He said you'd be alone and if you were hurt or in trouble, or if anything unusual occurred that required his attention, I was to call."

Angela wanted to stomp her foot so badly, it would almost be worth further injury. "That meddling, son-of-a—"

A low chuckle interrupted her tirade. She looked over at Hank, his eyes crinkled with laughter.

"You're right," she said. "My brother is an idiot." She glanced toward Mr. Thomas. "Thank you, Walter. Calling Stephen won't be necessary. I'm fine."

Oreo continued her low, threatening growls. Walter's gaze never left the dog. "I'll leave you alone then. I'll be right next door if you need me." He took a step back, then disappeared off the tiny porch.

Angela glanced over at Hank. "I need to get up now." His gaze, warm and compassionate, searched her face. If only he weren't her client, she'd lean in, ever so slightly.... "You'll need to let me go."

"Oh." His eyes widened while the arm she'd found so comforting disengaged. He helped her stand, then watched as she began her step-hop-step-hop up the stairs. Within moments Hank's hand wrapped around her upper arm, half-lifting, half-supporting her labored progress.

"I swear," she said, trying to dismiss the solidity of his support. "If you try to sweep me into your arms again, I'll blacken your eyes."

"I believe you." He chuckled, negotiating her smoothly to the landing. "I've seen how much damage you can do." A bit of temper flared but when she turned to reply, he held his hands up in mock submission.

"Look," Angie said. "I need to change. Thanks for your help and everything but I can handle it from—"

"Don't you need to go back down these stairs?" he asked.

"Yes, eventually, but I'm sure I—"

"I'll wait." He leaned against the newel post. "Take your time."

"Maybe you could wait in the kitchen?" she asked hopefully. "I feel a little nervous changing with you out here. Perhaps you'd like a cup of coffee or something?"

"You'll call when you're ready to come down?"

She nodded, figuring he'd only leave her alone if she agreed. "The kitchen is downstairs in the back. Follow the beeps." He looked confused. "The answering machine," she explained. "It's in the kitchen." She turned to negotiate the hallway, but listened to his footfalls down the steps and around to the kitchen. Oreo's tail thumped approval marking his progress.

Going down the steps was much easier than going up, especially without Oreo weaving through her legs. Proud that she'd managed without his assistance, she followed the welcoming scent of fresh-brewed coffee back to the kitchen. Hank sat at the kitchen table, reading the newspaper, one hand wrapped around a steaming Classic Limo mug. Oreo lay sprawled at his feet, as if tall, muscular men at her kitchen table were an everyday occurrence. The thought brought an unexpected ache deep inside.

She leaned against the doorway. "As you can see, I'm capable of managing on my own, so you don't have to wait any further on my account."

He frowned. "I thought you were going to call when you were ready to come down those stairs?"

"Hank, really I appreciate—" The telephone rang, interrupting her plea. She sighed, knowing instinctively who was calling, and would continue to call, if she didn't answer. "Excuse me," she mumbled.

She crossed the room to the telephone, glancing at the digital display on its base. Eight messages. *You'd think the woman had nothing better to do.*

"Hi, Mom. I just got in." She paused, watching Hank leave the table.

"Yes, I'm fine. Oreo and I were out for a walk." She watched him cross the hall to the dining room where he studied the colorful Tree of Life quilt hanging above the dry sink.

"Over to the reservoir. The woods are beautiful, the leaves are starting to peak." She answered her mother's questions without thought, all her attention focused on the man who picked up a paperback romance she'd left on the dining room table. One dark brow lifted in question. Well, what did he expect? Accounting texts? She turned her back to him.

"I know you called, Mom. I can see the messages, but I just got in. Honest."

She listened to questions so familiar she could answer them in her sleep. "Yes, I'm taking my pills... No, I'm not pushing myself too hard... Yes, I feel fine." Before her mother could start up again, she interrupted, "Listen, Mom, can I call you back? There's something I have to take care of. Yes, I promise I'll call you right back... Okay, Mom. Love you too."

She hung up the phone, grateful that the action silenced the irritating electronic beep, and looked for Hank. She found him in the tiny living room in the front of the house. He sat on the couch, one foot balanced on the other knee, just as if they were in Wilson's office. The triangle formed by his legs reminded her of her recent contact with that very region. Residual embarrassment collided with a bit of yearning warming her far beyond anything controlled by a thermostat.

"Look, Hank—"

"You didn't tell your mother about your ankle." Oreo sat by his side, content to have Hank's fingers scratch her between the ears. *Traitor*, she thought. Hank patted the cushions next to him, inviting her to join him on the couch. She hobbled over to the opposite wing chair instead.

"If I had even hinted about hurting my ankle, she'd be packing to come home before I could hang up." She eased onto the cushions and relaxed. The chair felt good after the earlier ordeal on the steps.

"Is there something wrong with that?" Hank's brows rose quizzically. "Your family obviously cares a great deal about you."

"I know they love me, but that kind of love can be smothering." She placed her injured foot on the coffee table. "All my life they've waited on me. Protected me. Never let me do for myself. Well, I'm not sick anymore. It's time, past time, that I stand on my own two feet." She glanced at her wrapped ankle. The irony of the situation, that she couldn't literally stand on two feet at that moment, didn't escape her. She glanced up at Hank half-expecting him to laugh, but he didn't. He waited for her to continue.

Before she could, her stomach rumbled, announcing to the world that she'd missed a meal. Hank shifted his position on the couch.

"You can't stay here by yourself, not with that ankle."

She started to protest but he held up his hand. "I know you're not comfortable calling your family. Is there someone else? A neighbor maybe? A friend?"

"Mrs. Kravitz next door is seventy-five years old. She'd have more trouble with the steps and Oreo than I would. You met my neighbor on the other side. Obviously Mr. Thomas..." she smiled, "...Walter wouldn't be comfortable with Oreo." She thought of Nicki, her best friend, but she was away for the weekend. "I can't think of anyone else."

"Well, that settles it," he said, patting one of her mother's quilted throw pillows.

"Settles what?"

"This couch feels pretty comfortable. I'll stay here."

"No! You can't." She gasped.

"Why not? You need someone to help you. You won't come to my house where I can see to you in private. So I have no choice but to stay here." He kicked off his shoes and stretched his body out full length on the couch. "Yes, this will do nicely."

"But my neighbors," she argued. "People will see you. I told you I could lose my job."

"Are you afraid I'll take advantage of you?" He smiled and liquid warmth poured through her body at the suggestion. "Relax." His dimple deepened. "I'm involved with someone else, remember?"

Elizabeth Everett, how could she forget? The image of the tall, dark model formed in her memory. Angie supposed this was his way of tactfully suggesting that she was not his type. Indeed, the exact opposite of his type. A strange sense of disappointment tugged at her heart.

"And," he continued, tossing the pillow from one hand to the other as if it were a football. "When I answer the phone, I won't hesitate to tell the person on the other end about your foot or my identity. Even if it's Falstaff himself."

Her throat constricted; her lips went dry. But with his gaze fixed so steadily on her face, she refused to moisten them.

He smiled, his eyes claiming victory. "So you see, Angel—"

"Angela," she corrected. He merely nodded acknowledgment.

"You can dig out some guest towels, or pack a bag to spend the weekend with me." He paused. A wicked smile tilted his lips, sending an anticipatory shiver dancing down her spine. "The choice is yours."

Chapter Five

"See what I mean?" Hank guided his Lexus past a brick column supporting the numbers 1107. "Nobody can find you here. Not even Falstaff." Even through the dusky light that settled so early this time of year, she could see the house would be difficult to spot from the road. The long driveway and banks of trees, many still holding their brightly colored foliage, obscured the view.

"And you'll be able to rest that foot," he continued his cheerful tirade. "So just relax. Enjoy the weekend."

Relax? She accepted that the house was private, and the ranch styling would be easier to negotiate. But relax? She stole a sideways glance. Not with this man. Something about him kept her on edge.

The curving driveway ended in front of a sprawling ranch of stone and dark-hued timber. No welcoming lights shone through the windows, as if the house didn't want her there anymore than she wished it herself. She shivered.

He noticed. "It's a shame we had to pick up dinner. I'm a pretty good cook, you know."

No, she didn't know. Other than the fact that he seemed bound and determined to make both her working and private lives miserable, she didn't know much about the man she'd agreed to hide away with. She bit her lower lip.

"We'll eat as soon as I bring in some wood for the fireplace. I'll have you warm and cozy in no time." He pushed a button on the windshield visor and a door to a cavernous garage slowly lifted.

"No one else lives here?" she asked, noting a bright red corvette in one of the packing spaces.

"That's Elizabeth's. She leaves it here so she'll have a car available when she visits."

"Oh." She sighed. As if she needed further proof that she posed no competition to the beautiful Elizabeth. The sleek flashy Corvette epitomized the New York model, while her tiny battered Civic... Shoot—her Civic! She hadn't arranged for anyone to move it from the reservoir's parking lot.

"I need to make a call," she said, tugging at the door handle. The engine noise, amplified in the garage, died with the turn of a key, reminding her of yet another complication. Her keys. How could she get her car keys to someone without revealing her whereabouts? "Oh dear." She slumped back in the seat with the car door still open.

"What's wrong?" Hank asked, quickly crossing to her side. He shifted the bag of hamburgers and fries so he could help her ease from the car.

"My Civic is still in the park and I'm the only one with the keys." Oreo jumped over the front seat, exiting the car moments before the door closed. "It'll be towed if it's left overnight."

"Don't worry. I'll take care of it," he said, leading her toward the door at the back of the garage.

"But no one can know I'm here. How can you—"

"Look, Angela." He stopped and faced her. "I know how important this is to you. I said I'll take care of it and I will." His hand slid up and down her upper arm, generating warmth that dipped much lower. "Trust me a little." He smiled. "Okay?"

She nodded, too dazed by her reaction to his touch to speak.

He opened the door leading to the main house and flipped on a light switch, illuminating the great room. "Make yourself at home." He pushed the bag of food into her arms. "I have a call to make."

A leather couch and chairs surrounded a small coffee table in front of an enormous walk-through fireplace. She hobbled over to the table and set the bag down. Oreo busily investigated all the corners of the room, her nails clicking on the hardwood floors. She glanced up at the tasteful and quite probably expensive furnishings. No magazines. No photographs. No half-dead plants or partially melted candles. The room felt lifeless, cold, impersonal. A lump formed in her stomach.

She dropped her purse on the nearest chair and limp-hopped to the French doors along the opposite wall. A switch by the door illuminated the grounds behind the house.

"My God," she whispered. Dark blue canvas covered the in-ground pool directly in front of her. The high fence of a tennis court loomed to the right. Ornamental bushes and what she supposed were the remnants of a garden led from the pool area to a wide grassy field beyond. She could see the outline of trees against the darkening sky. Not a light from a neighbor could be seen. Oreo's fluffy tail brushed against her leg. "What have we gotten ourselves into?" she whispered to the dog.

"Thanks, Tom. I owe you one." Hank's voice drifted from the hallway. "I'll meet you in thirty minutes." He walked into the great room a few moments later.

"I promised to get that fire going." He pulled a brown leather bomber jacket from a closet to replace his muddy windbreaker. "Oreo can come out with me and do her thing while I get some firewood." Oreo dashed across the room at the word "out", twirling in little circles at Hank's feet.

"Traitor," Angela scolded, too low for Hank to hear.

"Once the fire's going, I'll grab one of those burgers to eat on the run. You ought to rest that foot, young lady." He pointed to the couch then zipped up his jacket. "And eat something before the food gets cold. Don't wait for me." Man and dog disappeared out the same door through which she had entered only minutes before.

Men. Already he was telling her what to do, and for nothing more serious than a sprained ankle. She almost laughed, imagining his orders if he knew the full truth. She slowly made her way across the room. As tempting as the couch appeared, no way was he going to find her there on his return. She shouldered the strap of her overnight bag and with her arms braced against opposite walls, limped down the hallway of closed doors.

The first door on the left opened to a small no-frills bedroom with French doors to the back terrace. After checking to make sure the door to the hall had a lock, she fell on the bed, her ankle aching more than she cared to admit. She rolled to her back, checking for an adjoining bathroom. "Rats," she muttered, partially to relieve the eerie silence of the nearly deserted house. "There has to be a bathroom around here someplace."

Pushing herself off the bed, she negotiated her way back into the hall without the heavy shoulder bag. She opened a door on the opposite wall and knew immediately she had stumbled into his office. The fresh manly scent that had earlier evoked images of a light-dappled forest, now brought thoughts of a flashing dimple and warm, assessing, gray eyes. She drew a deep breath. His essence drifted through her, pooling deep inside. Instantly, she felt transported back to earlier that afternoon when he had held her in his arms. Her head had rested on his shoulder. Her ankle had throbbed like hell.

A shudder leaped up her spine. *Silly,* she scolded herself. *He's dating a model.* A man like Renard—handsome, intelligent, successful—a man like that would have no interest in her.

She quickly scanned his desk and the book-laden shelves, half expecting to see a photograph of Elizabeth Everett mocking her from an ornate silver frame. But there were no photos. A laptop computer, similar to hers, sat on the desk, waiting for its owner to bring it humming to life. A phone rested in close reach of the computer.

She looked past the elaborate wall unit of bookcases to the adjoining room. Curiosity and a few awkward steps carried her to his bedroom. The carefully made king-size bed framed by four massive bedposts caught her by surprise. Her bed at home still had the sheets tossed back from when she had left it that morning. Guilt twinges increased as she looked around the room. Clean. Sharp. Masculine. A prickling at her neck warned her she shouldn't be here, but she couldn't resist.

Oreo's nails rapidly clicked across the great room. Panic struck. She bit her lip. If he found her here in his room, he might draw the wrong conclusions. At least, that's what those television shows implied. A part of her hesitated, curious to explore those conclusions. But the more practical side of her nature urged her to run. Running, of course, was impossible. Even sneaking out of the room would be difficult, given her unsteady gait.

In a Heartbeat

Holding her breath to soften the pain, she hobbled slowly, quietly, expecting any moment to hear his heavy footsteps in the hall.

She made it to the door and peeked into the hallway. No Hank. Backing out, she pulled the door silently closed behind her. Her captive breath flew out in a soft sigh of relief. With a pasted-on smile to hide the burning on her cheeks, she advanced slowly down the hall. She made it to the great room and froze. The smile died on her face.

Hank stood by the chair in front of the newly lit fire, his hand buried deep in her handbag.

"Find what you're looking for?" Icicles could have hung from her tone.

"There you are." He smiled, oblivious to her concern. "I need your keys to get your car. I thought..." His brows shifted down as he groped in her bag. "What the hell?" He pulled one of her many prescription pill bottles out for closer inspection. Then another. And another.

Here it comes, she thought. *He'll want to know about the pills.* Pity would soften his eyes, lower his voice. He'll treat her like a fragile doll, an invalid, too delicate to touch, too temporary to care about. A lump twisted in her stomach.

He glanced up at her, four fat amber bottles clutched in his hands, with an equal number still in her purse. The unspoken question mirrored in his eyes. She moistened her lips.

"This is the medicine you mentioned earlier?" He lifted the clattering bottles. "These pills?"

She nodded, her voice buried beneath the lump in her throat.

"Is it HIV?" His voice caught, and concern radiated from his eyes. She hobbled closer.

"No." Her lips formed the word, but the sound disappeared in the heated air around them.

Gas from a hissing log popped, sending a shower of sparks to the grate. Frightened, Oreo scrambled behind her legs, knocking her off-balance. Immediately, Hank was there, catching her, offering his strength and support. Her hands went instinctively to his chest. She glanced up, disturbed by the

47

urgency in his eyes. "Tell me," he practically snarled. "Are you dying?"

"No," she repeated. Her pulse pounded in her ears, reminding her of the truth of that statement. The thought brought a faint smile. "I'm fine." She pulled her hands back, conscious that his hands remained on her upper arms. "At least, I will be as long as I keep taking those." She tilted her head toward the pill bottles scattered on the floor.

"Well." His audible exhale ended with a nervous laugh. His thumbs stroked the top of her shoulders in slow sensuous arcs. He lowered his mouth close to her ear, his warm breath swirled on the back of her neck, raising goose flesh down her body. "Then by all means, keep taking them."

Her heart pounded. Dangerous. She could almost hear her mother's voice, "Don't excite yourself. That can't be good for your heart." The memory stiffened her resolve. She stood a little taller. She looked directly in his eyes. Her resolve weakened. Maybe Mom was right.

With a quick smile, he got down on his hands and knees to gather the fallen pill bottles and stuff them back into her purse. Oreo hampered the search, believing this to be a new game invented for her enjoyment. Angie watched their antics, trying to hold her heart in check. When Hank brought her the restored handbag, she pulled out her key ring with its identification heart.

His hand closed around the keys. His dimples flashed. For a moment, she thought he might kiss her on the cheek. But he didn't. Instead he pointed to her purse.

"We'll talk about this when I return."

Her lips tilted up in a smile she didn't really feel. He left her standing firmly on her own two feet.

But they didn't talk later. He returned to an empty, dark house. She was gone.

Chapter Six

There was no answer on her phone. He didn't leave a message. He drove to her house, but it was dark, no one home. After a long restless night, he tried again on Sunday morning, afternoon and evening to no avail. He couldn't find her.

Hank pulled out the yellow pages and looked up limousine services. What was the name of that company she drove for? But before his finger had traveled far down the page, he realized Angela wouldn't be able to drive with her injured foot. He looked up the brother's name in the white pages, but to call him would be to betray Angela's trust, so he didn't call.

He didn't call, he didn't sleep, he couldn't concentrate and it all made him mad as hell. Why should he care so much about one mere slip of a girl? He didn't have time for this nonsense, and he certainly couldn't afford to get involved. Not now. His arrangement with Owens made that impossible.

Still, every time he tried to cram out thoughts of Angela with thoughts of business, the reverse would happen and Angie's face would chase other concerns away. He'd see her face, stubborn with poorly concealed vulnerability about her eyes, intelligent cornflower blue eyes, and a slim body, not bony like Elizabeth, but soft and feather light, made to fit in a man's arms. His groin responded to the memory.

Stop this. He chided himself. *It's those pills.* They were making him half crazy. She had mentioned she carried medicine in her purse, but he'd never imagined... And now she was out there somewhere, alone and crippled.

His phone rang. He eagerly answered, hoping Angela would be on the other end.

"Philip?" The man's voice was unmistakable.

"Yes, Father." An awkward silence ensued.

"I received notification of a bank transfer and I wondered if you knew anything about it."

"Transfer in or out?" Hank feigned innocence. The routing he had used to transfer funds into his father's account should have concealed his identity, but any good investigator could trace the transfer back to him.

"In. It's a mere drop in the bucket for the million that was lost." *On the stock you recommended.* Hank heard the accusation in his father's tone if not in his words. "But four hundred thousand will pay a few bills."

"How's Mother?" Hank asked abruptly.

"She sends her love. Listen, Philip." Hank cringed, hating the sound of that name. "You're not engaged in another foolhardy scheme, are you? We haven't recovered from that last stock deal. I don't want—"

"No, Father, I'm not involved in the stock market anymore." His father's loss in the market hung around Hank's neck like the proverbial albatross, displaying his market speculation as a disgrace to all who could see.

"I just wondered. I saw Jim Owens the other day; he seemed to think you had some sort of announcement to share with your family."

Hank remained silent. Damn Owens, he had said Hank had two weeks.

"Scandal crosses state lines, Philip. The only real asset a businessman has is his integrity. The family can't afford—"

"To smear the family name." Hank finished the familiar quote. "So you've told me time and again."

"Yes, well...if there's nothing else, I'll bid you good night then."

"Good night, Father."

At the click of the phone, Hank closed his eyes and let his head fall back on the couch. One week had already passed, and Owens was obviously watching the clock. As pleased as Hank was that this agreement with Owens would provide enough money to repay his family, he wondered if this wasn't another rash move. The business portion of the agreement, reversing the trend of losses, would be a challenge. But the second part of the agreement, regarding matters of a more personal nature, had his stomach churning in turmoil. Rash decision or not, a deal was a deal, and it was time to put all the parties into play. He couldn't wait any longer. He picked up the phone and dialed Elizabeth's number.

⋆⋆⋆

Monday morning, the conference room door flew open with a bang. "Where is she?"

Max struggled to catch the papers that caught the draft like sails in a regatta. "Excuse me?"

Renard glowered. "Where is Ms. Blake?"

"She had an unexpected doctor's appointment this morning. I guess she hurt her leg over the weekend." Max pulled at the tip of his tie. "She should be back this afternoon, though. Would you like me to leave a message?"

"You do that." Renard's fists slowly unclenched. "The moment she comes in, I want to see her. You got that?"

Max nodded numbly. "The moment she comes in," he repeated.

"Good," Renard snapped. He hesitated as if he had something more to say, then turned and left more sedately than he'd arrived.

"Jesus, Angie." Max muttered after the door closed. "What have you done now?"

⋆⋆⋆

A timid knock at his doorjamb broke Hank's concentration. Damn. Ever since he had stormed the conference room in search of Angela, everyone had been tiptoeing around him, avoiding eye contact. He'd have to do something about that. Later. After the red haze filtered away from his eyes. Damn that woman.

"Mr. Renard?" Cathy, his secretary, nudged her head around the door. "I'm leaving for lunch. Would you like me to bring you something?"

"No," he grumbled. Worry over Angela's wellbeing, anxiety over her apparent health problems, to say nothing of the chaotic nature of this company's financial statements, had his stomach in an uproar. Eating would just add to the indigestion. "I'll grab something later." Cathy started to withdraw. "Wait..."

"Yes, sir?" She shielded her body with the office door. "Did you want something?"

He had intended to ask her if Angela had returned yet, but the question might raise some unwanted flags. His secretary waited expectantly, half-in, half-out the door.

"On second thought." He leaned back in his chair and smiled, stretching his arms behind his head. "A sandwich might be just the thing."

Cathy opened the door a bit farther. "There's a deli down the street that makes a great Reuben sandwich."

"That sounds fine." His stomach turned at the thought of sauerkraut. He fought to maintain the smile. "Can you bring me back one of those?"

"I'll be back in an hour."

"Thanks, Cathy," he called to the closing door, hoping he'd soothed her apprehension if not his stomach. Opening the desk drawer, he fumbled for a roll of antacids and popped two. Now back to business. He ran his finger down the column of numbers on the paper in front of him. Something just wasn't right. The profits on the income statement were far below industry standards. If only he could concentrate without the face of a pale, blonde angel intruding on his thoughts.

"It's those pills," he muttered, remembering his shock when he discovered the nest of prescription bottles in her purse. If he knew for a fact that Angela was well, maybe he could concentrate on business. That's why he needed to see her, he told himself. The only reason.

Someone knocked on his door, a little more forcefully this time. *Good*, he thought. That friendly exchange with Cathy must have given her more confidence.

"Come on in, Cathy," he called, continuing to study the financial report. "Did you forget something?"

"I'm told you wanted to see me."

His head shot up. "You!"

She frowned. "That's the third time you've greeted me like that."

"I'll try not to make it habit-forming." Just seeing her lightened his spirits. He struggled to keep a smile from tipping his lips. She needed to understand what she put him through. "Come in, sit down. We need to talk."

She smiled tentatively, then hobbled toward the left chair in front of his desk.

He stood, then walked around the desk to close the door. "No crutches? How's the ankle?"

She angled her body on the chair, then lifted the injured leg, now encased in a white plastic brace, only to plop it down on the seat next to her. The very seat he had intended to use. She smiled up at him, almost as if she had placed her foot there to keep him at arm's length. "The doctor gave me this plastic ankle brace. See?" She tilted her leg from side to side. "It fits inside a tennis shoe. Not that it's very fashionable."

He noted her emphasis on "fashion" but couldn't grasp the significance.

Hank braced his hip on the edge of the desk and raised his foot to the same chair, inches from her tennis shoe. Ignoring her uncertain glance, he rested his forearm on the bent knee and leaned forward, effectively trapping her in the corner. Now he would get some answers.

"What happened to you Saturday night?"

"Didn't you see my note? I called my brother and asked him to pick me up."

"Some note, all it said was not to worry. It didn't say anything about where you had gone."

She shifted in the chair, his gaze following her movements. Her black slacks stretched tight across her thighs. Slender thighs. Encased in very sheer stockings beneath those slacks, he imagined. His entire mouth felt as dry as the *Wall Street*

Journal lying on his desk. He forgot for a moment what he wanted to ask.

She was too calm. Too well-rehearsed. He wanted to see her squirm and feel a fraction of the anxiety he had felt over her disappearance.

"You called your brother?" He leaned a little closer, cramping her space. "The idiot?"

"I shouldn't have called him that. He just gets overly concerned for my well-being."

"Yes, let's talk about that well-being." Now they were getting to the crux of the matter. "You were going to explain about those pills in your purse."

She shifted in the chair, her eyes downcast. A knot formed in his chest. He wanted to reach across and shake the truth out of her. Instead, he opted for a confession. "You know, I tried to find you Sunday. I went to your house and that zombie next door said you hadn't returned."

"I told you." She glanced up, her eyes narrowed. "I stayed with Stephen. It wasn't right that I imposed upon you that way."

"Imposed? I invited you. It wasn't an imposition." He stood, then paced around the perimeter of the office. "You want to talk imposition. Let's talk about how you landed in my lap headfirst. That was an imposition, but this—"

"Will you keep your voice down! Someone will hear," she hissed. "Besides, you know what I mean. You're involved with someone."

"That's got nothing to do with it. I invited you to rest your ankle, not appease my perverse appetites." He frowned down at her. "Tell me, were you afraid that I would take advantage of the situation—"

"No--" she injected.

"Or that I wouldn't," he finished.

She blanched.

"My God." He stuttered. "That's it. That's why you left!" A pretty blush covered her cheeks. She turned her face to the wall, but he reached over and gently turned her face to his. The vulnerability in those sweet blue eyes squelched the joy of his discovery. His breath caught. "I'm sorry. I shouldn't have said that. I was so worried and then—" His chin sank to his chest. "I'm sorry."

Her fingers gently wrapped around his palm, tugging his hand from her cheek. "It's not your fault," she said. Her words rode on a current of sweet breath that warmed his cheek. Her scent, soft and inviting, penetrated his thoughts. "I never should have—"

"Philip!" a woman shrieked.

Elizabeth Everett, wrapped in a body-hugging sweater dress, glared from the doorway. "Am I interrupting something?"

Damn. He hadn't expected her to arrive so soon. He hesitated, then straightened. "As a matter of fact, you—"

"You called and said we needed to talk. I drop everything, catch a plane to Ohio," she glared at Angela, "and find this."

"Knock off the dramatics, Elizabeth. Nothing was happening here." The woman was a hellcat. Owens's offer of a million dollars might not be enough. "Ms. Blake and I were merely discussing—"

"Discussing?" She stepped closer, a smug smile firmly in place. "Is that what you call it when some sweet young thing spreads her legs for you in your office?"

Angela's eyes widened into two blue ovals while his entire body went rigid. Clenching his hands into fists at his sides, he stepped between Elizabeth and Angela. "You have no right," he growled.

"Excuse me," Angela said behind him. "I think I should go."

Hank motioned behind him for Angela to stay. If anyone should leave, it should be Elizabeth.

"Right? I have every right," Elizabeth screeched. "Is this what you wanted to discuss?" She pointed an accusatory finger. "Her?"

"Calm down. It's not what you think," he repeated. Although his words were directed to Elizabeth, his thoughts centered on Angie as she brushed past him on her way to the door. He wanted to stop her, wanted to explain, but it would be impossible with Elizabeth in the room.

Angela slipped through the open door, turned and attempted to pull the door closed quietly behind her. Elizabeth stepped in the path of the closing door, leveling her glare at Angela. "I won't forget you." She narrowed her eyes. "Nobody messes with what's mine and gets off this easy."

Goosebumps lifted on Angela's arms. No one had ever threatened her before, especially with such pure hatred. She jerked the door free of the model's grasp and pulled it closed.

"Jesus," a man's southern drawl sounded behind her. "What was that all about?"

Angela swirled around, practically ramming the controller's chest. As the head of the accounting department and one of the few employees who had been with the company since it was founded, Tom Wilson could be crucial to her ability to earn that coveted promotion. He obviously hadn't been overly impressed with her at that meeting last week. Now this.

"Mr. Wilson." She stepped back, smoothing back the hair from her face. "I, uh, Mr. Renard had a visitor."

"A loud one from the sounds of it." He grinned at the feminine wail partially muted by the closed door. "Daddy won't be pleased." He turned to walk down the narrow hallway that connected "executive row" to the rest of the offices.

"Excuse me?" Angela hurried to catch up to him. She put her hand on Tom's arm, partly to stop him, and partly to ease some discomfort. The ankle brace hadn't provided enough support for all the jerky turns and twists.

"What happened to you?" Tom glanced down at the bulky brace.

"It's just a sprain. Nothing serious." She pulled her hand back from his arm and cocked her head up to him. "What did you mean when you said 'Daddy won't be pleased'?"

"That's Elizabeth Everett in his office, isn't it?" Angela nodded in response. "Her daddy owns this place."

"No," she gasped. "I thought someone named Jim Owens owned the company."

"He does. Jim is her father. He told me once that Elizabeth's agent made her change her name." Tom ran a hand through his thinning gray hair. "Jim wasn't too happy about that, either."

"So Hank...Mr. Renard," she corrected, "is dating the boss's daughter?" Her breath escaped as if someone had punched her in the stomach.

"Why the surprise?" Tom teased, one side of his mouth curled up to a sneer. "In this business it's not what you know, it's who you know." He nodded toward the door. "Why else would he be here? He's not old enough to know the business yet." He turned and continued down the hall, but not before she heard his lowered tone. "Not like he should."

Angela leaned against the wall. Mental tumblers clicked into place in a very unpleasant combination. *He's a user*, a part of her brain screamed. He's after her money. That's why there were no pictures of Elizabeth in his room. *The man is pond scum. If he used one woman to get ahead, he'll use another.*

The blood drained from her face. Hank already knew about her "other" part-time job. He knew about the rules on relationships between auditors and their clients, and yet he still coerced her into his house. She gnawed at her lower lip. Stephen's words from two nights ago haunted her.

"What do you know about this man?" he had lectured. "He could be a murderer, a pervert or something. How could you be so stupid, Angela?" Oh, how she had defended him then, she remembered.

"Don't be silly," she had argued. "He's no more a murderer than that guy next door. It wasn't that I didn't feel safe with him."

Of course, she really hadn't felt safe alone with him. That's why she'd called Stephen. She hadn't been afraid Hank would hurt her. It was something else, something she wouldn't begin to try to explain to her brother. A tremor twisted deep inside her.

"Oh God." Her head clunked back against the wall with a thud. "What have I done?"

You trusted him, a small voice reasoned. *And why not? What proof, real proof, do you have that he's not trustworthy?* She drew in a deep breath. There were two sides to every story, she calmly reasoned. *Don't judge him until you know his side.*

She closed her eyes. "Don't judge," she repeated, as if the sound of her words would chase the other thoughts from her head. "Don't judge."

"Angela? Are you all right?" a woman asked.

Her eyes opened instantly. Mouthwatering smells drifted from the white bag tightly clutched in Cathy's hand. The secretary's lips thinned into a line of concern. "Is it your leg? Can I get you anything?"

Angela sighed, pushing away from the wall. "I'm fine," she answered for the umpteenth time. "Just fine." She walked unsteadily down the hall.

Chapter Seven

"Max, I want to be out of here tomorrow," Angela announced as soon as she returned to the conference room. "Where do we stand?"

"Well, I finished testing that stack of accounts payable invoices you requested."

Angela eased down on one padded chair and propped her injured foot up on another. "Anything unusual?"

"Nope." He stretched, the white cotton shirt pulled tight across his chest. "Looked pretty complete to me."

"So every invoice had a copy of the purchase order and the receiving report, showing the warehouse received the goods ordered and invoiced, right?" Angie rattled almost routinely, her mind still occupied with her recent enlightenment. She shuffled the file folders, looking for the one with the audit program that documented completed versus uncompleted audit steps. The sooner she could distance herself from Hank Renard and his rude girlfriend the better.

"All except the direct ships."

She paused in her search. "Direct ships?" Her mind shuffled through all the interviews with the various department heads, searching for where she had heard that term before.

"Yeah, that's when the merchandise is shipped directly to a customer." Max tugged at the bottom of his tie. "Sara explained it all to me."

"Sara?" Angie drawled. "Another conquest?"

"No." He laughed. "Tom Wilson wasn't in his office, so I asked Sara about the invoices without receivers."

Yes, it was all coming back. The interview with Tom Wilson and the embarrassing confrontation with Renard. "Can you show me one?" she asked.

Max flipped through the stack of papers before sliding a page with navy blue letterhead across the table. "Most of the invoices from Timone Industries are direct ships."

"Timone Industries," Angela repeated, studying the letterhead. "It's a local company, but there's no street address, just a post office box."

"Is something wrong with that?" Max started thumbing through the stack of invoices. "Lots of these vendors list PO box numbers along with their street addresses."

"No," she hesitated, not ready to disclose her "other" job to Max. Having driven limousines all over town, she recognized most local street addresses. Several people knew of her brother's business, but no one knew of her chauffeur sideline. She quickly modified that thought. One person, one possibly pond scum of a person, knew her secret.

"Now this street I know." She tapped the ship-to address on the Timone Industries invoice. "Ritchton Street." She propped her chin up with her right hand. "That's not the best of neighborhoods." She tried to remember the street, but her memory only dredged up images of refuse-strewn alleyways and vacant office buildings. She shuddered and the images disappeared. "Were any of the direct ships from someone other than Timone Industries?"

"There were only seven direct ships in the sample. Most were from Timone, but I think maybe there were one or two from somewhere else." He looked up at Angie. "Is something wrong?"

"I just want to be thorough, that's all." An uncertainty made her hesitate. "Could you do me a favor, Max?" She smiled sweetly. "Could you make a copy of this invoice for me?"

"Oh, I see how it works now." Max laughed, taking the invoice from her. "You're going to milk this ankle thing for all it's worth, aren't you?"

"Maybe." She laughed. "Only if it'll work."

As soon as Max closed the door behind him, Angela strained to pull the heavy audit bag on the floor behind her

In a Heartbeat

chair around to her side, so she could search for a thick press board folder: the permanent file.

Like most accounting firms, Falstaff and Watterson maintained a complete file of copies of important documents, schedules that spanned years of operations, and other boring but important information. The detailed accounting system descriptions resided in the permanent file. Part of her job was to ensure these descriptions were up-to-date and accurate. If she wasn't aware of these direct ship invoices, there was a good chance they hadn't been documented in the accounts payable system description. She opened the overstuffed folder to the table of contents.

Section I. Background Information

A. Dun & Bradstreet Reports.

B. Product Literature

C. Press Releases & Newspaper Articles

D. Industry Audit Guides

Section II. Accounting Systems

A. Flowcharts, System Descriptions and questionnaires.

Angie's finger slid down the list of contents and paused at "newspaper articles". Every time a client, or a client's product, appeared in a newspaper or magazine, the firm clipped the article and stored it in the permanent file. It was a long shot, but...

She quickly passed the faded green workpapers and headed straight for the juicy stuff, the newspaper articles.

The articles were filed chronologically with the most recent on top. Not quite the most recent, Angela thought. The office probably clipped the announcement of the new CEO from the paper last week. She'd have to ask Max to stop by the office tomorrow to pick up any updates for the file.

The top article talked about Hayden's new product line. She flipped to the next page. A yellowed photograph of Jim Owens looked back at her. Nothing new here, she'd seen his picture before. She was about to flip to the next page when a small photograph at the bottom right corner caught her eye. Jim Owens stood talking to another man. To his immediate right stood a slender dark-haired woman. Angie squinted at the fine

61

print of the caption: Owens and his daughter, Elizabeth, discuss the future of Hayden Industries with...

It was true! Hank was dating the owner's daughter. Bile rose up in her throat. In her heart she had suspected it wasn't a love match, but she hadn't suspected Hank of something this low. This... She shook her head. No wonder the company was supplying him with that big fancy house. She remembered Tom's curled lip. *It's not what you know but who you know.* Well, she knew a lot more now, thank you very much.

The door opened. Angela let the file pages fall back in place.

"The copying machine outside is broken again, so I had to run up to Sales to make a copy." Max tossed the copy of the Timone invoice over to her. "Anything else?"

Angela hesitated, then pulled the invoice copy and a legal pad over to her. "I think I need to ask Tom Wilson a few questions about these direct ships. How about checking out the audit program to make sure you've signed off on your sections. Have you written your memo yet?"

Max frowned. "You know how much I hate writing those things."

Angela smiled. "All part of the job, Max, all part of the job."

He was still grumbling when she slipped out of the conference room.

CS80

"I'm leaving now, Mr. Renard. You have a good evening."

Hank glanced up from his desk, suddenly aware of the absence of ringing phones and slamming file cabinets. "Thank you, Cathy. I'll see you tomorrow." After she left, he checked his watch. Six o'clock.

He reluctantly stood and stretched the kinks from his shoulders. Elizabeth and another screaming confrontation would be back at the house waiting for him. He was in no hurry to jump into the fray, but Owens was calling the shots. Fishing in his pocket for his car keys, he found another set there. A set of keys with a tiny heart. He smiled. Unfinished business.

Hank walked down the hallway toward the opened door of the conference room. He found her standing at the end of the long table, staring through the picture window to the parking lot beyond.

"I hoped you might still be here."

She lurched, apparently startled by the sound of his voice. Her hand covered her heart. "You scared me half to death."

"I'm sorry," he said, stepping into the room. He began to shut the door, but at her anxious look, he pushed it open again.

"My brother should be here any minute." She stepped back.

Something had changed. Earlier she had been comfortable in his presence, almost teasing. Now...

"I only need a minute." He smiled. She averted her eyes. His smile faded. This wasn't going well. "I wanted to apologize. Elizabeth had no right—"

Angie snorted, casting her gaze up to the ceiling. "Elizabeth." She shook her head. "What did you call it last time? Her urban attitude?"

The reference threw him for a second, then he remembered silky blonde tendrils slipping from a chauffeur's cap. He leaned back against the wall, sensing that she needed the space.

"You never did explain why you were driving a limousine that night."

Her gaze shifted to him and lingered before she began an intense study of her fingernails.

"I'd appreciate it if you would forget you saw me that night. It's not the sort of thing Falstaff would approve of."

"Like staying at my house for the weekend?" At least that got him a reaction. She disregarded her fingernails and leveled her gaze on him. A cold, ice blue gaze.

"Exactly."

Her chilling tone punched him in the gut. His reference to Elizabeth hadn't brought about that frosty reaction, something else had. He took one step toward her. She glanced again to the open door. "Seems like Falstaff and Watterman have a lot to say about running your life. Why do you stay there?"

"I'm good at what I do. Public accounting pays well." She ran a finger down the table. "Their rigid code of conduct isn't any different from the other firms."

"So you're in it for the money?" Money as an incentive he could understand.

"I have my reasons. Private reasons." She tossed him a look that placed him lower than fish bait. "At least I'm honest about how I earn my paycheck."

"What's that supposed to mean?" Her glare suggested she knew something. Whatever she had discovered obviously placed him on some shit list.

A movement by the window caught his eye. A white stretch limousine pulled up to the curb.

"I have to go." She gathered her purse and computer case. "My brother's here."

He barred her way. "Not until you explain that last statement."

"Look," she sighed, "we'll be finished here tomorrow, then you won't have to see me until we come back to observe the physical inventory. Can't we just end this discussion and part as business associates?"

"No," he thundered. Then, more softly, "Tell me."

She looked straight into his eyes. "Jim Owens's daughter."

He stared at her a moment, at her accusatory expression. She was fierce, no doubt about it. A smile tilted his lips. "I suppose I should have expected this after Elizabeth's little scene earlier. I knew eventually someone would imply something. I just didn't expect it this soon."

He looked down at her shocked face. She obviously didn't see the humor in the situation. How could she? She didn't know all the facts. "And I didn't expect the someone to be you." She tried to push her way past him, but he caught her arm and spun her around. "Wait. I owe you an explanation."

She stared pointedly at his hand, making him feel like a brute for forcing her to stay. She glanced up. Her blue eyes narrowed in an expression of anger and deep disappointment. "You owe me nothing."

Her glare stabbed him to the bone. All humor dissipated. He had to make her understand. "Not true. Now listen—"

"Let me go--" She tried to squirm out of his grasp but he held fast.

"Not until I tell you—"

"Take your hands off her," a man demanded from the open doorway.

Hank sized up the stranger. "Who the hell are you?"

"Stephen." Angie took a breath and gestured toward Hank. "This is H.P. Renard, the man I told you about?"

"Oh yeah." Stephen smirked. "The one you said was as cold as the calculator he must have been named for."

Cold! She said he was cold—a cold, impersonal calculator? Hank swung his gaze to Angela. A flattering blush tinged her cheeks. At least she had the decency to be embarrassed.

"You can take your hands off my sister now." Stephen nodded to Hank's grip on Angela. "Or I can take them off for you."

Hank let go of her arm. "I wasn't harming your sister. I was just trying to—"

"I know what you were just trying," Stephen said. "And you won't be trying it again any time soon."

Angela rubbed the spot where Hank's hand had been. "You okay, sis?" Stephen asked.

Hank bristled at the insinuation, and waited for Angie to defend him, to admit that he would never hurt her, to reply that Hank wasn't that kind of man.

Instead she nodded and walked toward the door. Stephen turned toward him. "You touch Angie again and it'll be the last thing you touch."

Hank watched the blond strongman leave with Angie under his wing. So she found out about Elizabeth. *I wonder how she gained that bit of information? I wonder how much she knows?* An unsettling queasiness roiled in his stomach. It shouldn't matter. Angela wasn't part of this unholy arrangement with Owens. He was the victim, not Angela. Still, the accusations in her eyes when she spat out Elizabeth's name twisted in his gut. What did she say? Tomorrow was their last day? Why did that announcement disappoint him so? Maybe it was for the best. He had enough women trouble to deal with. He still hadn't decided how to approach Elizabeth with her father's scheme. Owens's two-week deadline was rapidly approaching and he was no further along now than he was when he was handed that first check.

He patted his pocket in search of a roll of antacids. Lately, he seemed to be living off the chalky stuff. Instead, he felt the sharp outline of notched metal, Angela's keys. A smile slipped to his lips. She may think tomorrow would be the last day he would see her, but she was mistaken.

"I've told you before, Stephen, I'm capable of taking care of myself. You didn't need to play the heavy back there." She slid in the front seat and waited for her brother to close the door and slip behind the wheel. She supposed she could have ridden in the back and stewed in silence, but riding alone in a cavernous limousine never suited her. Too much like riding in the back of a funeral hearse, and a reminder of all she had not experienced.

"Heck, Angie, you can't even walk the dog without getting hurt." Stephen glanced over at her leg before turning the key in the ignition. "How's the ankle?"

"It's fine, but that's not—"

"And your heart? I saw how red your face was back there. You were straining too hard, too stressed. That's not good for your heart."

"That was embarrassment, not stress, and—"

"Did you take your pills at lunch like you're supposed to? I think as soon as we get home you should lie down and take a nap."

"I'm not a child. In case you hadn't noticed, I'm a full grown adult."

Stephen snorted, an unfortunate family characteristic. "Full grown?" He laughed, looked over at her briefly, then back at the road. "You know you're not like everyone else, Angie. No matter how much you wish you were normal, it's not going to happen. You have to take special care, special medicines. I don't know why you insist on working. It's not good—"

"Don't tell me how to live. I'm not going to spend my life lying in bed being coddled." She glanced at the fading red ring about her wrist. No man had ever held her in so firm a grip, as if she was made of muscle and bone, not spun sugar. Hank was certainly not one to coddle her, but then he was too busy coddling Elizabeth. She turned her face to the window.

It was an old argument, one she and Stephen had been over too many times to count. So they stewed in silence while Stephen negotiated the rush hour traffic. She knew she wasn't like everyone else. She didn't need his reminder. She knew she was different every time she felt her heart beat, but that didn't stop her from having dreams and desires, just like a normal person. Just like a normal woman.

The limousine stopped at a red light in front of a popular bar and restaurant. Stephen glanced over at the crowded parking lot. "Timothy's is packing them in tonight. Not bad for a weeknight."

"No, not bad," she echoed, glancing over at the red neon sign mounted to the roof of the restaurant. The name turned her thoughts in a different direction.

"Stephen, have you ever heard of a Timone Industries on Ritchton Street?" she asked.

"Timone Industries." He tried the words out on his tongue. "Not much call for my ladies in that neighborhood. Why do you ask?"

"Just curious." She turned back to the window, wondering if Stephen realized how much he sounded like he belonged in another less socially accepted business.

"Right. Out of the blue, you just happen to ask me about some dive in a seedy part of town?"

"It's not a dive. It's a business associated with Hayden. I had some questions about the type of business."

"You better not be thinking about going down there. That's a tough area." He glanced over her way. "Maybe it's a good thing you can't just pick up and drive anywhere with that leg of yours."

She winced. Another reminder of something else she couldn't do. She shifted the offending leg away from her good, sturdy one. Stephen acted as if she had sprained both her ankles, not just one. She paused. Not just one... She looked over at Stephen's feet. It only took one foot to negotiate a car with an automatic transmission.

"And don't even think about getting one of my drivers to take you there."

"Wouldn't dream of it," she murmured. But her mind was already turning. A limousine would stand out like a sore thumb, but her dinged-up little Civic would probably fit right in. Her Civic! Damn. She forgot to get her keys back from Hank. That meant another private meeting. She couldn't very well ask for her car keys in public.

Of course, even if she had her car keys, she wasn't completely sure she could handle driving her car with her injured ankle. She glanced back at Stephen. There was only one way to find out.

"Who's on the board tonight?" she asked, hoping to feign small talk.

"I'm running dispatch. Pete's on call for driving. I sure could use another driver on board."

"No response to the help wanted ad?"

He shook his head. "Not yet, but I'm still hopeful." After a brief silence he glanced over at her suspiciously. "Why do you ask?"

"I was just thinking your apartment is crowded enough without Oreo and me." She quickly shushed her brother when he tried to interrupt. "You and Laurie could use some alone time. I thought maybe I could handle dispatch for you tonight. It would get Oreo and me out of your place for a little while."

Stephen's eyes narrowed suspiciously. "You're not harboring any ridiculous ideas about taking one of the ladies out on a run, are you?"

"With this leg?" She pouted sweetly. "Here I am, trying to do something nice for my big brother. But does he trust me? No."

He laughed at her exaggerated sulk. "All right, you win. It would be nice to spend a quiet night at home for once. You *are* planning to take that dog with you?" She nodded. "And you promise not to take a car out on the road?"

"Cross my heart." She reminded herself it really wasn't a lie. She wouldn't have to drive out on the road to test her proficiency on the pedals. Classic Limo's parking lot opened to a strip mall. There should be plenty enough blacktop for what she had in mind.

Chapter Eight

Hank turned the Lexus into the long winding driveway. He had asked Elizabeth to wait for him at home, but the place looked deserted—the curtains drawn, the rooms dark. It looked just as it had late Saturday night, or rather early Sunday morning when he had returned to the cold, lonely house after searching for Angela. His stomach gurgled, a precursor of the indigestion that was sure to follow. Ever since he agreed to Owens's scheme his stomach churned in constant turmoil. He reached in his pocket for some antacid tablets but found only empty wrappers. *That's okay*, he reminded himself. Relief was just inside in the bulk container he had put in the kitchen.

Even though he had spent most of the afternoon thinking over the imminent discussion, he was no closer to knowing how to proceed with Elizabeth than when he had called her yesterday. He turned off the engine. Of course, after that scene at Hayden, maybe she packed up and headed back to New York. The house sure looked empty enough. The thought brought comfort and a surprising amount of relief. Although her absence would mean he'd probably have to follow her to New York to accomplish his goal, it would be good to get out of this suit tonight. Kick back, order in a pizza, maybe catch a football game on the tube.

By the time the car nosed into the garage next to the familiar corvette, the dour mood surrounding him since Elizabeth's untimely arrival began to lift. *I wonder if Angie likes pizza.* The thought came out from nowhere, but he felt so comfortable around her, he suspected he knew the answer. *Yes, she does.* He chuckled to himself as he turned off the ignition and exited the car.

A stale acrid odor and a pale stream of light from the hallway beckoned him upon entering the dark house. Elizabeth probably forgot to turn off the lights. He flipped the wall switch to brighten the great room, dropped off his briefcase on the couch, then followed the light trail to his bedroom. Crossing through the office, he found her, naked and quite at home in his bed.

"Elizabeth?" he braced his arm in the doorway. "What are you doing?"

"You told me to come here, or have you forgotten?" She flipped the glossy page of a fashion magazine and tapped the ashes of a lipstick-rimmed cigarette into a half filled wineglass by the side of the bed. "It's about time you got home. Did *she* keep you late?"

"I wasn't expecting to find you here...like this." He loosened his necktie and unbuttoned the top button. Chilly autumn breezes pushed at the windows, but inside the temperature was quickly heating up. He pulled off his suit coat, taking the time to hang it properly on the wooden clothes valet in the corner.

Elizabeth flipped her long hair in what he knew was a practiced move, exposing the pink tip of one barely swollen breast. Her tongue glided over her lips in an overt attempt at seduction. "You like?"

His stomach roiled. He could see her ribs rising with each breath. Had she looked that gaunt two weeks ago? He slipped off his shoes, one after the other, positioning them by the suit coat. She waited for his response. "What do you think?"

After a long drag on her cigarette, she dropped the remaining stub into the wineglass. A steady stream of smoke poured past her lips. Was she angry or bored? Hank couldn't tell.

"I think you're taking too long to kiss me hello." She tipped her lips in a seductive smile, a pose he recognized from the perfume advertisements. He crossed over to her side of the bed. He leaned over for a light kiss, but she had other plans.

Capturing his necktie, she pulled his head down and met his lips with hers. Her sharp tongue pushed past his lips, filling his mouth with a vile nicotine taste. He reached for her shoulders to steady himself while he pulled back. The necktie tightened briefly, mirroring the clenching of his gut. He broke the embrace.

"Isn't that why you asked me here?" Her lower lip extended in a photogenic pout.

"I asked you to come here because we have something to discuss." He quickly removed his necktie, no need to provide her with a torture device. Not so long ago, he would have gladly reciprocated her advance. He glanced over toward where she sat on the bed. She had a woman's face, but lacked the soft fullness and curves of a woman's body. "Do you mind putting a robe on?" He forced his mouth to smile. "It's distracting to have a serious conversation with you so...casual."

"I need a drink." She scampered over the blankets and dashed from the room. He picked up some kind of flimsy garment that had been tossed over a chair and followed after her.

He found her in the great room, tugging on the handles of a cabinet over the wet bar. "Locked." She glanced over her shoulder at him. "I don't suppose you'll give me the key?"

"I have no idea where the key is. Not my place. Look Liz, why don't you and I sit—"

She sighed. "It doesn't matter, I know where Daddy hides it." She crossed to the fireplace and upended a cobalt blue glass vase. The resulting clink of metal on glass confirmed her familiarity.

"Elizabeth, I don't think alcohol is a good idea right now." She ignored him and crossed back to the bar, inserting the key with a practiced twist. "Your father has made a proposition that affects both of us. I think we should –"

"Looky here." She pulled a plastic bag full of a white powder from the unlocked liquor cabinet. "Now we can party!" She carried her treasure into the kitchen mumbling something about a knife.

He stood stunned by the couch. Drugs! There were drugs in the house and Elizabeth was obviously well-acquainted with them. This manic woman wasn't the Elizabeth he remembered. Had so much changed in a week, or had he just not been paying attention? Angela had warned him and he had stupidly defended his childhood friend. *Well, I'm not a fool any longer*, he thought with a vengeance.

He marched into the kitchen and while Elizabeth ransacked the drawers, he emptied the contents of the unattended bag into the sink and flipped on the faucet.

"How dare you?" she screamed, pummeling his back with her fists. "I wanted that. I needed that."

"No, you didn't," he said calmly. He turned and captured her wrists in his hands. "You may have thought you needed that but—"

"What do you know?" She pulled herself free and screamed at him like a crazed lunatic. "You have no idea about my needs. You don't know me at all." She backed up, her face twisted in a sneer. "Look at you. Mister Goody Two Shoes. Everyone does drugs. Everyone. You deserve to be stuck in this backwater town. You have no right--"

"I have every right, or at least I will soon."

"What...?" She rubbed her hands down her naked thighs as if trying to remove some vile scent that had somehow settled on them. "What are you talking about?"

"I'm talking about marriage. Our marriage."

His words must not have found purchase in her mind. She shook her head repeatedly and looked at him as if he were a total stranger. "You want to marry me?"

"Your father thinks it would be a good idea."

"You asked my father if you could marry me?" Her face softened.

He didn't bother to explain that her father had insisted on the marriage as part of the payment package. When Owens had first proposed the union, Hank had thought marriage to Elizabeth would be only a small sacrifice, a convenient arrangement for their mutual benefit, but now...now he wasn't so sure.

She stepped closer and rubbed her body up against him like a scrawny cat begging for cream. "I had no idea you wanted to propose. Before you said we were just friends." She sucked on his ear lobes. "I'm going to be so good to you, baby. Wait till you meet my friends." She pulled back. "We need a drink to celebrate." She hurried back to the liquor cabinet.

"Liz, about the drugs..."

She removed one of the cut crystal water goblets from the rack under the liquor cabinet, then selected a bottle of scotch. "We'll live in New York," she said. Amber liquid sloshed in the glass, over the rim and onto the carpet. "There's so many parties." She glanced at him quickly with something akin to a frown. "You'll have to loosen up. Now that you know about the drugs, I won't have to hide them anymore." She took a gulp from her glass and her face brightened. "I'm sure you can find a job easily in New York."

"No, we'll both have to live here in Columbus." It was another stipulation of her father's plan, a stipulation Hank approved of.

She stopped mid-gulp. Her eyes widened briefly while she struggled for her voice. "My career! I can't live here. You can forget that." She swirled the remaining liquid in her glass and studied it a moment. "I'm not against the marriage idea, matter of fact I've always..." She shook her head briefly then raised her gaze back to him. "But I'm not giving up my career. Nobody lives in Columbus, for Christ's sake."

Hank sighed. This wasn't going at all as it should. "Your father wants –"

"My father?" She threw her glass back at the liquor cabinet where it shattered. "What do I care what my father wants? This is my life and neither you nor he are going to ruin it for me." She ran back down the hallway. A door slammed and moments later he heard the click of the lock.

This was ridiculous. He walked over to the kitchen to retrieve a trashcan before returning to the liquor cabinet, carefully avoiding the splinters of glass on the floor. The whole idea of a marriage was ridiculous. He picked the larger glass pieces from the mess and tossed them into the plastic trash pail. He never seriously thought Elizabeth would agree to such a marriage, but Owens seemed sure that she would. And she did, didn't she?

Funny that the word "love" never came up in their discussion. Maybe not so funny. He shrugged. The concept of love had never infringed on his own parents' marriage. Marrying Elizabeth would be convenient. His father would approve of her place in society, his mother would approve...of a reason to drink

In a Heartbeat

in public. He shook his head. Of course at the time, he thought he was agreeing to marry his childhood friend, not this drug-sniffing stranger.

The clink of glass hitting broken glass in the pail reminded him of broken vows, broken promises, lost opportunities. His mind conjured up an image of Angela's face, but he quickly pushed it aside. This was not the time to dwell on some elfin chauffeur/auditor, who managed to intrude upon his thoughts at the most inconvenient of times. He wondered how Angela would have reacted to a similar proposal of marriage. *Clink.* Probably about the same as Elizabeth, without the acceptance, of course. She hardly knew him and from what he observed watching her work, she didn't commit to anything without lots of research. *Clink.*

One image chased after another, and he conjured up a vision of Angela, naked, petite yet curved in all the right places, blonde hair streaming out behind her as she stormed down the hallway. His groin tightened. Angela would never have made it to the bedroom without him. He would have chased after her, that's for sure. He glanced toward the hallway. He hadn't chased after Elizabeth.

He returned to the kitchen for a towel and used that to mop up the remains of Elizabeth's drink. Surely, Owens knew his daughter wouldn't want to give up her career, yet he was so adamant about the idea of their marriage. Something didn't make sense. He glanced down the hallway. He knew why he had accepted Owens' plan, but why did Elizabeth? There was only one way to find out.

He walked over to the locked door, prepared for a probable argument. But her voice on the other side of the door stopped him from knocking.

"Sean? It's me... Yes, well, I'm leaving tomorrow. I've already booked a flight... Can you meet me at LaGuardia? Ten o'clock... Of course in the morning. I want out of here as soon as possible... No, he didn't hurt me. Phillip wouldn't... Sean. I told you. He didn't hurt me... It's my father... Yes... Of course I do... I know you do, too. I'll see you tomorrow. Bye."

He waited a discreet moment after he heard the snap of the phone closing before he knocked.

"Liz, we have to talk."

"I have nothing to say."

"Come on Liz, It's the one thing we could always do well. Even when we were little kids, we could always talk."

After a brief hesitation, the lock clicked and Elizabeth opened the door a crack. "I don't want you to stay with me tonight."

He shook his head. "That's okay. There's plenty of bedrooms in this house. I'm sure I can find one to fit me." Even through the tiny crack in the door, he could see her smile.

"I'm leaving tomorrow first thing."

"That's why we need to talk tonight, before you go." He could almost hear her vacillating. "Have you eaten anything? Are you hungry?" Maybe he could coax her out with a meal.

"Do you still make those yummy rolls?" she asked, a bit of yearning in her voice. "No. Don't tell me. I can't eat anything that even looks like it contains calories."

He laughed. This sounded more like his old Elizabeth. "Come on out. I promise I won't tempt you with anything edible."

"Give me a minute," she said. "I want to put something on."

A few minutes later, she breezed into the great room wrapped in a shimmering red silk robe. Her jet-black hair hung limp down her back. A cigarette dangled between two freshly painted lips. Flopping onto the nearest corner of the couch, she searched briefly for an ashtray, then decided the stone hearth of the fireplace would suit her purpose. She flicked off some ashes. "You wanted to talk?"

Hank selected the chair across from her and leaned forward, his elbows on his knees. "Who's Sean?" Her eyes widened and he added quickly, "I heard you mention his name when I came to knock on your door."

She shrugged. "He's a friend. A photographer." She fidgeted a bit with the belt of her robe. "We've worked a bit together, know the same people, that sort of thing."

"And he's in New York," Hank added. She looked toward the ceiling and shook her head with a dramatic sigh before dragging on her cigarette.

"You asked before why I asked you to come here," he said.

"You already explained that. You wanted to ask me to marry you."

"No. Your father wants me to marry you. Why is that, Liz?"

She shook her head and pulled the robe across her knees. "I don't know. He's always thought of you like a son. He'd probably marry you himself if he could." She laughed at her joke. "Wouldn't that be a hoot?"

"I'm serious, Liz. At the time we made the deal, I didn't see anything wrong with us getting married. We've been friends for so long. My parents don't even have that in common. My mother has mentioned on more than one occasion that you'd be a wonderful daughter-in-law."

"Your mother wouldn't even know she had a daughter-in-law."

Hank winced. Elizabeth's observation was true enough, but he tried not to think of his mother's alcohol problems. He clasped his hands together. "I've begun to notice things about you that I hadn't before, and I think –"

"You don't want to marry me."

"I didn't say that." Did he imagine it, or did her lower lip tremble? Her fingers shook, but they often did. He didn't want to hurt her. "I don't think now is the right time for either of us to make that kind of commitment."

She nodded then dabbed the corners of her eyes. Damn. Nothing cut deeper than a woman's tears. He moved to the couch and put his arm around her shoulder. "Don't cry, Liz."

She cuddled into his shoulder and sniffed. "Sean said this would happen. He told me not to come when you called."

"I'm glad you came." Who was this Sean person? Hank squeezed her shoulder. "We needed to have this talk, to keep everything open and honest between us. We've always been honest with each other, haven't we?"

Well, maybe not. She hadn't been honest about her drugs. He owed Angela an apology on that score. But Elizabeth nodded in agreement.

"Daddy really said he wants me to marry you?" He nodded. She fingered the buttons on his shirt. "And he wants me to live here?" He nodded again. "Why?"

"He said something about this being a better place to raise children."

"Children? I can't model if I'm pregnant. I don't even think I can have children." She buried her head in her hands. "What am I going to do?" Turning her head, she glanced up at him. "What should I do?"

His shoulders ached from the added responsibility for Elizabeth's future. What had at first appeared to be a cut and dried proposition now appeared to be a monumental undertaking. Why hadn't Owens been upfront about Elizabeth's drug problems and career objections? What to do now?

"Philip?"

He cringed. He hated that name. "I'm not sure what your father is up to, but I need a little time. I have an idea. Are you game?"

She stiffened.

"Don't worry. You can still go back to New York tomorrow."

"In that case, count me in on one condition." Her lips turned up in a coy smile. "I want an engagement ring."

⋐З᎒᎒⋑

Raymond checked the address on a tiny piece of paper, Gekmon Hall. Yes, this looked to be the place. He smiled. These large universities might attract the stalwart scholars and virtuous philosophers, but they inevitably attracted people from the opposite end of the spectrum as well. The egghead with no social skills best kept far from view, or better yet, a scholar with ethics that came with a price tag. These were the people he sought when he'd first entered the hacker's chat room. It had taken far more patience than he thought he could stand, and far more time than he'd anticipated, but in the end he had found his man, Larry Smith.

He pulled the handles on the heavy doors to the old academic building and stepped inside. Not much changes from one University building to another, he noted. Bulletin boards still overflowed with meaningless papers. Shabby students lounged in equally shabby orange vinyl seats near humming pop machines. Voices and steps echoed in identical intensity down the near empty hallways. Raymond quickly located the building stairwell and started his descent to the basement.

Overhead florescent tubes lit the maze-like warren of hallways. Raymond followed the directions on the scrap of paper through a door marked NO ADMITTANCE, followed along a fenced-in area secured with a padlock, to a quiet, dimly lit, yet obviously protected corner of obscurity.

"Larry, is that you?" Raymond called to the T-shirt-clad back hunched before a flickering monitor.

"Who wants to know?"

"Andy," he replied, using a pseudonym. "We met on the Internet, remember?"

The chair squeaked and turned, revealing a gangly, baby-faced boy sporting a sparse goatee. PHREAKING WITH THE UNIVERSE blazed across his chest on a T-shirt that appeared to have only a passing acquaintance with a washing machine. "Yeah, the hospital guy. Did you bring my money?"

"That depends." Raymond moved closer. "Did you get my information?"

"Nothing to it." A large grin spread across the hacker's face. "I sniffed around a bit, hit a few walls, but I found a weak link in the pathology department. They had some archaic security structure. Easy to penetrate. Once in, I hooked up some databases and lifted all kinds of crap." He held up about five pages of paper covered with words and numbers.

"Let me see," Raymond reached for the report.

"Not so fast." The pages disappeared behind Larry's back. "I could get in deep shit over this. How do I know you won't blow my cover?"

"Don't you watch television?" Raymond sighed. "A journalist never has to reveal his sources. I'm going to use this to prove how hospitals haven't enough security over confidential information."

"No one will get hurt with this?" Larry asked. "I mean, I hack into databases just to see if I can, not to hurt anyone."

"Do I look like a criminal?" Raymond asked, practicing his most innocent "trust-me" look. "I'm a journalist, Larry, and I always protect my sources."

"Okay then." He pulled the papers from behind his back. "Did you bring the money?"

Raymond smiled; it always came down to money. "You bet. Five hundred dollars, right?" He pulled his wallet from his hip pocket, then counted out the bills.

Larry handed over the report in exchange for the crisp hundred-dollar bills. "Sweet," he said. "I've got my eye on a high-speed motherboard. This should put me over the top."

Raymond didn't respond. He turned and retraced his steps out of the underground maze.

"Pleasure doing business with you, man," he heard Larry call to his back. Raymond headed quickly down the hall, back up the stairs, and out the building door.

He studied the pages as he walked down the campus walkway to a nearby fast-food restaurant. Just as he had done with the other two hackers and their assigned hospitals, he had asked Larry for a list of all transplants performed at the university hospital over the course of a month, sorted by organ and date, that identified each recipient by name, address, age and social security number. Heart transplants were still rare enough that only one or two names on each list met the date criteria surrounding Miranda's death. He had already researched the candidates on the other lists and both were dead. One died on the operating table. The other died of complications after contracting a respiratory infection. This was the last hospital of the three that appeared on the screen of the organ transplant billing facility.

One last name to research. One last name between him and freedom. Concerns about being identified as Miranda's killer had twisted his dreams into grotesque nightmares. The uncertainty was eating him alive, and now...now he held the key. What was it Larry had called it? A weak link? Well, now he could eradicate the weak link and return to his perfect life without shadows of uncertainty.

He shuffled through the pages looking for the date he knew as well as his own birthday, May fifteenth. There it was, the final name on his list. He crumbled up the other pages of the report and tossed them into a trash can overflowing with greasy burger wrappers and ice-filled cups.

Carefully, he folded the paper into a neat two-inch square. This one felt right, it pulsed with the quickening of his own heartbeat. He hadn't been this excited since he first conceived of Miranda's death. Smiling, he silently began to plot his strategy. It was time to meet Angela Blake.

Chapter Nine

"I'd like my keys back, please." Angela was surprised Hank was already in his office when she arrived. She had asked Stephen to drop her off extra early on the excuse of having so much work to finish up. In reality, she hoped to catch Hank before the others arrived. But she hadn't expected him to be waiting for her.

"Angel. Come in. Sit down."

"My name is not Angel and I don't need to sit down. May I have my keys back now?"

"Why? I doubt you can drive with that thing on your leg."

"This thing on my leg is none of your business. My keys, please." She could have told him she drove Lilly last night just fine. But she didn't feel she owed him an explanation.

"How's Oreo?" he asked.

"How's Elizabeth?" she countered, instantly disliking the pettiness in her voice. He winced, then removed her keys from his drawer and laid them on the desk. She reconsidered the sharp edge to her words, attributing her nastiness to lack of sleep. The plastic cast was extremely uncomfortable. Even faithful Oreo had abandoned the bed after her constant fidgeting. She softened her tone. "I think Oreo's as anxious to move back home as I am."

"You could have avoided all that family involvement, you know."

His gentle reminder was akin to holding a lollipop just out of reach of a grasping child. She straightened her posture. "No, I don't think that would have been possible. Now, if you can tell me where you parked the car."

"It's in back by the shipping dock."

"Thank you." She reached across his desk, covering the metal keys with her hand. She was about to pick them up when he placed his hand over hers. Her whole body jerked at his touch. She bit her lip, hoping he hadn't noticed. *Calm down*, she willed silently. *He's just touching my hand.* She glanced down, noting that the little identification heart attached to her key chain lay exposed outside the cover of his hand.

"That heart." He poked at it with his free hand. "This is the reason for all those pills, isn't it? There's something wrong with your heart?"

"Not anymore." She shifted uncomfortably under his gaze. "Not exactly. I...I had a transplant three years ago."

"A heart transplant? You have someone else's heart?"

She recognized the pattern. First shock, then curiosity and finally pity. Something shifted within her. She wasn't sure if it was relief or despair that he knew the truth.

"My heart wasn't going to last much longer. When a healthy one became available, I took it." She swatted his hand away and pulled her keys close. "Now if we're through with the freak show." She turned to make a quick exit.

"Angela, wait." Darn the man was fast. He managed to block her exit before she could get to the door. He stood close, too close. His familiar scent, mixed with the lingering fresh smell of a recent shave, drifted to her nose. The metal keys dug into her clenched hand.

"I'm sorry," he said. "I didn't mean to embarrass you. I didn't know."

The building was beginning to come to life. File doors opened and closed, raised voices called in greeting, shoes shuffled on the carpet.

"I've got to go," she whispered.

"Wait, one minute." He continued to block the door. She mentally configured the quickest route to the nearest restroom. Somewhere to go where she could splash water on her burning eyes. "I had a long talk with Elizabeth last night. I explained that there was nothing going on between us. She's leaving this morning for New York."

She glanced up at him. "Your dates are none of my business, Mr. Renard."

He frowned at the use of "mister". "She was rude to you yesterday. I thought you'd want to know she was gone."

"For all the apologizing you've been doing, I'm not sure which of us should be more relieved." The words slipped out before her common sense could stop them. "I'm sorry." Heat infused her face again. "I'm not normally that rude."

"Must be the effect I have on you." He smiled but stepped aside, giving her free access to the door.

"If you'll excuse me, I need to speak with Max before he gets started." She almost collided with Tom Wilson as she stepped into the hallway. "Excuse me," she mumbled as they passed, hoping he didn't notice her high color.

From behind, she heard Hank. "Come on in, Tom. I wanted to talk to you about these accounts payable turn ratios."

Turn ratios? Angie turned quickly, but just caught a glance of the closing office door. Hank wanted to talk about Accounts Payable? Had he noticed the same inconsistencies she had? The little irritation in the back of her skull grew to a suspicious shadow. She walked over to Hank's secretary's desk. Max's flirtatious nature had encouraged frequent visits to the conference room by women delivering documents, coffee, baked goods, etc. Consequently, Angie was on a first name basis with all the female support staff.

"Cathy, can you do me a favor?"

"Sure, Angie, what's up?"

"Can you call Pete Burroughs in Purchasing and tell him I'm running about five minutes late? I want to ask Max to do a little research project for me while I'm meeting with Pete."

"I'll call Pete for you, but Max isn't in the conference room."

"He's not?"

"He mentioned you guys were wrapping up today, so the girls in Accounts Receivable baked a cake for him, kind of a farewell party."

"Don't they know we'll be back in a couple of months for year end?" Cathy shrugged. "Well, if you could deliver this message to Max for me." Angie scribbled a quick note on her legal pad, ripped it on the perforated edge and folded it up in a tidy square. "I'll just go ahead and meet Pete as scheduled."

Pete Burroughs, the Purchasing Manager, fidgeted behind his metal desk. He stood to shake her hand when she entered then stepped behind her to close the office door. Although Pete was one of the few in the department with an office, it was a modular office, little more than a cubicle with a door. Privacy was more imagined than real. She glanced at the collection of framed family photos angled on the credenza behind his desk. A child's joyful smile stirred a memory.

"How's your daughter doing?"

"Some days are better than others." He picked up the photograph. "The latest round of chemotherapy seems to be doing some good. We're hoping this will put the leukemia in remission."

"I'm so sorry for your family. This must be very difficult."

"It's always difficult when one of your children is ill. But that's—" He waved away any further questions. "Thank you for asking." He took his seat. "I thought we covered everything rather thoroughly last week when you and Mr. Renard came through. Was there something that we missed?"

"Direct ships."

"Direct ships?" He looked startled. A thin man, with deep-set eyes magnified by the thick black-rimmed glasses perched high on his nose, he looked like a surprised Chihuahua. His agitated condition made Angie uncomfortable. She glanced quickly at her notes.

"I understand you frequently request that goods be shipped to an outside location— "

Pete interrupted, "I wouldn't say frequently..."

"Well, then let's say, sometimes shipped." Angie countered.

He shrugged. "Sometimes our customers don't want to pick up their merchandise at the warehouse, so we ship it to where they tell us."

"Why not ship it directly to the customer?" She asked. "Why an outside warehouse?"

"I guess you'd have to ask the customer. I just do what I'm told." His lips thinned to a tight straight line. Obviously, this line of questioning wasn't going to get her anywhere.

"Okay." She changed tactics. "What can you tell me about Timone Industries?"

He shifted a bit in his chair, scratched his chin a few times. "They're a local company, I believe. We've done business with them for a couple of years now. What else do you want to know?"

"What do you buy from them?"

"I'd have to check that out." He wrote out TIMONE on a piece of paper. "With three hundred vendors, I can't remember them all. I'll get back to you with that information. Anything else?"

"Do you have a report that shows all the purchase orders issued with direct ship instructions?"

"Nope. That sounds like something you'd have to take up with Data Processing. Tom Wilson would have to ask for it."

Based on her earlier meetings with Tom, she doubted he'd request anything special for her. "Do you have a report that shows how much money you've spent with Timone?"

"I have a report like that for rebate vendors, those vendors that refund some of our money based on purchasing volumes, but Timone doesn't give rebates. You'd have to ask Data Processing, that's another—"

"Yes, I know. Tom would have to ask for it." She sighed, maybe a bit too audibly. This meeting was rapidly becoming a waste of time. "How about a phone number for Timone. Do you at least have that?"

"Now, Angie. I don't want you to be calling our vendors. They might panic and think we're in some sort of financial difficulty. I'll call and ask whatever you want, but I don't want any auditors calling them. Understand?"

Angie paused, disappointed at Pete's refusal to surrender any information, even a telephone number. "All right, Pete." She stood and walked out of the cubicle, but turned once she stepped outside his office. "We're planning to finish up today, so if you could get me that information today, I'd really appre—"

"I'll see what I can do." He closed the flimsy door. The whole partition that made up his office wall shook.

She walked back to the conference room in a quandary. She had nothing tangible to base any suspicions on, and if she was to bring this job in on budget, she couldn't afford to spend another day investigating a mere suspicion.

She found Max hunched over his laptop computer. "Hi, Angie. Got your note."

"Did you find anything?"

Max frowned. "You'd think nowadays, everyone would have a web presence, but I can't find anything on Timone Industries."

"Well, maybe they have a phone number." She checked the inside of a wooden cabinet and recovered the metropolitan phone book. Flipping through the business pages, she ran her finger down the newsprint. "It's not here."

"What?"

"Timone Industries. You'd expect any legitimate business to have a phone number in their local phone directory."

"So you think Timone isn't legitimate?"

"I'm not sure, but this whole direct ship thing just doesn't feel right. I don't want to accuse anyone of wrongdoing without some solid evidence, though."

"Wrongdoing?" He perked up in his seat. "That sounds serious. What are we going to do?"

Angie looked at Max, and noticed a little bit of chocolate frosting clinging to the corner of his mouth. "You've got a little bit of something…" She fingered the corner of her mouth.

"Oh, thanks." He wiped the sugar away. "Someone made a cake in our honor. I brought you back a piece." He pointed to a plump square of chocolate cake on a colorful napkin.

"*Our* honor?" she teased. "I guess it's just coincidence that it's your favorite, chocolate on chocolate." She used the plastic fork next to the napkin to cut out a piece. The rich taste seemed sweeter after the morning's disappointments. "Umm, this is good."

Max just grinned. "There's plenty more. I'm sure if you swung by Accounts Receivable, the girls would cut you another piece."

Inspiration struck. She pushed the paper napkin with the unfinished cake aside.

"Max, I have a mission for you. I want to know how much has been spent with Timone Industries for this year and last, if possible, but I don't want you to talk to Tom Wilson or Pete Burroughs."

"And how—?"

"Accounts Payable must keep track of how much money they pay to each of their vendors so they can issue tax forms at the end of the year. Can you talk to the girls there and see if you can get a copy of the report? If you can't get the information from Accounts Payable, try Purchasing. Pete Burroughs says they track the total dollars spent on rebate vendors, but I bet they do it on all their vendors, maybe they just don't print it on a report. Anyway, see what you can find out from the girls."

Max gave her a mock salute. "No problem."

"Just don't let Wilson or Burroughs catch you snooping around." That caught him up short. His irrepressible smile lifted at one corner and his eyes narrowed slightly.

"Are you on to something?"

"I don't know, but steer clear of them for now."

"The name is Bond...Maxwell Bond," he said in his best Welsh imitation. He glanced at his watch. "I'll be back in about an hour, Miss Moneypenny."

"Max." He hesitated at the door. She wasn't sure why she felt the need to caution him but the words just slipped out. "Be careful."

೦೩೮೦೮೦

Max still hadn't returned by eleven-thirty, and Angie's rumbling stomach reminded her of the consequences of skipping breakfast in favor of keeping Stephen's kitchen clean. As much as she wanted to move out of her mother's house, it would feel good to be back on home turf and not feel obligated to follow someone else's house rules. Besides, with her mother still in Florida, it was almost like having her own place.

The payable clerks probably hijacked Max for lunch, she thought with a smile, knowing Max wouldn't discourage their attention. Just as well. She needed to retrieve her car, preferably without an audience. She grabbed her handbag with its valuable stash of medications and attempted to negotiate the maze of hallways to the shipping dock.

She found the door that separated the office from the unheated warehouse. A blast of fresh air chilled her the moment she opened it. Darn. She grimaced. Her coat was still probably draped over the back of a chair in the conference room. She rubbed the outside of her arms briskly. A respiratory infection that might be merely a discomfort to most people could be a potential death sentence to her. Before she drove to lunch, she'd better retrieve her coat.

She spotted her car parked along a back fence in the general area described by Renard. Unlocking the car door, she even welcomed the tiny wisps of dog hair clinging to the upholstered seats. This car represented home as much as any place on earth, and she took a moment to savor it before starting the engine and driving it around to the front of the building.

She'd just parked and was walking to the front entrance when a scowling Tom Wilson headed directly toward her.

"I heard you've been pestering Pete Burroughs about that direct ship nonsense."

"Excuse me?"

Wilson sneered down at her. "I told you before you're making a big stink over nothing and I won't have it. Do you hear me?"

"I just asked Pete for—"

"I know what you asked for, and if you don't keep your nose out of things that don't concern you, you're going to regret it."

A chill tripped down her back, whether from the October wind or Wilson's threat, she wasn't sure. She shivered and hugged her arms to her chest.

"Is there a problem here?" Renard's voice called from the parking lot. Both of them turned in his direction. *Great, just what I need,* Angela thought. Why did he always show up when her lack of negotiation skills were on full display?

"No, no problem," she said. "Just a slight disagreement." *Drive on,* she mentally urged, *just drive on.* Wilson continued to glare, all semblance of a congenial Southern gentleman gone.

"Tom?" Renard asked through his lowered window. "Everything okay?"

"Everything's fine. We were...talking." Wilson frowned. Angie struggled to keep her smile glued in place. Obviously, her rendition wasn't good enough. He had to ask Wilson as well.

"In that case, why don't the both of you join me for lunch? I'm just going down the street to Timothy's. Some company would be nice."

"I can't." Tom turned away. "Maybe some other time. I've made plans." Tom stormed away toward his car. Angela watched, wondering why her meeting with Pete Burroughs had generated such a response.

"Angie?"

She watched Tom for a few moments until he had closed his car door and started the ignition. Half of her wanted to accept Hank's invitation, the half that remembered the feel of his arms and the sweet warmth of his breath; but the other half, the wise and sane half that knew about Elizabeth and her connection to his position, urged her to turn him down. She took a few steps toward Hank's car, looking both ways in the parking lot before she lowered her voice. "I don't think it's wise."

"What's wrong with lunch? We're two business people going out for a business lunch. Surely, Falstaff can't object to that."

A brief flare of indignation fired through her. "I wasn't even thinking about Falstaff."

"Good. Then there's no reason not to join me." He nodded his head toward the passenger side of his car. "Come on. It's your last day here. Let me take you out to lunch."

She glanced back at her Civic. Maybe lunch wouldn't be so bad, she thought. With everything else, she hadn't broached the subject of selling additional services, the one condition Falstaff had placed between herself and a promotion. "Can you wait while I grab my coat?"

Hank nodded and she dashed back to the conference room. Reappearing moments later, she crossed in front of Hank's car and slipped into the front seat. She was so careful to keep plenty of distance between them that it was a wonder she didn't smash her right side black and blue when she closed the car door.

"I won't bite, you know," he said after a quick glance in her direction. "Mind telling me what that disagreement was about?"

"Tom was just giving me his opinion of what I should or should not be doing in regard to my audit tests," Angie answered. "He seems to think we're asking too many questions."

"Well, maybe you are. Had you considered that? Maybe if you stepped back and considered the whole picture, certain elements would fall into place. If you think of the concept of..."

She didn't pay attention to the rest of the lecture. At least that's what it felt like. Hank could easily have been one of her doctors reciting complex medical procedures or her brother reading a litany of things she shouldn't, couldn't do. Indignation welled up from her gut until the tips of her ears burned. She shifted in the front seat, pretending to look out the passenger window. If he thought so little of her interpersonal skills, she would never be able to sell him on the idea of additional services. She saw her promotion slipping away like the rapidly passing landscape. Stupid, stupid, stupid! Did she ever really have a chance?

"Did you tell Tom that today would be your last day of field work?"

"I guess that's not soon enough for some people." She sunk deeper into the confines of her coat. "You included."

"Me? What did I do?"

Angie looked at him, then sighed. It was her own fault. She had allowed herself to imagine that just because she felt so right nestled in his arms last Saturday, he might have changed his views on her professionalism. But was it professional to pout this way? Probably not.

"I'm sorry. I shouldn't have said that. I've been on edge. I just assumed..."

"Assumed what?" he asked.

"I seem to be causing problems between you and your girlfriend. And you haven't been overjoyed with my work, and—"

"Wait a minute. What do you mean I haven't been overjoyed with your work? Why would you say something like that?" She saw his scowl when he glanced in the rear view mirror. Heck, she couldn't even grovel without getting him upset.

"You've criticized everything I've done since day one. You've doubted my word. You've questioned my ability. I've been both a professional and personal nuisance."

She tilted her head over her opened handbag, hoping her hair would shield her face from his view. There, she had said it. Although how the words had escaped past the constriction of her throat, she had no idea. She searched in vain for a tissue in her purse, pill bottles rattling from one side to the other. No luck. Instead she pressed her forehead against the side window, hoping the cool glass might calm the burning in her cheeks.

She squeezed her eyes shut to stem threatening tears, but one leaked out the corner and down her cheek. Once established, the wet track encouraged more. She discreetly tried to blot them away with the cuff of her coat, but that's when she noticed the crowded parking lot of Timothy's. As if it wasn't enough that she was crying in front of this arrogant, controlling *man*, now her humiliation would be on show for everyone inside the popular lunch spot.

She tried to sniff back the rapidly descending nasal drip, but her sniff emerged as a loud snort, followed by a barrage of tears.

The traffic light changed and the car moved forward, past the entrance to the restaurant. He didn't say anything and she didn't ask. She closed her eyes and fought to bring her emotions under control. *It's the pills*, she tried to tell herself. Sometimes the combinations and massive quantities played havoc with her emotional stability, but she suspected that she couldn't blame this debacle entirely on medication.

Eventually, the tears subsided and she felt more in control. A tap on her knee brought her face away from the window. Hank held out a precisely folded, pristine handkerchief.

She tried to smile in response but a few more tears escaped, ruining the effect. She swabbed her cheeks, blotted her eyes, then emptied her nose in the soft cotton that smelled so much like him; fresh, crisp and manly.

"Angie," he said, his tone as gentle as the cloth in her hand. "Your work has been fine. I'm the one who's been the problem."

He waited a few moments, probably expecting her to disagree, but she didn't. She couldn't trust her voice just yet.

"It's important that I succeed in this job for reasons I can't go into right now," he said. "The timing of your interim audit work provided a means for me to learn about the operations of the company in a way that wouldn't have been possible otherwise. But your goals in performing compliance testing are different from mine. If I've seemed overly critical, it wasn't because of your work. It was because I needed to accomplish something else. I was frustrated. In hindsight, it was probably unfair to watch over your shoulder the way I did."

She faced forward and squeezed his handkerchief into a tight little ball. He looked over at her expectantly, but she didn't respond. She could control either her words or her tears, but not both. So she stayed silent and squeezed the cloth tighter. After an uncomfortable period of quiet, she heard him sigh.

"You know, Angie, I don't know anyone in this town. What I could really use is a friend."

She took a deep breath. "I don't think Falstaff— "

"Don't tell me we can't even be friends. Surely, they don't want us to be enemies, do they?" She shook her head from side to side. "Okay then. Friends." This time his audible sigh had a dramatic quality. "I feel better all ready."

She couldn't stop the smile that pulled at the corners of her mouth. "I suppose it's all right. The partners play golf with clients and some invite them to parties and such."

"Do you play golf?" She heard such eagerness in his voice, she hated to disappoint him, again.

"No. Golf was one of those activities my mother forbid. I'm not sure which was considered worse, the fresh air or the exercise." He seemed surprised.

"I thought exercise would be a good thing."

"It is, as long as it's not too strenuous, which when you think about it, isn't exercise at all." He laughed at the irony which in turn lifted some of her embarrassment. She relaxed a bit. "I guess we can be friends, as long as we're not too close."

"Not too close," he agreed with a nod. His eyes never left the road. "So listen, as one friend to another, do you have any idea where we are?"

Her jaw dropped several inches before she focused on the herd of cows grazing in the pasture to her right. Hayden was situated on the urban border between industrial Columbus and the surrounding rural community. It didn't require extensive travel to reach open pastures and dilapidated, picturesque barns, but it still came as a shock. "I remember passing Timothy's parking lot, but I guess I just didn't pay attention after that."

He shrugged. "I just thought you weren't ready to —"

"You were right. Thanks for giving me some time." She sniffed, and tears gathered at the corner of her eyes. *Don't*, she scolded herself. She took a deep breath and pointed to a white steeple rising above the bare trees in the distance. "That's Granville. It's a sleepy little college town. We can find someplace to grab a bite over there."

"See, where would I be without my friends?" he teased.

"Utterly and totally lost," she answered.

Knowing her eyes were undoubtedly red and swollen from her emotional outburst, she had hoped he would stop someplace where they could eat in the car and she might avoid curious glances. He chose, however, an inviting restaurant, quaint and historic, if the brass plaque beside the entrance was to be believed. She lost her concern about her appearance the moment they stepped inside.

Tables, covered in white linen, were scattered throughout many small connecting rooms and patrons were disbursed accordingly, allowing each a sense of privacy. She and Hank were seated in a sunny room with ancient white plastered walls and gleaming antique furniture. The scent of smoke from a wood-burning fireplace lent a sense of intimacy to the open surroundings. One other couple sat at the opposite end of the room. No one here would recognize her, much less criticize her appearance or judgment. She shed her coat and felt an emotional burden lift from her shoulders as well.

After a quick study of the menu, they ordered. Angie leaned back in a surprisingly comfortable wooden chair and Hank leaned forward, cradling a glass of iced tea.

"What's it like having someone else's heart?"

The question surprised her, although she had been asked it many times in the past. But never quite so directly.

"Someone else's healthy heart," she said, stressing the word healthy. "It's wonderful, invigorating, stimulating. I can do things I never could do before."

"Like what?"

"Like get out of bed." She smiled. "Hold down a job. Go to a restaurant." There were many more personal things she could add to that list. Things she had confided to a diary but hadn't had the opportunity to experience with another person. *And probably never will.*

"How long does this one last?"

"A lifetime." Her pat answer caused him to practically choke on his iced tea. She felt a little remorse at shifting the discomfort of these all too familiar questions. But not much. She waited until he took another sip and was breathing easily again. "Actually, as long as I'm careful about taking my medication, I should be okay for another twenty years."

"Do you ever wonder about the donor? What kind of person they were, that sort of thing?" he asked in a breathless voice. Apparently he hadn't recovered as much from his choking incident as she had supposed. She took a long sip of her iced tea and thought about how to answer his question. Their waiter appeared with their lunches, giving her a few extra moments to compose her thoughts.

"I know she was a young woman, although older than I was at the time of the transplant." She pushed the green pepper garnish off the mound of chicken salad. "That's really all I know."

"Don't they have agencies that can tell you more?"

She shrugged, not wanting to answer. She didn't want to know more about the donor, although it was difficult to explain to strangers. Every June, when her family celebrated her successful transplant, Angie knew another family somewhere was grieving over a different sort of anniversary. She may not be responsible for that person's death, but the guilt was the same.

After an awkward silence, Hank said, "It must have been difficult growing up with that kind of condition."

"It was quiet," she replied without pause. "My family was afraid that any kind of excitement, loud noises, or physical exercise, just about anything would throw me into heart failure. My life was tiptoes and whispers.

"School?"

"Home-tutored," she managed to slip in a few bites between words. "Less risk of those nasty childhood infections that way."

"You don't sound too happy about it."

"I missed so much growing up, birthday parties and Halloween parades, high school dances and football games. I suppose you always want what you can't have." She struggled to keep the wistfulness out of her voice. "I wanted so much to be like the other kids, but I had to sit on the sidelines. I always got to hand out the candy, never dress up in the costumes."

"Can you do those things now?"

She smiled. "Perhaps, but it's a little different now that I'm all grown up." His dimple flashed, and she anticipated a comment about her diminutive size. She pointed her fork at him. "Don't even think about it."

He threw up his hands in surrender, "What?" But they both laughed at the unsaid joke and worked on their lunches a bit. Hank broke the fork-clicking silence.

"Maybe it's not too late. You can still experience all those things you missed through your children."

She placed her fork on her plate, the food had lost its appeal. "I can never have children. The doctors say it would be too risky to put such a physical strain on my heart." She took a deep breath. "And then, of course, all those medications I take would cross over to the fetus." It hurt. She knew all the logic, but it still hurt. "I suppose it's a small price for a chance at life."

"But there are other ways..."

She looked at her watch. "Can we go back now? I don't want to leave Max alone too long, although knowing Max, companionship is one thing he never lacks."

In a Heartbeat

"Cathy brought me a piece of the cake. Are you really finishing up today? I didn't mean to scare you off." He sounded sincere and for an instant she almost regretted announcing her intention to wrap things up. Now that he knew the whole truth about her heart, she had expected he'd be anxious to see her go. Her medical condition made most people nervous. But Hank... Well, he hid any discomfort well.

"It's not you," she lied. "Our field budget is just about spent. There's a few loose ends, but I think we can resolve those from the office."

"Figures." He flagged down the waiter for the check. "Just when I find a friend, she runs off."

"Well, maybe I won't run too far," she said, feeling empowered by his mention of their pact. "I'd like to talk to you about additional services."

"Additional services?" he repeated, placing an appropriate number of bills on the table. "Sounds expensive." He helped her with her coat as her confidence slowly deflated. "I'm not sure now is the right time, but we'll discuss it on our way back. Shall we?"

☙❧

"Bummer." Max studied the decided tilt of the Honda Civic and the spill of black rubber around the left front tire. "You got a spare?"

Bummer summed up her day perfectly. First the public argument with Wilson in the parking lot, then the emotional outburst in front of Hank, followed by his refusal to consider additional services, followed by the discovery that she had caught part of her coat in the car door. It had dragged in the muck from Granville back to Hayden. Not unlike her own self-esteem, she added. Now this.

"I don't understand." She set her bulky audit bag on the curb. "Everything was fine at lunchtime. This tire wasn't even low." She groaned. "Why me? Why now?"

"Who knows? Maybe you picked up a piece of glass." Max stripped off his suit coat and dropped it across the audit bag. He rolled up his sleeves, then loosened his tie. "Got your keys?"

She handed them to him. He crossed to the trunk and removed the jack and spare tire. "Ever change a tire?" Angie shook her head. "Then watch and learn."

Angie watched so intently, she missed the shadow that fell over the precariously tilted car.

"Is there a problem here?"

Angie bumped into the adjacent car in response to his voice. Her hand fluttered to her heart.

"Mr. Renard," Max called in greeting. "Angie's having a little bit of a problem with a flat."

"I see." Hank slipped his hand under Angie's arm to help steady her. "Do you need any help?"

"No, I think I've got it here." Max pulled the bad tire off the rim and rolled it to the back of the car for closer inspection.

Angie removed Hank's hand from her arm. "Thank you for your concern, Mr. Renard, but you can see Max has everything under control."

"I'll be darned," Max glanced up to Angie. "I think you better take a look at this."

Both Hank and Angie hurried to the back of the car.

"Here's the problem." Max pushed down on the sidewall, exposing an inch wide slash in the rubber. Hank and Max exchanged glances.

"What is it?" Angie asked. "What's wrong?"

"It looks like this was no accident." Max said.

"Someone slashed your tire." Hank added.

"Who would do something like that?" Angie poked around the gash as if the perpetrator had carved his initials in the rubber. "Why would someone want to slash my tire?"

"Good question," Max said. He looked at Angie, then Hank, before fitting the tire in the trunk. He rolled the spare to the naked axle.

"You'll have to replace that tire," Hank said. "Do you have insurance?"

She nodded. "Why would someone do that?" She shaded her eyes with her hand as she looked up at Hank. "Do you think it could be a mistake? Someone thought my car was someone else's?" She glanced around the parking lot, hoping to see another Civic parked nearby. Not a one in sight.

"Could be." He followed her gaze around the parking lot. "Or it could be something else. Either way," he lowered his voice, "be careful."

෦ෂ෯෨

"It's good to be home, isn't it, girl?" Angie bent down to brush her hand along Oreo's back before she slipped the key into the front door lock. The dog raced inside before her, but she followed close behind. She closed the front door and stumbled into the nearest chair. "Let me catch my breath for a minute." Oreo finished her inspection of the house and returned triumphantly to flop at Angie's feet with her favorite squeaky toy.

Immediately, the phone began to ring. "Let the machine get it," she instructed the dog, then laughed when Oreo cocked her head at the suggestion.

"Angela? It's Mom. Are you sure it's wise to move back to the house? Stephen was quite upset that you moved out and were driving home by yourself. I'm not sure I approve." Angela grimaced, remembering the argument she and Stephen shared when she drove the Civic to his place after work. It sure didn't take him long to get Mom on his side.

"I'm a little worried, dear, with your foot and all. Stephen said the weatherman is calling for sleet turning to snow tonight. Call me when you get in so I'll know you're all right. Perhaps I should find someone to stay with Ceal and come home. You shouldn't be all alone with... What's that?" Angie could hear background voices but couldn't make out the words. The tape continued, "Ceal sends her love. I have to go now. Call me. I love you." *Click.*

Angie pushed herself out of the chair and walked to the kitchen. She drew a large glass of tap water and stared out the back window. Given the weather forecast, perhaps tonight wasn't the best night to investigate that strange address for Timone Industries. *It's probably nothing,* she told herself. She squinted out the window, but it was too dark to see anything.

No point driving out in bad weather to check out a legitimate address.

"You feeling neglected?" she asked the plants on the windowsill, giving them a drink from the glass in her hand. "I bet Stephen forgot all about you when he stopped by for the mail." The phone rang. Angela sighed and dumped the rest of the water unceremoniously on the dieffenbachia. She picked up the receiver. "Hi, Mom, I was—"

Click. She looked at the receiver as if it could tell her who had just hung up on her. "Okay, if you don't want to talk, that's okay with me." She headed for the kitchen to fill Oreo's dog dish. "We sure could use a nice, quiet night at home, couldn't we, girl?"

The dog's tail wagged a few times, then stopped. Oreo issued a low warning growl, seconds before someone knocked on the door.

"Just a minute." Angela frowned at the dog, which ran down the front hallway at full bark. She placed the filled dish on the floor, then cautiously opened the door enough to peek outside. "Oh, Mr. Thomas, uh, Walter." She reached down and caught Oreo by her collar.

She shuddered, something about that man... What did Hank call him, a little weasel? Holding the dog by her side, she opened the door a little wider.

"I just stopped by to see how you were. Your brother said you had an accident."

"That's very neighborly of you," she said dismissing the other adjective that had sprung to mind. "It was nothing serious, just the leg." She feigned a quick laugh and tried to gesture to her plastic cast, but Oreo pulled so hard in an attempt to lunge at the man, it threw her a little off balance. Walter jumped back a foot or so.

"Oreo," she scolded. "Stop that."

"I'm just next door if you need anything," Walter added in full retreat. "I'm glad to see you back."

"Me too." she replied, but he was already halfway across the front yard. "You bad dog," she lectured as she closed the door. "That wasn't very nice." Oreo drooped her ears and head.

Even her tail lowered an inch or two before slowly resuming its steady sideways swing.

Alone once again, Angela surveyed the living room. A shiver tripped down her spine, but she brushed it off. A few lit candles would banish the stuffiness, she decided, and an evening wrapped in one of her mother's quilts with a cup of hot chocolate and an intriguing romance novel would chase the uneasiness from her bones. But first, a call to Mom before the phone started ringing again.

Chapter Ten

Safely ensconced in the firm's library, Angela studied the audit workpapers spread on the conference table. The walls of leather-bound books and the hint of wood polish normally instilled a comforting sense of tradition. Today, however, an anxiety pricked at her consciousness, disturbing the serene environment.

"How many documents couldn't they find?" she asked Max.

"Just three, but Beth said Accounts Payable hired this goofy file clerk about six months ago. She only lasted two months, but they still haven't cleaned up the damage she did to the filing system." Max's brows lifted. "Is that so bad? They found forty-seven of the fifty I asked them to pull."

"That's not the point, Max. We requested a sample of invoices. Missing anything in a sample could mean we're looking at the tip of an iceberg. There could be lots of missing invoices."

"Or it could mean they couldn't find three invoices." Max ran his fingers down his scarlet and gray striped tie, accidentally triggering the little metal insert that played the Ohio State University fight song in tinny notes. Angela leaned back in her chair.

"You're starting early, aren't you? The big game's not till this Saturday."

"It's never too early for football. The whole city is gearing up for the game. Some alumni you are," he scolded, "I'm surprised you're not wearing scarlet and gray."

Angie reached in her pocket and rolled a buckeye, the symbol of the university's football team, across the table.

"I knew it." Max caught the nut as it wobbled to the table edge. "Do you have tickets?"

"Are you kidding? My alumni status earned me a bleacher seat for a non-conference game. I gave it to my brother. He's a bigger fan than I am." She didn't add that she'd never attended a football game. Her imperfect heart and an over-protective family wouldn't allow it.

"A bunch of us are going to Timothy's to watch the game on the big screen. You can always join us." Max rolled the buckeye back to her.

"We'll see." Angie slipped the charm back in her pocket. "Meanwhile, I think we should get back to business."

Max slid the workpaper over to his side of the table. "What do you want me to do? I could write up the missing invoices for the letter of recommendations," Max offered. "Or I could go back out there and look at some more invoices." He tilted his head, accurately reading Angela's mind. "Of course, if I go back out, we'll probably overrun the budget for interim work."

"Something about this whole thing isn't right." She hesitated, staring at the papers. "Were the missing invoices all from the same vendor?"

"Nope. Three different invoices, three different vendors." Max slipped his hands deep in his pants pocket. "What's it going to be?"

She hesitated for a moment. "I definitely want you to write this up for the letter of recommendation. At the very least, not producing the documents shows a lack of control over processed invoices. Then, take another look to see if there's some commonality between the three. Were they all processed in the same month? Were they for the same item? Would the same accounts payable clerk have been responsible for them?"

One of the office secretaries poked her head around the library door. "Angie? Mr. Falstaff wants to see you."

A solid weight plummeted through her stomach.

"Be right there," she called in what she hoped was a confident tone. She glanced up at Max, noting his conflicting expressions of sympathy and curiosity. "See if you can find something to tie this down a little tighter." She pushed away from the table. "Then we'll figure out what to do."

Angela managed her way down the hallway to the corner office with hardly a wobble. As long as she stayed off her feet for most of the day, her plastic brace and unattractive tennis shoe remained the only evidence of her mishap last week.

The secretary's desk was empty, but the door to Falstaff's office stood ajar. Angela paused to knock on the doorframe before entering.

"Angela, come in. Come in." Falstaff didn't rise, gesturing instead to the two chairs in front of the paper-strewn desk. "Have a seat." She selected the chair closest to the door, sitting uncomfortably erect on the edge of the seat. "I understand you've made quite an impression on Mr. Renard."

Panic quickened Angie's heartbeat. Who told? She tried to remember if anyone had passed the two of them in the car that first night, or had someone overheard an argument? Maybe after he dismissed the need for additional services, Hank had decided to dismiss her as well and called Falstaff. No, Hank's invitation for friendship was sincere. Wasn't it?

"After his initial reaction, I had thought there might be problems. The thing is—" He removed his wire rim glasses and let them hang from his fingers. "Renard's offered Falstaff and Watterson four seats to the Ohio State football game this weekend. He insists the audit team attend."

"I beg your pardon?" Angie asked, stunned that she wasn't the recipient of a client relations lecture.

"Hayden Manufacturing has a box at the stadium. Excellent seats. Owens invited me a few years back. That was some game, let me tell you." He squinted in Angela's direction. "Quite a coup for you and young Max to be invited."

"Can we accept? I mean," Angela stumbled. "Wouldn't this threaten our independence and all that?"

"A football game?" Falstaff laughed, barely able to resettle his glasses on his nose. "Seriously, this gives you a perfect opportunity to talk to Renard about extended services, and I'll be right there to help you along."

"You'll be there?" Her initial sense of bewilderment rapidly descended into panic. She hadn't mentioned Hank's earlier dismissal of the entire subject, hoping Falstaff would forget this condition of her promotion.

"Of course, I'll be there. It should be a great game and I wouldn't want to insult our host by turning down his invitation. We still need a fourth. Who's the tax partner assigned to Hayden?"

She answered, but her mind had already tuned out of the conversation. What could be worse than being put on the spot in front of her boss and associates, with a man who had already turned her down, and at a game totally foreign to her. All this on top of a vague suspicion that something wasn't quite right in—

"Angie?"

"Oh, sorry." Her focus returned to the conversation at hand. "Did you ask me something?"

"I wondered if you had found anything specific that we could parlay into extended services?" He toyed with a pencil, glancing at her over the rim of his glasses.

"Well, we've had a bit of a problem with missing vendor invoices, but I'm not sure—"

"Splendid. We could review and make recommendations about the whole accounts payable process. Excellent work. We'll talk to Renard about it." Falstaff settled back in his chair with a satisfied grin. "Keep it up, Angela. You'll be a partner before you know it."

Angie recognized her cue to leave. After an obligatory thank you, she returned to the library. Max glanced up from his worksheet.

"How'd it go?"

Horrible. "Not bad," she answered. "Renard's given us seats to the game this weekend."

"You're kidding!" Max's jaw dropped. "I heard the scalpers are asking $600 for tickets, and we get to go free?" At her nod, Max jumped up and danced around the room to the tinny refrains of his tie. Angela slumped in the chair.

"Why so glum?"

"Nothing important." She certainly didn't want to discuss the possibility that the game on Saturday might destroy all hope for advancement within the firm. Nor did she want to disclose her ignorance about football in general. That would lead to questions she would prefer to avoid. She sighed. There had been much speculation on the radio and television about winners and losers of the game on Saturday. Unfortunately, she suspected she already knew who would lose, and it wouldn't be either of the teams.

She shifted position so she could rest her foot on the opposite chair. The best she could do now was wrap up this Hayden assignment and bring it in under budget. Maybe that would be worth something. Perhaps Falstaff would reconsider his ultimatum if she excelled in other areas. She glanced at Max. "Did you discover anything about the missing invoices?"

"As a matter of fact, I did." His smile extended from ear to ear. "They're all direct ships."

"To that same address on Ritchton?" An uneasiness filled her at his nod. She'd put off investigating Ritchton Street before for one reason or another, but so many uncertainties seemed to hover around that address.

"Is there anything else, Angie? I've got some buddies I want to call, rub in the good news."

She waved him off while she pondered her next move.

Her gaze settled on Max's stack of computer printouts. Pulling them closer, she rifled through them and found a report showing the total amount paid to all the various vendors. Yes. Leave it to sweet-talking Max. She flipped to Timone Industries. At one hundred thousand dollars, Timone wasn't one of the largest of Hayden's vendors, but it wasn't one of the smallest either.

Why didn't Pete Burroughs know this report existed? Or did he? Why the big secret?

Max returned, whistling the university fight song. "This is too cool. I hear that some of the local corporations have the best seats in the stadium. I can't wait till Saturday."

"Max, can I entice you into a little more subterfuge?"

"What's up? More digging around for reports?" he asked. "Are there women involved?" He bobbed his eyebrows up and down.

"Just me, I'm afraid," she laughed. "This time I had something a little more physical in mind."

"Even better." He twirled the ends of an imaginary mustache.

"Stop that," Angie scolded, laughing right along with him. "I want to check out Timone Industries on Ritchton Street, but I don't want to go alone. Can you come with me?"

"Maybe. When do you want to go?"

"As soon as possible." She glanced back down to the computer report. "I'd like to settle this thing in my head. Maybe it's nothing but..."

"Can't go tonight, and I've got a date for tomorrow. I plan to be doing some celebrating after the game on Saturday... Is Sunday too late?"

"Can we go at night?" Angie asked. "I don't want anyone to see us."

"Wow." The laughter left his face. "You're really serious about this, aren't you?"

"It's probably just my wild imagination." She brushed it off, as if crazy ideas about investigating suspicious addresses at night were an everyday occurrence. "I just want to check it out."

CB❀BO

That evening, Angie set a big bowl of popcorn on the coffee table in front of the television, next to a legal pad and a pen. She refused to look like a complete idiot on Saturday. She might not have any control over Falstaff's appearance, but thanks to the Internet, she'd already researched the rules of the game. She crossed to the desk to retrieve some of the material she had printed out. Oreo advanced, her nose twitching delicately at the fluffy white kernels.

"Back off." Angie gave her a gentle push. "This isn't for you. I have some serious work to do." She pushed a button on the remote controller and the television screen came alive with pictures of dancing cheerleaders.

A knock at the door interrupted. Great. Her brother must have changed his mind about her emergency plea for help.

"Stephen. I didn't think you could make it." She pulled the door open. Walter Thomas stood on the porch. Her jubilant greeting died in her throat.

"I'm sorry for disturbing you." He shifted a small brown paper bag from one hand to the other. "You were obviously expecting someone else."

"Just my brother." She peeked down the driveway, hoping Stephen, or Max or anyone would suddenly appear at the outside door. No luck. "He promised to stop by and teach me about football."

"I won't keep you then."

A low growl issued from behind her. She closed the door a little so her body would block the entire opening. "I'd invite you in, but the dog..."

"Yes, yes, I understand. Actually, I brought something for the dog. Oreo, isn't it?" He reached in the bag and withdrew a rawhide bone. "I thought maybe we could make friends."

The growls intensified, interspersed with frustrated whimpering.

"I don't know." Angie glanced at the canine nose forcing its way between her leg and the doorframe. "I don't think she's ready for this."

He offered the bone to the protruding nose, but Oreo backed up and began barking furiously. Walter shoved the bag and the bone into Angie's hands. "Maybe you should just give this to the dog later."

"Thank you, Walter," she called to his retreating back, "I'm sure Oreo will enjoy it." He disappeared into the night.

"That wasn't very nice." She closed the door, scowling at the dog. Oreo's head drooped a few inches but her tail started a slight wag. "He even brought you a gift, but I doubt Mom wants a chewed up bone in the house." She walked down the hallway and dropped the bag on the kitchen counter. "We'll save it for outside."

She returned to her seat on the couch. Oreo sat by her side, looking up with woeful eyes full of apology.

"Can't say as I blame you though." A shudder slipped down her back. "Something about that man gives me the willies." Oreo stood up, her tail in full swing.

"Come on," Angie invited. "Let's watch some football." After tossing Oreo a few kernels of popcorn, she began counting the players on each team. If I'm going to learn this game, might as well start with numbers.

ಌଚ଼ଉଞ

On Saturday, she quickly realized the television hadn't done justice to the actual game experience. Max had parked the car and ushered her quickly through the crowds streaming toward a massive concrete stadium. She was jostled and bumped from all directions by people dressed in all manner of outrageous combinations of scarlet and gray. The air crackled with pre-recorded band music, amplified radio broadcasts and loud conversation, all floating on the aromas of freshly popped popcorn and long-simmering hot dogs. Max steered her towards a ramp that opened into the interior of the stadium. The noise and excitement magnified ten times when she emerged from the tunnel passageway to a blustering October wind. The intensity of the thousands of cheering football fans already seated smacked into all her senses at once, overwhelming and invigorating. She loved it.

"Come on, we just can't stand here." Max tugged on her elbow. "We have to go up there." He turned and pointed up a very steep and very narrow column of concrete steps.

They weren't the first to arrive. Tom Wilson and Pete Burroughs were already seated in "the box" which in reality consisted of two rows of four wooden folding chairs placed on a narrow concrete ledge. Angie hesitated. Another lump of discomfort dumped into her already roiling stomach. She pasted on a smile, gritted her teeth and followed Max to their assigned seats in the back row, opposite the two Hayden executives. The four seats in the front row remained empty.

"This is great," Max said after the cursory greetings. "We're right at midfield. High enough to see the entire field, without resorting to the upper deck. I'd never get seats like this on my own."

Angie merely nodded, focused instead on the field. The players below were running in systematic patterns unlike anything she'd seen on television. Panic chipped away at the little bit of confidence she'd earned through her research.

"Uh-oh, here comes trouble." Max's binoculars pointed to the bottom of the concrete steps.

"What do you see?" she asked, abandoning her study of the statistics displayed on the electronic scoreboard.

"Falstaff and that tax partner, Peters."

She could see the two men pulling themselves up the steep incline with the help of a handrail. About fifteen people behind them, she noticed Renard. She hadn't seen him for three days, and although she knew he'd be here, seeing him again gave her a jolt. She watched his slow advance.

"Angie, are you okay?" Max lowered the binoculars a bit. "You look a little pale."

"I'm fine, Max," she replied automatically, while deep inside she knew she was not.

She stood when the partners arrived, and introduced them to the other box inhabitants. Hank reached the box before everyone could sit down. Handshakes were exchanged once again amid new introductions. Falstaff and Peters sat down in front of Max and Angie, allowing her a sigh of relief. Surely, she couldn't be expected to talk business with Hank when he sat on the far side of the box. Besides, with Falstaff seated next to Renard, her expertise would probably not be needed. She could sit back and enjoy the game.

They all stood while the band took the field, and clapped to the invigorating marching rhythm. Hank leaned back behind Falstaff and waved for her attention.

"How about coming up here and sitting on the other side of me?" he yelled over the enthusiastic fans cheering for the entering players. Falstaff glanced over his shoulder and winked. She couldn't gracefully refuse. The others shuffled chairs and bodies, allowing her to negotiate the edge of the concrete ledge. One misstep and she imagined she would roll head over heels down that sharp incline, all the way to the turf. She gulped, quickly gaining her seat and already missing the security of the back row.

Hank leaned closer to her ear. Instantly, Angie recognized the woodsy scent that singled him out from the thousands of men in the stadium. His warm breath stirred the air around her sensitive earlobe. Her fear forgotten, she instinctively moved closer, drawn to his heat.

"Cathy's coming," he said. "She asked if she could sit next to Max. You won't tell him, will you?"

These were not the words she expected. Neither was her resulting disappointment although she wouldn't admit the reason why. "Is that why you invited us to the game?" she asked. "For matchmaking?" While the rest of the stadium cheered madly for who-knew-what, a part of her caved in and collapsed.

"No. Cathy's request came after the invitation." He leaned close again, sharing words for her ears alone. "I wanted to share a football game with a friend."

She blossomed inside. It was the only way she could describe that tender, opening sensation that lifted her spirits and warmed her to the tips of her fingers. The man had the ability to make her insides shrivel and expand at a moment's notice. And she was expected to talk business with him? She bit her lower lip.

"We've missed the kick-off," she said.

"So we have." His gaze skimmed over her face. All her nerve endings went on high alert. He should be watching the field, not looking at her.

"Some people say the kick-off is the most important part of the game."

"Perhaps, but I'm a strategy man myself." He focused on her lips. She moistened them quickly with the tip of her tongue. His smile spread slowly, pulled by deepening dimples. "I like to watch the plays develop," he said. "Slow and sure with a focused target in mind."

She wasn't sure if he was talking about football, or the intense yearning building inside of her. She swallowed.

"You know the home team supplies the balls for the game," she said in an effort to regain control over her emotions. "They have to have thirty-six footballs available."

His eyes crinkled as he looked toward the field. "Is that so?"

"Yes, they'd have to have twenty-four available if this were a domed stadium."

"Well, Angie," he raised his voice and squinted at the field, "you sure know your football."

Cathy arrived and took the only empty seat available, the one next to Max. All the men in the box seemed enthralled with the game and engaged in little conversation other than an occasional yell at no one in particular. Angie relaxed and actually started to enjoy herself. She laughed at the animations on the giant scoreboard and stood with the others in something called a "wave". Although she never managed to see an actual infraction of the rules, due to her research, she understood the arm gestures of the referees before the announcer explained them to the uninformed public. By the end of the second quarter, she was yelling and cheering with the rest of the box occupants. She was feeling good.

Falstaff leaned over towards Hank. "Angela tells me you're having some problems with your accounts payable."

"Oh." Hank sounded genuinely surprised.

"Tell him, Angela," Falstaff prodded. "Tell him what you've noted during the interim work."

All the pageantry of the bands and cheerleaders down on the field couldn't lift the rock of apprehension that settled in her stomach. She heard shuffling behind her and knew Wilson had edged forward at the mention of accounts payable. She could well imagine his glare boring into her back.

"Well, I noticed the warehouse was unattended when the overhead doors were open. That could lead to theft, you know." She dared to glance up. Hank nodded thoughtfully in response. "It's outside the role of our interim work, but we could monitor the warehouse for this condition and maybe make recommendations..."

"Tell him about the missing invoices," Falstaff said, not letting her take a breath.

"Your staff couldn't provide a number of the payable invoices that we specifically requested. This could be an indication of several problem areas, such as unauthorized payment, or payment to fictitious vendors, or—"

"Poor filing procedures?" Hank asked.

"Perhaps," Angie conceded. "Hopefully, that's all that's wrong. But the missing invoice can be the first warning of something potentially much more serious."

Hank seemed to consider the possibility. At least he appeared to be taking the matter in earnest and she found some comfort in that. Angie glanced over toward Falstaff. His face beamed brighter than the shiny brass of the tubas marching onto the field.

Hank shifted towards Falstaff. "I suppose you're suggesting some sort of additional study your people can perform for a price."

"We can do that, most assuredly."

Hank washed his hand over his face. "Your people have done a good job, a competent job for Hayden thus far. However, I'm faced with certain financial constraints that will probably preclude me from utilizing anything beyond the contracted audit. But I'll tell you what. If you'll put together a proposal, I'll give it some serious attention." He stood up. "I need to excuse myself for a few minutes. Anyone want anything from the concession stand?" He glanced quickly around before leaving the box for the stairs.

Competent. Angie could almost feel herself glow. He said they had performed a competent job, to Falstaff no less.

Falstaff reached over and grabbed Angie's hand. "Good work. I knew you could do it. Things look fairly positive. Perhaps I underestimated your marketing skills. We'll talk more about this in the office on Monday."

She slumped back in her wooden chair exhausted, surprised at what a toll the anxiety of this moment had caused. The plastic ankle brace felt like the only part of her body that hadn't gone completely limp. Someone tapped her shoulder from behind. She twisted her body as best she could in the tiny space available and faced Tom Wilson.

"I heard you had some trouble in the parking lot the other day." He smiled, not a particularly pleasant smile, more of a cat-concealing-a-canary smirk.

"It was only a flat tire. Max changed it for—"

"Maybe you should be more careful, Angie. I wouldn't want to see you get hurt."

"Get hurt? But how—?"

Tom stood and stretched. "Think I better go make a run of it before halftime is over," he announced and followed the same path as Renard.

Angie briefly pondered the strange conversation, but the marching antics of the band and the constantly shifting amplitude of the sound soon captured her attention. Eventually Hank and Tom returned. The late afternoon sun had shifted enough to throw deep shadows across the field and add a chilly briskness to the ever-present wind. Angie cheered the hometown team on to victory in the final two quarters. The thoroughly delightful afternoon ended all too soon. With the victory bell tolling from the far end of the stadium, she reluctantly stood to leave. The two partners thanked Hank for the seats and quickly joined the crowds surging down the steps.

"Thank you for the tickets." She held out her hand to shake Hank's as had the two partners before her.

"Yeah, these were great seats." Max moved the folding chairs so he could stand besides Hank. "Angie, we've got to go."

Hank blocked Angie's exit. "Is that wise? Can you manage the steps with that cast on your leg? You could wait here until the crowd thins down."

She took one look at the mass of humanity crowding the narrow concrete aisles, and wished that was an option. "Max is my ride. I promised him we wouldn't stick around after the game. I think I can manage." She glanced up to his eyes. "Thank you again. This was truly a gift."

"I'm glad you enjoyed it."

She started to step around Hank to join Max on his other side when a quick shove from behind sent her tottering on the narrow ledge. Her breath caught. Her arms flailed at the empty air. Just as she felt herself falling backwards, Hank caught her arm and pulled her back to safety. He held her steady while her insides jittered like one of those cheerleader's pom-poms.

"What happened?" Max asked. "Did you trip?"

"Pete stumbled," Wilson said. "He must have bumped you."

"Yeah, I must have bumped into you or something." Pete scowled back at Tom. "Sorry about that."

"Are you all right?" Hank held her shoulders in a death grip. His face drained of color.

"Yes, I think so." Her heart pounded fiercely in her ears. "Just let me sit down for a moment."

"I'm sorry I'm so clumsy," Pete said. "You sure you're okay?"

"It's a wonder you didn't tumble down the stadium," Cathy said, standing discreetly behind Max.

Angie nodded. Hank frowned. "Max, why don't you go on? I'll take Angie home."

She started to protest but he held up his hand in warning. "Those steps are difficult enough to descend in a cast, and after that scare, you'll need a moment to recover." He looked up at Max. "Go ahead, I'll take care of everything."

"Are you sure?" Max looked at Angie, his eyebrows raised.

She smiled. After all the ranting and raving she had done about Renard, it was no wonder Max was concerned to leave her alone with him. "It's okay, Max. You go ahead. I'll be fine. Thanks for the ride over here."

"Sure thing, Angie. We're still on for that project tomorrow, right?"

She nodded and he left followed by Cathy, Pete and Wilson. Soon she was alone with Hank in a rapidly emptying stadium. "Thanks for waiting with me. I'm not sure I could have handled those steps." She cocked her head towards him and squinted. "You always seem to be around when I need rescuing. Why is that?"

"And you need rescuing so often." He laughed. "Are you ready to take on the steps now? You look like you're breathing a bit easier."

They walked to the handrail, but she hesitated. Somehow going down appeared far more terrifying than coming up. "Let me go first," Hank said. "It's not as bad if you can't see the bottom."

"And if I trip?"

"Then we go down together." They both laughed and she followed behind at Hank's deliberately slow pace. They reached the bottom and he took her elbow to steer her toward the tunnel passage. "Did you really enjoy the game?"

"Oh yes. I liked the cheerleaders and mascots and the bands..." She tried unsuccessfully to describe how alive she felt to be a part of so much commotion. "It's not at all the same as watching the game on television."

"No, that it's not," he agreed. "I'm glad you liked it. I've never been able to convince Elizabeth to come to a football game."

"Why not?"

He shrugged, then took her hand. "I wonder if you could do a favor for me, Angela?"

"What kind of favor?" she asked, staring at her hand in his. She was sure Falstaff would disapprove but, darn it, the warmth and strength of his hand covering hers felt too good to protest. Everyone who knew them had left. Maybe she could allow it just this once...

"I have to attend a charity ball and Elizabeth can't—"

She pulled her hand out of his and stopped dead in her tracks. "Oh no, you don't. We've had this discussion before. I told you, I'm not allowed to socialize with clients."

"I've thought of that," he said, tossing the ends of her scarf over her shoulders. "No one will know who you are. It's a masquerade ball. For Halloween. You'll be in costume."

"Masquerade?" She hesitated. She'd never dressed in a costume before, not that she could remember.

"The art museum has a fundraiser." He slipped her hand in his again and steered her towards a car parked at the far end of the stadium lot. "I'm expected to go and I don't want to do it alone. I wouldn't ask if there was anyone else I could invite..."

"What about Elizabeth?"

"She's tied up with a shoot in New York that weekend."

Her defenses weakened. First a real live football game, now a masquerade ball. "I...I don't have a costume."

"Leave it to me. I'll have you covered head to toe, I promise. No one will recognize you."

"No, I can't." She shook her head, and pulled her hand back from his. What was she thinking? There's no way Falstaff would sanction a masquerade ball. In truth, she'd love to go. A lump formed in her throat. She'd never been invited to a dance, much less a costume ball. "It's not that I don't appreciate you asking me." The words caught in her throat, betraying her with an off-key gasp in the middle. She turned and hurried toward the car.

"Angie, wait up--" He ran the few steps after her. "What's the real reason you won't come with me?"

"I told you. It's not allowed." She forged ahead, wishing she hadn't sent Max on his way. She stopped, took a deep breath and turned towards Hank. "Don't they have businesses that lease out women for occasions like these?"

"You mean escort services?" He stopped and looked at her as if she had just suggested he take Oreo as his date. Heat tinged her cheeks. Grabbing her arm, he pulled her toward his car.

"I hadn't realized I was so pathetic that I needed to hire a stranger for companionship." He swore softly under his breath.

She had insulted him. He'd been a perfect gentleman and come to her assistance every time she needed it, and she had insulted him. "I didn't mean to imply..."

"To imply what?" He looked at her with round pleading eyes, the same expression that had earned Oreo all those extra treats the veterinarian constantly scolded her about. He shook his head. "Never mind. If you can't stand to share my company, I'll give the tickets away. I just thought you'd enjoy it."

"And I would. I've never..."

"Never what?"

"Never dressed in a costume before, never pretended to be anything other than what I am." Hadn't she already told him as much at the restaurant? Why was he badgering her?

"And what exactly are you, Angie?"

"Clumsy." She nodded to the plastic cast on her leg. "Uncoordinated." She turned her head away from him. "Boring." Her voice dropped. "A freak."

"What?" He stopped, causing her to swirl around to face him. "What are you talking about? What makes you think you're a freak?"

A lump formed in her throat making the words stick and burn. She tapped her hand to her chest instead.

He pulled her into his arms, holding her tight. She buried her face into his shoulder.

"You're no freak, Angel," He laid his cheek on top of her head. "Not you." He hugged her tight. "And no one could ever say you were boring."

Tears filled her eyes. She hoped his jacket would absorb the wetness so he wouldn't see. She swallowed, forcing the lump down further. "You didn't say anything about my being so clumsy."

Laughter shook his chest beneath her cheek. She smiled. Whereas she couldn't face his pity, laughter was another matter. She pulled back out of his arms and swiped at her eyes.

"You know, my father used to call me Angel." They continued their progress toward the car. The crisp October air relieved the burning heat in her cheeks. "My mother thought I wasn't going to live. The doctors told her my chances weren't very good, so she named me Angela to put me under the protection of the angels."

"But you showed them." He squeezed her arm. "Now do it again. Come to the masquerade ball with me."

"Even if I could go, it wouldn't be any good. I can't dance." What was it about this man that brought out all her secrets? Well, almost all her secrets.

"Nonsense. Everyone can dance. You just move to the music." They reached the car. He unlocked and opened her door before crossing over to the driver's side.

"It's not nonsense. I've never even been to a dance," she said once he was inside. "I don't know where you put your hands or how you're supposed to step. I can't do this."

"You told me you hadn't been to a football game until today and you learned about that quick enough." He started the engine but they remained in the parking lot while the car warmed up.

"That was different," she said. "I don't think you can learn to dance over the Internet."

"You'll never learn if you keep turning down invitations."

Angie felt her lips turn up in a sneer. Little did he know. She'd jump at an invitation to dance if it was from anyone else but him. But then no one else had ever asked.

"Tell you what." He slipped the car into drive and stared straight ahead while negotiating their way out of the lot. "How about I let you practice dancing with me. That way when a real date comes along. You won't refuse him."

"This isn't a real date?" A withering sense of disappointment fluttered about her ribcage.

"We're friends, remember?" He smiled at her quickly, then turned his attention back to the road. "I'm asking you to this dance as a friend, not a date. I don't see how Falstaff can object to two friends supporting such a worthy cause as a museum fundraiser, but we'll be disguised anyway, so he'll never know. What do you say?"

She watched the fall foliage pass by the window. The contagious pop rhythm from the car radio worked its way down to her toes, tapping within her shoes. A part of her longed to accept his invitation, yet another part, the more rational and sensible part, argued that accepting would be a mistake. She glanced over to him.

"Won't you be embarrassed when I step all over your feet? I'm serious about not being able to dance, and Halloween is in two weeks."

"We'll work something out." She thought she saw his dimple deepening. "We can always try a few practice dancing sessions after work."

"What kind of costume?" It couldn't hurt to pretend she was going.

"Any kind you like, scary, fancy, just say the word."

"I have a scar." She traced the incision that bisected her chest. He reached across and took her hand.

"Don't worry," he said. "No one will see." He squeezed her hand with such tenderness she feared the familiar embarrassing tears would return.

Her heart beat so furiously she was afraid it would leap from her chest into his lap. She wanted this. She wanted it so bad. Odds were such an opportunity would never come again. If there was one thing she understood, it was odds. A shiver slipped through her at the thought of lost chances, lost dreams, lost opportunities to experience life.

Falstaff hadn't objected to her attending this football game. Heck, he encouraged it. Would there really be a problem with her going to a dance with a client? After all, it benefited a worthy cause.

"Trust me," he said with another squeeze.

She tried to see his eyes, but he continued to watch the road. She had already trusted several secrets to him. What was one more, more or less? She bit her lip and made a leap of faith.

"Yes, I'll go with you." A wave of excitement tingled through her, drowning out her previous apprehensions.

That night, her mother called. Angie answered after the first ring. "Guess what, Mom? I'm a modern day Cinderella. I'm going to a ball!"

Raymond watched the lights come on in the empty house and noted the time in his black book. All alone in a big old house. She was almost making this too easy. Soon, very soon, he'd meet her face-to-face.

Chapter Eleven

"Are you sure about this?" Max stood in the hallway, rain from his wet coat dripped puddles on the floor. "You look entirely too cheerful to be going out in this weather, especially on some wild goose chase. It's raining cats and dogs out there." He glanced down at Oreo and scratched between her ears. "No offense, Oreo."

"Germs cause viruses, not rain," she snapped. At his crestfallen expression, she reminded herself this was Max, not Stephen or her mother. She softened her tone. "Cheer up. At least it's not snowing." Oreo sat at her feet, tail swishing with enthusiasm. "Sorry, girl. You can't come with us. I doubt Max wants wet dog hair all over his car seats. You guard the place."

She locked the front door, pulled her raincoat hood up over her head and followed Max to his car. In truth, she had misgivings about the weather, but she had been in such a good mood since accepting Hank's invitation that even the rain couldn't bring her down. "Thanks for coming with me, Max. Especially as we're off the clock."

"I couldn't very well let you do this thing by yourself. Ritchton Street isn't in the safest neighborhood." He opened the driver's side door and slid in behind the wheel. "Although I doubt any self-respecting crook would be out in this mess." Angie fastened her seatbelt and he turned the key, revving the motor slightly before pulling the car out on the street.

Icy, cold rain pelted the windshield, occasionally drowning out the rock and roll playing on the car radio.

"Okay, you've made me wait long enough." Max glanced at her quickly. "What happened after I left the game yesterday?"

"What do you mean?"

"I mean, between you and Renard. You've got a smile about as wide as you're tall so I'm thinking something good happened." He winked at her.

The smile froze on her face. A rock of discomfort settled in her throat. Was she so transparent? She hadn't even told her mother she had an escort for the ball, letting her think instead that she was going solo. How could Max have figured it out? Her good humor vanished like the red taillights of passing cars.

"You got him to agree to additional services, right? Am I right?" In the dim dashboard light, she saw Max beaming. "That means your promotion is in the bag, right? When were you going to tell me? We should be out celebrating, not prowling around some old warehouse."

"Well, he hasn't exactly committed yet," she said, scrambling to think how to keep Max from discovering her secret.

"What did he say? Man, when I think about his expression when Falstaff first introduced you, I doubt Renard would have believed you if you said rain was wet. Now he's eating out of your hand. I bow to the master." He tipped his head toward her. "What exactly did you say?"

"I'm...I'm not sure it's anything specific that I said." What could she say? And what would she say to Max if the promotion fell through? She shifted the seatbelt across her chest. She hadn't deliberately lied to anyone but felt caught in a web of deception just the same.

"Well, then it must be something that you did." He wriggled his eyebrows in a suggestive leer then glanced her way. "Don't look so stricken, I'm only teasing." He laughed. "After all those lectures you've given me about social involvement with clients, I know there's nothing going on that isn't strictly business."

Thank heavens it was dark in the car, the tips of her ears burned from embarrassment. Max didn't know how close he was to the truth. "Look, there's the exit." Angie pointed to a lit green sign. "Maybe we better focus on the job ahead."

"Good idea. What exactly are we looking for?" Max asked after a quick glance in the rear view mirror.

"I'm not sure." Angie snuggled deeper into her coat, not knowing if the rain, her discomfort at Max's suggestions, or anxiety over this spy mission caused the icy shivers down her back. Whatever it was, she needed to focus on the present task. She took a deep breath. "Something about this direct ship business just doesn't feel right. Maybe if I see that this is a legitimate business, I can accept Wilson's explanations and put this audit to rest."

"At least till we come back to do year-end work in February. Hey, if you get promoted to Audit Manager, do you think I'll be in charge of the rest of the audit?"

Apparently, Max's enthusiasm wasn't entirely based on her good fortune. No wonder he wanted to celebrate. "Is that why you agreed to coming down here off the clock?"

"I figured a little advanced client knowledge wouldn't hurt if your promotion came through."

They turned off a well-lighted thoroughfare into a dark, dismal neighborhood. It wouldn't improve with daylight, she thought, any more than the rain would wash away the grime and filth from the graffiti-marked walls. The car's headlights illuminated puddles that percolated with raindrops like primeval ooze. No other car passed or followed them along the street.

They turned onto Richton Street. Max squinted uneasily at the windshield. "Angie, I'm not so sure this is a good idea. It's not too late to turn around."

"What was that address?" she asked, squinting out the side window. "Do you see any building numbers?"

"Twenty-six, thirty-three," Max answered. "Should be on your side."

They drifted cautiously down the street, each scouring the old brick turn-of-the-century buildings for identification.

"There it is." She tapped on the window, pointing to white numbers tacked above a windowless metal door. Max pulled into the deserted truck dock, dodged some broken glass, then shifted into park.

"There's no business sign, no identification," Angie said. "Don't you think that's strange?"

"In this neighborhood?" Max studied the surroundings through the car windows. "It was probably stolen. Look," he turned to face her, "I'm sure your brother wouldn't want you here at this time of night. Why don't we just go home?"

His words just sealed her commitment. "There'd be too many questions if we came during the day. Besides, as soon as we wrap up this interim work, we'll both be assigned to new jobs. No..." She pulled on the door handle. "We came all this way, let's get it over with."

Max sighed and turned off the engine. With that one motion, the headlights switched off and plunged them into darkness. "Did you at least bring a flashlight?" he asked. Angela patted the bulge in her coat pocket and exited the car.

The hungry emptiness swallowed her flashlight beam. *Big help this is*, she thought. The darn thing probably illuminated her more then the path in front of her. Avoiding the deeper puddles of water, she carefully made her way to the front door and twisted the doorknob. Locked.

Max joined her with a second flashlight. "What's the plan?"

Plan? What plan? She wasn't sure what to look for, much less how to find it. Rain pelted her shoulders and arms and dripped off her nose. If only she could see inside the building, maybe then she'd be satisfied and they could get out of this downpour. "Let's find a window."

"Nothing on this side," Max said, flashing his narrow beam of light around the front of the two-storied building. Wooden boards covered the places windows might have existed long ago. Angie pointed to an alleyway along the side. "Maybe over there."

Fortunately, the building blocked much of the wind and stinging rain. However, the flashlight beams bounced off the thick paint covering the bank of windows along this side of the building. Heavy security bars on the outside of the first floor windows prevented close inspection. They followed the length of the building down the dark alley littered with refuse and broken wooden pallets.

"Bingo." Max pointed his flashlight beam to a multi-paned section about eight feet off the ground. A jagged shadow in the far middle pane suggested a broken window, at least the light disappeared into the murky interior.

"Great. But how can we get up there?" Angie trailed her light down to the base of the building and a few feet further down the alley. The beam found an industrial refuse container on the opposite side of the alley, about a foot down from the broken window. "Can we do something with this?"

"We can try."

In spite of the intense urine and decaying trash scent, they pushed against the sticky metal, trying to move it closer to the window. They only dislodged a few fist-sized rats that skittered out from behind the container. Angie shrieked and jumped back, dropping her flashlight in the process. It rolled underneath the metal box, providing heat and light for a whole generation of rats.

"Don't worry about it," Max said, looking at the faint beam shining under the container. "It wasn't helping much anyway. Besides, this isn't working."

She agreed, holding her sticky hands out to catch the rain before smearing them down the front of her coat. She studied the industrial-sized rat home. "Maybe if you give me a boost, I could climb on top of that thing and see through the window."

"You? No way." Max shook his head even as Angie continued her protests. "If anyone is climbing, it makes more sense if I do it. I'm taller and you have a bum leg." He scanned the bin. "Look, there's a lid. If we can get it closed, I can stand on it." Angie grabbed two wooden planks from a nearby broken pallet, then handed one of them to Max. Together, they pushed the heavy metal lid around on its hinge until gravity pulled the lid the rest of the way. Bang! The metal shuddered and belched fetid trash stench.

Max handed her his flashlight.

"Be careful," she said with unspoken gratitude

Using a broken crate to give him some extra lift, Max hoisted his lean body to the container rim before bracing himself with the building wall. Feeling helpless below, Angela kept her flashlight trained on the rim of the container. A can hit the pavement behind her. She spun around, swinging her flashlight beam erratically at the opening of the alley. Nothing.

"Hey, come back here with that," Max yelled. "Don't leave me in the dark."

125

"Sorry, I thought I heard something." Her hood slipped back allowing a trickle of liquid ice to work its way down her back. She shivered. "Probably a cat searching for dinner."

"Well, he's found the right place." Max balanced himself precariously on the corner of the container. "Can you hand me a light?"

Angela fixed her hood, then stretched on tiptoes to give him the flashlight. He trained it on the broken window.

"Can you see anything?" she shouted up. The rain finally started to ease up, but cold blasts of wind chilled her to the bone.

"Not really." The beam flashed along the perimeter of the building. "I'm not close enough. From this angle, all I can see is the ceiling."

"Then come back down before you fall." Angela called, disappointed.

"Easier said than done." Max looked back the way he came and opted instead to jump off the container. He landed in a crouch splashing water in all directions, including the front of Angie. "Sorry," he apologized.

"A little more water isn't going to make any difference at this point." She scrubbed at her face with the sleeve of her coat. "Come on, let's get out of here." She shivered. "This place gives me the creeps and I'm in desperate need of a hot shower."

"Now that's something I think I can definitely help you with," Max said, slipping his arm around Angie's shoulders.

"Max," she pushed him away from her side. "You're incorrigible."

CB∞BO

The phone rang in the Wilsons' household.

"I'll get it," Tom called up the stairs, switching on the light in the den. He picked up the receiver on the second ring.

"Hello?"

"Tom, it's me. I just got back. She was there just like you thought she'd be."

"Are you sure? How do you know it was her?" He lowered his voice to a whisper and pushed the den door shut with his free hand.

"There were two of them, a man and a woman. The hood on her coat fell off and I got a good look. It was her all right."

"Did she see you?"

"No, I made sure of that."

"Could you tell if they saw anything?"

"They were climbing around Argo's trash bin. I couldn't hear what they said, it was raining too hard. But I don't think they could get close enough to see inside."

The man was probably that assistant of hers. Wilson gnawed at his upper lip. But what if it wasn't? What if it was Renard? Angie and Renard had been thick as thieves lately, and then there was that business about—

"Tom? What do you want me to do?"

"Go home." He groused into the receiver. "Go home and go to bed and act like nothing's happened."

"But what if—"

"Go home," he ordered. "Let me think about this. We'll talk tomorrow."

"All right then. Good night."

Tom hung up without returning the sentiment. He rubbed his forehead. The Ritchton street building was locked up tighter than a bank vault. That nosy auditor's expedition probably turned up nothing more than a wet wino or two. But still...

"Tom? Is everything all right in there?"

Wilson opened the door for the flannel-encased woman who represented little more than a joint tax return. "Everything is fine, Alice. Go on back to bed."

"I heard the phone. I thought maybe one of the kids..."

"No, it was just business."

"Are you coming to bed soon?"

He looked at her homely face and generous proportions. The years hadn't been kind. "You go ahead. I'll be up shortly. I have some work I need to finish."

Was it doubt that flashed across her face before her lips turned up in a sad smile? A pang of guilt shifted in his gut. She couldn't know about the other women. He'd been too careful. It must be a trick of the light.

She turned and padded silently up the stairs.

"Good night," he called up after her.

She didn't return the sentiment.

Chapter Twelve

"Good morning," Max greeted Angie in the conference room the next morning. "You look about as good as I feel," he added with a yawn.

"That bad, huh?" She would have liked to deny the truth of his statement, but a glance in the mirror that morning had suggested otherwise. "Both my mother and my brother called to check up on me after you dropped me off last night."

"How's your mom doing?"

"Fine. My aunt Ceal is mending so well that Mom thinks she'll be coming home the week after next."

"That'll be nice. I suppose it gets lonely in that house all by yourself."

"I've kind of enjoyed it, actually." Angie said. If nothing else, her experiences over the past two weeks confirmed that it was time she moved away from home. "But I need to snag that promotion to have any hope of finding a place of my own." She took a sip from her bottled water. "And that means we have to put together an excellent letter of recommendations so we can convince Renard to hire us to do more work."

"What do you want to do about that warehouse last night?"

"Let's draft up the letter without reference to the warehouse and see what we've got." She picked up a legal pad and positioned it in front of her. "Then, if we're still not sure, I'll take it up with Falstaff."

Max nodded and they spent the rest of the day pulling together their notes and drafting their recommendations. Contrary to his comment at the game, Falstaff didn't meet with her on Monday. Instead, he suggested they review everything on

Wednesday with a thought of scheduling a meeting with Hank at Hayden Industries on Thursday. That only gave her a few days to design a program of procedures for the additional services and figure a budget.

Concentrating was difficult, though, as her mind kept drifting into daydreams centered on the upcoming ball. What kind of costumes would Hank find? Where did one even find costumes? Would she make a complete and utter fool of herself on the dance floor? Hank promised to teach her, but what if she was unteachable? She needed practice, lots of practice. That need drove her to calling Stephen later in the afternoon.

"Hi, sis. I'm glad you called. I have some good news."

"What's that?"

"I found a new driver. Now you don't have to worry about helping me out with the homecoming traffic."

Actually, she hadn't worried about it at all, she thought with a twinge of guilt. Stephen had been so insistent that she couldn't handle his ladies with her ankle cast that she'd assumed he wouldn't have asked her to drive under any circumstances. That and the fact that she had so many other things to worry about, her brother's business had fallen low on the list.

"...you'll like him. His name is Raymond and he just came into town."

"That's great, Stephen, I know you were worried about finding someone."

"Yeah, just in time too. So what did you call me for?"

The audit room was empty but she lowered her voice just the same. "I was wondering if you could teach me to dance."

"Dance? Why on earth do you need to know how to dance? What kind of dancing?"

His voice was so loud it hurt her ear. Yet she didn't want to hold the receiver away for fear someone else would overhear their conversation.

"Sssh. Ballroom dancing." She assumed that's what they did at a ball.

"*Ballroom* dancing." He laughed and Angie wanted to reach through the phone line and shake him. "I don't even know if *I* know how to ballroom dance."

"Well, slow dancing then." She looked furtively right and left, checking to make sure no one could hear her. One of the secretaries and another associate stood at the other end of hallway by a soda machine.

"That depends. Who're you planning to slow dance with?"

"Stephen!"

"Okay. Listen. Normally I'd be happy to teach my little sister to dance, but right now isn't the time. With Raymond coming on, I'll be tied up with training. I want him to be able to run dispatch and scheduling as well as drive the ladies. Maybe we can do this in a couple of weeks. Hey, maybe after you get rid of that ankle cast. You probably couldn't dance real well in that thing anyway. Okay?"

"Sure, Stephen. Thanks. I'll talk to you later. Bye." Leave it to her brother to add that last little uncertainty to her quickly dwindling confidence. It was a mistake to call him. She replaced the receiver on the phone next to her computer. If she needed to learn, she'd have to do it herself. After all, she taught herself about football. She glanced down at the computer. Maybe she could do the same with dancing.

಄ೞ಄

It had been a long day. Oreo's enthusiastic greeting at the door practically knocked her over. As expected, the answering machine beeped that messages required her attention. She hit the play button, jotting down the messages meant for her mother. Hank's voice on the machine jarred her attention.

"Angie. Just wanted to let you know that I'll be out of town for a few days. What do you say we get together Saturday for those dance lessons? If you come early enough, I'll make you dinner. Did I tell you I'm a good cook?" Yes, he had, she remembered with a smile. "I understand Falstaff has set up a meeting for Thursday. I'll see you then. Bye."

That gave her a whole week to fret about dancing. All in all, she looked forward to crashing in bed early and recapturing some of those lost hours of sleep. After dinner, a little TV, and Oreo's walk, she checked to make sure the house was locked up tight. Then she took her evening medications and talked long-distance with her mother before climbing into bed with a good book and a comforting dog. In short order she fell fast asleep.

⋘≽⋦⋧≼⋙

The dog was barking.

"Oreo. Be quiet," she mumbled, still half asleep. She slid her hand across the mattress, searching for Oreo's furry body. The dog wasn't there and the barking continued. She squinted her eyes at the fluorescent digital clock on the nightstand. Three o'clock a.m. "Oreo," she yelled a little louder. "It's just Mrs. Kravitz's cat." Still, she sat up, pulled on a robe and turned on the light.

Following Oreo's frantic barks, she went downstairs toward the kitchen, turning on house lights along the way. Oreo stopped the frantic barking, substituting a few threatening growls and intermittent barks. Angie flipped the switch that flooded the room with light. Oreo turned, tail wagging and tongue dripping from the side of her mouth to greet her.

"What are you doing down here?" she scolded. "Come on, you'll wake up the neighbors. Come on." She patted the side of her thigh, but Oreo wouldn't leave her post. "Come on, puppy." She grabbed a dog biscuit from the pantry. "It's time for bed." With one last hesitant glance at the door, the dog came to her side for the treat. "That's better," she said. "Now, no more barking."

She turned off the light and started down the hallway back to the stairs. Oreo issued one more warning semi-bark then followed slowly behind her. "Stupid dog," she half-uttered under her breath. Loyal to a fault, but stupid for barking at some similarly inclined cat.

What if it wasn't a cat? It was pretty close to Halloween. What if some kid was trying to scare poor Mrs. Kravitz? Pulling her robe tighter around her, Angie walked over to the kitchen window and peered into the yard beyond. Nothing. No movement that she could see. Nothing out of place. "Probably a cat." She yawned and retreated back to the bedroom in hopes of pursuing an abruptly interrupted sweet dream.

The next morning, Oreo ran to the back door the moment Angela stepped into the kitchen. "You want out, girl?" Angela opened the back door to let the dog into the fenced back yard. "Not too long, it's still pretty muddy out there.

Oreo immediately dashed outside, sniffing the ground in erratic circles as if pursuing some trophy animal. Angie watched from the warmth of the kitchen, waiting for the dog to drop down into her morning squat. Oreo continued investigating the yard. *That's odd*, she thought. Normally Oreo was quick to finish and come in for a morning treat.

Angela grabbed a sweater from the coat stand by the door before stepping out on the stoop and down the two steps to the small patio behind the house. Brown and yellow leaves liberated by Sunday's storm clung to her slippers as she crossed the concrete. She stopped at the perimeter.

"Come here, girl." She slapped her side. The dog ignored her. Angie reached down to remove one dew-damp leaf from her heel when she saw a clearly defined footprint in the dirt of her mother's perennial garden. A large man's footprint, judging from the size. Goosebumps rose up on her arms. Was Oreo barking at an intruder last night? From the direction of the footprint, he may have even tried the back door. A shiver danced down her spine.

Oreo trotted up next to her. Angie reached down to pet her head. "Good girl," she praised with newfound respect. Maybe Stephen wasn't so far off the mark after all. Together, she and Oreo walked the yard, searching for new clues. She didn't find any more footprints, nor did she find any evidence that the intruder tried to enter the house. "Probably scared him off with the lights," she told the dog. Still, she checked the locks on all the windows and doors before leaving for work.

෴

"Hey Angie, what's up? You look like you're a zillion miles away," Max said, leaning over her cubicle. "Planning how to decorate your new office?"

She offered a weak smile. The constant reference to her not-a-sure-thing promotion was becoming more of a nuisance than a compliment. "I think I might have had a visitor last night."

"You don't know?" Max moved around to sit on the radiator that created the third wall of her cubicle.

Angie described the previous night's proceedings.

"What are you going to do?" he asked.

"What can I do? Other than one footprint, there's no evidence anyone was there. It's not like they caused any damage or anything."

"How do you know? Maybe they went down the street and broke into someone else's home. Maybe that footprint is the best evidence of another break-in."

She hadn't thought of that. "I guess I should call the police." And call Mrs. Kravitz when she got home to make sure she was okay. She didn't want to worry the poor thing about a possible break-in, but it wouldn't hurt to check in on her.

"Doesn't it seem strange, though?"

"What do you mean?" she asked.

"First, someone slashes your tires. Then someone tries to break into your house."

"We don't know that," she quickly protested. "There was no evidence of a break in."

"Still, doesn't it seem strange that the two things happened within a week of each other?"

"Do you think they're related?" Frankly, she hadn't thought about a connection between the two incidents. She shook her head. "Why would someone intentionally want to harm me?"

"Only you can answer that," Max said. "Maybe you should move back in with your brother until your mother comes home, just in case."

"Don't be ridiculous," she scolded. "It's just coincidence and I doubt I'm anyone's target." Still, a shiver danced down her spine. She remembered Elizabeth's contorted face when she threatened bodily harm if she "messed" with Hank. But Elizabeth was in New York, wasn't she? Tom Wilson warned her something bad might happen, but she assumed that was an

In a Heartbeat

empty threat. She wasn't doing anything to harm Tom Wilson that she could see, so why would he want to harm her? No, the two incidents were not related. "You're probably right about the police, though. I'll call just in case."

About an hour later, she called the police. They hadn't received any reports of break-ins in her neighborhood. Relieved, she listened to their promise to pay particular attention to her street on their nightly rounds before hanging up the phone. It was probably just a prank. Pushing intruder concerns to the back of her mind, she focused on the task at hand. The jury was still out on her marketing ability. She needed to impress Falstaff tomorrow with her efficiency and effectiveness and that required concentration. She organized her papers and bent to work.

Dusk settled in before Angie completed the trip home from work. Pink and purple streaked the western sky, while crimson and bright yellow trees added a false brilliance to the fading light. A sudden gust of wind liberated fistfuls of leaves, showering her car and the small town streets in a golden shower. Angie turned onto her street.

Three plump, uncarved pumpkins graced a corner of Mrs. Kravitz's porch. Halloween was still a good two weeks away, too early for the transformation from benign vegetable to traditional decoration. Last year Mrs. Kravitz carved a portrait of Elvis in one of her pumpkins. "From a kit", she had said with a wink. At seventy-five, she was still pretty spry. A burglar might be surprised if he targeted her house.

"Stop it," Angie scolded herself as she turned into the driveway of her own unadorned house. Her mother kept various holiday decorations down in the basement. Angie made a mental note to check out the collection later in the evening.

After collecting the mail from the front porch box, she entered the house and dodged Oreo's voracious greeting. As expected, the answering machine beeped with its typical irritating urgency. Angie walked to the kitchen, thumbing through the various envelopes, separating them into bills and junk. Oreo whimpered by the back door, waiting impatiently.

"Just a minute, girl." Although normally she let Oreo run free in the backyard while she listened to the phone messages, this time she decided to let the blasted machine beep a bit longer. "Come on. Let's take another look at that footprint."

Oreo made a beeline for the back fence. Tail wagging frantically, she sniffed then pawed something on the ground.

"Leave it be" she scolded, walking to the garden shed to retrieve a shovel and bag. Too bad her brother wasn't making an unannounced visit. Scooping up stiff dead birds right before dinner pretty much ruined her appetite.

"What in the world..." That was no bird. Oreo growled as she approached. A thick, raw porterhouse steak conveniently lay in the grass by the back fence. Using the shovel as a buffer between her and her threatening dog, Angie picked up the butchered meat between two fingers and carried it at arm's length back to her kitchen. Oreo danced beneath the prize, trying to grab it from her fingers, but she held it out of reach.

Although the surface of the meat had hardened, the interior was still moist as evidenced by the many cuts into the steak. Using a knife to probe the cuts, she discovered a rather large cache of buried pills. Poison, she suspected, or an overdose of sleeping pills. A burning rage shook her. Someone tried to poison Oreo and she had a sneaking suspicion who it could be. She threw the tainted meat into the sink, out of reach of the dog, and marched to her neighbor's front door.

"I need to talk to you, Walter," she yelled, banging on the front door. "Open up."

He opened the door slowly, as if oblivious to her frantic pounding. "Is there something wrong?" the sun-adverse, neat-as-a-pin zombie asked. "Can I help you?"

Her contorted angry face reflected in his glasses. "Look you...you...dog killer. I know you don't like my dog, but that doesn't give you the right—"

"Dog killer?" The man blanched to a pasty gray. "I've never killed any dogs. I never would kill a dog. I don't know what you're talking about."

"You put a raw steak infested with poison pills in my back yard," she shouted through the screen door. "I should call the police and I would have if Oreo –"

"Someone tried to kill your dog? Oh my." He opened the screen door so she could enter. "Who'd do something so cruel? Would you like me to call your brother?"

His obvious concern caught her off guard. "My brother? No... You didn't put the steak there?"

"Me? Oh no. I'd never kill a living thing. I see too much of death at work." He led the way back into the neatly appointed kitchen. She followed, her boiling anger rolling back to a simmer. "Besides, I don't dislike your dog. Your dog isn't fond of me, but I thought maybe that was because of the chemicals." He removed two coffee mugs from a perfectly aligned row in the cabinet. "Coffee?"

The diminishing spike of adrenaline left her confused. She leaned against the doorjamb. "Chemicals? What chemicals?"

"Formaldehyde mostly. I work in a funeral home preparing the corpses. That's how I first met your brother." He smiled. "Not as a corpse, of course." He chuckled, at least she thought that strangled hiccup might be a chuckle.

"Sorry, a little funeral home humor." He pushed his glasses back higher onto his nose. "We contract limousines sometimes with Stephen." He held up a jar. "Is instant okay? I rarely need to fix it for more than one so I tend to drink—"

She shook her head. "Water would be fine."

He nodded and pulled a large plastic water jug from the refrigerator. "Tell me what happened to your dog. Is she okay?"

"Someone tried to poison her with tainted meat. I found it in time before any harm could be done." She studied him carefully. Although he still had that surreal coordinated-catalog look, he was less intimidating than she remembered. "Where exactly do you work?"

"Robbins Funeral Home over on Walnut." He gestured toward the kitchen table.

"Oh." She knew the place, not that she had driven for any funerals, but she knew Stephen did a steady business with them. Angie took a seat at the kitchen table.

"You didn't happen to see someone suspicious throwing something into my back yard, did you?" Look who she was asking about suspicious.

"No. Not really," he said after some thought. "But I just arrived home shortly before you."

"You know what time I came home?"

"I saw your car from my front window." He swallowed the water in his glass in one long swig. "I'm sorry I can't help you with your mystery."

"By any chance, did you hear or see anyone prowling around my house last night?" Angie sipped from her glass, watching Walter over the rim.

"You had a prowler last night?"

"I think so."

"Did you call your brother? I'm sure he'd want to know about this."

"No." she said a little too quickly. "And I'd appreciate you not calling him either. I'd like to handle this on my own."

"I don't understand." Walter clasped his hands in front of him on the table, almost as if he were praying. "Why do you want to handle this alone? I think I've handled just about everything alone and it's not enjoyable."

The lenses of his glasses magnified his watery, hazel eyes. Guilt from all the mean thoughts and words she had ever expressed about him congealed in her throat. He was lonely. Why hadn't she seen that earlier?

"Walter," she said impulsively. "Do you know how to dance?"

His eyes widened, his ears reddened, and his Adam's apple bobbed noticeably. "I'm... It's been a long... I'm really not sure," he finally managed, averting his glance. "Why do you ask?"

"I need to learn and I hoped maybe you could teach me."

He bounced his clenched hands lightly on the table. "Do you think it's wise in your condition?"

Now it was her turn to be embarrassed. How much did he know and what exactly did her idiot-brother tell him?

"Dancing can't be good for your leg," he said. "Does it hurt much?"

"Oh." She breathed a sigh of relief. "It aches a bit when I've been standing on it too long. At night especially." She stretched her leg out and studied it as if this were the first time she had considered such a question. "The plastic cast is more awkward than uncomfortable. Perhaps if that prowler comes back, I could use it to bash him one."

"I have a better idea." Walter left the kitchen table, walked down a hallway and returned with a heavy wooden baseball bat. "Maybe you should keep this for a while."

A gentle warmth bloomed in her chest. She suspected this was his own means of protection. Sharing it demonstrated his friendship. "Thank you, Walter. I'll feel much safer with this in the house." She stood. "I need to get back, though. Oreo's waiting for me."

He walked her to the door. "I'll keep my eyes open for any strangers."

"Thank you, Walter." She took his hand and warmed it briefly in hers. "Thank you very much."

That evening she lay in bed listening to every crack and creak in the house. She checked the locks on every door and window at least twice, and left the outside lights on as a deterrent to would-be burglars. Walter did the same, she noted. Oreo curled up at the foot of the bed. Walter's baseball bat lay within reach on the side. She tried to take the edge off her fears by lighting a candle, but the autumn fragrance didn't soften her mood.

Walter was right. It certainly wasn't enjoyable facing her fears alone. She wished there was someone she could talk to, confide in. She refused to tell Stephen or her mother about the prowler. No need to worry them, or invite them to orchestrate her safety. She couldn't tell Max about her relationship with Hank and how that had evoked a threat from Elizabeth. About the only one she could talk to, the only one she wanted to talk to, was Hank. But he was out of town probably visiting Elizabeth at this very moment. Jealousy jabbed her thoughts.

And why not? She had never felt so protected as she did in his arms that day in the woods. She could almost feel those arms around her now, pulling her close, pressing her against his chest. The room warmed with the memory and she relaxed within its power. She thought of his eyes and how a simple glance, a raise of the eyebrow, a flash of his dimple sent every nerve ending in her body in a sizzling furor. He listened to her as if he cared what she had to say, not to solve her problems for her. He listened and—

The phone rang.

"Angela? It's Hank."

"Hank?" Her breath caught and she rose up on her elbow. How did he know she was just thinking of him?

"Falstaff hasn't tapped your phone lines, has he?"

"What?"

"Because if they have, I know you won't talk to me."

She heard the laughter in his voice and relaxed for the first time that evening. She lay back down on her pillows. "Why are you calling me?"

"I was lonely and needed to hear the sound of another voice. I thought of you. Are you in bed? I'm sorry. Did I wake you?"

"I'm in bed, but you didn't wake me." A few pregnant moments of silence passed. Almost as if he wanted to say something, but couldn't find the words. She understood the feeling.

"What were you doing?" His voice had dropped a notch and a tantalizing heat spread from her cheeks down to her toes. It was almost as if he knew what she'd been thinking.

"Thinking."

"Of me?" The understated laughter was back. She imagined his eyes crinkling with laugh lines and his dimple begging to be explored.

"A little," she lied. "How's Elizabeth?"

"Elizabeth?" There was a hesitation. "I don't know. I haven't talked to her in a while. I guess she's off on a shoot somewhere."

"Oh." Damn her jealous imagination. "Your message said you were out of town, I just assumed you were visiting her."

"No, this is business."

Not pleasure, she added mentally. Was he referring to the telephone conversation or his trip?

"I'm visiting some of Hayden's major customers, looking for some feedback on how we can improve product, service, support. That sort of thing."

So this *was* a business call, nothing more. A lump of disappointment settled in her throat.

"Listen, I really called to say thank you for agreeing to go with me to that charity ball. I know what a difficult decision that was for you to make. And I know you've probably second guessed that decision about a dozen times already."

She nodded, then realized he couldn't see her through the phone line. Funny, she imagined she could see everything about him, just by the sound of his voice. "At least."

"Well, I appreciate it and I won't let you down. I promise, Angel."

She couldn't even get the words past the lump in her throat to correct him. His nickname for her hung in the air between them.

"I guess I should let you get some rest. I'm looking forward to Thursday. I can't promise I'll buy in to the additional services, but I will enjoy seeing you again. Good night. Sweet dreams."

"Good night," she said, cradling the receiver in her hands as if his essence lingered there, not a plastic handset. Reluctantly, she replaced the receiver and snuggled deep beneath a layer of quilts. Her dreams most likely would be sweet, now that he had called. She hugged her pillow, letting her imagination take wing. Just a few nights ago she had called herself a modern-day Cinderella.

"And, like it or not, that makes you, Hank Renard, *my* Prince Charming."

Damn. Raymond ducked behind a low shrub. The whole neighborhood looked ablaze with lights. He hadn't missed the increasing police surveillance every three hours, either. *That's all right, Miss Angela Blake. You go on thinking bright lights will save you. I can wait. I have time. And when you least expect it. I'll be there with a razor at your throat.*

Chapter Thirteen

Wearing her power suit for luck, Angie flanked Falstaff as they waited in the conference room for Hank. The door opened and Wilson and Burroughs walked in together. Surprised, she forced a cordial smile on her face.

"Gentlemen," Falstaff boomed, extending his hand. "I'm sure you remember Ms. Blake here." Angela held her hand out as expected.

"Of course, Ms. Blake." Wilson took her hand in both of his. "So good to see you again." He glanced quickly down at her ankle brace. "I'm glad you recovered from Saturday's near slip."

Near-slip my eye. More like a flagrant push. Angie held a tight smile and pulled her hand from Wilson's grasp. Resisting the urge to rub her palm down her skirt, she diverted her attention to the open conference room door. Hank entered, wearing a power suit of his own. At least it had a power over her. The Italian cut spanned his broad shoulders, then neatly tapered, emphasizing his trim waist and flat abdomen. His crisp white shirt contrasted nicely with the charcoal gray jacket and set off his handsome facial features to perfection. She nearly drooled. Falstaff looked like an out-of-step drudge next to Hank.

"Good morning, everyone, sorry to be the last to arrive." He turned to Falstaff, "I've asked Pete and Tom to attend as I believe you're proposing to focus on their areas." He gestured to the conference table, inviting everyone to sit.

"Excellent idea," Falstaff replied, taking a seat at the side of the table. Angie selected the chair to his left, opposite from Tom Wilson. Hank assumed the seat at the head of the table. "Let's start with the letter of recommendations and then move on to the proposal for additional services. Shall we?"

For the most part, the meeting was uneventful. Angie listed control violations, Wilson and Burroughs aggressively rebutted each of the points. However, she struck a nerve when she mentioned direct ships.

"You have no proof," Wilson debated. "So a few invoices have been misfiled. Big deal. That doesn't prove anything."

Angela looked to Hank. He didn't say a word.

"In a test situation, the absence of an invoice does indeed prove something." Falstaff said. "Perhaps, you're right. Perhaps it only proves the existence of a poor filing system, but it could also be a sign of something more important." He took off his glasses for emphasis.

Angela had seen this ploy before. Without the distorting glass in front of them, his eyes appeared old, experienced and wise. That, she supposed, was the point.

"It would be a mistake to ignore or downplay the significance of missing invoices," he said. "Especially without collaborating receiving reports as in the case of direct ships."

Burroughs cradled his weak chin and scribbled something on the legal pad in front of him. Wilson glared at Angela. A cold shiver slipped down the small of her back.

"Well now." Hank broke the silence. "I assume your additional services are designed to probe further into the matter of missing invoices and direct ships."

"Yes, an audit focuses primarily on the capture of financial information, but we've designed some procedures to thoroughly explore these areas and provide the kind of answers any dynamic management team needs to operate productively." Having delivered the standard additional services rhetoric, Falstaff returned the glasses to his nose. "We can go over each procedure if you like."

Hank held up his hand. "Not necessary. I'm sure Ms. Blake has put together an efficient and effective program."

His tight smile in her direction expanded ten-fold in her heart. She struggled to suppress visible signs of her gratitude. Maybe that promotion wasn't totally out of reach after all.

"However," he continued, his voice dripping with authority. "This company can ill afford to invest a lot of money only to learn we need to improve our filing system. So I'll make a proposition to you." He shifted slightly toward Falstaff. Angie's skin prickled at the shift of tension in the room. "If your additional services can explain why my accounts payable ratios are so lousy compared to the rest of the industry and why my costs of production are so high, I'll be happy to pay the freight for your investigation. But," he held up his hand to stall Falstaff's reply, "if you come back and say my dynamic management team is operating productively and things are as they appear on the surface, just a few missing pieces of paper, then I pay nothing and you pick up the cost."

It was a gamble. Angie knew Falstaff viewed the purchase of new office wallpaper as a risky venture. Disappointed that she'd have no excuse to return to Hayden Industries until the inventory count at year-end, she slumped in her chair. Still, Falstaff couldn't blame her for failing to sell additional services if he, himself, turned the proposal down.

"So, what do you say?"

Falstaff glanced at her. She smiled in sympathy. Poor guy, it must hurt to leave money on the table like that. He turned back toward Hank.

"You've got a deal."

What? What just happened? Angie straightened while Falstaff and Hank shook hands. When was she supposed to fit this in? She already had new assignments to attend to.

"I want to go on record as saying this is a mistake." Wilson rose from his chair. "This will just be a waste of my time." His eyes narrowed specifically at Angela. "You won't find a thing." He stormed out of the conference room with Burroughs dragging behind.

"Well, I guess this means we'll be seeing more of you, Ms. Blake," Hank said, coming around the table to shake her hand. He held her hand firmly in a formal gesture, then his grip gentled and lingered. Her gaze lifted to his. "I look forward to that."

Warm honey spread through her veins. "Yes," she said. "I do too."

"Come along now, Angela." Falstaff's hand pressed against her back. "We have much to discuss. Scheduling and all that."

Hank looked over her shoulder to Falstaff. "Call me with your time frame." His glance shifted back to Angela. He squeezed her hand briefly before releasing it. "Goodbye."

"Goodbye," she answered, but he was already out the door.

Falstaff glowered over his glasses. "I'm betting a lot of money on your hunches, young lady. You know that, don't you?"

She swallowed, suspecting this was more of a threat than a compliment. "Yes sir."

"Good. Then don't let me down."

That evening, she raced through her front door and grabbed the ringing phone before the answering machine engaged. Expecting to hear her mother's voice, she was delighted to hear Hank's.

"You did good today, Angela. Did you get the promotion?"

Her jaw dropped. "You knew about that?"

"I suspected as much. You kept dogging me about additional services even after I said no. I thought something had to be up. What do you say we do something to celebrate?"

"I see," she smiled. "First you get me promoted, then you get me fired."

"You got yourself promoted." His enthusiastic praise made her tingle all over. "I made that proposal in my own self-interest. Given the market, we should be making hand over fist in profits. Unfortunately, we're not and I can't find the problem."

"So you've delegated the quest to me."

"In a manner of speaking. It's a no-risk proposition. I'll gladly pay if you find something significant. So," his voice changed from that of a business associate to a friendly confidant, "what shall we do to celebrate? You could come over here for dinner."

"Thank you for the invitation, but I'm already committed this evening. Stephen wants me to meet his new driver, Raymond, so the three of us are going to Timothy's. Besides, no one's promoted me yet." *But they will soon*, she thought with

145

unexpected confidence. She was scheduled for a performance review at the end of the month, right after the Halloween ball.

"It's only a matter of time," Hank assured her. "How about tomorrow night?"

"Sorry. Walter and I are going out to a movie."

"Walter? You're going to a movie with the zombie? When did this happen?"

"You shouldn't be so hard on him," she scolded, knowing full well she said the same things herself not so long ago. "He's really a sweet, lonely guy."

"There's a reason that guy is lonely."

"Ssh," she said trying not to laugh.

"So I won't see you till Saturday?" He sounded disappointed, and that lifted her spirits.

"Guess not."

"Will you come over early enough for dinner?"

"I'll try."

"Good. Then I'll make us something special. See you then."

"Bye," she replied, before hanging up the phone.

෬෫෨෩

Although traditionally packed on the weekends, Timothy's maintained a moderate dinner business on weekdays. Angela found a parking spot with very little problem. A small limousine with the license plate PICKFORD straddled a couple spaces. She smiled; she wasn't the first of their party to arrive.

"Angela," Stephen called, waving her over to the table. He didn't rise when she approached the table, but his handsome companion did.

"Angie, I want you to meet my new driver, Ray." She extended her hand to the stranger with the smug smile. "Ray, this is my kid sister."

"So pleased to meet you." He took her offered hand, shocking her with his cold, bloodless touch. Goosebumps formed on her arms. She released his hand immediately.

"Come, sit down." Stephen waved her to an empty seat that placed her at the table between them.

"With all Stephen has told me, I feel I know you already." Raymond shifted his body towards hers. "You look familiar. Have we met before?"

He had beautiful features—long, thick eyelashes, a strong, compelling chin, black, wavy hair. However, his cold black eyes gave her the willies. She shifted uncomfortably. "No, I don't think so. I'd remember you."

She ordered from the hovering waitress while reminding herself not to prejudge Raymond. Look how mistaken she had been about Walter.

Stephen babbled on about the livery business and his plans for the future. Angie paid more attention to her food than the conversation around her. She felt Raymond's gaze on her, roaming, assessing and passing judgment.

"What did you do to your foot?" he asked when Stephen paused for air.

"I tripped and sprained my ankle," she replied. "Didn't Stephen tell you I'm a real klutz?"

"No, but he did say you had a sheltered childhood due to a physical malady."

Darn him. She glared at Stephen, but he studied his food with great intent.

"Are you well now?" Raymond asked.

"Yes," she answered, no need to go into details with nosy strangers.

"You'll have to be careful walking your dog with your foot in that cast."

Silent alarms sounded in her head. "How did you know I had a dog?" she asked, laying down her fork. Suddenly, she had lost her appetite.

He reached over and removed a long, curly hair from her sleeve. "Your pet travels with you." His smile didn't reach his eyes.

She wrapped her hands around her forearms and rubbed. "Isn't it cold in here?"

"Oreo sheds on everything." Stephen inserted himself back into the conversation. "She's a good dog, though." He smiled at Angela as if his compliment to Oreo made up for his sharing family secrets.

"I have an idea." Stephen turned toward Raymond. "Do you know how to dance? Angie asked me –"

"It's okay." She grabbed his arm to stop him from saying more. "I've made other arrangements. I don't think I'll need your help in that department." Her heart raced. The last thing she needed was that frigid thing touching her in an effort to learn to dance. She'd take her chances looking foolish with Hank on Saturday night. Stephen might be disappointed but he'd just have to live with it.

"Look, I'm not feeling very well. Do you mind if I leave before dessert?" She stood, reaching for her coat on a nearby hook.

Concern tinted Stephen's face. "Are you okay, Angie? You're not coming down with something, are you?" He turned to Raymond. "The slightest virus can be a serious thing to someone in Angie's condition." He stood to help her with her coat. "Maybe I should call the doctor."

"No." She patted his hand, suffering a little guilt over the necessary deception. "I think I just need some rest. It's been a tough week." With a bit of hesitation, she offered her hand again to Raymond. "It was nice to meet you."

"Nice to meet you, Short Stuff."

Trying not to recoil from his touch, she forced a smile then gave Stephen a kiss on the cheek before saying good night.

Once outside, she turned full-face toward the crisp October wind, hoping the gusts that sent dried leaves skittering across the parking lot would chase away lingering traces of that man's touch. She clutched her coat tightly to her chest and scurried across the lot. Something sinister about him made her skin crawl and her heart pound. She unlocked her car and scooted behind the wheel, turning her heater on full blast. But the coldness stayed, too deep for the heat to reach. She shivered, searching for the comfort that only a very loud dog and a very hard baseball bat could deliver.

Chapter Fourteen

Saturday night. Angela shut off her car's engine but remained behind the wheel. Taking a deep breath, she stared at the stone façade on Hank's temporary home. A tiny thrill tripped down her spine. So this is how it felt to pull up to a man's house all alone in the dark. It was so wanton, and yet liberating and exciting. She could practically hear both her mother and Stephen objecting. Placing her hand over her heart, she felt the steady rhythm there. *Stop this*, she scolded. *It's not like I'm a pubescent teenager chasing after a school crush.* Hank's house provided more room and more privacy for dance lessons. It made sense that she come here, she reasoned. Practical. Then why did it feel so wicked? And why did feeling wicked feel so delicious?

The garage door started a slow glide up. Hank walked toward her from the well-lit bay. She pushed her car door open before he could reach it, but he pulled it wider and extended a hand to help her out.

"I thought I heard your car. I was afraid you'd change your mind."

She wanted to say something witty, something to show she was well-accustomed to visiting men at all hours of the night, but nothing came to mind. Or nothing that she would dare say.

The sharp clean scent of pine trees surrounding the property invigorated her senses. Smoke drifted in the wind. Somewhere a cozy fire burned in a homey fireplace. The thought made her comfortable and warm.

Utilizing his offered hand for support, she left the car. He closed the door behind her, but didn't relinquish her hand. He stood close, too close for comfort, but with the car frame at her back she had nowhere to retreat. For a brief moment, she wasn't sure she would even if she could.

"I have a surprise for you," he said.

A gust of wind whispered through the tops of the pines and eddies of fallen leaves scattered across the driveway. Aided by the wind, her hair pulled free from her heavy neck scarf and blew across her face. But it was Hank's fingers that tenderly pushed the resistant strands back behind her ear. Her nerve endings electrified under his touch and followed the trail of his fingers across her forehead and down the side of her far-too-sensitive face. Words poised on the tip of her tongue, melted and slipped away in the charged silence. Her heavy eyelids started a slow descent.

"Don't you want to know what it is?"

Oh, she wanted many things, like his fingertips to continue their torturous journey past her ear to the back of her neck. She wanted to close the distance between them. She wanted to tip her lips up to his advancing kiss. She wanted... Oh my God! Her eyes opened wide. What was she thinking! He was a client.

"I'm thinking...dinner?" She pulled her lips into a quick smile, thankful that the early onset of evening masked the heat radiating from her cheeks. "Maybe we should go inside?"

"Oh. Of course, yes." He dropped her hand. "You must be cold." She nodded, although the rapidly spreading warmth beneath her skin rendered her heavy coat and scarf superfluous. At his gesture, she led the way into the brightly lit garage and on into the house.

The enticing aromas smacked her senses like a pie-in-the-face on one of Stephen's silent movies. "Something smells wonderful."

"I baked," he replied with a shrug.

"I brought some music." She held up a stack of five CDs, then slipped out of her coat for Hank to hang in the closet. "I aimed for variety 'cause I'm not sure exactly what kind of music they play at these things."

He took the square jewel boxes from her hand and shuffled through them. "Rock and roll, jazz, Gershwin," he lifted an eyebrow, "disco? That's quite a collection."

"My parents indulged me with music. They thought it was safe enough." She turned to go into the great room, noticing he had already pushed the furniture back against the walls. A fire hissed and crackled in the fireplace. "I usually have the radio or some CD playing."

"I thought we might eat first, then work it off in the dance lesson. If that's all right with you?"

"My mouth is watering so bad now, I don't think I could concentrate otherwise," she teased, half in earnest. The inviting aromas of fresh baked bread and a roast of some kind fairly overwhelmed her.

"Then go into the dining room while I put on some music."

She hadn't explored the dining room the last time she was there. Even though he had invited her to do so, it still felt uncomfortable exploring the unfamiliar room on her own. Not that it stopped her.

Her breath caught at the spaciousness. Both her mother's tiny kitchen and dining room could fit neatly in the space of this one room. A highly polished oak table dominated the center of the room, one half covered with a crisp white tablecloth and laid with gleaming china. Two candles flickered, the light reflected in the flashing silver of the place settings and in the glass front of an immense china breakfront. The sweet vibrant notes from a violin concerto flowed into the lavish setting.

"I hope you like Beef Wellington," he said, slipping into the room behind her. He pulled back one of the chairs. "If you'll have a seat, I'll bring in the salad."

"I can help," she said quickly, suddenly hesitant at being trapped in this room, at this table. Opulence like this was meant for someone else, not Angela Blake of backwater Westerville. "Why don't I carry something in?"

"Please sit," he insisted. She hesitated a moment, then sat in the offered chair. He leaned close to her ear. The tiny hairs at her nape stood up and took notice. "Next time you can help, but tonight it would be my pleasure to serve you." His soft voice and warm breath swirled around her ear and took hold deep inside. She was lost, submerged over her head. But drowning in his voice and touch seemed preferable to waking from this dream.

"Would you like some wine?" He pulled a bottle from the ice bucket by the side of the table.

"No. Not for me," she said, covering her wineglass with her hand. "It doesn't work well with my medications."

"Oh, I'm sorry. I forgot," he said. Ice crunched as he reinserted the bottle. "I just forgot. Let me get those salads."

He forgot—that meant he thought of her as normal. She relaxed in her chair. The warmth of his acceptance simmered down to her toes. Who would believe those two words could sound so sweet.

He returned with two plates of salad and some of the yummiest rolls she had ever tasted.

"Where did you find these?" she asked, helping herself to a second one.

His dimple flashed in the candlelight. He stood and removed their empty salad plates. "I made them."

"No," she exclaimed. "They don't teach this in business school." In moments, he returned with two larger plates.

"I'm serious," she said. "Where did you learn to cook like this?" She looked at the plate set before her, brimming with the pastry-covered beef, potatoes au gratin and asparagus. She groaned. "I can't eat all that."

He laughed. "I've got plenty of leftover takeout containers that can serve as a doggie bag."

She sliced into the pastry-covered beef, releasing steam and meat juices. The tiny morsel of meat practically melted in her mouth in a burst of flavor. "Oreo will have to fight me to get hold of this. Delicious."

"Thank you." Although candlelight offered the only illumination, she thought his face brightened at her compliment. Obviously, he was proud of his culinary skills.

"Now I wish I hadn't eaten so many of those rolls," she said, enjoying that her compliments lit his eyes with pleasure. She scooped a small forkful of potatoes. "Your mother must be a fabulous cook."

He looked confused. "My mother?"

"Didn't she teach you to cook this way?"

The light lifted from his face and receded in the dim corners of the room. "No. My mother never went into a kitchen unless it was to locate the sherry."

She recognized the unexplored pain behind his words, but didn't want to lose the earlier mood. "But someone had to teach you to cook like this."

He put his fork on his plate and reached for the water goblet. "There was someone. Our family cook, Mrs. Thurgood. When I was growing up, I spent a lot of time in the kitchen. It was warm there...accepting..." He took a drink from the goblet then shrugged. "She taught me the joy of pounding dough."

"You mean kneading?" she asked, enthralled at the changes in his expressions as he relived the past.

"Not the way I do it." He laughed. "Eat up or we won't have time for that dancing lesson."

The rest of the meal passed with idle conversation. She helped clear the dishes, but he insisted the pots and pans could wait till morning. The dance lesson, he said, could not. With only one week to the big night, she agreed. She drifted out to the great room while he put away the perishables. With the furniture cleared to one side, the gleaming hardwood floors presented the perfect surface for an evening of dance.

She paused by one of the tables along the wall. Two large rectangular boxes were stacked one upon the other, the top one bearing the name MASQUE MAGIC.

"The costumes!" She reached for the top box, wanting to shake it as if it were discovered under a Christmas tree. "You didn't tell me you had the costumes!"

"That's the surprise I mentioned earlier." He crossed the floor to join her.

"What kind did you get? Is this one mine?" She didn't give him time to answer before she slipped her fingers around the sides, jostling the top back and forth to separate it from the bottom. "You know, I have to admit, ever since you talked me into agreeing to go to this dance, I've been pretty excited about wearing a costume." The top came free and she tossed it aside. But before she could explore the contents of the box, Hank put his hand on the obscuring white tissue paper.

"They didn't have a lot to choose from," he said with an apologetic tone. "I guess people reserve these things pretty early. I did the best I could."

"I'm sure you did, but it doesn't matter. I'm so excited." Giddy with anticipation, she became the little girl she hadn't had much of a chance to be. "I've never dressed up in a costume before. I could look like a frog and be happy."

"Are you sure?"

His hesitancy gave her a moment's discomfort, but she couldn't restrain her enthusiasm. She tugged at his arm. "Let me see!"

He stepped back, allowing her room to dig into the box. She eagerly attacked the tissue paper. "As long as my face is covered so no one can see, that's all I—"

Nestled within the rustling tissue paper lay a treasure of blue and gold. Her breath caught. "Oh, Hank..." She lifted the delicate costume by the shoulders. Sheer, wispy fabric petals of pale shimmering blue and translucent green unfolded from the box. Gossamer wings tipped in gold like those found on a dragonfly dripped from the back of the sparkling tunic. It was something from a dream, or at least a bedtime story, far more beautiful than anything she could have imagined.

"Is this for me?" Awe constricted her throat.

He laughed. "Do you think I could fit in that thing?"

Heat warmed her cheeks. "What is it?" she asked, surprised to hear she had spoken the words.

"A fairy," he said. "Or a sprite, I'm not sure I know the difference."

"It's beautiful," she said with a note of wonder. And a miracle of construction. It even had a high bateau neckline that would cover her scar, just as she requested. The entire bodice was sprinkled with glittery sparkles dancing with light. "Perfect," she added.

"I knew you'd like it. But it won't be perfect until you try it on." His face sparkled as if some of the fairy dust scattered on the costume had managed to get caught in his smile. That same dizzy, sinking feeling she had felt earlier resurged, but passed in her excitement.

"May I?" She clasped the garment to her chest. "I'll need the mask."

She quickly checked the inside of the box and found the tiny mask; elegant, sparkling, and not the least bit concealing. A lump formed in her throat. The ensemble was more beautiful than anything she had ever dreamed of wearing, but vastly inappropriate. How could she be anonymous with her face revealed? Her emotional carousel stopped. Time to drift back to reality.

"The costume is really beautiful," she slowly folded the material back into the box. "But, I don't think this will—"

"Wait," he said, pulling the second box out from under hers. "You haven't seen the best part."

"It doesn't matter. It was a lovely thought, and I appreciate you picking out something so beautiful for me." She couldn't bear to turn around and look at him. Instead she focused on the bit of whimsy she would never get a chance to wear. She carefully folded the tissue back over the light airy petals. Tears threatened the corners of her eyes. She swiped at them before putting the top of the box back on. Another fantasy neatly contained and filed away, like so many others. "But it just won't do," she whispered.

"I know it's not what I promised," he said from behind her.

His voice sounded different, muffled, but she didn't give it much thought. Her disappointment was too consuming. After all, he had promised to keep her identity a secret, hadn't he? *Trust me*, he had said.

"No, it's not at all what you promised." Anger sparked and she smacked her hand on the box lid before turning to face him. "You said you'd..." The words died in her throat.

A massive deformed head balanced on top of a man's grotesquely misshapen body. Eyeballs bulged from their sockets, a huge bulbous nose sneered over enormous yellowed teeth protruding at unlikely angles. Tufts of bristly black hair poked up in improbable places. Worst of all, it laughed at her.

"Do you like it?" Hank asked from beneath the monstrous head.

"What is it?" she asked, consciously willing her heart to slow a bit after the fright.

"I forget if it's an ogre or a troll." Hank replied. "All I know is it's ugly," he took the mask off his head, "and hot."

"A troll?" She stooped to retrieve the box that had fallen to the floor. He knelt down beside her.

"I couldn't find anything that covered you completely, so I thought if I was the one under wraps, we could still go to the ball. No one will know that I'm with you."

"You think?" A glimmer of longing flared in her heart.

"Either that, or we can switch costumes. You go as the ogre and I'll go as the fairy."

The image of Hank in the diaphanous costume generated unrestrained laughter.

"Does that mean you'll still go?" he asked. His fingertips touched hers on the sides of the box at their feet. That same electrical current that she had experienced earlier raced up her arms and settled in her chest. Momentarily stunned, she lifted her gaze to his and lost all sense of time and place in their inviting warmth.

"Will you?" he asked, all trace of mirth gone.

She watched his lips wrap around the vowels. Magnetic, his voice pulled her closer. Her eyelids lowered as if to verify this was all a dream.

He leaned forward, the scent of his deep, woodsy cologne surrounding her. Perhaps she had been transformed to that magical wood sprite, whimsical, free and daring. Miracles happened every day. She knew. She was a product of one. Lulled by the fantasy, she leaned closer, scant inches from his tempting lips.

She was about to be kissed, truly kissed, and her heart pounded all the more fiercely for it. Not a brotherly peck on the cheek, either. Or a sloppy sophomoric kiss exchanged between two experimenting teenagers. This would be shared between a man and a woman, a true kiss, like the kind exchanged by lovers.

But he's a client! Her brain screamed. *He's not a lover. He's not even a date!*

She froze. And he must think she's the perfect fool to be begging for a kiss this way. She pulled back abruptly, averting her eyes.

"I'm going to go try this on," she said, then stood before hurrying down the hallway. Glancing back over her shoulder, she saw he continued to kneel, his chin dropped to his chest. She slipped into the first bedroom and leaned heavily against the door.

"Good," he called after her. "After you've changed, we'll begin that dance lesson."

Hank heard the door click shut and let out his breath in a slow stream. What was he doing? What had started as a benevolent gesture to treat Angela to some of those lost experiences was quickly growing out of his control. Caught in a swirling maelstrom of emotions, he wasn't sure how to escape. Wasn't sure he wanted to escape. He rose from his knees and walked over to Angela's stack of CDs lying on the table. He slipped them into the CD player and pushed random play. A rich bluesy melody filled the room.

Great, he thought with a grimace. *All I have to do now is dim the lights, pour some wine and light some candles.* Damn, he had made promises to Owens and overtures to Elizabeth. The door clicked open down the hall, but he continued his mental tirade. He shouldn't be getting involved with a...a...

"Angel." The word, spoken in reverence, slipped out at the sight of her.

"Do you like it?" She pirouetted in front of him, lifting the petals of the skirt to reveal trim firm thighs encased in clinging tights. His mouth went dry.

Magnificent. The costume must have been cut with seduction in mind. Gauzy layers of almost transparent fabric revealed nothing but suggested everything, from the gentle swelling of her breasts to the narrow curve of her waist. His groin tightened.

"Look at this." With childlike glee, she pulled at a tiny ring hidden beneath the petal layers at her waist. "There's a cord or fishing line or something that slips around to the back. When I pull this ring..." Gossamer wings unfolded behind her with life-like precision.

"Gorgeous." The word slipped from his lips as if in prayer. She glanced up from the device at her waist, her eyes the same shimmering blue as the magical garment she wore. He cleared his throat. "You'll be the envy of every woman at the ball."

"Do you think so?" Her eyes seemed more liquid than before. "I've never been the envy of anyone for anything." She stepped closer.

His grip tightened on the empty CD cases in his hand. He glanced down. If he wasn't careful, the hard plastic covers would crack.

"This song is one of my favorites." She started to sway from side to side. "I hope they play music like this at the ball." The shimmering petals of the costume moved with her body accentuating the rhythm. She lifted her arms like some ancient mythical goddess. "Shall we dance?"

Dancing. Right. That was what she was here for. "Do you mind if I get something to drink first? My throat's kind of scratchy." He tugged at the collar of the troll costume as if that were the cause of his discomfort. "As a matter of fact..." He crossed his hands and pulled off the tunic that made up the body of the costume.

"Maybe I should change too," she said, her eyes betraying her disappointment.

"No. You stay the way you are. You look...fabulous." He hurried off to the kitchen for a glass of water. "I'll just have to be careful about what I wear underneath that thing. Certainly not jeans and a sweater." He rubbed his sweaty palms down his jeans. How was he going to teach her to dance with palms sweaty as a teenager?

"I have to tell you." She drifted over to the kitchen to join him, the petals of her costume swaying with each step. "I've been thinking about this costume ball ever since you first mentioned it. I'm still a little nervous that someone will find out that it's you and me. But this is..." She floundered for words, her eyes sparkling to match the faint sprinkling of glitter on the wings.

Hank sipped the cool water from his glass, watching the wondrous play of joy across her face.

"It's all so perfect." Her eyes glowed and her voice was magic. Her words mingled with the seductive music and wove their way into his soul. He was going down fast.

"You say that because you haven't seen me dance." He hoped his self-deprecating humor would relieve the pressure to sample those lips that spun the magic.

"And you're supposed to be the teacher." She laughed, and the song ended. "Shall we?" she asked, hand extended.

He took one last gulp of the water and followed her out to the middle of the floor. A fast-paced rock and roll tune erupted from the speakers. "The important thing is to feel the beat," he said, shifting his weight from one foot to the other. "Can you feel it?"

Obviously she could, he reflected, as her body moved from side to sensuous side.

"Just let the music take over and get inside you. Do what you feel." He could have been talking to a wall. She was already doing just that. Her eyes closed. Every movement of her arm, every swing of her hip synchronized perfectly with the music. Her lips tilted in a luring smile as if she enjoyed a secret known only to her. The petals of her costume and the swing of her hair only emphasized the sensuality of her movements. Her face glowed as if she was intoxicated.

"You lied to me," he called over the music. Her eyes opened abruptly, she stopped moving.

"Excuse me?"

"You're a born dancer." He continued his clumsy side-to-side motions. "You put me to shame. I thought you said you couldn't do this."

Her lips turned up in that mysterious smile. "This I can do by myself with no one around."

The thought of her dancing in this sinuous fashion behind closed doors brought new pressures. Perhaps her parents restricted her dancing, not so much to protect her heart, but to protect her partner's. Heaven knew his heart was pounding out a furious tempo. His hands turned clammy and, dammit, damp again.

Mercifully, the song ended and he retreated to the kitchen counter for his glass of water and another discreet swipe at his pants leg.

The next song slowed down the pace considerably. "Now this is the kind of dancing that takes two." She swayed in invitation.

He crossed the room and stepped up close. "Let's see." His right hand found her waist. "Put your hand on my arm... That's right." He clasped her hand in his left and held it loosely aloft.

"Now what?" she asked, her head bent in concentration, staring at her feet.

"Now we take little steps, first one then the other to the music." He demonstrated. She mimicked his movements perfectly, still watching their feet. He guided her in a slow, smooth circle.

"Is that it?" she asked, finally looking at him rather than their feet.

"That's all there is to it," he said, enjoying the feel of her agile waist beneath his fingers. He glanced at her face and frowned. "You look disappointed."

"It looks different on television, or in the movies."

"How so?" he asked.

"For one thing, they don't stand two feet apart."

"Oh." He stepped closer, feeling heat creep up the back of his neck. "I didn't want to crowd you." His hands slipped to the small of her back and encountered the wing contraption. "That won't work," he muttered before moving his hand back to her waist. Still, he was close enough that her breasts softly brushed the front of his shirt. Was that his imagination or were those taut, hard nipples gliding across his chest. He stepped on her foot.

"Sorry," he apologized as he fumbled to find the beat. "I told you you were better at this than me."

"The only time I've ever done this is when I stood on my father's feet when I was a little girl."

"And now, I'm attempting to stand on yours," he teased. Her resulting laughter calmed the flutter of jitters in his stomach. They danced close, his chin at a level with her forehead. Her hair smelled fresh and clean, not the unwashed-but-disguised-by-cloying-perfume heaviness of Elizabeth's hair. In one impulsive moment, he rested his cheek against the raw silk softness. These same silky strands had splayed across his thighs that eventful afternoon in the woods. Other regions of his body remembered the afternoon as well and he instantly wished he still wore the camouflaging tunic from the costume. He stepped back from her. "I know one step that might razzle-dazzle you."

"Show me, please."

"Okay, when I press the inside of your knee with mine, it means we're going to spin around in a circle. Are you ready?" At her nod, he pressed her knee and took three fast steps, spinning her with him in the process.

"That felt like flying." She beamed. "I love it. Can we try it again?"

"We're out of music," he said as the song issued its final chord. Although the music ended, he held her close in stance, hesitant to let her go. He looked down at her tilted face, her eyes glowing with excitement, wispy blonde tendrils across her flushed forehead. "Are you still disappointed?"

In answer, her lips reached up to his. Without thought, he met her halfway.

It was a petal-soft kiss. Delicate, inviting.

A kiss of innocent sweetness and youth. That kiss said more of her inexperience than words ever could. His hands moved instinctively around her back. He longed to lift her, pull her closer so she could see what her innocence had done to him. But that darn wing thing got in the way. Vaguely aware that her arms had somehow become entangled around his neck, he set her back a step.

"I'm sorry. I shouldn't have done that," she said.

"No. No. It's my fault. I wanted to kiss you," he admitted, hoping to take some of her discomfort away.

"You did?" Her eyes softened. He fought the overwhelming urge to lift her up and carry her back to one of those empty bedrooms.

"Do you still...?"

"Want to take you to the dance?" he finished her sentence. She might have suggested something else and he couldn't lose control like that again. Kissing her had definitely cost him control. "Yes, of course," he said, although touching her was leading him down a path of ruin. "I'm looking forward to it."

"Good," she said on a breath. Relief flooded her face. He wanted to tell her how much he enjoyed her kiss, how he longed for it to linger. How he longed to take it deeper.

"Maybe we should call it a night," he said instead. "Would you like to change?" *Do you need me to help*, he almost added.

"No." she said, her face tilted studying him. "But I don't think these wings will fit under my coat."

He chuckled. His hands clenched into fists once she had turned toward the hallway. It would be so easy to follow her, to watch as she slipped off that flimsy concoction from her delicate shoulders, to taste those tempting breasts that reduced him to a clumsy teenager. Instead, he muttered an obscenity beneath his breath and walked over to the CD player to eject the discs. At least the action gave him something to do other than fantasize about what was happening on the other side of the door.

She quickly emerged, the cardboard box under her arm. "Do you think we're ready?" she asked.

"For the dance?" He knew he was ready for something more than what she was asking. More than ready. "Yes, I think we are."

"Then I'll see you Saturday? Should I drive here?"

He wanted to do this right, to pick up her up at her house and not ask her to come to him. But he understood her concern, and after all they'd done to conceal their identities, it would be unfortunate to blow their cover now.

"I've got an idea," he said. Retrieving her coat from the closet, he held it out to assist her putting it on. "How about I charter a limo with nice dark windows?"

She smiled. "I should have thought of that. I know just the place." She slipped her arms into the coat and he caught an enticing glimpse of her neck. His lips lowered to kiss that sensitive patch of skin, but he caught himself just in time. Instead, he whispered in her ear.

"I thought you might."

Then she was gone.

Chapter Fifteen

The week preceding the ball passed much too quickly. Her days were spent in the office or at the site of Claymoor Construction, another client, performing interim work. Her evenings were devoted to all manner of preparations for the dance. She experimented with make-up and hairstyles, finally deciding on a tousled style full of random curly tendrils. The just-tumbled-out-of-the-woods effect required several hours of battle with a curling iron and a can of hair spray, but the end result was worth it. She wished her mother were home to share this with her. Funny, she thought, all the effort she was putting into a promotion so she could move away from home, yet now that she was on her own, she missed her mother.

Finally the long-awaited day arrived. The news had predicted rain and the depressing gray clouds gave credence to the warnings. But none of that concerned Angela. Her excitement about the coming evening could burn away the gloomiest skies. The rain held off. Blustering winds offered the only evidence of the storm front moving in. Even the fact that Stephen sent Raymond to maneuver the sleek white limousine through downtown failed to darken her mood.

"What time do you want me to return to pick you up?" Raymond asked Hank after he had exited the limousine.

"I'm not sure. What do you think?" Hank asked Angie as he helped her from the back of the car.

She glanced over at Ray, standing by the door in his new Classic Limousine livery. Had she known he would be driving, she would have driven herself. The man definitely made her uncomfortable, though she wasn't sure why. "I've no idea. Maybe we should just take a taxi back."

"You can always call me when you're ready," Ray said. "I'm always at your beck and call."

"No. Neither one of us brought a cell phone." She put her hand on Raymond's arm and forced herself not to recoil. *Remember Walter*, she reminded herself. "I appreciate you bringing us here, but I think we can manage to make it back on our own."

"If you insist." He tipped his cap and walked back to the driver's side of the car. A shiver slipped down her spine, but Hank propelled her toward the building's entrance before she could dwell on it further.

"May I take your wrap?" the hideous monstrosity, her date, asked.

She smiled, and dragged one of her first-time-ever manicured fingernails down the front of Hank's rumpled, ragtag tunic.

"Your voice is much too sweet to go with that costume." *Sweet? My God, Listen to me. I'm flirting.* A sudden rash of heat burned her cheeks. She never realized she was capable of flirting.

"May I take your wrap, you ...you ...fairy?" he said in a deeper gruff tone. She laughed, then quickly covered her mouth to avoid one of her famous snorts.

The wings on her costume were too delicate to crush under the heavy weight of a coat, so she had settled on a woven shawl that she could wrap loosely around her shoulders. Hank helped remove the shawl with oversized fake plastic hands. Angie watched him plow through the press of witches and ghouls, devils and angels, human-sized food items and walking, talking animals. No one would recognize him in that costume, she reassured herself. Which was wonderful, because already she knew, she wouldn't have missed this for the world.

The ballroom was lavishly decorated to resemble a mad scientist's laboratory. Neon tubes flashed bright colors through dry ice mists. A drummer in a skeleton outfit provided a backbeat to a group of goblins wielding instruments. Music and conversation filled the room with deafening harmony.

"Would you like to dance?" Hank practically yelled in her ear. She looked at the packed dance floor.

"Where?" she shouted in reply.

He squeezed her hand. "We'll make room."

They stepped onto the dance floor and the other couples seemed to compact, affording them a little room to dance, albeit closely.

The music took over. Even with the clunky plastic cast wrapped around one leg, her feet quickly found the rhythm and she moved as the notes carried her. She couldn't see Hank's face to see if it registered approval or not. She was dancing, in a crowd of normal healthy adults. Life was wonderful.

After several fast-paced songs, the band elected to slow things down a bit. Hank extended his grotesque hand and took her glitter-spangled one. Someone bumped her from behind, pushing her closer to Hank. Her hand slid up to the top of his shoulder.

"Having a good time?" he asked, his voice muffled by the mask but audible to her ear.

"Wonderful." The simple word couldn't contain all the joy she felt. "How about you?"

"I'm about to melt away in here, but I'm enjoying myself." They swayed through a few more verses. "Do you mind if after this dance we go get something cold to drink?"

She began to pull away. "We can go now if you like. There's no reason..."

He pulled her back against his chest, continuing the dance step. "The next dance is soon enough. Besides, we haven't done our spin yet."

She smiled against his shoulder, content that he must be enjoying the dance as much as she.

"Have I told you tonight what a fabulous dancer you are?" he teased.

"That's because I had a fabulous teacher."

"Oh?" She could hear the smile in his voice.

"Yes. He had the biggest, hairiest feet I've ever seen," she teased, looking pointedly at the plastic overshoes that completed the Troll costume. "But he sure could dance."

"Hold tight." His knee pressed against the inside of hers. They spun neatly around in a tight circle. Chilling air from dry ice clouds tingled on the back of her neck, as her hair, curled just for this occasion, lifted in the artificial current. The music sounded the final notes just as her world stopped spinning. Before she could catch her breath, he lowered her in a dramatic dip over one arm. Her heart pounded, each beat reinforcing the joy of life that filled her. She felt vulnerable, defenseless before the man in the mask, but at the same time secure and desired. The song ended, the couples clapped, and in their own little corner of the dance floor, Hank slowly raised Angie back to her feet.

"We never practiced that before," she said, chest heaving while she caught her breath.

"What can I say? You're an inspiration." They stood chest to chest for a moment. She wished he wasn't wearing that silly mask. She couldn't see his face, his eyes. She couldn't read his thoughts. He tugged at her hand. "Let's get that drink."

Hank guided her to an empty table. "What would you like?"

How could she answer that question? She'd like to explore the trembling emotions that erupted inside her every time he took her in his arms. She'd like to sample his lips again like she did last weekend, only this time longer and maybe...deeper. A small vibration originating below her belly tingled upward, sparking nerve endings in its path. *He's a friend*, she reminded herself in an effort to find her voice; *he's a client.* "A soft drink would be fine." She needed something to moisten her suddenly parched throat.

"The bar is over by that bubbling cauldron." He pointed to a group of costumed celebrants huddled in a far corner. "Wait here and I'll be right back."

Angie sat on the edge of the chair, afraid sitting back might damage her wings. She waited patiently, marveling at the imaginative costumes. She tapped her finger on the rack of test tubes used as a table decoration. One test tube sported a long stemmed rose, another a glittery substance, others held weights that secured balloons bobbing overhead.

Inexplicably, she felt she was the object of someone's surveillance. Goosebumps rose on her arms. Twisting in her seat, she studied the people sitting at the surrounding gaily-decorated tables.

Most of the occupants acted oblivious to her scrutiny, but at one far table, a man faced her directly. A brimmed hat pulled low on his forehead shielded his face from the already dimmed lighting. She squinted to separate him from the shadows. He was dressed in black, except for a white tie. Still facing her, he rose from behind the table and...

"Angela, is that you?"

She turned quickly toward a familiar voice. A devil, complete with a black cape, a red pointed tail and a pair of bifocal glasses stood to her right.

"Mr. Falstaff?" she asked, peering at the red painted face and black goatee. She couldn't get any other words past the lump of dread that formed in her throat.

He laughed, his horns shaking in rhythm with his ponderous belly. "I thought that was you on the dance floor." He nodded to her leg. "That plastic cast gave you away." He pulled out a chair and sat down next to her.

"That's a...a...great costume." She cleared her throat and quickly scanned over Falstaff's shoulder, hoping to spot Hank before he could approach the table. No luck, not a single troll in sight.

"This?" He leaned his plastic trident against the tabletop. "It's my wife's idea of a joke, I think. She came dressed as an angel. But she doesn't look half as angelic as you, my dear. What a lovely outfit."

Her cheeks warmed under his gaze. "I admit it's a change from a business suit."

"Yes, quite a change indeed." They sat at the table a few moments in awkward silence. "I must admit I'm surprised to see you here. I didn't realize you were a patron of the arts."

Angie planned to reply when she saw Hank twisting through the crowd trying to protect the contents of the two plastic cups in his hands. *Go away*, she tried to telepath. Even hidden beneath his costume, someone who knew him might recognize his voice. She knew she would, no matter what kind of mask obscured his face.

She looked back at Falstaff. "I'm sorry. I couldn't hear you over the music. What did you say?"

"I was asking who you were dancing with a moment ago. You made such a handsome couple." Speculation glinted in his shrewd eyes.

"My brother," she answered quickly, noting Hank's imminent arrival. "I don't think you've ever met my brother." Hank arrived at the table, two drinks in hand. She raised her voice to a near shout. "Stephen, I'd like you to meet my boss, Mr. Falstaff." In an aside to Falstaff, she added, "he can't hear well under that mask."

Hank nodded once, then placed the drinks on the table before extending his hand to Falstaff.

"Actually we've met once before, at the company picnic last July. Do you remember?" Falstaff shouted, vigorously pumping Hank's hand. Hank bobbed his head as if agreeing with the devil. "If you can't hear well under that mask," Falstaff shouted, "maybe you should take it off."

"No!" Angela shouted. Both men looked at her. "He can't." She bit her lower lip, then leaned toward Falstaff's ear. "He doesn't like to be seen in public. He's self-conscious about his scar." She traced a path down her cheek in explanation.

"A scar? I don't remember a scar."

"It's recent. Happened in a car accident," she lied while silently vowing never to invite her brother to another company function.

Falstaff turned back to Hank. "If all you got was a scar, sounds like you were pretty lucky." Hank continued bobbing his head. Falstaff lowered his voice to a normal level. "Looks like the band is taking a break so it's safe to track down my wife. I'm not a big dancer, you know, and she always insists." He stood. "It was nice to see you again, Stephen."

Hank nodded again and extended his hand for a parting handshake.

"I'll see you in the office on Monday, Angela."

She smiled, relieved to see him leaving so soon. "I'll be there."

"Yes, well," he collected his trident, "enjoy the ball." After a quick nod, he melted into the crowd.

Angie nonchalantly sipped her drink, watching Falstaff until she was certain he was no longer a threat.

"Do you want to leave?" Hank asked, his own drink untouched.

She nodded. "It's not that this hasn't been wonderful. It's just..."

"It's okay." Hank patted her hand. "I understand." They both stood to leave. "To tell you the truth, I'm anxious to get this darn mask off." Angie looked past him to see if the mysterious man in black still watched her from the corner. The table was vacant.

Hank collected their garments from the coat check booth and they stepped briefly into the chill night air before sliding into the backseat of a taxi.

"Thanks for not driving tonight," she said as the cab pulled away from the curb. "I was afraid someone might recognize your car otherwise."

"It's okay, Angie." He reassured her again. "I promised you that we, or at least I, would be completely incognito and I meant it." He gripped the bottom of the plastic mask with both hands. "But, do you mind if I took this off now? I don't think anyone can see."

"Oh yes, please." She helped him shed the torture device. His sweat-plastered hair combined with the rivulets of moisture running down his cheeks went straight to her heart. He did this for her. She leaned close to his ear. "Thank you."

His dimple deepened. "So you had a good time, if only for a little while?" He mopped his face with a handkerchief.

"It was wonderful, like a dream...better than a dream."

"Better than a dream?"

She nodded. "I'll remember all of this, the costume, the decorations, the dance, long after I wake up."

His hand sought hers for a gentle squeeze. "What did you like the best?"

She leaned back in the seat, closed her eyes and reveled that her hand still nestled inside of his. How could she tell him all that this evening of firsts meant to her? First costume, first dance, first date. *Not a date*, a voice tried to remind her. She refused to listen.

He jiggled her hand. "Come on, you can't go to sleep on me. The evening is too young." She reluctantly opened her eyes, not quite ready for reality.

"Tell me," he teased. "What did you like the most?"

"That you asked me." The words slipped out before she could pull them back.

The jovial humor faded from his eyes, replaced by something else, something that warmed every inch of skin touched by the fantasy costume. Delicious.

"Angie?" He kissed the back of her hand. Her spine melted into the upholstery. "There's something I need to tell you..." His breath bathed the back of her hand, causing the tips of her breasts to tingle. "Something I need to explain."

"Here you go, folks." The cab driver pulled the cab up to the curb in front of her house. "Thirty-seven fifteen Plum Street."

"Wait for me?" Hank whispered, releasing her hand. As he settled with the driver, Angie allowed herself a moment to recover before she let herself out the side door. She drew deep breaths of the autumn-tinged air into her lungs, sharp, cold, a whisper of smoke, a hint of dead leaves. The fresh air chased away her amorous illusions. *I'm only a substitute date. Get hold of yourself.*

"Angie?" She jumped a little, not realizing he was there.

"Figures." He looked off in the distance, a smile teasing his lips. "My natural face is scarier than the mask."

They laughed all the way to the front door. She fished out her house key from her tiny whimsical drawstring bag purchased just for this evening, slipped the key in the lock and turned till the tumblers clicked. The dark empty house loomed in front of her. The phone was ringing, probably her mother wanting details about the evening, or Stephen wondering why she dismissed the limo. Let them wait. She wasn't ready to discuss this magical evening with others. She turned to face Hank.

"I think this is the part where I turn back into a char woman," she said, recalling her favorite fairy tale. She held out her hand for a handshake. "I had a wonderful time."

He looked briefly at her outstretched hand. "I think you may have your fairy tales mixed-up." His arms closed around her back and pulled her close. "I'm the bewitched one."

His lips met hers, softly, inquisitive. The tip of his tongue slid around the seam of her closed lips before retreating. He pulled back, slowly. Her arms wrapped around his neck.

"Now I can return to my former handsome state," he whispered, then arched an eyebrow. "I was handsome, wasn't I?"

She nodded slowly, still dazed by the kiss.

His hands slid down to her waist. "I had a wonderful time tonight, Angela." He kissed her softly on her cheek. "Thank you for coming with me. I'm in your debt." He stepped back and took all that glorious warmth with him. She shivered in its absence.

"Good night now," he said, before turning toward the cab.

"Wait." She had to stop him, but she wasn't sure why. She wrapped her hand around one of the posts, feeling the need for support. "Maybe you'd like to come in for some coffee or something?"

He smiled. She barely saw the flash of his dimple in the porch light. "Coffee would be nice," he said, signaling to the cab. He returned to the porch.

She led the way to the kitchen, mentally scolding herself for not buying some fancy gourmet coffee, the kind he had served her last weekend. But then, she hadn't considered anything beyond the ball itself. After silencing the insistent answering machine and putting Oreo out in the yard, she retrieved a mug from a cabinet. Standing on tiptoe, she tried to reach a tin of coffee her mother kept on a high shelf. Her fingertips barely grazed the side of the tin.

"Here, let me get that for you," Hank said, stepping up behind her. He reached over her head, but his arm kept bumping into her delicate wings. "Tell you what," he said, stepping aside. "Why don't I make the coffee while you go change out of that contraption."

Embarrassing warmth tinged her cheeks at his suggestion that she undress, but she recognized its practicality. Although perfect for dancing, the wings made even sitting difficult.

Leaving him in the kitchen, she climbed the steps, slipped out of her costume, then stared at her reflection in the full-length mirror. No matter how magical the evening, a seven-inch scar still bisected her chest. No amount of fairy dust could change that reality. Disenchanted, she reached for a T-shirt. Just as well. As much as she might dream otherwise, Hank had clearly said that this was not a date. He already had a "normal" girlfriend, one without hideous scars. The scent of freshly brewed coffee drifted up the stairs reminding her that he waited below. She reached for her jeans. He probably expected her to drive him home anyway. She took one last glance at the mirror. For the first time in her life, she wondered if just being alive was enough.

"Just in time," Hank said, pausing in his arrangement of biscotti on a plate. "I hope you don't mind, I raided the pantry and found this."

"Sure, no problem." She picked up the plate and a glass of water. "Shall we go into the sitting room? It's more comfortable there."

She sat near the arm of the couch, expecting him to select the nearby chair. Instead he sat next to her, his weight on the cushions shifting her body closer to his.

"You were beautiful tonight." Her face warmed under his compliment. "And witty, and charming, and graceful—"

"Not graceful," she protested, thinking of her leg brace. Her brace! She'd forgotten to put it back on when she'd changed upstairs. Was that why she felt lighter than gauze?

"Definitely graceful," he said, looping his arm around the back of the couch behind her. "But you look much more comfortable in this." He tugged at the short sleeve of her T-shirt. *Looks can be deceiving*, she thought as his fingertips raised excited goosebumps on her forearm.

He was so close, intimately close. She put her glass on the table, afraid to risk exposing her shaking hands.

"Thank you for inviting me for coffee," he said. "I wasn't ready for the evening to end."

"You too?" she said, surprised to hear her own thoughts echoed. She twisted a little to face him. "Tonight was like magic." She closed her eyes to recall every delicious moment. "It was—"

His lips captured her unspoken words and transformed them into pure sensation, eliciting responses more powerful than words could allow. Her body reacted instinctively, as if to an awakened memory of internal urging. His tongue played along the seam of her mouth and she opened, giving him access. The tight spring of tension coiled beneath her ribcage loosened, sending warm rippling waves of desire along her nerve endings. A deep groan rose between them. She didn't know who initiated it, but the sweet vibrations from the sound resonated through her body like a tuning fork.

He tugged on her arm, loosening it from where it wrapped around his shoulders. Following his lead, she let her hand slide down his torso, exploring the ribs and muscles she had fantasized about while staring at his stiff oxford shirts. He led her hand to the hard bulge at his crotch, then released her.

Not sure what she was expected to do, she explored the area with her fingertips, pressing and stroking. She felt more than heard another groan, and knew this time it was coming from Hank. Cupping the area with her hand, she felt him pushing, straining against her.

He pulled his lips from hers. "Angel, you know I want you." He kissed her neck, just below her ear. "You can feel how much I want to bury myself deep within you." She pressed, just to see if she was interpreting his words correctly. His eyes squeezed shut and he swore under his breath. She thrilled with her newfound power.

"I think I've wanted you from that first time you attacked me in the woods." His lips pulled into a slight smile, "But we have to talk."

"No, we don't," she said. Her body cried for more of his caresses, for the friction of skin on skin. Instinctively she knew talking would move them in the opposite direction.

"But Angel." He dragged his fingertips down the side of her face, brushing stray hairs behind her ear. He kissed her neck. "I have to explain."

"No. I don't want to hear it." She pushed on his chest so he would pull back enough to see her face. "Hank, you've given me so many firsts these past weeks. Can't you give me one more?"

He looked drowsy, dazed, not at all like the controlled, self-possessed executive she knew him to be. She resisted the urge to kiss him again. He needed to understand what exactly she wanted, needed.

"You want me to make love to you?"

Yes! Yes! Yes! Every inch of her body responded. She nodded slowly.

"I'm not sure that's a good idea. There are things about me you don't understand."

"I understand that I want this." She struggled to keep the pleading tone out of her voice. "I may never have another opportunity."

"Angie, I'm sure there'll be—"

She covered his mouth with her hand, knowing what the rest of the sentence would be. She'd heard it too many times from her mother, from her brother, and from her doctors. But she knew better than them all that each moment was a gift, not to be thrown away. She wanted this moment of shared physical intimacy more than she had ever wanted anything before. "Please, do this for me."

He hesitated. She watched a battle play out in his eyes, then he pulled her fingers aside and kissed her softly, gently. A goodbye kiss, she thought, panicked. Already his hands had pulled back, away from where she longed for them to be. "It's not that I don't want to make love to you. Lord knows there's nothing I want more right now but—"

If her words hadn't convinced him, her actions would have to. She pressed her body full against him. She sucked hungrily at his lower lip, then with desperate bravado, she slipped her hand inside the waistband of his pants.

He drew back and studied her face. Did her eyes reflect hungry intent the way his did? If so, he had to know how much she wanted this.

"Okay, okay you win," he said. "But if we're going to do this, we're going to do this right." He scooped her up in his arms. "Just tell me where."

Although her mother had a bed large enough to accommodate them, making love in her bed would be sacrilegious. Her own room held too many childhood memories for comfort. Stephen's bedroom had been turned into a storage room not long after he moved out. "Here," she said after her quick analysis. "We can put that quilt on the floor." She pointed to the Tree of Life quilt her mother had pieced together when Angie had her transplant.

Holding her securely in his arms, Hank looked first at the quilt, then at the floor, then at her. "Where are your car keys?"

"In my purse in the hall closet. Why?" she asked. He carried her into the hallway. "Where are we going?"

"To my house."

"Why?" she asked, trying to peer around his determined jaw to his eyes.

"Beds."

Chapter Sixteen

He had only given her part of his reasoning. Hank slowed for a traffic light. Even though rug burn was a small price to pay for fulfilling a fantasy he'd carried inside since that day in the woods, the real reason for returning to his house was far more practical. He had only anticipated a stirring good-night kiss or two at the end of the evening, nothing that would require the kind of protection that he kept tucked away in a bedside table. Judging from Angie's inexperience, condoms were not the sort of thing she could produce on a moment's notice. At least this way he could love her the way she deserved to be loved. She'd be isolated enough that she could scream at the intense pleasure he intended to give her. Heck, they both could.

"What are you smiling at?" she asked from the passenger side of the car.

"Oh, I was just thinking...planning," he said.

"I was talking to the dog," she said, scratching the furry head that poked between the front seats. "Thanks for letting me bring her along. I hated to leave her alone tonight after having been gone earlier."

"As long as she stays out of our room," he reminded her. *Our room.* He liked the sound of that. It had a permanence that felt right.

"You'll be good, won't you, girl?" She rubbed under Oreo's furry chin.

Hank turned into the long driveway and parked Angie's car in front of the garage. "We'll go in the front," he said, realizing as the words left his mouth that he was stating the obvious. Anticipation must have him rattled. Still, he didn't want to spook Angie with the sight of Elizabeth's corvette. He had tried once again to explain that even though he didn't love Elizabeth, he still had a commitment to her until he could talk to her father. But Angie had stopped him again before he could begin.

She was determined to do this. He'd give her that. He smiled watching her direct her pet to the front of the house. Yes, he'd give her that and much more.

Angie lingered in the great room to give Oreo time to settle in. Meanwhile Hank hustled back to his bedroom to make sure everything was ready. He pulled some candles out of one of the drawers. He had searched the house for them one afternoon when the power went out, believing the outage would last into the night. It hadn't, but he kept the candles near just in case. Tonight they would serve a less utilitarian purpose. He placed them in front of the mirror to maximize the romantic glow. Slipping out of what remained of his troll costume, he tossed it, along with a couple of shirts and a pair of jeans into the closet. That left him in his T-shirt and a pair of plaid boxers. It would have to do. He looked around. *Music*, he thought. *Angie likes music.* What did he have that would set the mood? Too late. Her light step sounded in the hall outside his room.

The door between the office and hallway closed with a soft click. God, he was nervous. Hard and nervous, not unlike the time Elizabeth first initiated him in the secrets of intercourse.

Then Angie appeared. Cool, confident, determined, she had to be a little scared, this being her first time. But she didn't show it, not his Angel. Framed by the doorway leading into the office, she said, "I have one condition."

"What's that?" He aimed for nonchalance but suspected that he failed miserably. He walked towards her, enjoying her look of discovery when her glance drifted down to his crotch. He felt himself stretch further in response.

"No lights." She flicked the switch, but the candles cast shifting soft pools of illumination across her hair, her cheekbones, her lips. He wrapped his arms around her and thrilled at the way her arms reached around his shoulders in response. He lifted her in his arms, enjoying the weight of her.

"That's fine with me. You look beautiful by candlelight." He nibbled on her earlobe as he carried her to the bed. "I've wanted to see what you look like under those power suits for weeks on end." He kissed her lips lightly, placing her carefully on the pillows. "Tonight I get to see all of you."

"No." She pushed back on his shoulders, forcing space between them. "You can't see me. That's part of the deal."

"Why?" He pushed her hair back behind her ear. God, he loved the feel of her hair. Soft as silk, shiny as the moonlight, it flowed beneath his fingers like a woodland stream tumbling over sun-drenched stones.

"Tonight, I want to be beautiful," she said.

"But you are beautiful..." He slid his hands down her sides, feeling the lithe body beneath her clothes. Didn't she know? Hadn't she ever looked in a mirror? How could she miss the freshwater blue of her eyes, the infusion of pink that spread on her cheeks whenever someone paid her the slightest compliment, the sweet lushness of her lower lip that teased and beckoned. Even now—

"Trust me," she said. "You wouldn't say that if you saw my scar." The delicate wings of her eyebrows lifted in a plea, she worried her bottom lip for just a moment. "I need to have all the lights out, even the candles."

"But if we do that, you won't get to see me either," he teased, half in jest, half in earnest. He wanted to watch her, see pleasure shudder through her body, see if her sweet blush extended to all her other parts.

Her gaze moved slowly from his face to his shoulders, to his chest and lower. She appeared to logically consider his argument as if he had proposed a change in accounting methods. How could she be so calm and collected when he was fighting to maintain sanity? With a quick practiced jerk, he pulled off his T-shirt and dropped it to the side of the bed.

Her eyes widened briefly before her fingers followed her gaze to the crisp furring of chest hair. "I see what you mean," she said with a certain measure of awe.

His fully erect shaft strained against the loose fabric of his boxers. His fingers clenched into fists. Lord, what sweet torture. She was killing him.

"Can you promise me you'll keep your eyes closed?" she asked, her fingers exploring the breadth of his chest.

"I don't know if that's a promise I can keep," he said tightly. Her fingertips ventured lower, following the path directed by his chest hair. If they didn't reach some kind of agreement soon, he would explode.

"I've got an idea," he said, inspired. He dashed to the closet, rummaged on the top shelf, cursing under his breath at everything in his way. It had to be up here somewhere... There-- his hands wrapped around the suitcase he had used on a transcontinental flight to Italy to see Elizabeth. His fingers searched inside until they slipped over satiny cloth. "Found it." He kicked the fallen clothes back in the closet and turned, holding his prize, the black sleeping mask he had used to catch some shuteye. "Will this do?"

"I don't know. Try it on."

He pulled the mask over his eyes, then turned his head from side to side. He heard the mattress springs squeak. The scent of her perfume stirred nearby.

"Can you see me?" she asked, her voice coming directly in front of him.

In truth, he could see a little where the mask didn't lie flush on his cheeks, but with the dim flickering candlelight, he could see very little. "No."

"Then come with me." Her fingernails glided down his forearm. He jumped a little inside his skin, not realizing she was that close. His reaction must have pleased her judging by her soft chuckle. Her fingers slipped down to his hand and interlaced with his fingers. Pulling his arm, she guided him across the room.

"Stand here," she ordered. She was enjoying this! Then again, so was he. His cheeks tightened in a smile. This experience was proving to be a "first" for him as well.

"Now that you've brought it to my attention," she said. "I want to take a good, long look at you."

Her fingernails scraped against his belly before slipping beneath the elastic at his waistline. That about did him in. Without sight, he couldn't anticipate and without that ability to anticipate, every nerve ending leapt to attention, ready for anything—or almost anything. She stretched the band and eased the boxers down his legs, releasing his rock hard dick for her close inspection. His breath caught. He imagined her studying him as intently as she did numbers on a computer screen. A warm breath swirled around the tip of his shaft, and his toes curled. God, what sweet torture!

"Have you seen enough?" he asked tightly, imagining her innocent tongue moistening her lips just a hair's breadth away from his manhood. Something soft brushed the top of his thigh, testing a new kind of control for him. What was that? Her hair? His erection reached for what he couldn't see. He had never been this hard in his life.

"Touch me," he ground out beneath clenched lips. "Touch me so I know where you are."

"Here," she said, stroking the length of him with her fingertips. A low moan issued from his throat and she abruptly stopped. "Am I hurting you?"

"Not in the way you mean." He reached in the void for her hand and led it back. "Explore to your heart's content."

She slowly dragged her fingers over his testicles, up his shaft, tracing every bulging vein.

"I didn't know men were so velvety smooth, so soft," she said, rounding her fingers around his sensitive tip.

"Soft is not the word I'd use," he said with a gasp. He heard her light chuckle a moment before another hand touched the small of his back and traveled down, thoroughly exploring his buttocks.

"Hmmm. I see you have dimples here too."

He broke into a sweat and lost restraint. Now that he knew where she was centered, he reached out and wrapped his arms around her shoulders, pulling her fully clothed body tight against him.

His lips found her neck then licked and kissed the sensitive skin beneath her ear. Pleased to feel her tilt her head to give him greater access, he explored the inside of her ear with his tongue until he heard her gasp.

"It's my turn," he said. His hands found the edge of her T-shirt and lifted before she could complain. "You can't have all the fun."

"Why not?" she purred, but she allowed him to pull the fabric over her arms and head. Encouraged, he ran his hand down the delicate skin of her raised arm and further down her sensuous curved side until he found the waistline of her jeans. His fingertips followed just inside the rough denim, skimming over her taut belly till both of his hands met at the zipper.

Virgin flesh untouched by any other man. His fingers quivered and his knees almost buckled. By touch alone he manipulated the zipper, releasing the fabric and exposing the private side of Angela Blake. God, he wanted to see.

He held her shoulders to help her balance as she stepped out of the pants, all the while fantasizing about her undergarments. Did she wear those frilly temptress concoctions that Elizabeth preferred? Probably not. Not his Angel. The sight of her staid conservative cotton undies would tempt him more than any lace and satin garment of Elizabeth's. His fingers located the shoulder straps of her brassiere and with a finger underneath each he followed the straps down to her chest.

As much as his body urged him to rush, he refused. As insecure as Angie seemed about her body, standing before him exposed must be difficult. He forced himself to go slow and gain control. As long as she kept her hands on his forearms and not below his waist, he figured he had a chance.

He kissed her forehead, her cheekbones, her lips, letting the tip of his nose navigate the seductive angles of her face. His hands busied themselves massaging her breasts through her brassiere. When her hard, turgid nipples strained against the fabric, he unfastened the clasp and pulled the fabric free from her chest. He filled his hands with her flesh.

"Are you okay?" he whispered between kisses. At her nod, he bent to lave one breast with his tongue while massaging the other with his hand. He suckled until a shudder rippled through her body and a low moan teased his ear.

"Better show me to bed," he said.

She took his hand and led him to the mattress. *This is it,* she thought, *the big moment.* Could he tell how nervous she was? How inexperienced? She didn't even know if she should sit on the edge of the bed or lie down. She opted for the latter as he had placed her in that position before. He felt for her shoulders, then his knee nudged her legs apart. Within moments, he lay down on top of her.

So this is what a man feels like. A silent, inward breath passed her lips. The weight of him wasn't unpleasant or heavy, as she had imagined it would be. It felt...right, timeless. She tightened her arms around his back.

"Relax," he whispered in her ear. Easy for him to say. His erection pressed her inner thigh. She hadn't imagined how hard or how long that living length of flesh could be. She understood what was to happen tonight. She was twenty-six, after all. But understanding and experiencing were two different things. However, she still wore her panties, and he couldn't do anything with those on. She forced herself to relax.

Hank caressed and suckled her breasts. She arched her back, offering him more, and he took it greedily. Pleasure rippled through her in waves. She didn't know it could be like this. She tried to pull his head to her lips but he just smiled and pushed her arms down to the bed, holding them there. His kisses moved from her breasts to the scar that lay between.

"Hank," she said, trying to twist away, but he refused to budge. Her entire body lay exposed to his assault and he centered on her obvious imperfection. Humiliation chased away her earlier euphoria.

His tongue trailed the length of the scar, then flicked back and forth over the ridge of it. Pinned under him, she suffered embarrassment in silence. Words couldn't squeeze past the lump in her throat. Tears gathered at the corners of her eyes before streaming to the pillow. How could he do this to her? She had trusted him.

"I can feel your scar, Angel," he said. "It's not ugly at all." He trailed his tongue down it as if to prove his point. "It's magnificent, just like the rest of you." His voice expanded deep inside her. He kissed her stomach. "Sometimes you don't need your eyes to see."

Tears continued to flow, but not from embarrassment. He hadn't rejected her, but instead made her feel special. His lips moved down her body, kissing every conceivable part of her. In that moment, she would have told him how much his acceptance meant to her if he hadn't slipped his hand under the waistband of her panties. She practically jumped off the bed.

He shifted and eased the panties off before reclaiming his place between her legs. She braced herself, seconds before his fingers parted her pubic hair to expose the moist flesh lining beneath.

"Relax, Angel," he said, easing her legs wider apart. "I want you to enjoy this." She clenched her teeth, knowing that pain accompanied a woman's first time. But he assaulted her with his tongue, not his penis. My God, he was kissing her—down there! He was... Electrifying sensations ripped through her, each stronger than the preceding. She twisted, but he was relentless. Her fists clenched and pounded on the mattress, tremors shook her thighs, and strange noises issued from her throat. Still the sensations mounted until they exploded in waves of radiating contentment. Her body stilled, then went limp, but her heart pounded out a furious rhythm. She was safe; she was alive; she gasped for air.

"That was...incredible," she said in breathless bursts.

He kissed the inside of her leg. "I wanted you to feel the pleasure of loving, without the pain of the first time."

"You mean that wasn't?"

"No. Technically, you're still a virgin." His voice lowered to a more somber tone. "We can stop here if you like. You don't have to go through—"

"No. I want it all. I want to feel you inside me." She meant it too. No one else. Just Hank. Always Hank.

He nodded. "Believe me, that's where I want to be, but Angel?"

"Hmmmm?"

"I've got to take off this mask to put on a condom." He hurried to add, "I won't look at you, if you don't want me to. But I really need—"

"It's okay." Considering what he had just done, the places he had explored with such attention to detail, her earlier concerns seemed suddenly childish. She wasn't a child any longer.

He shoved the mask to the top of his head, opened a drawer in a bedside table and removed a foil square. It took only a few moments before he was back.

He repositioned himself, then looked up at her. "My God, you're beautiful." She felt a fresh tingling across her chest, then with one surge and an internal pinch, he was inside of her. He settled his weight across her torso and soothed the hair away from her face. "Are you okay? Was that too much? I thought the pain would be less if I was quick."

The concern in his voice, combined with the silly mask perched on the top of his head, made something swell deep inside. He had no concept of the pain she had endured in the past. That he should worry so much about that pinch, and a little accommodation... She smiled, remembering how large he had expanded—okay, a lot of accommodation. Still, his concern endeared him further in her heart.

"I'm fine," she replied. "More than fine."

He moved inside her. Long strokes, powerful strokes. He established a rhythm and her body rose to meet his thrusts in a similar tempo. She tried to see his face, but couldn't see past his chin. He continued to drive into her with determination and need until at the height of one thrust, he stopped, held tense, then relaxed on top of her. She relaxed with him, dismissing her sore muscles in favor of enjoying the comfort of his weight, and that he joined her like a key in a lock. She squeezed her muscles tight around him. He groaned.

"You can feel that?" she said, amazed.

"Oh baby, you have no idea."

That felt good. She was raw and sore and trapped under a man three times her size, but she wasn't without control. Smiling, she listened to the reassuring sound of his heartbeat. This was good, a miracle in itself. A silent prayer of gratitude winged upward.

He slowly pulled out of her and she instantly missed the close contact. "I'll be right back," he said, padding off for the adjoining bathroom.

The squeak of a stubborn faucet and the rush of running water issued from the bathroom. She smiled at the flickering candlelight dancing on the ceiling. She felt complete and mystically transformed. For the first time that she could remember, she felt normal. Normal and experienced, she modified. She didn't think she could look at life and men, especially Hank, the same way again.

"Here, try this." He sat on the side of the bed, the mask comically propped on his head, and pressed a warm, damp cloth between her legs. "It might make you feel better." Her hand replaced his. He stroked the inside of her arm.

"Any regrets?" he asked with poorly concealed concern.

"Yes." She smiled. "I regret I couldn't see your face when you were inside me."

Relief washed over his face. A small smile pulled at his cheek. "There are other positions, you know, where that is entirely possible." He brushed his hand through his hair and tangled it in the black satin.

They both laughed, he at the discovery and she at his expression.

"I'm sorry I made you wear that," she said, stroking his naked thigh. Her fear that he'd reject her seemed so irrational now, in light of what they had shared.

"I'm not," he said. "It provided a heightened experience, although I doubt I can ever wear it again without thinking of this night." *And you.* He didn't say the words but his smile conveyed the sentiment. A warm, liquid contentment expanded within her chest. She wanted to hold on to the moment, but her body had other ideas. Her mouth contorted in a gaping yawn.

"I know it's been a long night. Why don't you get some rest?" He reached for the damp cloth. "Let me take that."

"You're coming back?" she asked, hoping he couldn't hear the alarm in her voice. He couldn't leave her in this bed alone, not tonight.

"Of course. Just let me take care of this."

"Okay then," she said, or she thought she said, she wasn't sure which. She thought she'd just rest her eyes for a moment till he returned. Just for a moment...

He tossed the washcloth in the sink, trying to avoid looking at the bloodstains. My God, what had he done? He couldn't even raise his eyes to the mirror. She was so trusting, so full of passion, so... His gaze fell to the sleep mask clenched tight in his hand. So magnificent. She deserved someone better than him, that's for sure. Someone who didn't make commitments to people they didn't love. He turned out the lights, stepped back into the bedroom and glanced at the petite form huddled in his bed. He smiled, warmed by the sight. A petite form with the heart of a giant sleeping away in his bed.

He blew out the candles that had burned down to glowing pools of wax, then slipped into the bed beside her.

Almost immediately she turned toward him and snuggled closer. His arm instinctively wrapped around her shoulders. He kissed her forehead and drifted off to sleep.

CRSO

Early the next morning, Oreo's loud sniffs at the crack of the door woke her from a fabulous dream. Not for the first time, she wished her mother had reconsidered her decision not to put in a pet door. Of course her mother wasn't the one getting up first thing in the morning to let the dog out.

"I'm coming," she muttered against the pillow and tried to rise from the bed. She couldn't move. Something held her at her waist and…pressed against her back. She forced her eyes open and saw a man's arm. Memories of the previous night came streaming back. She relaxed. So this is how it felt to wake up next to a man. Nice, very nice. A warm, lazy sluggishness swept her from shoulder to toe. She snuggled backwards to press her back against Hank's chest. His arm tightened around her and his warm breath stirred the tiny hairs on the back of her neck.

Spooning, she thought. *That's what they call this.* Lying like two spoons nestled in a drawer. Oreo whimpered outside the door. Knowing the whimper would soon turn to a bark, Angie reluctantly lifted Hank's arm so she could slip off the side of the bed.

She found a white terry cloth robe several sizes too big hanging on the back of the bathroom door. Repositioning the belt so that it tied at her waist instead of low on her hips, she crossed the room and slipped out the door.

Oreo's tail began a steady sway the minute Angie opened the door. She headed through the great room to the sliding glass doors with Oreo on her heels. Together they went outside into the chill morning.

Angie hopped from one foot to the other, wishing she had thought to search for slippers, while Oreo dashed past the covered pool and onto the frost-covered lawn beyond.

"Hurry, hurry, hurry," she said, crossing her arms to hold the heat in. Steam puffed with each exhale. Oreo explored the expansive lawn oblivious to the cold. Angie's gaze alternated between the dog's movements and the new day spreading in glorious pink and gold across the eastern sky.

A flash of light burst from the western side of the wide, deep lawn. At least she thought she saw a flash. Tugging the robe tighter around her, she searched the base of a line of pine trees for movement. Other than the few birds that had decided to forego migration, everything was still and peaceful. An uneasiness settled over her. Something didn't *feel* right, although she'd be hard-pressed to explain what. Oreo trotted to her side, apparently finished with her morning constitutional.

"Good girl," she said, patting the dog's head. "Let's go inside." Oreo headed immediately for the door. After one last glance to the row of pines, Angie followed.

"Hope you're hungry." Hank called from the kitchen when she stepped through the sliding glass door. He stood at the kitchen counter, a chef's apron tied over his naked chest. "The pan is heating up. Give me a couple of minutes and we'll have some bacon and eggs."

"I'm sorry. I didn't mean to wake you," she said, closing the door behind her. She thought to grab the lapels of the robe to cover her scar, but then resisted. After last night she supposed she had little to hide. The realization was empowering. She let the lapels fall back into place and crossed the room toward the kitchen.

"Something smells awfully good," she said, taking a deep drink of freshly brewed coffee. Hank laid a couple of slices of bacon in the pan. "Sounds good, too."

If the sight of her scar in the light of day repulsed him, Hank didn't show it. She relaxed further.

"I thought you'd like some breakfast." He cracked a couple of eggs and dropped them in the pan, then pointed a long turning fork toward the bar stools at the counter. "Have a seat."

"Let me get Oreo some—"

He intercepted her the moment she stepped into the kitchen. Closing his arms around her, he pulled her against his chest. "Good morning," he said. His distinctive male scent wrapped around her as securely as his arms.

The kiss chased the chill from her bones and warmed her like bread popping from the toaster. He tasted of toothpaste and mouthwash, reminding her that she hadn't performed that little bit of hygiene, but it didn't seem to matter to him. She lifted her hands to either side of his face with full intent to slide them down to his shoulders, but the rasp of his morning stubble intrigued her fingertips and they stayed. She welcomed and encouraged the deepening of the kiss with knowledge born from last night's passion. He growled deep in his throat, delighting her.

"Angel," he murmured under his breath. He rubbed his scratchy cheek against hers for a moment. He pulled back. "How are you feeling this morning?"

At this very moment, she felt fabulous, womanly, and very, very normal. "Great," she said. "Why?"

"After last night, I wasn't sure if you had..." He focused his gaze somewhere below her face.

"Regrets?" she said, guessing at the word that seemed stuck in his throat.

His gaze lifted to hers, but they both smelled smoke from the burning bacon at the same time.

"Shit!" He turned toward the stovetop. Bare buttocks flashed at her beneath the tie of the apron.

"You're naked!"

"Not exactly." He moved the smoking pan to a cool burner, flipped on the exhaust fan full blast before turning off the stove. "After all, I was frying bacon and you've got my robe. I had to wear something."

They laughed and sat on stools to drink coffee and eat toast.

"You looked worried when you let the dog in. I was afraid you had misgivings about last night," Hank said, nursing a mug of coffee.

"No. Last night was wonderful. I have no regrets." She squeezed his hand for emphasis. How could she regret loving this talented, wonderful man? "I just thought I saw something outside a few minutes ago. A movement, a flash, something and it surprised me."

"Probably a deer," he said, obviously relieved at her answer. He squeezed her hand back, then removed their plates to the sink. "There's a lot of them out here. You should see them at dusk. Then they really come out."

It wasn't a deer, Angie knew that much, but she wasn't exactly sure what she saw. "It's probably nothing," she said, ignoring the shiver that vibrated her spine. "Probably just my imagination." She took one last sip from her cup, then slipped off the stool. "I better get dressed or I'll be late for church."

"Church? You go to church?"

You would have thought by his dropped jaw that she had said she was going to Venus. She smiled, "Of course, silly, it's Sunday. I'd invite you to go with me, but people can't see --"

"Us together," he finished her sentence with a nod. "I guess I don't know many single people our age who go to church voluntarily."

"I suppose that's because you don't know many people on the receiving end of a miracle." She gave him a quick kiss on the cheek, remembering that he had treated her to some pretty miraculous experiences himself last night. "Besides it's time I get back. My mother will be coming home soon and I need to clean the place up a bit."

After she had changed and had rounded up Oreo, Hank walked her to the door. "Call me later?"

"Definitely" he said.

This time she initiated the kiss. Another first.

She flipped the car radio to her favorite station and sang along with all the love songs. A beautiful morning was following a magical night. The slight aching between her legs proved that it all hadn't been a dream. She wouldn't suddenly wake up wanting what she knew she'd never experience. At the first stoplight, she lowered the passenger window so Oreo could stick her head out and smell the wind. The chill breeze felt pleasantly refreshing and verified that she was awake, alive and happier than she could ever remember being. The morning was perfect until she noticed the swirling red and blue police lights in her driveway.

Chapter Seventeen

"What's going on?" Angie murmured, pulling in front of the house. She left Oreo barking in the car, the window cracked enough to release the captured sound.

"Ms. Blake?" A uniformed officer greeted her.

"Yes, that's me."

"We received a report last night that someone smashed your front window." Angie looked at the large window facing the quiet residential street. A dark jagged hole, like some gaping wound, stared back. "We found a brick inside, but your brother says nothing else appears to be missing."

"My brother?"

"Yes. Apparently your neighbor called him this morning when we couldn't locate you. He's in the house now, but since you're back we'd like—"

Angie headed for the house before the officer could finish.

"Stephen?" she called from the front door. Her insides shook like a dying leaf clinging to a wind-tossed branch. "Stephen, where are you?"

"Here. Angie, I'm here." She heard his footsteps pounding on the upstairs hallway. "Thank God. I was so worried." He reached the ground floor and pulled her into a bear hug. "Are you all right?"

"Yes," she reassured him. "What happened?"

"The breaking glass woke Walter. He came over here to see if you were all right, but you weren't home." Stephen pulled back to look at her face. "Where were you last night?"

"Do the police think it was a burglary?" she asked, already suspecting the answer was no.

"Nothing seems to be missing, at least not that I can tell. But you didn't answer—"

"Are you the young lady who lives here?" Another uniformed officer entered the hallway from the kitchen.

"Yes, that's me." She separated from Stephen.

"We've checked the house and property outside. If anyone was here, they've gone now. Is there someone who might have some sort of grudge against you that might pull this kind of prank?"

"No. No one that I know of," she answered truthfully.

"Fired anyone at work? A jealous boyfriend or girlfriend? Anyone like that?"

"No," she assured them. "No one."

"I understand you filed a complaint a week or so ago about a prowler?"

"What?" Stephen exploded. "Why didn't you call me?"

"Calm down, Stephen. I didn't think it was serious. If there was a prowler, he didn't do anything. It was probably some kid celebrating Halloween a little early." She knew it sounded lame but she didn't want Stephen involving himself in her life anymore than he normally did.

"Well, we'd like you to take a look around to verify that nothing's missing all the same," the officer said. "Do you live here alone?"

"At the moment, it's just my dog and me," Angie said, scanning the sitting room. Other than shards of glass scattered among the furniture and rug, everything appeared in order.

"Dog?"

"She's in my car." Angie moved on to the dining room.

"She wasn't here last night either?"

"No, Officer. She was with me. Neither one of us was here last night." She glared at Stephen. "Which was probably a good thing given the circumstances." She moved on to the kitchen.

"Well, miss. You might want to board up that window until it can be fixed. Your home insurance will probably cover the cost of replacing it..."

"I brought some wood to do just that," Stephen said.

"I don't think there's anything else we can do here," the officer said. "Here's my card." He handed her an official-looking business card. "If you think of anyone who might be responsible for this, or if you discover something is missing, call the number on the card. Otherwise we'll keep an eye on the house during our patrols."

I've heard that one before, Angie thought, but she nodded consent. The officer left to join his partner outside. Angie watched the patrol car back down the driveway before disappearing down the street. She retrieved Oreo from her tiny Civic.

"Angie, is everything okay?" Walter crossed his front lawn to intercept them. "I hope you don't mind that I called Stephen. I didn't know what else to do. You weren't home and I thought someone should..."

"It's all right, Walter." She patted his arm in reassurance. "You did the right thing." The sound of a hammer pounding wood made them both glance back toward the house. Stephen had set to work boarding up the window. "But how did you know that I wasn't home?"

"I heard the glass shatter and looked out the window. When I didn't see anyone out on the street, I came out here. There wasn't a single light on in the house and I didn't even hear Oreo bark once. So I knew you weren't home."

Or we were both dead on the carpet, she thought with a grimace. No sense spooking Walter. "You did the right thing," she repeated.

"Why would someone throw a brick through your window?" Walter asked.

"Why would someone try to poison my dog?" She sighed. "I haven't a clue and it's beginning to spook me."

"If there's anything I can do to help, I'm right here next door," Walter said, his eyeglasses reflecting the mid-morning sun.

"Thanks, Walter, you've already been a big help." She turned and led Oreo up to the house, bracing herself for a confrontation with Stephen. He was finishing when she entered. She retrieved the broom and dustpan from the kitchen before entering the darkened sitting room.

"Pack up your clothes," Stephen said the moment she stepped in the room. "I'm taking you home with me."

"No." She began sweeping the broken glass shards into a tidy pile. "I'm staying here."

"Are you crazy? Someone tried to break in here. You could have been killed!"

She stopped sweeping only long enough to make her point. "They threw a brick through the window, Stephen. That's hardly attempted murder."

"How close to attempted murder do they have to get?" He hesitated then collected his tools. "Pack your bags."

"No." She planted the broom and stood her ground. "We don't even know if that brick was targeted for this house. Maybe they thought someone else lived here." She stooped to brush the pile of glass into the plastic dustpan. "I'm not running from this house because of some stupid prank."

"And if it's not a prank?" He watched her for a moment, then took the dustpan from her hand. "Give me that. You could cut yourself with that broken glass." She stood and put her hands on her hips. "I don't like the idea of you staying here alone," he lectured. "It would be different if Mom were home. What if something should happen?"

"Walter's next door. If I need help, I'll call him."

Stephen snorted, a guttural opinion of Walter's attributes. "What if I ask Raymond to stay here with you? There's room and—"

"No." Angie interrupted. She could feel her own face blanching at the thought. How typical of Stephen to think that he was such a superior judge of character that he would suggest a man, who was little more than a stranger, stay with her.

"Why not?"

"He gives me the creeps." She tried unsuccessfully to suppress the goosebumps rising on her arms.

"He's not so bad... You just have to get to know him better." Stephen took the bits of glass back to the kitchen.

"I'd prefer not to." Angie said an instant before bits of glass clattered into the trash bin. Stephen came back into the room.

"Tell you what, I'll let you stay if..." Angie's skin bristled at the word "let" as if he had that kind of control over her. "Mom agrees to come home before next weekend. And," he held up his hand as if expecting an argument, "I can have Raymond stop by periodically to check up on you."

"Fine," she said. Anything to get Stephen out of her hair. She had her baseball bat. She had her dog. She could put up with some minor intrusions by that creepazoid if it would make Stephen happy. Besides, she knew her mother was flying home this week anyway. The plane ticket was a gift from Aunt Ceal. It would be her mother's first airplane flight. *Hah*, she thought with a smile, *another first.*

∞§∞

Monday morning dawned in a glorious array of deep velvety pinks across a deepening blue sky. Angie glanced in her rear view mirror on her way to work. "Red sky at morning, sailors take warning," she recited, recalling the childhood rhyme. Hopefully, the scenic panorama was only a prediction of weather.

Last night, after she had put the earlier vandalism behind her and convinced herself it was a random act, she thought long and hard about her relationship with Hank and its effect on her work. She had reached a painful decision. She'd have to tell Falstaff that she was no longer independent with regard to Hayden Industries, without explaining the details, of course. No one had to know about that. Her pulse quickened with the memory, and her body tingled wanting more. "Stop that," she ordered herself, knowing that this desire was not something that could be silenced with a verbal command. Pulling to a stop at an intersection, she glanced in the rear view mirror. Did she look different? Would everyone know that she was now experienced?

The light turned and she moved forward with the traffic. Would she be able to look at Hank in the office, or say his name without melting into a languid pool of passion on the spot? For that matter, could he look at her and still maintain that aloof executive exterior? And Elizabeth, how would she take the news that Hank had chosen a lowly accountant over a glamorous fashion model? Not that Hank had promised anything. Still his eyes told her more than words could. He loved her as much as she loved him; he just hadn't realized it.

Love... She almost rear-ended the car in front of her. Her first real relationship and already she was calling it love! For one pregnant moment she could feel the life-defining thump of her heart pushing life-giving blood through her body. Her failing heart had taught her what it was like to miss out on a childhood. Hank had given that back to her, plus a taste of what it meant to join with a man. If only for those things, she would love Hank.

Max could finish the audit and perform the additional procedures. The firm would still get the additional billings and hopefully, she would still get the promotion. Surely Hank would understand that she couldn't do the work as he stipulated it. Of course, it would have helped matters if he had called last night. She had wanted to discuss her decision with him. She'd tried calling his house, but there was no answer.

She pulled into a parking spot and shut off the engine. Yes, requesting removal from the Hayden engagement was the right decision, to do otherwise would be unethical. She could give up the promotion, but she couldn't give up Hank.

"Best to get this over with," she told her image in the rearview mirror. She exited the car, shifted her shoulders back, lifted her chin, then marched into the building and up to the office. After exchanging "good mornings" with the receptionist, she headed straight for Falstaff's office.

"Angie, good morning. Don't you look nice today," Teresa, Falstaff's secretary, greeted her from behind her desk. She dropped the newspaper she had been reading and peered closer at Angie over the gold-rimmed bifocals balanced on the tip of her nose. "You have a glow about you today, what's different? New make-up?"

In a Heartbeat

Already Angie could feel heat creeping up her cheeks. Undaunted, she smiled. "Must just be the light." She nodded toward the office. "Is he in? I have something I want to run past him."

"No, he called earlier this morning. Said he had to run out for some big powwow. I don't imagine he'll be in till this afternoon. Would you like me to give him a message?"

"No." Angie shook her head. "It can keep till tomorrow." She turned to head back to her cubicle in the staff room.

"Angie, wait," Teresa called. "Have you seen this?"

Angie turned, the quick move causing a twinge in her ankle. Teresa ruffled the newspaper at her. "This should probably go into Hayden's permanent file. Why don't you take it with you."

Angie stepped closer to the desk. "What is it?" She bent over the paper and saw Hank's picture.

"That new CEO... What's his name?" Teresa frowned for a minute. "You know, the good-looking one..."

"Renard", Angie answered, quickly scanning the headline. *Hayden announces executive engagement.*

"That's the one. He's going to marry that model, Elizabeth Everett. They've announced their engagement." Teresa chortled. "The handsome ones never last long, do they?"

Angie felt the blood drain from her face. She leaned against the desk for support. "Engaged?"

"Hmmm." Teresa adjusted her glasses and looked up at Angie. "Are you feeling all right? You look like you're going to faint."

Angie struggled a moment for breath. "I'm okay. I think I just turned too fast on my ankle," she lied. Picking up the paper, she folded it and shoved it under her arm so Teresa wouldn't notice her hands shaking. Then with an exaggerated limp to disguise her true injury, she hobbled back to her cubicle.

CBSO80

It took a full box of tissues to repair the damage from her crying jag in the women's restroom. Afterwards, she tried to call Hank at work. He was out of town, she was told. Some emergency, Cathy said.

"Emergency my foot," Angie murmured after hanging up the phone. He must have hot-tailed it to New York so he could propose to Elizabeth.

Granted, he had never made promises to her. He had tried to tell her something on several occasions, but she had stopped him. Was this what he was trying to say? After all she knew he was dating Elizabeth and she, not Hank, initiated the idea of intimacy. Begged. She'd practically begged him to bed her. The burning in the corners of her eyes started anew.

She hadn't expected this emotional attachment. All the magazines implied that intercourse was little more than shared aerobics. But Hank knew. He was experienced at this sort of thing. Was it his plan all along to destroy her heart, her soul? Was it pity? Show the little cripple a good time then dump her? A tear dropped from her cheek onto the betraying face in the newspaper. H.P. Renard, the caption said. Named after a calculator, she reminded herself. One of these days she'd learn to trust her instincts and not her heart. She wiped the wetness from her cheeks. Cold-hearted bastard.

"Angie," Teresa called from the door to the staff room. "Mr. Falstaff would like to see you now."

"Oh, that's okay." Angie struggled to find her voice. She turned the newspaper over so she couldn't see Hank's newsprint smile. "I worked the problem out, I don't need to talk to him anymore."

"No, Angie. Mr. Falstaff would like to see you now." The emphasis on the "you" made it clear to everyone in the staff room that Angie was not calling this meeting. Max shot a concerned glance towards Angie.

"Probably wants a progress report," she said, picking up the manila folders she had just dropped on her desk. Tucking them under her arm, she followed Teresa down the hall to the corner office.

Angie attempted what she thought was a chipper smile before entering the paneled vestibule. "Good morning, Mr. Falstaff. You wanted to see me?"

"Sit down, Angela, we have some serious business to discuss." His ominous tone overpowered her attempts at being perky.

"If it's about Tempco, I've brought the audit papers." She placed the manila folders on his circular conference table, then selected one of the surrounding chairs.

Falstaff rose from behind his massive desk and walked over to the table. "I want to talk to you about your relationship with Hayden Industries."

Her heart stalled. Did he know something he shouldn't? Or was he preparing to push her for more billings. "Yes, sir, what would you like to know?" She shifted uncomfortably in the chair.

Falstaff dismissed her question with a wave of his hand. He lowered himself into one of the chairs. "Did you have a good time at the ball Saturday night?"

"Well...yes ..." she stammered.

"That wasn't your brother you were with, was it?" His penetrating stare made it all the more difficult to continue the lie. Dishonesty was never her strong suit anyway.

"Mr. Falstaff, I don't ..."

"I had a phone call this morning. Never mind from who," he held up his hand to silence her unspoken questions. "The caller said you've been having an illicit relationship with Henry Renard. Is that true?"

The heat scorching her cheeks probably answered his question. Words refused to surface.

"I might not have believed the caller if he hadn't sent me this." He removed a large glossy photograph that showed Angela in Hank's robe. The lapels opened enough to expose a zipper-like scar down the middle of her chest. "I've been a guest at the Owens's house a time or two. I recognize that setting."

"Let me explain..." Angie said, although she wasn't sure how she could explain away the damning photo. Her heart raced. That flash... That must have been... "Who sent this?"

"Not important." He refused to look at her face. "It's not up to me to preach morals to my employees. I was young once. I know something about romance. I suspected your date Saturday night wasn't your brother. The way you two looked on the dance floor..." He pushed his glasses to the top of his head and covered his eyes for a moment with his hands. "But a client, Angela?" He peered at her from over the tips of his fingers. "I expected more from you than that."

Angie swiped the moisture collecting on her cheeks. "Please, Mr. Falstaff, I know it doesn't look good, but..."

"Why didn't you come to me when this thing first started?" he admonished. He stood up and began pacing the length of the office. "I could have reassigned you. I thought you had a solid future here, Angela. I hate to lose you."

"Lose me?" she sniffed, watching as he turned his back toward her.

"You know the rules. You've compromised this office, the audit and our reputation. You've left me no choice as to disciplinary action." He turned back to face her. "We are letting you go, Angela."

"You're firing me?"

He nodded. "Max can finish up the year-end work on Hayden. You're to gather up your personal belongings and vacate the premises immediately."

"I'm fired?" she repeated, shock holding her captive to the chair.

"I'm sorry, Angie, I truly am. I know I'm not your father, but if I can offer a piece of advice. I don't know what you and Renard had going together, but the caller implied you had spent the night with Renard fairly early on. I didn't believe it at first, but clearly this was not idle gossip. Given the notice in the paper this morning, I'd urge you to be more selective in your conquests next time. Maintain some standards, for Heaven's sake."

She stood, leaving the papers untouched on the table, then exited the office in a zombie-like state. Outside Falstaff's office, Teresa quickly lowered her voice and whispered into a phone receiver. Angela slowly walked down the hall to her cubicle.

She scanned the narrow shelves and picked up a framed photograph of Oreo with a Frisbee and a box containing an extra supply of her prescriptions.

"Angie, what's going on? Where are you going?" Max's head appeared over the side of her cubicle. He glanced at her face. "My God, what's happened?"

She held up her hand. "Not now, Max. I can't talk now." She slipped her personal items in her purse and turned to leave.

"Can I call you later at home?"

She didn't reply. She just walked to the exit of Falstaff and Watterson and let the door to that chapter of her life close behind her.

Chapter Eighteen

"Open up, Angie, I know you're in there." Hank pounded on Angie's front door till the hinges rattled. The contents of the paper bag he clenched in one hand shifted with the motion, splattering chicken soup. Oreo's incessant barking from the other side of the door added to the chaos.

"I swear I'll break this door down if you don't open it," he threatened. How could anyone tolerate this racket? If her car wasn't parked in the driveway, he'd have thought she wasn't home. He began pounding again.

The strange little man from next door stepped out on his porch. "Is something wrong?" he called.

"Everything would be fine if she'd just open the damn door," Hank answered, his voice rising to a near shout. Oreo's barking turned to a frustrated whimper. He could hear her sniffing and snorting at the bottom of the door.

"Maybe she doesn't want to talk to you," the neighbor said with stiff bravado. "Maybe you should leave."

That was right. He'd forgotten that Angie had befriended the little zombie. It shouldn't be a surprise. She had that effect on people. She'd had that effect on him. He looked back at what's-his-name, the neighbor, and softened his tone. "I heard she might not be feeling well."

Holding the stained paper sack aloft, he remembered Angie's vigilance regarding her medically suppressed immune system. The thought renewed his anguish. "She could be seriously ill," he yelled at the neighbor. "She could need help."

"Should I call her brother?" The neighbor suddenly became a collaborator. "I have his number."

Angie's dead bolt clicked a moment before the door opened the length of the safety chain. "I'm fine. I don't want to talk to you. Go away."

Oreo stuck her long white snout out through the crack. Before Angie could retract the dog, Hank had his foot in the door. He winced as Angie tried repeatedly to slam the door closed. As petite as she was, she could still pack a wallop.

"Angie, please-- I've got to talk to you."

"Go away."

"Let me explain." He worked his fingers around the edge of the door.

"Explain it to Elizabeth."

"It's a mistake," he pleaded, grimacing as his knuckles shared the same torture as his instep. The pressure eased on both extremities. "I never proposed to Elizabeth."

"You're not engaged?" Although nasal in tone, her question held so much longing it made his throat ache. He pressed his cheek against the door, imagining she pressed hers on the other side.

"Please, Angel. We need to talk, but not like this." He pitched his words soft and low like a prayer, which indeed it was. "Please let me in." He slid his fingers up and down the edge of the door, blindly hoping for a touch of her hand. "Please?"

"All right, step back a minute."

He hesitated, suspecting that once he withdrew his foot and hand, the door would slam shut, forcing him to start all over again. But if he was going to beg for her trust in him, he needed to begin with some trust in her. He slipped his hand and foot from the door. It closed and in answer to his silent prayer, the safety chain slid back. The door reopened. Oreo ran out, jumping in a fervent display of affection.

"Come in," she said, still hidden behind the door. Her invitation sounded more like resignation. Hank petted the dog briefly. Oreo's tail repeatedly bashed his leg. At least someone was glad to see him.

Once inside, Angie pushed the door closed with her back. Her fuzzy pink robe clashed with her red nose, the only spot of color in a pale, drained face. She pushed unwashed hair over her shoulder, then crossed her arms defiantly in front of her chest. She looked like Hell and Heaven all rolled into one.

"Max said you weren't feeling well so I brought you some chicken soup." He held up the crinkled paper bag, the bottom threatening to break loose in moisture-weakened spots. "I think I spilled some."

She sighed; her whole body shook with the effort. "You talked to Max?"

He nodded. "I was in New York when I started receiving calls congratulating me on my engagement. That's when I learned of the newspaper article. I called Falstaff and Watterson and asked for you. When they told me you weren't available, I asked for Max."

"Not available," she repeated. A chortle-like laugh caught in her throat and started a coughing spasm. He stepped closer to help her, but she held up her arm to keep him at bay.

"Come sit down, Angie. You look like you can barely stand."

Her head jerked up. "I'm fine. I don't need your help."

"Then sit down for my sake," he grumbled, tired of playing by Miss Independent's rules. He crossed into the sitting room, depositing the tenuous bag of soup on a magazine near the couch. "If you faint on me, I'd have to catch you, and you certainly wouldn't want that." *Aah, but I would*, he thought, remembering how she had felt in his arms.

"No, I certainly wouldn't." She tugged her robe more tightly around her and stomped to the couch. Hank hid his smile and called Oreo over for a scratch between the ears. That way the dog couldn't inadvertently trip her up.

"You're walking better," he observed.

She shrugged. "My leg's gotten a lot of rest this week." She flopped on the couch. "Satisfied?"

"Almost." He picked up a quilt from the floor and shook it, sending myriad dog hairs adrift. "Put your feet up."

Somewhat begrudgingly, she leaned on one elbow and pulled her legs up to the couch. He laid the quilt over her, then tucked it tight around the curves of her body.

She batted his hands away. "What are you doing?"

If he had any thoughts of exploring those luscious curves under the pretense of tucking in the quilt, the accusation in her eyes stopped him cold. "You're sick," he said, feeling a bit like a scolding father. "You need to stay warm."

"I'm not sick," she grumbled.

"But your eyes are puffy. I heard you sniffling. Max said... Don't you have a cold?"

She dismissed his concerns with a wave of her hand. "If you talked to Max, then you know why I wasn't available when you called."

He nodded. "Max and I had quite a long conversation. He said you were let go."

"Let go," she repeated, dejection echoing in her voice. "As if I wanted to leave." Tears welled in her vulnerable blue eyes, tugging at his heart. "They fired me, Hank."

He rested his hip on the thin edge of couch near her feet. He felt totally useless. Her small body shook under her sobs, and not for the first time, he suspected. He reached over and plucked a tissue from the well-used box on the coffee table and offered it to her, all the while stroking her hip through the quilt. "I'm sorry, Angel, so sorry," he repeated over and over, as if the mantra would alleviate some of his guilt. Even Oreo padded over to offer sympathy, negotiating her nose between Angie's arms.

"I should never have made you go to that ball," he said. "I never dreamed they would fire you for going to a dance with me."

"You didn't make me." She swabbed at her eyes, then blew her nose, a sound worthy of a moose. "I could have said no."

"You did, several times," he reminded her, "but I persisted. Something about no one would recognize us, I believe." He shifted his weight and dropped his elbows to his knees. "Damn, I was so careful not to let anyone know it was me under that mask."

"I've thought about that." *A lot.* She didn't say it, but Hank heard the added sentiment loud and clear. "I think Falstaff knew you weren't my brother, but he didn't know I was dancing with Hank Renard." She patted his knee, and he covered her small hand with his own much larger one.

"Then how did he...?"

"Someone sent him a photograph. Remember when I saw movement in the woods Sunday morning? Guess it wasn't a deer after all." She managed a sarcastic sneer. "Whoever it was said we'd been intimate for some time."

"A photograph?" He pulled back, shocked. "But who knew that we were together that night?" He mentally reviewed a list of anyone that met that criteria. It was a very short list, a limousine chauffeur and a taxi driver.

"I don't know," she said, crinkling her brow. "And I'm tired of guessing who slashed my tires, who tried to poison my dog, who smashed my window, who—"

"Wait a minute." He noticed the wood covering the window for the first time. He hadn't focused on anything but Angie and had assumed the lamps were lit to offset the gloom of the overcast day. "When did this happen?"

Angie recited her recent litany of troubles. "Walter said something that's had me wondering if the brick and the photograph weren't somehow related."

Walter, Hank nodded, that was the twerp's name. "What's that?"

"He said after he heard the window break, he ran outside. He knew I wasn't home because no lights came on and Oreo didn't bark."

"You think someone was trying to find out if you were home? They could have just rung the doorbell, or telephoned."

"Yes, but that's not vindictive enough. Maybe when they didn't see any lights, they went to your house."

"But how did they know you'd be there?" He was baffled. "They must have camped out by my house all night just to catch you. Seems like a lot of work, just to make you lose your job."

Angie's eyes narrowed to puffy slits. "You know, I never had problems like this until I met you. Do you think everything is somehow related? Do you know who's behind all this?"

"No. But I'll sure as hell find out." He patted Angie's small cool hand. He would weed out the culprit and the sonofabitch would pay. He glanced at her red-rimmed eyes and guilt twisted in his gut. Oh yes, they would pay...and pay.

"Did Max say he knew why I'd been fired?" she asked.

"You don't think Max..."

"No, but he's pretty observant. If he had a suspicion about us, maybe someone else thought along the same lines."

Hank straightened from his hunched position. Angie scooted back on the couch, affording him more room. She continued her therapeutic petting of Oreo's head.

"He said he was just as surprised as everyone when he heard the news, and at first, didn't know the reason. But afterwards there were memos and training sessions about client-auditor independence. He put two and two together. Something about restless nights."

"Like I said, he's very observant," Angie muttered.

"He also said," Hank glanced at her with what he hoped was a stern expression. "That you and he had a late night expedition a few nights back." He patted her on the rump. "Want to tell me what that was about?"

"Sounds to me that Max was awfully talkative." She pulled her lips into a tight line.

"Not at first," Hank acknowledged. "He suggested I call you here, and you know how successful that was." He glanced her way and she smiled weakly. No wonder she was immune to his banging on the door, she'd already had plenty of practice not answering his calls.

"I just couldn't..." she said, and he patted her hip again before continuing.

"I called Max again and was rather insistent on details." That was an understatement. Hank smiled remembering the threats and promises it eventually took to get Max's cooperation. "I don't think he would have told me anything if he thought I approved of what Falstaff did."

"What did you promise Max?" She sneered. "Tickets to another football game?"

"No, I promised him I'd give you a job."

"What?" She practically kicked him off the couch. "What are you talking about?"

"Think about it, Angie. It makes perfect sense." He stood and moved to a chair where his rump wasn't in danger of being further abused. "I can't force Falstaff to rehire you." He didn't tell her that he had tried, and got nowhere. Falstaff brought up that bloody independence issue again, saying that clients could not dictate those kinds of terms to auditors. He glanced over to Angie and she nodded, obviously more familiar with these rules than he. "And I can't change auditing firms, that's a board of director's decision. The only thing I can do is hire you."

"But, Hank—"

"I've already checked with Falstaff. He said clients hire staff from the auditing firm all the time. To be honest, I think he feels badly about what happened and was pleased to hear that you had employment." Hank smiled, pleased with his resolution of her predicament.

"No."

"No?" He sat stunned. This was the part of his plan when she was to throw herself into his arms in gratitude. Looking at her now, the only thing she was liable to throw was the cooling container of chicken soup. "Why not?"

"I can't work for you, Hank." She pulled herself to a sitting position. He had the distinct impression that the room had suddenly gotten darker and colder. "I think it's time for you to leave."

"But, Angel—"

"I've told you not to call me that." She closed her eyes tightly and for an instant, when she opened them, he thought he saw moisture collecting around the rims. "Please go now, I don't think you should come here anymore."

He sat glued to his chair. He wasn't about to go anywhere. "Is this about Elizabeth?" He clenched the arms of his chair so tightly his fingertips were numb. No one was going to make him leave before he said what he came here to say.

"Do you think I could work day-by-day with a man who...who...uses people for his own pleasure then tosses them away?"

"Is that what you think of me?" he asked. He held his breath waiting for her answer. Of all people, he had thought Angie knew him better than that. That she didn't... His heartbeat pounded out the intervening seconds.

"No." Her voice registered barely above a whisper. "Not really." Relief and something else surged through his bloodstream. "But you haven't explained about that wedding announcement."

"I haven't proposed to Elizabeth," he insisted. "I told you that earlier."

"You said you were in New York."

"Yes, but not to propose marriage. Elizabeth overdosed on cocaine Saturday night and was taken to the hospital. I went to New York to make arrangements for her admittance to a rehab center. She didn't want her father to know."

"But then ...?"

He held up his hand to stop her question. "Her father ran the notice as part of an agreement he and I made months ago."

Her eyes narrowed. "What sort of agreement?"

He stood to pace. There was no easy way to say this. No easy way not to hurt her. "Do you remember when you accused me of using Elizabeth to secure this job?" She nodded. He took a deep breath. "You were partially right."

"How partial?"

"Elizabeth and I were neighbors when we were children. She developed a sort of crush on me that she never outgrew. Her father promised to do certain things for my family and give me this opportunity to prove myself if I promised to marry Elizabeth."

"He bought you off."

Hank cringed. "Something like that." He turned to face her. "I'm not proud of what I promised. I never expected to meet someone like you. I thought—"

"Someone like me?" Her eyes widened and her lips turned up in a soft smile.

He saw an opening. "Someone strong and kind, smart and honest." He sat next to her and took her hands in his "Beautiful and innocent, trusting and trustworthy." Her cheeks began to glow. He lowered his voice and leaned in closer. "Independent and self-assured." His lips brushed her damp cheek, tasting salt. His gut wrenched. He had never intended to hurt her, never planned to be the cause of so much pain.

She gently pushed him away. "Go on about this arrangement."

"I thought maybe Elizabeth and I could work something out. I thought we'd have a marriage like my parents." *Cold, loveless.* "They essentially co-existed." If he hadn't met Angie, he'd probably be married to Elizabeth right now. He couldn't repress a slight smile. "At the time, it made perfect business sense."

"So what you're saying is that even though you didn't propose to Elizabeth, it's really only a matter of time."

"I won't lie to you, Angie. I've never reneged on a promise. I ..."

"Get out."

"You can hate me if you want—"

"I do."

Her contempt reduced him to fish bait. He cast about looking for words that would win her favor again. Even the dog looked at him with disdain. She couldn't toss him out of her life like that. He wouldn't let her. "But you still need a job."

"I can always drive for my brother."

"Your brother will let you drive with a cast on your leg?" He looked down and noticed she wasn't wearing the plastic cast.

"My ankle is strong enough."

"Come work for me, Angie," he pleaded. Heck, he'd get down on his knees if he had to. "Max said you had some concerns about Hayden's operations. The financial ratios show something isn't right. Together, we can—"

"Together?" Her laugh turned into a choking fit.

"If you want, I won't talk to you. I'll avoid you like the flu." He pleaded. "Everyone at Hayden will think we hate each other. Whatever you want."

"I want you to leave. Now."

She'd rejected him. He had played his trump card and she still rejected him. There wasn't anything else to say. She tossed back the quilt in a struggle to stand, but he restrained her. "Relax. I'll go. You don't have to get up." He headed for the door. With one final swallow of pride, he turned back. "If you change your mind about the job, be at my office Monday morning, eight o'clock." He let himself out.

After he left, Angie slumped down on the sofa. Did he really expect she could work with him after all that had happened? It was hard enough to see him today without falling into his arms and weeping over the loss of her job and the breaking of her heart. Every time he spoke, she watched his lips, the same lips that had explored her so intimately and thoroughly just a few nights ago. At one point, she had closed her eyes so the sight of him couldn't tempt her. Instead, the resulting loss of sight reminded her of that silly mask. A tingling tension had raced from the tips of her breasts to the depths of her womb. And he expected her to forget everything? To forget her own humiliation at his engagement? The idea was ludicrous. Infuriating.

Obviously he would do anything for money, even marry someone he didn't love. But she had standards, she had pride, she had...no job, no promotion, no life. Tears welled up in her eyes again. How could her entire world disintegrate in such a short period of time?

The doorbell rang. Angie straightened, pulling her robe lapels together at her neck. He came back! She wiped the wetness from her cheeks, her imagination racing faster than her feet. He came back to apologize and tell her he could never marry Elizabeth, that she was the only one he could love. She ran for the door.

Opening it wide, she looked for a broad shouldered, commanding, sensual man, but found instead a six-year-old, curly-haired child dressed as a pumpkin.

"Trick or treat."

Angie glanced beyond the orange and green costume to see a mother frowning at her from the driveway. Beggar's night. Westerville always set aside a special night for the door-to-door ritual and this apparently was it.

"Just a minute," she said to the little girl before turning back into the house. What to do? She hadn't purchased any candy for the occasion and her mother never kept sweets in the house. She saw her purse and retrieved her wallet. Returning to the front door, she plunked two quarters in the little girl's plastic pumpkin, already partially filled with candy.

"Thank you," the pumpkin said before carefully negotiating the steps off the porch to rejoin her mother.

Angie stepped out on the porch and saw a long procession of costumed children down the street dashing from house-to-house. *Why tonight?* She moaned. *I'm not ready for this.*

Tell that to all those little expectant faces, her subconscious lectured. *They don't care about your personal problems. Life goes on.*

She dashed upstairs, quickly changing into jeans and a heavy sweater before running next door to beg for some of Walter's candy. Fortunately, he was well stocked.

Armed with a bowl of brightly wrapped chocolates, she sat on her porch and dispersed the candy to the parade of imaginatively attired children. One little girl, dressed in a store-bought fairy costume, received a fistful of candy, rather than the tightly rationed portions handed out to her peers. Angie's fairy costume may have been more expensive, but she recognized the sparkle of magic in the girl's eyes that she herself had felt the evening of the ball.

As the cardboard wings flounced off the porch, Angie reflected on the gifts Hank had unknowingly given her, memories of things she might not have otherwise experienced. It was time to stop weeping about what might have been and allow her life to go on. Her steady heartbeat sounded its approval, and she relaxed for the first time in days.

Headlights moved slowly down the street before turning sharply into her driveway. A white limousine glowed softly in the moonlight. The front passenger door opened and her mother stepped out.

"Mom" Angela set the bowl with the dwindling supply of candy aside and rushed to hug her mother. "I didn't know you were coming back today."

"Aunt Ceal couldn't take her anymore," Stephen quipped from the other side of the car.

Her mother squeezed her tight, then set her back a pace. "Let me take a look at you. Did you take your medications? Are you feeling all right?" Her eyes narrowed. "You look different, somehow. Older."

In a Heartbeat

Angie could feel her cheeks warming even in the cool night air. "Probably just the moonlight."

"You're probably right." Her mother laughed. "How much can a person grow in a month?"

More than you would suspect, Angie silently answered. "How was your trip?" Stephen pulled some suitcases from the back and joined them as they walked toward the house.

"Wonderful," her mother answered. "Ceal mended quickly and we got to spend time together. Plus, I took orders for three quilts while I was down there. Isn't that wonderful?" She squeezed Angie's hand. "You know we can always use the money."

Reality settled over Angie like a shroud. The loss of her job meant the loss of her health insurance and coverage for her expensive medications. The sale of a few quilts wouldn't begin to cover their needs. "Mom," she said. "We need to talk..."

Chapter Nineteen

Angie angled her car into the employee parking lot at Hayden. The prospect of having to eat crow in front of Hank Renard curdled in her stomach. Stephen couldn't offer her the kind of insurance benefits she needed even if she worked full-time. He had Raymond working for him now and Raymond's medical needs weren't as demanding as her own. She took a deep breath and stepped from the Civic, tightening her coat against a frigid wind.

"Angela, what are you doing here?" Tom Wilson loomed at her elbow. "I thought you had finished with your field work."

"We were...are," she stumbled, wishing she had checked the rearview mirror before exiting her car. She hadn't quite worked out how to explain her presence. "I...I just wanted to clear up a few points with Mr. Renard."

"Are you sure it's not something I can help you with?" he asked smoothly. "Henry hasn't recovered from his trip last week. He has a very full schedule."

"He's expecting me," Angie added quickly, scolding herself for not parking in the visitors' lot. If she had, she'd be inside the building by now.

"Is he really?" Was it surprise or sarcasm she heard in Wilson's voice? "He didn't say anything about a morning appointment to me."

"I didn't know you functioned as his secretary," Angela replied.

He laughed, little puffs of heated air lifted around his head. "I guess I deserved that. I meant to say that I also have a morning meeting with Henry. I didn't realize he was so tightly scheduled."

Angela reached for the door handle, but Wilson beat her to it. He held it open and she mumbled her thanks as she passed into the warmth of the building interior. "Stop by before you leave, Angie," Tom said, following her inside. "I found some of those missing documents you were requesting." She nodded and he turned down the hall towards the accounting department.

Angie hesitated before she slipped out of her coat, then tossed it over her arm. Relieved that the receptionist hadn't arrived yet, she continued down the hall. Would he gloat when he saw her? Would he retract his offer of employment? Her heart pounded with each step. Was she a fool for coming here?

She reached his office door and raised her hand to knock when it opened from the inside. She looked up from the broad chest filling the doorway to the talented lips that filled her dreams. She smiled weakly.

"You said something about a job?"

"Angie!" Hank latched onto her arm and roughly pulled her into the office before pushing the door closed. He held her at arm's length a moment, then somewhat self-consciously crammed his hands into his pockets.

"I thought you'd decided to work for your brother." He meandered behind his desk, then picked up a silver pen and tapped it on the desk.

"I changed my mind," she lied. He didn't need to know Stephen refused to hire her fulltime. "You were right when you said I should do something accounting related. That is, after all, what I've been trained for." She placed her coat over the back of a chair and clasped her hands behind her back, unsure what else to do with them. Holding her breath, she forced her gaze to travel from the knot of his necktie, past his smile to his eyes. Even as she tried to suppress it, desire surged through her bloodstream. Her knees threatened to buckle. "Do you still want me?"

A smile unfolded slowly across his face, his dimple flashed, his eyes crinkled. "More than ever," He moved toward her with outstretched arms.

She stepped back out of his reach. "I mean for the job." Her heart pounded in her throat, raising her voice an octave. "Is it still available?"

He hesitated, dropped his arms and walked back to his desk to examine the silver pen. "We have to iron out some details, but, yes. It's still available."

"What kind of details?" she asked suspiciously.

"Salary. Duties. Title. Whether or not you still hate me."

"I do." She thought she saw him wince ever so slightly. The reaction didn't give her the pleasure she thought it might.

He coughed. "Then this is to be strictly business?"

"If I'm to work here, yes."

He exhaled a held breath, then studied her a moment. "Sit down." He stepped around his desk to his chair. "You never told me about your excursion with Max. What were you after?"

"I'd rather not say. It was just a hunch. Something I wanted to check out. We didn't find anything so there's no point rehashing the whole thing." She stalled. If she was to work with these people on a full time basis, she'd best not burn bridges by verbalizing her suspicions.

"I see. The reason I ask is that I've had a few 'hunches' myself. I think I mentioned that the inventory turnover statistics don't come close to the industry norms. I should be seeing stockpiles of excess inventory in the warehouse, and I'm not."

"You think someone is stealing?"

He nodded. "I don't know who or how. But I think maybe you've come to a similar conclusion."

It was her turn to nod. "I've noticed some aberrations in your accounts payable. Nothing really obvious, but suspicious. That's what Max and I went to check out, but we didn't find anything."

"Here's my plan. I want to hire you to investigate further and see if you can find any evidence of fraud or misappropriation of assets. You'll report directly to me."

"Do I have some sort of title?"

"Director of Internal Audit." He chuckled beneath his breath. "Maybe that'll scare the guilty party and flush them out. Are you game?"

She cleared her throat. "What about compensation?"

"Falstaff told me how much they were paying you." Apparently, nothing about her life was private, she thought disgruntled. "I'll increase your pay by fifteen percent and pick up your insurance payments until you're covered under our plan. You can work it out with the personnel department."

That was a relief. "What about my office? Where do I work?"

"That's a tough one." He thought for a moment. "For now you can use Jim Owens's office next door."

She nodded and looked around, uncertain what to do next.

"Angie." She looked up; his voice had lost its hard executive edge. "I'm glad you decided to come here. I'm sorry for what happened, but that's not the reason I'm hiring you. I really do need your expertise."

She cleared her throat to move the lump settling there. "I guess I should get started then." She turned toward the door, but Hank beat her to the doorknob.

"I understand it's a tradition here that the boss takes new hires to lunch on their first day." His lips twisted in that sideways smile she loved. An ache formed in her chest. It wasn't going to be easy working so close to him.

"Tradition? When did this tradition start?"

"Today." He smiled and pulled the door open. Angie stepped into the hallway and saw Tom Wilson approach the office. Hank followed her out. "I'll see you about eleven-thirty, then?" He glanced up. "Tom, I want you to meet our new internal auditor."

"Angie?" He stopped in his tracks. "You're going to be working here? Full-time?"

"Yes. I guess that means we'll be seeing a lot more of each other."

"But what happened to Falstaff and Watterson?"

"Mr. Renard made me an offer I couldn't refuse." She turned to Hank, "But I'm afraid I'll have to decline your offer of lunch."

"I guess congratulations are in order." Wilson held out his hand.

Angie accepted his clammy handshake, purposefully avoiding Hank's frown. No way would she accompany him on a private lunch. Some temptations were too powerful. Best to avoid them all together. "I'll stop by in an hour or so to pick up those invoice copies," she told Wilson. "Right after I set up my office and talk to personnel."

"R...Right," Wilson replied before following Hank back into his office. The door must have caught a draft. The wall shook when it slammed.

○§○§○

After retrieving the missing documents from Tom Wilson, Angie requested and received the vendor file for Timone Industries. Fortunately Owens's office had a locking door for privacy and a large table for her armload of papers. She submersed herself in detail. Tracking the movement of individual transactions through stacks of paper completely absorbed her thoughts. Sometime later a knock at the door jolted her concentration.

"I just wanted to check and see if you were still alive." Hank lingered at the door. "Most of the crew left at five."

She glanced at her watch. Six-thirty. "Oh no. My mother's probably having a fit." She quickly stood and grabbed her coat from the rack in the corner. "I didn't realize how late it was. Thanks for checking on me." She pulled open a desk drawer and removed her purse before hurrying past Hank without a word.

"Wait--" His footsteps thudded behind her. "I thought we could discuss what you've uncovered over dinner?"

"No time." She pushed open the outside door. "Maybe later." She walked briskly to her car, leaving little puffs of steam in her wake.

The interior of the Civic was slightly warmer than the air outside. She started the engine and put it in gear, not waiting for it to warm up. After backing out of her spot, she braked slightly before shifting into Drive. The car was slow to respond, probably the cold. After turning onto the main street, she pulled the safety belt over her shoulder and fastened it by her hip. The forced air pouring out the vents contained a little heat, and the fog on the windshield rapidly retreated.

The oncoming headlights thinned out as she left the industrial park and entered a residential area. Approaching a four-way stop at the top of a small hill, she sought the brake pedal and pushed down gently. The brake offered no resistance. Her foot slapped the floor.

A minivan pulled into the intersection in front of her, turning in her direction.

"No!" She screamed. Her car rushed towards the minivan's midsection. She caught a glance of the teenage driver's panicked face one second before she jerked the steering wheel toward the curb. The front bumper of her car narrowly missed the taillights of the minivan, but the car's back end continued in a collision course. The crunch of metal exploded like gunshot. The seatbelt pressed hard against her chest. The car shuddered then stopped.

Hank absently drove home while rehashing his conversation with Angie over and over in his head. What did he say that caused her to avoid him all afternoon? Would every day be like this? His mind churned over the day's events while his car moved forward on autopilot. Flashing beacons of police cruisers and flares on the roadside up ahead intruded on his thoughts. He reassessed his surroundings. Schrock Road. He smiled. His subconscious had pulled him towards Angie's house. And if his subconscious mind wanted him to go there, who was he to consciously refuse?

He neared the flares and slowed down. Two cars were off to the side of the road. He edged his car past the policeman signaling traffic and glanced right at the wreckage. Angie sat in the driver's seat of one of the mutilated cars, her hand pressed to her heart as if pledging allegiance. She nodded to a police officer through the open car door.

"Angie!" He yelled as if his voice would travel through his closed window. He cleared the flares and jerked his car to the side of the road. With little regard for oncoming traffic, he exited his car and ran back to her.

"What happened? Are you hurt?" He turned to the policewoman before Angie could respond. "Is she all right?"

"I'm fine." Angie put her hand on his coat sleeve.

"She seems a little shaken up, but otherwise okay." The officer paused in her writing. "Are you her husband?"

"No." They answered simultaneously. "Just a friend," Hank added.

"Well, I think I've gotten all the information I need here. Give me a few minutes to finish this paperwork and you can give your friend a lift home." The officer stepped back and headed for her vehicle.

"Your heart, you're pressing your heart," Hank said. "Do we need to go to the emergency room? Should someone check you out?" His own heart pounded as if he had run a marathon to reach her rather than a few yards. His thoughts jumbled in chaotic disorder. The sight of Elizabeth in the hospital hadn't thrown him into this kind of panic.

She rolled her eyes. "I'm fine," she repeated patiently, patting her chest. "A little confused, but fine."

"Confused? Did you hit your head? Maybe you have a concussion."

"Will you stop that?" She pushed him away from his close examination of her skull. "I swear you're as bad as my brother. I meant I don't understand how this could have happened."

Although his instinct was to gather her up in his arms and rush her to the nearest emergency room, he resisted. He forcibly slowed his breathing to match her calm exterior. "What do you mean?"

"This morning I didn't have any trouble with my brakes. But when I came to this stop sign, my car wouldn't slow down."

"Are you sure you didn't step on the gas by accident?" he asked, looking pointedly at her ankle.

"That's what the policewoman asked. I don't think she believed me when I said the brakes didn't work until she tried them herself."

"She tried them?"

Angie nodded. "Her foot went right to the floor. No brake fluid, she said." Angie tilted her head. "I was lucky this intersection is on top of the hill. The car had already slowed a bit before I tried to stop. Fortunately, no one was hurt."

To be honest, Hank could care less about the people in the other car. All his emotions and concerns focused on the woman in front of him. A policeman halted traffic and the other injured vehicle limped away from the curb. The approaching tow truck with flashing yellow lights was destined for the Civic.

The policewoman returned Angie's license along with a citation. Angie directed the tow driver to Classic Limo's garage. After all the details had been sorted out, she slid into the passenger side of Hank's car.

"Maybe you shouldn't be alone tonight," he said. "You know you can stay at my house."

"Just take me home." She sounded tired. "My mother came back this weekend. I won't be alone."

He was about to protest. He wasn't suggesting a lewd rendezvous, just some support. He glanced at her face and the words died in his throat. She looked drawn, defeated, and in no condition for a debate. He started the engine and headed toward her house.

"Darn," Angie muttered under her breath. As if things weren't already bad enough, the white limousine parked in her driveway signified they were about to get worse. "Stephen must be visiting. Just what I need, a lecture from both Mom and my brother."

"Would you like me to come in with you?" Hank asked.

"They're my family. I can deal with this alone." In truth, this was one confrontation she didn't want to deal with by herself, but she'd never admit it. If she did, Hank would stay, and that would definitely fuel the flames. "Thank you for bringing me home, but --"

"I'd like to meet your mother," he said.

"This wouldn't be the best time, Hank. Maybe later." *Maybe never*, she thought. This relationship can only end in pain. Best to move on.

"When?"

"I don't know. Just later." She reached for the door handle but he grabbed her arm before she could exit.

"When, Angie? Give me a date. Tell me a time when I can see you away from the office. Can't we be friends again, the way we were before?"

It was tempting to believe nothing had changed. But she knew better. She knew she wasn't the same child she was a month earlier.

The front door to her house opened, spilling light out onto the porch. Her mother stepped outside with a sweater wrapped around her shoulders.

"Angie, is that you? I thought I heard your car." Little puffs of steam from her breath rose like smoke signals. "Who's that with you?"

Angie glanced back at Hank. He smiled much as he had the night she had raved about his culinary skills. "Will you do the honors?" he asked. "Or should I just introduce myself?"

She sighed. "Come along. I'll introduce you." She exited the car and hurried up the walkway without waiting. Hank caught up to her at the porch.

"Mom, I'd like you to meet someone. This is my boss, Mr. Henry Renard."

"Mr. Renard," her mother nodded, her expression placid. Angie recognized the look from countless bedside vigils and hospital conferences. Her mother hid both tragic secrets and restrained joy behind that reserved mask. Which was it this time? The clue to her mother's true feelings lay in her eyes. Many people assumed Angie inherited her analytical skills from her father, but she knew better. One had only to watch her mother's eyes to see true critical assessment.

Tonight, however, the porch light didn't reach her mother's face, making close observation impossible. Angie couldn't tell whether or not her mother approved of the man beside her. But then, what did it matter? There would be no future with Hank Renard.

"Angela, where's your car?" her mother asked.

She cringed. "It's kind of a long story..."

"Then you better come inside before you catch your death of cold," her mother directed. Angie started up the steps while Hank hesitated. "You too, Mr. Renard."

Once inside, Angie and Hank repeatedly bumped elbows as they both tried to remove their coats in the tiny hallway. "I expected you home earlier." Her mother held out coat hangers for the both of them.

"I did lose track of time at Hayden, but that's not the reason I'm late." Angie took a deep breath, bracing herself for the reaction. "I had a car accident."

"An accident? Are you all right?"

"I'm fine. I'm fine," she recited, making her way down the hall. She glanced at the empty sitting room. Her brother must be waiting in the kitchen. No sense rehashing the details twice. She'd tell them both about the brakes and then hustle Hank out the door. "Before you start on me, Stephen, I want you to know --"

Raymond sat at the scarred kitchen table, cradling a Classic Limo mug. A sudden shiver raised goosebumps on her arms.

"What are you doing here? Where's Stephen?"

Raymond raised an eyebrow, glancing about the room. "Not here."

"I can see that." Hank stood at her back. She fought an odd urge to lean back and surround herself with his strength and warmth. She reminded herself that Raymond was no threat. He was just a driver. Still...he shouldn't be here.

"I see you've met Raymond," her mother said from behind them. "He volunteered to bring me home from the quilt store when I couldn't reach you. So are we going to stand around, or sit like civilized human beings?"

A distinctive scratch on the back door announced Oreo's impatience. Angie crossed the room to open the back door. Oreo burst into the kitchen in a flying mass of black and white, working the room for attention before settling down by Hank's leg. Her mother poured coffee while Angie reiterated the details of her accident.

"And no one was hurt?" Raymond asked. She shook her head.

"It was probably a good thing that you left so late," Hank added. "Just an hour earlier and the rush hour traffic would have been heavier. It could have been much worse."

"Speaking of leaving, it's time I move on." Raymond rose from the table. "Thank you for your hospitality." Her mother followed Raymond to the door. Angie remained rooted to her chair.

"Such a polite, young man." Her mother said on her return. "I know Stephen depends a great deal on him."

"I suppose it's time for me to be going also." Hank turned to Angie's mother. "Mrs. Blake, it's been a pleasure meeting you. Perhaps, in the future, we can—"

"I'll show you out." Angie said on a rush of breath. She certainly didn't want him infusing himself into her family. Now was the time to tell him so. She handed him his coat from the hall closet and slipped on her own. "I'll be back in a minute," she called to her mother. They exited the front door with Oreo at their heels.

"Thanks for stopping when you saw my car." She paused on the front porch to wrap a scarf around her neck. "But why were you driving down Schrock Road? Don't you normally take the parkway further north?"

"You stayed locked in that office all day. I wanted to stop by and see if you found anything."

She glanced over at him. "You could have waited until tomorrow. If I find anything important, you'll be the first to know. I told you our arrangement is to be strictly business. That means no after-hours social calls and no family meetings."

His broad shoulders, emphasized by the brushed camel coat, drooped a bit under her harsh criticism. She instantly regretted her words. He gave her a job, he always seemed to be there when she needed him, and all he had asked for in return was friendship. He shouldn't be blamed for her unrealistic expectations. She recanted. "But as you asked..."

They walked down the long driveway devoid of the white limousine. "There's a couple of shady transactions that I'm researching. I've been trying to track the sale of merchandise that is delivered to the Ritchton warehouse. So far, I've only managed to confirm about forty percent of the sales. If my numbers are right, that warehouse should be stuffed to the rafters."

"That's no problem," he said. "We'll go down there tomorrow and check it out."

"Not so fast. I think someone inside Hayden is behind all this. Several people are involved in buying inventory. With desktop publishing, it would be a snap to phony up necessary paper to cover their tracks. Or they could move merchandise from one location to another. If we tip our hand by visiting the warehouse, we may never find out who's behind this." Oreo dashed ahead to dribble at the base of a light post. It never ceased to amaze her how much one dog bladder could hold.

Hank stuffed his hands into his coat pockets. "I can't exactly sit around and let someone steal the company blind."

"You could take an inventory count," Angie said. "The count would quantify the problem. Besides the billings would have to be current to maintain a good cutoff, and that would force the direct ship billings to be processed so we could see if there's a problem. Plus, if Hayden inventory is being maintained off site, we'll have a valid reason to inspect and count it."

"Tom Wilson was planning a physical inventory for the end of December. Can we take one sooner? I don't want to let these people steal for two more months before we do something about it."

A car veered down the quiet street. Angie called Oreo back to her side to deter her from chasing after the speeding car. An explosion blasted from the side window of the car. Oreo yelped.

"My God!" she yelled as each house up and down the street turned on their lights. Neighborhood dogs barked in a lively cacophony. "What was that?"

Her answer lay in a quiet bundle of fur lying on the ground. "Oreo!" she cried, rushing to her pet. Hank beat her there. The too familiar stench of blood rose to her nose.

"She's been shot," Hank said. "Is there a vet somewhere nearby?"

"There's an emergency animal clinic not far from here," she said, kneeling down to get close to the wounded dog. She lifted Oreo's head into her lap.

Her mother shouted something from the porch. Hank yelled back and took off in a run. Big sorrowful brown eyes gazed up at her. "Sssh, puppy. You'll be all right," she cooed, stroking the dog's head. A tear dropped on the dog's nose.

"Wrap this around her to stop the bleeding." Hank spread one of her mother's old quilts on the grass before gently lifting and placing the dog on it. He wrapped the quilt securely around the injured animal, and after Angie was situated in the car, placed the dog in her arms.

Police sirens sounded in the distance but Hank and Angie didn't wait. Hank sped off while Angie shouted directions from the back seat.

She cradled and cooed to the dog as if she were a child. Oreo's glazed eyes and soft whimpers tore at her heart. "Why would anyone want to hurt you? Why would someone shoot my dog?"

"Maybe they weren't aiming at Oreo." Angie saw Hank's face clench in a grim frown.

"What do you mean?"

"Maybe they meant to shoot me...or you."

"No, why would anyone...?" She didn't finish the question. It was becoming a too familiar refrain. All these "accidents" couldn't be coincidental. But why were they happening at all?

Hank pulled up to the emergency clinic entrance and they carried Oreo inside. The veterinarian took the dog out of Angie's arms and rushed behind swinging doors. Hank and Angie waited in silence for the vet's prognosis.

The captive stench of dog urine and disinfectant inside the clinic burned her eyes, so she closed them for increasing stretches of time. The long stressful day pulled heavily at her limbs, and the eerie late night quiet of the waiting room lulled her senses.

"Angie, we have to talk," Hank said, his voice deeper and closer than she'd anticipated.

She lifted her heavy lids, surprised to discover her head on his shoulder. "Bout whaaat?"

"Wake up now, this is serious."

She rubbed at the corners of her eyes. "Can we get some fresh air? Clear my head?"

Hank told the receptionist that they'd be just outside if needed. Angie stretched, waiting for Hank before they exited at a far more leisurely pace than they had arrived.

Cold air washed over her face, invigorating her brain. Hank sat on a bench just outside the main entrance to the animal hospital. After a brief spell of arm swinging and stretching, she settled next to him.

"Do you still carry a supply of medications in your purse?" He cocked an eyebrow at her. She nodded. "Because I've been thinking you shouldn't go home tonight."

"What do you mean?" She asked, irritated. "Where else am I going to go?"

"I don't think you should be alone."

She audibly sighed. "We've been through this before, remember? You met my mother tonight. Have you forgotten already?"

He frowned. "Your mother isn't going to stop whoever is taking potshots at you. At least, her presence didn't tonight. They know where you live. I just think you shouldn't be there when they come calling again."

The attack tonight frightened her more than she cared to admit. She hadn't talked to her mother since they had rushed to the hospital, but she imagined the whole incident had frightened her as well. "If it's too dangerous for me to stay," she said, "isn't it too dangerous for my mother as well?"

Hank hesitated. "Could she stay with your brother a few days?"

"I suppose so." Better her than me, she thought. "But if Mom is at Stephen's, where would I stay?"

"With me."

"Somehow, I don't think my mother will approve." She could easily imagine her family's reaction when she told them she'd be staying with Hank.

"As much as I'd prefer your mother's approval, that's not my main concern." He shifted, his face a somber mask. "Think about this logically. You won't be alone and your mother will be safer staying with someone else. My house is large enough to accommodate you and Oreo...and your mother if she insists, although she'd be safer at Stephen's. There's a good chance these people, whoever they are, don't know my address or that you'd be staying with me."

Angie didn't point out that someone already knew enough about their relationship to have taken a candid photo of her at his house. She was too tired to think of alternative places to stay and, in truth, she felt more protected from outside danger with Hank than without him.

"And don't give me that breach of independence line," he said, obviously misinterpreting her silence. "You work for me now, remember?"

"I don't recall that living with the boss was part of the job description." Her lips tightened.

"I'm not suggesting you move in to share my bed." He raised an eyebrow. "Although if you want..." The invitation dwindled away once he glanced at her face. "I guess not." He stood. "I'm just concerned for your safety. The decision is yours to make."

The automatic doors opened with a swoosh. "Miss Blake?" The receptionist stayed in the vestibule and called out to them. "The doctor would like to talk to you now."

Chapter Twenty

The doctor wanted to keep Oreo overnight. The bullet had passed clean through the muscles of her shoulder and upper leg, narrowly missing the dog's spine. Blood loss was a concern, but the vet assured Angela that given her pet's age and health, full recovery was probable with adequate time and rest. Hank drove her straight from the animal hospital to the police station to file a report.

Angie figured at this rate, she would soon know the entire Westerville police staff on a first name basis. She answered the same questions with the same vague answers. No, they didn't know of anyone who might have a grudge. No, they didn't see the car. It blended in with the dark night. Yes, she was the same Angela Blake who had reported an earlier vandalism and attempted break-in.

The officer sighed. "There's not much to go on. You two are the only ones who saw the car, yet neither of you got much of a description or a license plate number." Angie shifted under the policeman's hard stare. "Although each of your recent complaints seems insignificant on the surface, taken together they don't paint a pleasant picture. Someone is trying to harm you, Ms. Blake. Yet you don't know who or why." He hesitated as if Angie could suddenly provide the solution to the puzzle. She couldn't.

"If I were you, Ms. Blake, I'd take precautions." He pulled out a business card case. "Maybe it's a good time to go on a vacation, get out of town." She hardly thought that was a solution. As long as these people were on the loose, she wouldn't feel safe anywhere. Still, the officer's comments added credence to Hank's analysis. "If either of you think of anything more, call me." The policeman placed a card on the table. "We've never had a drive-by shooting here before. Some things we'd like to leave for the larger cities."

They left the station and returned to Hank's car. Once en route, Angie bit her lip, glancing over to Hank. "Is there someone who might want to shoot at you?"

Hank shook this head. "Elizabeth's father is pretty upset with me at the moment, but not enough to kill me. That would pretty much defeat his purpose."

"And what purpose is that?"

"To get Elizabeth married off."

"I wouldn't think that would be such a difficult problem. After all she's beautiful and ..."

"She comes with a lot of baggage."

Angela hesitated, stumbling over the question that had plagued her since they met. "Do you love her?"

"Lord, no." He rubbed his hand on the back of his neck. "We've been friends since we were children, and I understand her more than most, I suppose. But love?" He shook his head.

Angie looked out the window, feeling relieved and buoyant at his admission. The slumbering landscape rolled by in the light of an occasional streetlight. Skeletons of once lush trees stretched bare limbs to the moon. Dried leaves raked into piles the height of a small child rose from the lawns like some all-consuming fungus. Long stretches of darkness replaced the occasional passing house light. She sat upright with a start.

"This isn't the way to my house."

He stiffened. "I thought we decided you should stay with me."

"But I need clothes, toiletries,..."

He relaxed behind the wheel. "You can call your mother and ask her to pack a suitcase. Maybe Stephen could drop it off tomorrow." Hank steered the car up the long driveway into the garage. "Why don't you give her a call now?"

"How well do you know this man?" Her mother asked after hearing Hank's idea. Angie detected an ounce of suspicion in her voice.

"Pretty well." An understatement. After all they had shared, she knew Hank better than she knew her own brother.

"Do you trust him?"

"Oh yes," she said without hesitation. She trusted him to do the right thing, the noble thing. Even if it meant marrying a woman he didn't love.

"How long are you planning to stay there?"

"I don't know. I guess until we find out who is responsible."

"And how do you plan to do that?"

It was a good question, but one to which she didn't have an answer. "I wish I knew. I'm tired of police reports. I'm tired of waiting for something terrible to happen."

"Maybe it's time for you to take the initiative."

Her mother's observation hit her like an overstuffed file cabinet. She was trained to analyze. Why wasn't she doing it now? Why was she so willing to be a victim?

"I trust you know what you're doing, Angela. Be mindful of your heart. I'll send Stephen over with clothes and your prescriptions. Be careful and know that I love you."

Angie replaced the receiver yearning for one of her mother's hugs. They had always eased her worries in the past. A hug wouldn't do it this time, but maybe her mother's advice would. It was time to be proactive, to figure out who was behind this series of accidents. She would start with a list and look for a pattern. She fished a pen from her purse and glanced around the tabletops looking for some paper. Hank was nowhere in sight.

An envelope with the top slashed by a letter opener lay on one of the tables. She smiled, the very table where she had first discovered the costume boxes. The back of the envelope would have to do. She'd make a list of all the different suspicious events and dates and possible suspects. She carried the envelope around to the sofa, flipped on the light and settled down to think.

"What are you doing?"

She looked toward the hallway. Hank stood with his arms full of brightly colored silks and satins. Lace spilled out from between his fingers. A fuchsia feathery boa trailed behind him. He stared at the envelope in her hand.

"There you are," she said. "I didn't know where you disappeared. Looks like you have your hands full."

"So do you." His voice held no humor. She looked at the envelope.

"You mean this?" She held it up by a corner. "I needed some paper but all I could find was this. Do you mind if I write on the back? I thought if we --"

A pale green check fell out of the slit opening and fluttered to the floor. "I'm sorry," Angie said. "I didn't mean... "

She picked up the check and gulped. "Five Hundred Thousand Dollars--I've never seen a handwritten check that large." She looked at the payer's name, Jim Owens.

Hank dropped his colorful bundle on the opposite end of the sofa, then walked behind her and leaned over her shoulder. "Bribe money. It's the second installment."

His breath stirred the back of her neck sending delicious tingles down her spine. She twisted around to see him. "I know you said he was paying you to marry his daughter, but five hundred thousand dollars? And this is the *second* installment?"

He nodded, then walked to the wing chair across from her and sat down. "My family lost a lot of money in a stock deal on my recommendation, more money than they could afford to lose. This was my only opportunity to recoup the loss. Does the amount make my actions more palatable?"

She thought for a moment. What would she do for half a million dollars? Heaven knew, with debt from her operations and medications, she could use the money. She looked across at Hank, his eyes pleading for acceptance, his shoulders slumped from exhaustion or shame, she wasn't sure which. Maybe she had judged him a little too harshly. She slid the check back in the envelope and laid it on the coffee table between them. "What are all those?" She nodded to the colorful pile of garments.

"Elizabeth keeps nightgowns here so she has more room in her suitcase to pack. I thought you could borrow something to wear for tonight."

Angie pulled the top garment off the stack, a bright pink floor-length satin gown sized to fit a six-foot model. She considered her own short stature. "I think I might be more comfortable in something of yours rather than Elizabeth's. Do you have a pajama top or a T-shirt or something?"

"I don't wear pajamas." For a moment she thought he blushed, but it might have been a reflection cast by the bright gown. "I didn't think T-shirts would make sense for Ohio this time of year. I have some clean undershirts. Would you like to try one of them?"

She thought about wearing one of his undershirts, one that had rubbed up against his chest and had been tucked in his pants. Her cheeks started to burn. It would probably carry his scent, no matter how many times it had been washed. She gathered up the rest of the garments in her arms. "I'll just look through these. I'm sure I can find something."

She took the lingerie back to the room across the hall from Hank's. Sorting through the vibrant stack, she found a blue baby doll nightie that probably teased the top of Elizabeth's buttocks. On Angela, it dropped to mid-thigh. Still, it didn't drag on the floor. She checked her reflection in the mirror. The puckered, gathered bodice scooped low, exposing her scar and an ample amount of cleavage. She chuckled. She had cleavage! After so many years of turtleneck sweaters and concealing blouses, she had forgotten. The form-fitting bodice molded to her figure, detailing every curve. Scandalous. She loved it.

Just for fun, she slipped on a long, sheer, boa trimmed robe, then walked the length of the room, letting the garment drag behind her. With a sultry pout and some fake eyelashes, she could be one of Stephen's classic movie queens.

A knock on the bedroom door interrupted.

Hank stood on the other side, a legal pad his hand. His eyes widened, his jaw slacked open. She rather enjoyed rendering him speechless.

"I found one that fits," she said, twirling in front of him.

"I see." He swallowed. "You look fantastic."

She pointed to the legal pad. "Is that for me?"

"Yes, you were looking before, and I found, well, I thought..." he rambled. "Can I get you something? Anything? A glass of water? I know you don't drink scotch. Maybe a glass of warm milk?"

She yawned. "I'm pretty tired. I think I'll just go to bed." She pulled the legal pad very slowly from between his frozen fingers. "Good night, Hank." She closed the door but still heard his muffled "Good night."

◊◊◊

The room was too quiet, or too noisy, or too dark, she couldn't decide which. More probably, she was too scared. Having charted everything that had occurred, she came to one conclusion. Someone at Hayden didn't want her there. Nothing happened the week she was unemployed, but the moment she showed up at Hayden, trouble followed. It had to be connected to her suspicions of theft. No one was targeting her dog. They were targeting her. Oreo just got in the way.

Outside, the wind blew in sudden gusts and the house responded with unfamiliar creaks and sighs. She missed Oreo and the comfort of her mother's familiar quilts. She tossed and turned and hammered the pillows into misshapen blobs. A tree branch scraped across the window and she sat straight up. Her heartbeat pounded in her ears. She'd never fall asleep in this room.

The last time she had slept in this house, Hank's arms curled about her. No tree branches scared her then. Nothing scared her, then. Deep in her memory, she could almost feel his breath on her neck, his chest pressed against her back, his manhood pressing her... Her mouth went dry.

"Water," she announced to the empty room. "I'll get a glass of water."

She opened the door to the hallway and noticed Hank's door ajar. She crossed the hallway and pushed through the outer office without a sound.

"Hank?" she whispered from the doorway. She didn't want to wake him if he was asleep but if he wasn't...

"Angela?" He sat straight up in bed. "Is everything all right? Where are you?"

"Here," she answered. "I couldn't sleep. Maybe I'm a little scared. I don't know. After everything that—"

"Come here," he said, sliding to make room for her on the mattress. "Let me hold you."

She crossed the dark room, buoyed by the timbre of his voice. He held the sheets apart, inviting her to slide between them. Any lingering doubt about the appropriateness of her aggressive behavior vanished the instant his arms closed around her, pulling her tight against his chest.

"I feel safer all ready," she said, relaxing into the warmth of his embrace.

"You are safe, Angel. You'll always be safe with me." He kissed the top of her head while his fingertips swirled in lazy circles on her back.

Indeed, she felt both protected and accepted. Her lips pressed against his chest in silent gratitude.

"I couldn't sleep either," he said. "I'm glad you came to me. I was afraid if I went to your room, you'd—"

"Slam the door on your face?" Her fingertips on his chest mimicked the pattern of his on her back. She dipped lower, stretching to circle his navel with her little finger.

"Something like that." His knuckles skimmed down her side. Even through the nightgown, his touch excited every nerve ending in her body and set them tingling. She stretched her fingers lower, teasing the tight curls she had inspected before. She felt his sharp intake of breath. The sheets rose a little higher.

"Angel, if we start this, I can't promise I'll stop. So if you have—"

"Ssh." She placed her fingers over his mouth. "I don't know what will happen tomorrow, but I'm alive today." She kissed the tip of his chin. "And I'm here now." She propped herself up on her elbow and faced him. "I want this. I want you."

He smiled tightly. He hooked a finger in the bodice of her nightgown, pulling it down until her straining nipple poked over the top. He captured it with his knuckles, playing an adult game of hide and seek. "You sound like a woman in control. Next you'll be telling me you want to be on top."

"On top?" She liked the sound of "a woman in control". That's what she wanted to be, needed to be. "Yes. I want to be on top." Although she wasn't exactly sure what that entailed, she'd always been a quick learner. She pushed back the sheets and blankets and rose on her knees to study the situation.

He twisted to reach the nightstand. "Better let me take care of this first."

"No," she pushed him back, a new idea dawning. "Not yet." Remembering her response when he laved her with his tongue, she bent down and rimmed his erect shaft with her tongue.

"My God!" He groaned. "Where did you learn that?"

"From you." Delighted with her newfound power, she continued experimenting, licking, sucking, and in some cases, teething all aspects of his manhood, from the smooth rounded head to the rough skin at the base. "Do you like this?" she asked, already suspecting the answer. "Do you want more?"

"Come here" He grabbed one of her legs and pulled it across his chest. Soon her knees straddled his neck while his penis bumped her lips. With his forearms securely trapping her buttocks, he separated her with his fingers then tongued the most sensitive parts of her anatomy. Just that quickly she had lost control. He had usurped her power, but she didn't mind a bit. She tried to duplicate with her lips all that he did with his own, but he was too skilled. Her legs quivered with the mounting internal tension before exploding waves of pleasure racked her body. She collapsed on his torso.

"Did you like that?" he mimicked, then kissed the inside of each thigh. "Do you want more?" She pulled her legs back to his side, then rested her head on his belly.

"I like being on top." Her voice sounded weak as if her heart was sick. But the strong, pounding rhythm surging through her veins reassured her it was not.

He stroked her hair from crown to shoulder. "That's not what I meant when—"

"No?" Her interest piqued. "What did you mean?" She rose up on her knees.

"Maybe we should save it for another time," he said. "You're probably pretty tired."

"No. Show me." She didn't add that there might not be another time. After a day like this one, she didn't want to take "another time" for granted.

"Then you better let me take care of this first." He slid his legs over the side of the bed and reached inside the nightstand. "I doubt if I can hold it much longer."

Once he had applied the condom, he instructed her how to straddle him. This time facing his head, not his feet. With his help, she eased herself down, taking him slowly inside. Hank understood her urge to move. His hands guided her hips in a rocking motion. Soon she took over the rhythm and continued the motion until the internal tension built again, higher and higher. Just as the sensation peaked, Hank gripped her tight and held her still. Waves of passion washed across his face. She was powerful, sexy and very, very satisfied.

After a moment, Hank pulled her down for a kiss. He locked his arms around her. She rested her head on his chest. "I like being on top," she whispered.

"I can tell," he whispered back. "But I need you to move." She slowly raised her body from his, then slid to his side. He pulled the cover up over her shoulder, then kissed her cheek. "I'll be right back," he said, before heading into the bathroom. She closed her eyes and waited for the tilt of the mattress and the return of his delicious warmth.

03ഐ80

The alarm clock jarred them both awake. Hank reached and pounded the irritating thing into silence. "You go back to sleep. I need to go into work."

"No!" Panic jolted her more than the electric alarm. She grabbed his arm. "I don't want you to go."

"I don't want to go either, Angel, but I'm expected. If I don't show, it might signal the bad guys that something is up."

"You think it's someone at Hayden, don't you?" He nodded. She collapsed back on the pillow. "So do I."

"You stay here," he insisted. "If someone is trying to scare you off, let's let them think they've succeeded. That should stop these attacks. I need to talk to Wilson about taking that physical inventory." He kissed her. "I'll make some excuse and come back early. You'll be safe here. I'll check all the locks. You just stay and get some sleep. You had a late night."

"You did too," she said, a smile spreading at the memory. He kissed her, hard. The thick male length of him stiffened against her thigh. Her hand began a slow exploratory venture down his side, but he caught it in his.

"Hmmmm..." He groaned deep in his chest. "Tonight," he whispered, caressing her ear with his warm breath. "Tonight, Angel, we'll have more time. Get some rest while you can."

She feigned sleep while he dressed and left the room. Once she heard the garage door close, she hopped out of bed. Slumber could wait until her safety wasn't at issue. After her shower, she dressed in her wrinkled clothes from yesterday and took her morning regiment of pills. She walked around the silent house. Now what? She couldn't just sit and wait for Hank's return. She needed to occupy her mind, work with her hands, do something constructive.

"I shouldn't have left everything at the office," she muttered to herself. Of course without a computer, research would be difficult, unless....

She wandered back to Hank's office. Sure enough, a flip of a switch and a fully equipped workstation sprang to life with beeps, whirls, and flashing lights. The main menu displayed an icon linking into Hayden's system. Perfect. All she needed was a password and she'd be in business. She telephoned Hank.

"Somehow I knew you wouldn't listen to reason and go back to sleep."

"I would have but all the warmth left with you."

"Are you cold? The thermostat is in the great room on the far side of the fireplace."

She laughed. "Thank you, but that's not what I meant. Listen, I'd like to do some research on the web, but I need a password." He gave her one. "How about for the company dial-up?" He gave her another. "One last thing, can you bring home the papers I left in Owens's office? I think I can finish what I started using your setup."

"Is everything else all right? Have you talked to the vet?"

"My next call."

"Stay safe, Angel. I'll be home soon."

The vet wanted to keep Oreo another twenty-four hours. She was progressing well, but she shouldn't be moved just yet. Angie agreed and gave permission for her to stay. She glanced at her watch. It might be a bit early, but she had to call her brother sometime.

"Stephen? It's Angie."

The phone receiver erupted with shouting. She moved it away from her ear. "What in the world is going on? Mom says someone shot Oreo and you had an accident. Now she can't stay in her own house. She's staying here. What the hell is—"

"Slow down. I can't answer if—"

"Where are you? Are you at home? Is Mom there?"

"I'm okay, Stephen. I'm staying at Hank's place. You remember, you picked me up from here about a month ago."

"No you're not. I'll be there in five minutes. Then I'll find that sonofabitch and I'll..."

"Stop it-- Hank is helping me."

Stephen snorted. "No offense, little sister, but you don't have the experience to deal with a man like that. You can stay here with Mom until this whole thing blows over."

"No. I'm a big girl now. I make my own decisions." Her whole body shook with her proclamation. "I choose to stay."

"You could have called me last night. You didn't need to run off with a stranger." Hurt resonated in his voice. She hadn't realized how much he relished his big brother role. She softened her voice.

"I know I can always call you. But Hank was already there." Before he could utter another insult, she hurried on. "He's a good man, Stephen. He's not a stranger. I won't listen to you say bad things about him." That stopped him. "I just wanted to let you know that I'm all right."

He sighed. "That's all I care about, Angie."

"Thanks, Stephen. Thanks for caring. Just care enough to let me grow up."

"I'm not sure I'm ready for that. I may need some time to adjust."

"Fine. And while you're adjusting," she said in a lighthearted tone. "I had the Civic towed to Classic Limo. Can you check it out for me?"

"Sure. First thing. Where can I reach you?"

She gave him Hank's number and expressed her thanks. Stephen reluctantly agreed to deliver a suitcase of clothes to carry her over for a few days. Time to get to work. She'd barely hung up the phone, when it rang. She froze. It could be Hank or her mother, but then it could also be the shooter trying to find her. The phone jangled its fourth discordant ring.

"Henry Renard. Leave your name, number and a short message."

Concise. Direct. In charge. So like Hank. The caller hung up. Hank or her mom would have left a message. Better let the machine pick up any and all calls, just to be safe. Preferring not to be disturbed, she turned the ring volume down and headed back to Hank's home office.

With a little help from Max, she received a faxed copy of their original audit workpaper. Engrossed in tracing shipping documents, she jumped at the sound of the doorbell. Must be Stephen with the suitcase.

"Just a minute." She clicked onto the next screen and jotted down a note. The doorbell chimed again.

She walked to the front door, "Hold your horses, I'm coming."

With one hand already releasing the lock, she checked the peephole. Her heart sank. Raymond waited outside.

Chapter Twenty-One

For a man who thrived on stress, Hank was having a helluva time concentrating on business. He'd tried to call Angel several times this morning, and each time the machine answered. Smart girl to screen calls, but then why wasn't she returning his messages? Was she even there? His gut twisted, then relaxed. Classic Limo had her car. She couldn't go anywhere. But what if she was hurt? What if she couldn't answer the phone because something had happened? What if...?

"Maybe we should discuss this when you can stay focused." Tom Wilson gathered up the papers he had brought in for Hank's review.

"I'm sorry. What were you saying?"

"I was saying that this is the worst possible time to do an inventory count. The warehouse is hopping with that sales promotion. We could lose business if we shut down for the day. And you and I both know that won't help the bottom line."

"God, I am so sick of hearing about 'the bottom line'. If we can't figure out how to stop the hemorrhaging, neither one of us will have to worry about the bottom line again. We'll both be out of a job."

"Maybe not both of us."

Hank glanced up. "What do you mean by that?"

"Nothing, nothing." Tom straightened his papers. "Hayden's been here for forty years. I don't think it's going to disappear overnight."

Hank snorted, surprising himself. When did he pick up that habit? "You have personnel. Find enough people to count.

I'll call Falstaff. We're going to count that inventory if it's my last official act as CEO."

As soon as Wilson left, the phone rang. Hank picked up, hoping it would be Angela. It wasn't.

"You bastard. What have you done to my sister?"

"What happened? Is she hurt?"

"She better not be or there won't be enough of you left to make a bowl of chowder."

"Slow down, cowboy. Angela was just fine when I left this morning. Has something happened?" The knots in his stomach clenched tighter.

"That was no accident yesterday. Her brake line was cut."

On some level, he wasn't surprised. The failing brakes combined with the shooting were too coincidental not to be related.

"Did you hear me?" The phone blasted in his ear. "Someone's trying to kill her, dammit!"

"Which is why I didn't want her to stay at her house." Hank fought to keep his voice calm and rational. "Whoever this is, they obviously know where she lives."

"And you think hiding out at your place is enough protection? I've been trying to call her for a good hour, but I keep getting your damn machine."

"Yeah, I've been getting the same."

"I sent Raymond out to check on her. She shouldn't be alone. You know, nothing like this ever happened to her before you came on the scene."

"If you think I'm responsible in any way for—"

"I don't know what to think. I just know nothing better happen to my little sister or someone's gonna pay." *Click.*

Stephen's threat made it perfectly clear who the *someone* would be. Hank replaced the receiver. Not that he blamed Stephen. He had a powerful urge to do bodily harm as well. He just didn't have a face to connect to his brutal punishment. Stephen was right about one thing. Angela shouldn't be alone.

"Mr. Renard, I was just coming to see you about—"

In a Heartbeat

"Later, Cathy." He grabbed his coat and headed toward the door. "I don't know if I'll be back this afternoon. If it's an emergency, leave a message on my machine."

ଓଚ୦ଓ

"Raymond. What are you doing here?"

"Stephen asked me to deliver this." He held up the suitcase her mother had used on her Florida trip. "And he wanted me to stay so you wouldn't be...alone." His gaze crawled the length of her, lingering, assessing.

Angie suppressed a shudder and reached for the suitcase. "Thank you for bringing this, but you don't have to stay. It really isn't necess—"

With a sharp twist, he jerked the suitcase back, causing her to practically wrap herself around him to keep her balance. She glanced up. A sickening smile curled his lips. "Stephen said you'd be difficult. He said I should insist."

She straightened without the suitcase, her ankle complaining from the awkward twisting. "Come in, then."

He passed her in the entry way and she glanced longingly at the crisp, clear day, hesitant to close the door.

"You should lock it," he said behind her. She looked at him, confused. "The door. You should lock it. There's lots of crazies out there."

And how do I know you're not one of them? She purposefully left it unlocked.

"This is a nice hiding place, Short Stuff." He dropped the suitcase on the sofa before walking across the room to the sliding glass door. "Not a lot of unnecessary clutter. Not a lot of froufrou plants." He pushed back the heavy drapes as if he owned the place, then peered out into the yard beyond. "I almost feel that I've been here before." He spun on his heel to face her. "There's a name for that, isn't there? When you feel like you've been somewhere before."

"Déjà vu?"

"That's right. Déjà vu." He smiled as if she had solved one of the world's great mysteries. She supposed the expression was

243

meant to be flattering, but it made her...uncomfortable. He took a few steps closer. "I experience déjà vu with people sometimes, as if I met them in a dream, or in another life. Does that ever happen to you?"

"I suppose it happens to everyone. That's why there's a name for it." She felt the tabletop behind her, searching for a book or some heavy object to discourage him from coming closer. Her hands came up empty. He stood no more than an arm's length away.

He laughed. "How true. But I'm particularly interested in you. Do you ever feel you've met someone, say like me, before? Especially in light of..." He dragged a finger slowly down her chest, tracing the scar beneath her too thin shirt.

She shuddered, pushing his finger away. "Stephen shouldn't have told you about that."

"I understand. You're uncomfortable that I know these things." His eyes gleamed.

Stepping around him, she crossed the room, anxious to put distance between them.

"Aren't you the brave one?" he said, nodding to the sliding glass door. "I heard someone took a potshot at you last night. You'd make a great target through that window."

She yanked the drapes shut. "You're the one who opened them."

"I'm sorry. I didn't mean to upset you." At least he looked contrite. "Why do you suppose someone wants to kill you?"

She almost missed it. The slight curl of his lip, the spark that lit up his eyes. He was enjoying this! She took a few steps back.

"I'm fine here by myself. I think you should leave."

"But your brother insisted that I stay. I'm your protector. You should be grateful." He walked into the kitchen and began to inspect the contents of the cabinets. "Coffee?" he asked.

"I'd be grateful if you left." She walked to the front door. "I'll explain everything to Stephen."

He pulled Hank's professional quality butcher knife from a wooden block, obviously ignoring her not-too-subtle suggestion. Testing the point with his finger, he smeared the resulting bubble of blood between his thumb and his forefinger. A smile pulled at his lips. He never even flinched, Angie realized, alarms going off in her head.

The door opened behind her. She jumped, her hand instinctively covering her heart.

"You should keep this door locked," Hank said, stepping over the threshold. "You never know..."

The rest of his words were lost as she practically leapt into his arms.

"Had I known I would get this reception, I'd have come back earlier." His voice warmed her ear and soothed her pulse. "Hi," he said, facing the kitchen. "Stephen told me I'd find you here. Thanks for watching over Angie. I can take it from here."

"I can stick around a bit. In case you need to leave or something. I can—"

"I said, I can handle it. I'm sure Stephen can use you back at Classic." The stern rumbling of his words vibrated against her cheek, making her feel secure.

She didn't turn to watch Raymond depart, even as she heard his footsteps approaching. She clutched Hank's back tighter, wishing she could melt into him, hide within his bones.

"I'll see you later," Raymond said, passing her. She knew he hadn't meant Hank. An icy tremor shook her spine.

"Are you okay?" Hank asked, pushing her back to arm's length.

She shook her head. "There's something about that man... I just don't feel comfortable around him."

"Well, he's gone now. How about you sit down, and I'll bring you a cold drink."

"No. I'm in the middle of a project. I'd like to see it through." She walked back to his office, knowing he'd follow.

"What did you find?"

"You know how we talked about how someone might be scared that I was too close to something they didn't want discovered?"

"Like the inventory in that warehouse on Ritchton Street?"

"Maybe...or maybe it's something right under our noses." She ruffled through a stack of papers. "I had Max fax me a copy of the testing we did on accounts payable, where we first encountered direct ships." She handed the sheet over to Hank.

"So?" He glanced at the spreadsheet.

"First, I checked out the names of the companies sending direct ships to that warehouse with the Secretary of State. I could find a listing for all the vendors except one, Timone Industries. If the sample on that spreadsheet is accurate, Timone is the biggest supplier to the warehouse."

"Timone... What do they sell?"

"According to their invoices, it's some part with lots of letters and numbers." Her voice rose in pitch. "The thing is, I don't think they supply us with anything."

"What do you mean?"

"Think about it, Hank. The merchandise isn't shipped to one of our warehouses, so there's no receiving report prepared. So what if someone *said* they shipped merchandise but they really didn't. Then, they send us an invoice..."

"A dummy invoice," Hank supplied.

"Right, Hayden pays it and someone gets money for nothing."

"Not a bad scheme."

"An extremely lucrative scheme," Angela modified. "Look at this." She pointed to his computer screen. "Before I left work yesterday, I built this spreadsheet showing how much we paid to all the different vendors for the last three years, this year, and year-to-date."

"When did you do this? I've been asking for a similar report and was told Data Processing was still working on it."

"All the information was in Hayden's computer. You just have to know how to tap in to get it out." She looked up at Hank. "Who told you data processing was working on it?"

"Tom Wilson"

"And who approves checks to Timone Industries?"

Tom Wilson. They both knew the answer to that one. "But the accounts payable clerks approve the direct ship invoices for payment. Are you suggesting they're in on this dummy invoice thing too?"

"All the clerks do on direct ships is match the invoice to the purchase order to make sure the stuff was ordered and the prices and quantities are correct. If everything matches up, they approve the invoice."

"So the real perpetrator may not be Tom Wilson at all. It's someone in the purchasing department."

Angela recalled her interview with Pete Burroughs, the little man with the terminally ill daughter, and hoped she was wrong.

"What else have you got?" Hank asked.

"I searched property records for the owners of the Ritchton warehouse."

"How do you know how to do all this?" Hank stared at her with a degree of awe.

"Stay confined to a bed for years on end and see how proficient you become with a keyboard and a modem."

"So what did you find?"

"It's a real estate company, Truman and Gabriel Real Estate. They own lots of property in that end of town." She picked up the phone and stared dialing.

"Now what are you doing?"

"Stephen? Yeah, it's me. I wonder if you can do me a favor?" She made a face into the receiver. "Hank's here. He sent Raymond back a few minutes ago." She paused, listening to her brother. She frowned. "No, Hank didn't tell me about the brakes. Listen, I need you to check something out for me. Can you find out who's renting a warehouse from Truman and Gabriel Real Estate? Yeah... The address is 2633 Ritchton... 2633, right. And Stephen? Be careful, okay?" After a moment, she hung up and glared at Hank.

"You didn't tell me my brake lines were cut."

"Does it make any difference at this point? Why do you think Stephen can find out who is renting that warehouse?"

"Stephen keeps telling me that when you own the biggest limousine service in town, you make lots of contacts. He comes in handy sometimes."

The phone rang. Hank picked it up on the first ring. "Hi, Cathy. No, it's okay. I told you to call me if..." He ran his fingers through his hair. "Isn't there anyone else there who can handle it? What happened to Wilson? I see. Okay. I'll be there... Tell him I'll be there in twenty minutes... Okay... Goodbye."

Hank looked at Angie. "I hate to leave you here alone. Especially, now that we've narrowed down the target of that bullet. But I have to go back."

"Be careful. Just because they've concentrated on me, doesn't mean they won't turn their attentions on you."

"That's true. I hadn't thought about that." He slipped on his coat.

"Hank. Is she worth it?"

"Who?"

"Elizabeth. Is she worth putting your life in danger?"

"I didn't come here for Elizabeth. She was just part of the deal. I came here to clear my reputation and pay back my family. Are you asking me if they're worth it?"

"No. I already know the answer to that one."

"Okay then, lock up behind me. Don't let any strangers in here. You know where to reach me if you need anything."

⊰✧⊱

"Angie, you won't believe who's renting that warehouse."

"You're calling from the limo, aren't you?" Angie replied. "You keep fading in and out."

"I'm on the highway, must be those overpasses. Listen, I talked to my contact and the company paying the rent checks is Timone Industries."

"Timone?"

"Yeah, I asked for an address and she said the checks only list a P.O. Box. Does that help?"

"That's great, Stephen." She wrote down the mailing address that he gave her, knowing full well it would match the address on the invoices. "Thanks. I'll get right on it."

She had hoped Stephen would uncover a person's name and a real street address. But that, she supposed, would be too easy. Fortunately, while she waited for Stephen's call, she had

In a Heartbeat

gone ahead and done some investigative work on Timone's post office box.

Post office boxes were located all over town, anywhere from supermarkets to satellite post office branches. She used the Internet to discover which post office would deliver mail to Timone's address. Then she called that post office to find the location of the box. In this case, the box was located inside the post office itself.

Now, how to discover the people behind Timone. If, as she suspected, Timone was a fictitious entity and the owners were connected to Hayden, then she should be able to recognize them if she could just flush them out. Right now, the only physical information she had on them was the location of their warehouse and their post office box.

"How do I know when they'll go to the post office?" she asked the computer screen. "What would they go there for?" She glanced at the spreadsheet lying next to the computer. The answer was obvious. "Money. They'd go to pick up checks."

Her fingers raced across the keypad. *Thank you, Hank*, she thought as his access code opened the accounts payable files. There might be a pattern to the payment schedule for Timone. If she could figure out when a check would be mailed...

"Well, duh..." She stared at the computer screen. Unlike the rest of the vendors, Timone's invoices were paid immediately. That alone should have raised a red flag. She scanned the list of payments. The last check was cut...yesterday. "Oh my God," she said, staring at the monitor. That check should be waiting in the post office box right now.

She stood to pace. What to do now? Call Stephen? No. He'd never drive her within fifty yards of a bad guy. He couldn't very well recognize any of the Hayden people by himself. Call Hank? No. He'd be noticed. She smiled. She'd notice him. Besides, he was tied up with something important or he'd never have left her. That left only one person.

But how could she get there? Stephen had her car at the shop. She spotted the trailing edge of a feather boa from Elizabeth's discarded nightgowns draped over a chair across the hall. She smiled. Elizabeth.

Everything was proceeding as planned, better than planned, she thought as she sat behind the wheel of Elizabeth's fire engine red corvette. She smiled. No one would imagine sheltered little Angela Blake behind the wheel of such a sporty, adventurous car. She had found the keys under the floor mat. Now she almost wished someone familiar, though non-Hayden related, would come along, just so she could show off the wheels.

Even though she had been sitting in the car for two hours, her heart still pumped adrenaline every time a new car pulled into the lot. She'd already scoped out the location of the actual box. Box 269 was almost disappointing in its lack of individuality. A smallish box, located in the midst of a bank of smallish boxes, all displaying the same metallic fronts and sequential numbers.

Who would have thought that such a plain, boring box could hide a fraud scheme costing Hayden hundreds of thousands of dollars? Angela checked her watch. The sign posted above the boxes indicated that the mail had already been distributed. Hayden's check should be resting comfortably in one of those metal pigeonholes. Her stomach growled, it was almost one o'clock. She should have packed a lunch along with the plastic bottles of water. She drank those sparingly as the post office didn't offer public bathrooms, and she didn't want to risk missing her prey if she hurried off in pursuit of one.

A car pulled in the post office driveway. Angie watched the car's progress in her rear view mirror. It looked familiar, but after several hours of watching cars, they all had familiar qualities. Still there was something about the determined set of the driver. The car pulled into a parking spot two cars down from her own. She squished down in the bucket seat, hoping to be less conspicuous. A man got out of the car and turned briefly in her direction. Tom Wilson! She knew it. Satisfaction couldn't cancel out the effect of the adrenaline pulsing through her system. Tom turned and headed for the post office's main door.

The fact that Tom was here was not enough proof. He could be here on Hayden business. After Tom entered the building,

Angela slipped out of the red monster and followed. She would have to see him open the box and physically remove the check.

The post office had three alcoves dedicated to the metal boxes. TImone's box was in the second one. She could walk down the hallway, past the second alcove, and hope Wilson's interest centered on the box's contents, and not on people. It was all a matter of timing. She walked slowly towards the first alcove, affording Wilson enough time to find his key and open the door. She walked purposefully by the opening to the second alcove. A quick glance to her right confirmed her suspicions. Wilson pulled an envelope out of the box. She had him. She had...

"Angela Blake." Angie jerked her head in time to see Suzy Schaffer, ex-high school cheerleader and former next-door neighbor. "How are you? I haven't seen you in ages."

Of all times to have her wish to see non-Hayden people answered. Angie could feel Tom's glaring gaze boring into her back. "Hello, Suzy. I didn't expect to see you here."

"Was that you in that red corvette out front? I thought it was you, but it's been so long."

Angie heard the tiny metal door slam. With her peripheral vision, she saw Wilson turn her way.

"You know it's so good to see you up and walking and everything," Suzy chatted on. "I always felt so bad when you were confined to that bed."

"Hello, Angela." Tom stepped to her side. "I thought you were home sick today."

"Uh-oh, busted." Suzy gave her a sympathetic look. "I better be going. Say hi to your mom and Stephen for me." She smiled. "Especially Stephen."

Angie twisted her lips in a parody of a smile before turning to Tom. "I guess you caught me playing hooky. Do me a favor. Don't tell Hank that you saw me."

"Hmm.... And you're here for...?"

"Stamps." She answered quickly, remembering that a self-service stamp machine resided at the end of the hallway. "With my ankle, it hurts to wait in lines at the window." She made to walk past him toward the machines when she saw the "out of order" sign. "Shoot."

"Did that young lady say you're driving a red corvette?"

"I had an accident a few nights ago and a friend lent me their car."

"Nice friend."

"Yes." She agreed, turning toward the main entrance, anxious to escape the awkward conversation.

"That looks a lot like Elizabeth's car."

"Does it? I wouldn't know." She pushed the front door.

"Aren't you forgetting something?"

She paused.

"Stamps?"

"Thanks." She stepped aside. "I almost forgot."

"That surprises me, Angela." His lips twisted in a light sneer. "I get the impression you don't forget much." He let the door close in her face and walked briskly to his car. While Angie watched through the front plate glass windows, his car roared to life and backed out of the parking space much too fast for safety. It sped down the main street, burning rubber toward Hayden. Once back in Elizabeth's car, she picked up the car phone to call Hank and tell him of her discovery.

"Put that down." A voice said from the back seat. She replaced the handset and swerved to look behind her. A not too steady gun barrel slanted up at her.

"Mr. Burroughs?"

"Turn around and face the front." She did as she was told. "I don't want to use this, Angie, but I will if I have to."

"But why...?"

"Because you went and stuck your nose into things that didn't concern you. Now start the car and drive to the freeway and no funny stuff." His voice, rising from the floor of the back seat, held more confidence than the hand holding the gun.

"I'll do what—"

"No talking," he hissed. "I don't want anyone poking around, looking to see who you're talking to. Now drive."

She pulled Elizabeth's convertible out of the parking lot and turned in the opposite direction from Hayden. Glancing in the rearview mirror, she saw a police cruiser several cars behind her. She jerked the wheel in a sharp turn and aimed the car for the curb until the sight of a looming telephone pole caused her to correct. The muzzle of the gun poked into her side.

"You have a death wish, Angie? I said no funny stuff. You get pulled over and I'll shoot you first, then the cop. Got that?" The gun pushed painfully into her ribs. She nodded.

She didn't think Burroughs could fire an incompetent clerk much less purposely kill someone. Still a discharge from a gun could do more damage than Burroughs bargained for. She glanced in the rearview mirror. The cruiser turned off into a strip mall parking lot. Damn! Her heart thudded against her ribcage.

She glanced to her right. Her purse, with the cell phone inside, lay almost in reach. If she could nonchalantly just reach over and...

"Leave it," he said. "And keep your eyes on the road."

"Why you, Pete?" she asked, glancing quickly at the metal under her elbow. "I never imagined you'd be a part of this."

"I said no talking. Don't you do anything you're told?"

"Relax. No one pays any attention to people talking to themselves in cars. I could be singing, or on a phone call, or..."

"Shut up and drive. Get on the freeway heading south."

She turned onto the entrance ramp and merged with the traffic. The wind caused by the rapidly accelerating car blocked out the sound of any conversation. She saw Burroughs's face in the rear view mirror. He hunched forward in the backseat, the gun never more than a few inches away.

"Turn off at Riverview, then take Ritchton." If there had been any doubts before, his words confirmed their destination.

Once they arrived at the warehouse, he signaled her to exit the car. She reached across the seat to grab her purse.

"I said leave it," he snarled.

"But my medicines. I can't—"

He poked the gun in her side. "Worry about this, not your purse."

He hustled her inside. Once her eyes adjusted to the dark interior, she noticed crates and corrugated boxes stacked haphazardly.

"You've been busy," she commented.

"No thanks to you," he snarled. "I've been bringing stuff in ever since Renard started making noise about a physical. That was your idea, wasn't it?"

"What are you going to do with me?" She looked around for an avenue to escape. Besides the narrow door they had come through and the closed receiving bay, there were two windowless doors along the back wall. He marched her to one of them.

Burroughs fished in his pockets, then slipped a key into a grimy lock. He pulled the door open, releasing a foul smell of stale urine and mildew. The stench alone made her gag.

"In there." He shoved her into the dark, dank closet. The door scraped shut. The lock clicked.

She spun around, pounding the door with both fists. "Let me out of here. I can't stay in this place. Let me out!" She pressed her nose by the crack in the door, hoping some fresh air might displace the fetid interior. The rancid air pressed in on her with a weight of its own, much like a casket, much like death. "Please, Pete," her voice broke. "I'm scared."

"There's a light switch by the door. You might as well quiet down 'cause you're going to be there awhile."

Footsteps retreated. "No! Come back." She pounded some more. "Don't leave me here! I need my pills." The far door slammed with finality. She was trapped in this hell on earth. "Please, come back," she whimpered.

Her fingers slid down the sticky surface of the wall until they dragged over a light switch. With a flip, her consigned hell flooded with light and the rusty rattle of a long unused ventilation fan. A grimy stained toilet commanded one corner of the tiny room. An equally disgusting sink and filth-covered mirror filled out the back wall. She looked around, hoping one of the outside dirt-caked windows opened to the bathroom. No such luck. Her prison had four scum-encrusted walls, not much larger than her bedroom closet.

In a Heartbeat

With horror, she glanced at a sticky black residue on her hands where she had pounded the door. Germs must thrive in this cesspool. Stumbling over to the sink, she turned the faucets. Brown water trickled out, adding flecks of rust to the stained basin. Once the water began to clear, she thrust her hands under the cold stream. With some difficulty, she chiseled away the dusty, dried sliver of soap cemented to the sink. She swiped her hands on her jeans rather than risk the stiff towel lying on the floor. Fortunately, the fan lessened the sharp ammonia smell, but nothing helped the appearance of the bathroom.

She kicked the gray towel to a spot near the door. A mouse dashed out from its folds. Angie shrieked, pressing herself tight against the sink. The rodent sought safety along the floorboards. Her pulse pounded in her ears. She willed herself to calm the frantic pace. "Relax," she said, her voice lost in the rattle of the overhead fan.

The mouse itself disappeared, but the floor bore witness to its frequent visits. She stomped on the gray rag, before using it with her foot to swipe a small area on the floor. Dust and dirt scattered in all directions. She sneezed repeatedly, then sat, touching as little of the floor as possible.

"Hello?" she yelled. Shoot. With the fan on, she wouldn't be able to hear footsteps when Pete came back. *If* he came back. She shuddered. With the ruckus overhead, no one would be able to hear her call for help.

Tears flowed freely down her cheeks. She didn't bother to swipe them away. Someone had to come back for her. They had to. She couldn't survive otherwise. And when they did, she would need to hear them coming. Her enemies already had advantages. They didn't need surprise on their side as well. She glanced up to the ceiling fan/light.

Someone had to come. Someone had to hear her call for help. Her fingers reached up to the light switch. She bit her lip, and after one last look at the path of the mouse, switched the lights off.

CRSOR

Tom Wilson's smile disappeared moments after leaving the personnel department. Something was up and he was willing to bet that Angela's sudden appearance at the post office had something to do with it. He walked up to Cathy's cubicle where he knew a half-full decanter of coffee would be sitting on a burner. How much did Hank know? Tom emptied some of the pot into a mug. What was Angela doing at that post office? Was she on to them? Absently, he pondered the possibilities while Cathy efficiently fielded phone calls. She turned towards him,

"Mr. Wilson? I have Pete Burroughs on the line. He's trying to track you down. He says it's important that he talk directly to you, no messages."

Tom nodded before swallowing the hot liquid. "Can you put it in the conference room? Thanks, and can you tell Hank when he's off the phone that I'll be just a few more minutes. Thanks, hon."

Great. With everything else on his plate, his nervous nellie of a co-conspirator required handling again. He closed the conference room door. "What's up?"

"I've got her locked up, that's what. But I don't know what to do with her."

"Who? Who have you got locked up?" Tom gripped the phone receiver tighter, a sinking feeling in his stomach.

"Angela Blake, that nosey auditor. She saw you at the post office this afternoon, so I grabbed her before she could blab what she knows."

"Calm down, Pete." Although the words did nothing to calm the sudden churning in Tom's stomach. "Where are you?"

"I'm at Timone. I've got Angela locked in a bathroom. What do you want me to do with her?"

"Now's a fine time to ask," he growled. "You should have thought about that before you kidnapped her."

"So what do I do?"

"Do I have to think of everything? Just...just leave her there." He mopped his forehead. "Are you sure she can't escape?"

"Yeah, I'm sure."

In a Heartbeat

"Good. I need some time to think. Come back here and we'll talk."

"What about her car? It's pretty snazzy, somebody will see it here."

"Then get rid of it."

"How?"

"What do I care? Just do it then get back here before people start asking questions." He slammed the receiver down and allowed himself a few moments to compose himself. Any possibility of hiding his tracks from future scrutiny had vanished. Burroughs's actions confirmed that nosey bitch's suspicions. What other possible motivation would explain kidnapping and detaining an auditor? And Pete would crack under pressure. No doubt about it.

Over the last few years, Timone had generated hundreds of thousands of tax-free income. He and Burroughs could have quietly shut it down, waited a few years before starting up another phony company, if that auditor had minded her own business. But not now...

An idea crept through his panic. Why not just shut everything down? No one else showed any interest in Timone Industries. With Angela out of the picture, no one else knew about the payout scheme. He could quietly pull the plug until the whole business was forgotten. People disappeared every day. A smile grew on his face. What's one more, more or less? He straightened his tie, collected his papers and opened the conference door.

೧೩೮೦೮೦

The miniscule light that had leaked under the locked door had faded. Her stomach had ceased its loud protestations of hunger hours ago and resigned itself to lack of sustenance. Angie glanced at the phosphorous dots on her wristwatch. Nine o'clock. She didn't need to place her hand over her heart to know it was beating. Its fierce pounding shook her entire body. The heavy air made it difficult to breathe, difficult to take deep breaths. Even her dark-adjusted eyes couldn't find a hand in front of her face. She might as well close her eyes as keep them open.

The lack of light accentuated the sounds and smells of the prison. What she'd give for that can of Lysol tucked away in her car. The smells were bad, but the sounds... She never imagined how many sounds existed in an isolated room in an abandoned warehouse. The tremble of air in the water lines, an occasional drip, and periodically the soft scurry of tiny feet.

A few times, she felt her way to the basin and splashed the brackish water on her face to keep her alert. She even succumbed to drinking some of the foul stuff.

Through it all, her mind kept slipping back to the ones who had often offered assistance in the past. How she wished they were here now. Stephen, her mother, Hank. Most especially Hank. She should have listened. She should have stayed behind locked doors. But no, she had to prove to them all how capable she was. How independent she was. She didn't need anyone's help...until now. A trickle of tears cleared a path down her cheek. She was hesitant to brush the tears away with her filthy hands and risk inviting more germs into her respiratory system. That thought almost brought a laugh. As if it mattered if she got an infection. Burroughs probably wouldn't let her live to see a tissue, much less the people she loved.

The people she loved. She wanted to say so much to them, now that she physically couldn't. In this hellhole she didn't even have one of her mother's quilts to cling to. She never told her mother how much those quilts meant to her. And Stephen. What would he do without her to preach to and bully? He'd probably have "I told you so" inscribed on her tombstone. At least now he could get on with his own life. Marry the girl of his dreams and build a family. Same with Hank. A shiver shook her spine. Hank would be able to marry his model and father beautiful children. A sob caught in her throat. She pictured his face, recalled his scent, felt his touch. The trail of tears became a torrent. Her shoulders shook with each agonized gasp. She never told him she loved him, never wanted to be that vulnerable. Now he'd never know.

Through her sobs, she thought she heard glass shattering.

"Hello?" she cried. "Is anyone there?" She pounded on the door. "Can you hear me? I'm locked in this room. Can you help me?" She screamed and banged louder.

There was no response, just the scurry of tiny feet on the opposite side of the room. "Hello?" she called without any real force.

Death had never scared her before. She had faced that possibility too often to be afraid of it, but now it was different. Before she had never felt truly alive. Now...now that she had known what it was to love, to feel passion, she wasn't willing to surrender to death. Hank. If only she could see him one more time, feel his breath on her cheek, feel him surging inside her. This was the regret. Leaving the one she loved behind.

Hours passed. The cold concrete beneath her cheek hummed with a faint vibration. An engine maybe...a car? She held her breath so the ragged sound wouldn't distort her hearing. She tried to sit up. The effort took all her strength. She tried to call out for help, but only a dull hoarse rasp issued from her dry, cracked lips. Footsteps. Someone was coming.

"Angie. I'm going to open the door. I've got a gun. Don't try anything." Burroughs's voice filtered through the door.

As if she could. That stiff, rank poor excuse for a towel had more strength than she did. She suspected the slow motion echoing of thoughts was due to fever racing through her body. Without her doses of anti-rejection medicine, infection set in quickly.

"Maybe she's dead." The voice sounded like Tom Wilson. "If she is, it would make things a lot easier."

The door supporting her back fell away. She tumbled out into fresher air, smacking her head on the floor in the process. She tried to open her eyelids but they wouldn't budge.

"Angie, can you hear me?" A cold hand touched her cheek. "She's burning up."

"Damn. That means she's still alive."

"She needs a hospital." Arms slipped around her back and under her legs.

"A hospital? Are you nuts? We want to kill her, not save her. If we just dump her in the reservoir, she'll die without any ties to us."

In a clumsy, awkward movement, someone lifted her. Her legs and arms dangled in the air and her head lolled to one side. A memory stirred. Someone else had carried her before. Different then. Strong, muscular, caring. "Hank," she murmured.

"She's awake. I'm taking her to a doctor," Burroughs said. "You told me no one would get hurt when I agreed to go along with this thing. You said no one would find out."

"No one will find out if she disappears. We wouldn't have to do this if you hadn't kidnapped her in the first place. Now I have to clean up after your mess, and I will. Just put her down."

By the jostling, she guessed the one carrying her was moving.

"Put her down, Burroughs. I've got your gun. I'm warning you."

"You'd shoot me? Just like that, you'd..." Her rescuer turned abruptly. A shot rang out and the floor smacked her back and thighs. A sharp pain ripped through her arm. Something softer than the floor but equally uncomfortable cushioned her head. Her thin grip on the conscious world slipped away.

Chapter Twenty-Two

Hank pounded his fist into a ball of dough, sending tiny floury clumps to the ceiling. Where the hell was she? He folded the flattened dough in half and turned it.

"I told her to stay here. I told her to keep the door locked. But did she listen?" His fist ground into the yeasty mass until his knuckles scraped the counter. He had called Stephen the minute he returned home and found Elizabeth's car missing. Stephen had no answers. That bodyguard he had assigned to Angie never returned. Hank called the police and recited the litany of threats and accidents. They promised to look out for the car and call him the minute they heard anything.

Pacing hadn't helped him work out frustrations. He was afraid to go out looking for her in case she came back. He was about to start pounding the walls when he thought of dough instead.

Bam! Not that this mess would ever see the inside of an oven. Bam! The pot in the coffeemaker bounced on the hot plate.

The phone rang as his fist was in mid-descent. He grabbed it before the second ring. "Did you find her?"

"Mr. Renard, it's Mrs. Blake. Angela's mother."

His breath caught in his throat. She was too calm for someone whose daughter was missing.

"Mr. Renard, are you there?"

"Yes. I'm sorry. Did you—"

"The police just called. Angela has been taken to OSU Hospital. We're on our way now."

"Has she been hurt? What happened?"

"I've told you all I know. I'll know more once I'm at the hospital. I just thought you should know."

He didn't know if he said goodbye, or just hung up on the poor woman. He ran for his car and sped toward the medical complex. It wasn't until he noticed the bits of dough and flour clinging to the steering wheel that he realized he hadn't stopped to wash his hands.

After parking the car, he ran into the hospital and found his way to the Intensive Care Unit. Two pairs of eyes turned toward him in the hallway outside the ICU.

"You've got a lot of nerve coming here." Stephen started toward him. "If it hadn't been for you, Angela wouldn't be fighting for her life right now."

His throat squeezed tight, making each breath painful. "Fighting for her life?" He looked at the two drawn faces in the hallway. "Can someone tell me what happened?"

"They found her at a warehouse with two of your people. She's been shot. One man is dead. The other has a bullet in him. Must have been a real blood bath."

"Angela's been shot? Is it serious? Do the police know who—"

"There's more to it." Mrs. Blake put a restraining hand on Stephen's arm. "You know of Angela's prior surgery?"

"You mean her heart?"

Mrs. Blake nodded. "The transplant saved her life but also made her extremely receptive to viruses. She needs to take medications every day, several times a day, to fool her body into accepting the new heart."

"Yes. I know all this."

"Then you realize how serious it is that she hasn't taken her medication. Plus, she picked up a bug that has escalated into a full viral infection. These things alone would land her in a hospital."

"Her body was trying to fight off that infection." Stephen picked up the conversation thread. "Then she was shot. If Angela doesn't make it. If she can't pull through, I'm going to --"

"Mr. Renard?"

They all turned to see a tall man in a brown sports jacket walk towards them. "Mr. Henry P. Renard of Hayden Industries?"

"That's me."

"I'm Detective Fisher with the Columbus Police." He quickly flashed a badge. "May I talk to you for a few minutes?" Hank agreed. "Let's go down this way then." Together they walked down the hall, out of earshot of the others.

"Mr. Renard, are you aware that two of your employees were shot earlier this morning at a warehouse belonging to Timone Industries?"

"Timone?" Damn, she must have decided to go investigating on her own. "Who was shot?"

The detective glanced down at his notes. "Thomas Wilson was found dead on the scene. Pete Burroughs is in surgery with a gunshot wound." The detective glanced at Hank. "Can you tell me what those two men were doing at Timone Industries, and what they were doing with Ms. Blake?"

"She was right." Hank muttered under his breath.

"Sir?"

"Angela...Ms. Blake suspected Wilson and someone else, probably Burroughs, of stealing from Hayden. She decided to investigate on her own." Hank stopped walking and turned to the detective. "But Angie would never shoot anyone. I don't understand why Burroughs and Wilson were shot."

"Is Ms. Blake your girlfriend, sir?"

Hank narrowed his eyes. *Girlfriend* sounded demeaning for all that Angela meant to him. "Why do you ask?"

"Do you own a gun, Mr. Renard?"

The question hit him hard in the stomach. "No. You think I had anything to do with this?"

The detective scribbled on a pad. "Easy enough to check." He glanced up. "I've got one gun and three bodies. The man holding the hardware sure didn't look like he committed suicide. I'm thinking maybe a jealous boyfriend..."

"That's ridiculous." Hank snarled. "I haven't been anywhere near that place." Down the hallway, the ICU door opened, and a doctor extended a hand towards Angela's mother. His stomach clenched. He should be there, learning about Angela's condition. But he was here with this—

"Where were you around midnight, Mr. Renard?"

"I was home calling the Westerville police every five minutes to see if they found Angela. Now, if we're finished here." He started to walk back towards Angela's family.

"Easy enough to check. Listen, Mr. Renard," the detective called to his back. "Don't go disappearing on us. We'll have more questions for you later."

"What did the doctor say?" he asked as soon as he reached Stephen and his mother. Stephen gathered his mother into a hug. Over her head, he glared at Hank. "The bullet passed through, but the blood loss is serious. They say the next twenty-four hours are crucial."

Hank's knees began to buckle, and he slumped against the wall. Cradling his head in his hands, he squeezed his eyes shut to quell the burning. Angie, his angel, could be dying just a few feet away.

"Can I see her?"

"No." Stephen replied sharply. "You're not family. You're not even wanted here. Haven't you done enough damage?"

"I need to see her."

"Well, she doesn't need you."

The truth of Stephen's words struck him in the gut. What did she need him for? He had taken her zest for life, taken her innocence, and given her nothing in return, all for some sham engagement. He pressed his hands tighter against his face, blotting the tears that gathered in the corners of his eyes. Stephen was right, who needed a loser like him?

Firm, gentle hands stroked his forearms. He looked over his fingertips. Compassionate blue eyes gazed up at him.

"She's unconscious now." Angie's mother patted his arm. "No one can see her. I know you want to help, but there's really nothing you can do here. There's nothing any of us can do, except pray. Angela has to fight this battle on her own." She took his hands in hers.

"I need to tell her..."

"Later, when she's stronger." She squeezed his hands. He took solace in that small embrace. "It will be a long wait before we know anything. Perhaps you'd like to freshen up?"

He glanced down at his flour-encrusted hands. He probably left a smeary mess on his face as well. "Yes, I'd like to do that...and maybe stop at the cafeteria. Can I bring you anything?"

She shook her head. Stephen didn't even acknowledge the offer. Hank walked back towards the elevators, searching for a restroom along the way.

CRSOSO

You'd think a hospital cafeteria would offer something larger than standard Styrofoam cups of coffee. He took a swallow and grimaced. What they lacked in volume, they made up for in strength.

"Mr. Renard?"

Hank turned to see a petite brown-haired woman clenching and unclenching her hands.

"I thought that was you. I'm Anita Burroughs, Pete's wife." She extended a shaky hand. "We met at your welcoming banquet. Remember?"

"Oh yes," he said, although he didn't remember her at all. All of his memories centered on a feisty, elfin chauffeur that caused him to be late for the reception. He shook her hand.

"I'm so sorry about what happened," she said. "Do you know how the girl is?"

"We're still waiting to hear. Her condition is not good."

"I'm sorry to hear that. The doctor said she saved Pete's life, in a way. If that bullet hadn't passed through her first, it could have killed my Pete."

Hank looked a little closer at the woman. "Do you have any idea what happened in that warehouse, Mrs. Burroughs?"

"You can call me Anita." She poured herself a cup of the hospital-strength coffee and doctored it with sugar and cream. "According to Pete, he was carrying that poor young woman when Tom Wilson threatened to shoot him. He turned and a gun fired. That's all he said."

"Why was he carrying Angela?" Memories of the times he had held Angela in his arms rushed forefront to his mind but he fought them back. He needed to listen without distraction.

"Angela, that's her name? I think he said she was sick, and he was taking her to the hospital."

"But why was he at that warehouse? Why was Angela? Did he say?"

"I only spoke with him for a few minutes before they took him for surgery." Her red-rimmed eyes squinted up at him. "Didn't you send him there?"

He shook his head.

"Then Pete will have to tell you that himself. I just don't understand." She frowned. "I thought Tom Wilson and he were friends. Why would he shoot Pete? Just because he wanted to take that girl to the hospital..." She shook her head. "Sometimes you just don't know people."

"Did Pete say who shot Tom Wilson?"

Her eyes widened. "Someone shot Tom? Pete didn't say anything about that. He said he was lucky to have pushed the nine-one-one button on his cell phone before he passed out."

"Mr. Renard." Detective Fisher approached the coffee machine. "I was told I might find a Mrs. Burroughs here. I wonder if you could direct me to—"

"This is Mrs. Burroughs." Hank made the introductions.

"Then, I wonder if Mrs. Burroughs and I might have a few words in private."

Hank excused himself and left.

He wasn't anxious to join Stephen in the ICU waiting room, but he couldn't very well leave the hospital. If there was a chance he could see Angela again, give her some of his strength, let her know he was waiting, then he had to stay. And if that meant putting up with false accusations, so be it. He left the cafeteria and walked the long hallway that led to a bank of elevators. On the way he passed a door with a wooden sign to the right. The chapel. A voice whispered in his head. *All we can do now is pray.*

In a Heartbeat

On impulse, he opened the door and stepped into the nearly deserted room. One woman knelt in the first wooden pew facing a stained-glass depiction of a wizened man surrounded by angels. *My mother put me in the protection of the angels.* He slipped into the last pew and sat. Flickering candles issued inviting warmth to the room, so different from the antiseptic atmosphere of the rest of the hospital. Imitating the woman in front of him, he slipped to his knees and bowed his head. *I don't know how to do this.* The woman in the front pew turned quickly to look back at him. Had he spoken out loud? Her face softened.

She stood and left the pew. As she passed him, she reached down and patted his shoulder. "Listen to your heart," she said, then continued on her way.

The chapel door closed with a soft click. He glanced up at the stained glass portrait.

"God, I'm probably doing this all wrong. I don't even know if you can hear me. I haven't been in a church since I was a boy. I'm probably not allowed to ask for anything." He clenched his hands tighter. "Let Angie live. Don't let her die."

You always want what you can't have. Angela's words pushed their way into his mind. He quickly amended his prayer.

"I'm not asking for me. Lots of people...even animals...love her, not just me."

You can't lie to God. He knows everything.

"Then He knows I love her." His own words surprised him. Words he had never admitted, but in his heart, knew were true. A clarity and strength filled him. Angela had to recover. She had to.

"Make her strong, God. Give her back to us. Give her back to me." His knuckles whitened. There had to be something more he could do. Something more he could offer. "If you let her live," he whispered. "I promise to believe."

It crossed his mind that he must believe already. Otherwise why was he here? Why did a tightness pull at his chest, and his heartbeat pound in his throat?

Someone else was in the chapel, an awareness pricked at the nape of his neck. He looked behind him and to the side but no one was there. He was alone.

He left the chapel and walked back to Intensive Care. Angela's mother sat alone in the waiting room, absently turning pages in a well-thumbed magazine.

"Where's Stephen?" he asked.

"I sent him home to pick up a few things. We're liable to be here awhile."

"Has there been any—"

"No. No change." She waved him off, "but that's a good sign. Every moment a doctor doesn't give us bad news is a good sign." Stress and strain ringed her eyes, but never touched her voice.

"I can see where Angela gets her optimism."

"I've been through this before." She sighed, then smiled. "I thought you went home for some rest."

"I got some coffee, then I visited the chapel."

She patted his leg. "Thank you."

They sat in silence a few more moments. Mrs. Blake studied him. "Would you like to see her?"

"Yes, of course, but how?"

He followed her through the door to the nurse's station. While she talked to the nurses, Hank looked beyond to a fragile figure on a nearby bed. Angela, pale, without her usual vibrancy, lay still among the beeping monitors and pumping machines. She needed him. She would never admit it, but she needed him.

"Sir, you can't go over there."

"Excuse me?" He stopped and looked back. He hadn't been aware of leaving the nurse's station.

"Your sister is very vulnerable to infection right now. You shouldn't go any closer."

"Vulnerable." He repeated in a daze. Of course she's vulnerable. She'd always been vulnerable.

"Hank, we should go." A hand tugged at his arm. "She needs to do this on her own."

The last time she did something on her own, it landed her in the ICU. He clenched his fists. "Not this time."

He allowed Angie's mother to lead him from the ward. But once outside in the hallway, he walked into the waiting room and settled into a sagging chair.

"Really, Hank, you might as well go home. There's nothing you can do."

"I can wait," he said, settling in. "I can be here for her. It may not sound like much. But it's everything to me."

She was weightless, yet anchored without restraint. A paradox, she noted briefly, one of many. Her senses were heightened in that she could see, but the parameters that normally restrict form kept shifting. Colors and patterns faded in and out. Muted sounds dimmed further and further. Memories of scents intrigued and confused. What kind of a world was this?

Was she standing? She couldn't feel the solid support of two legs beneath her, nor was she supported beneath her back. She thought about turning her head and the patterns shifted, even though she hadn't moved.

"Is that me?" The thought, not the words, resonated in her brain. Below, a tan blanket covered a pale, child-like body. The bed sheets had more vibrancy then the girl's skin; her lips tinged faintly blue as if frozen. Yet she wasn't, Angela realized. She was neither hot nor cold, nor was she in any pain. She just was, and it was wonderful.

Angela.

Did someone call? Her mind stretched to the melody of her name. An all-pervading calmness welcomed her. She had no questions, because she already had all the answers.

Are you ready to come home?

She knew home was not the tiny house on Plum Street. Nor was it Hank's house where she had experienced so many wonderful emotions.

Are you finished?

Contentment colored her thoughts. Indeed, all emotions were colors, this one a buttery rich yellow-peach. And freedom.

Freedom from pills and constant vigilance. Freedom from struggle and chest squeezing pain. Freedom from words and weighty concerns. Her thoughts were suddenly streaked with the lavender of a dawning morning.

Commotion beneath her chased away the colors. A man inched toward the bed. Hank... Her vision was much sharper than it had ever been before. Even from her hovering spot near the ceiling she could see every grief-drawn line in his face.

The colors faded to a smoky gray. His dark, sunken eyes had lost the vitality she remembered, replaced with a sorrow that caused an almost physical pain. Stubble, several days old, covered his jaw, a fine contrast to the ashen skin beneath. She longed to cup his cheek and soothe his worries. He needed comfort that only she could give.

His hand reached out and clasped that of the body on the bed. Rich vibrant warmth embraced her in streaks of velvet red and a deep fluid violet, the colors of love. She longed to entwine her fingers with his, give back some of the comfort he gave.

"Don't leave me, Angie. We haven't finished yet. I haven't told you..."

Angela, have you finished here?

She knew that he loved her. Her senses, so acute, told her so. She glanced at the still, pale figure on the bed. Life hurt in that world, not like her current concern-free state. The grief and pain on Hank's face dimmed the colors. If only she could tell him she loved him. If only --

Before Angela could finish the thought, she slipped back into the physical confines of her body. She couldn't lift her eyelids, couldn't even squeeze Hank's hand.

"Sir, I've told you before. You have to leave. You're not helping her," A woman's voice scolded.

Against the dry, scratchiness in her throat, Angie forced a whisper. It took every ounce of energy she possessed. "Won't leave."

An incredible fatigue racked her body, pulling her into a dreamless sleep.

"Did you hear? Did you hear what she said?" Hank massaged his thumb over her tear-dampened hand and hastily wiped his eyes.

"Sir, you're going to have to leave. Don't make me call security."

He kissed Angie's limp, lifeless hand. "You're going to pull through this and I'll be waiting. Thank you, God."

"Sir!" The nurse pulled urgently on his arm. "She needs her rest."

"Yes," He stood, feeling stronger. "Let her rest."

He left the ward and almost danced back to the waiting room where both Mrs. Blake and Stephen slept. He didn't want to wake them, but the energy pulsating through him made quiet waiting impossible. Instead, he visited the chapel. He wasn't sure what had pulled him to Angie's side at that precise moment. The urgency to see her, hold her hand, make sure she was all right had roused him from a restless sleep. He fell to his knees. "Thank you, God. Thank you."

"I thought I'd find you here." Mrs. Blake stood in the center aisle behind him. "The nurses said you forced your way in to see Angela. What's going on?"

"Did you see her?" he asked, barely able to contain his enthusiasm. When she shook her head, he took her hand. "Everything's going to be all right."

"But how?"

"She told me." He patted the back of her hand and left her confused and bewildered in the chapel.

Now that he knew, truly knew that Angela was going to be all right, he needed to resolve the small matter of an engagement. Angie would need to focus all her energy on healing. By the time she would be allowed visitors, he planned to be a free, unencumbered man.

CR§OBO

The hospital kept Angela in the ICU for a full week. Finally, she was moved out of the ICU and into a regular private room. A tube still pumped antibiotics into her arm, but she wasn't under the constant scrutiny of the ICU nurses. Well-acquainted from past experiences with the rhythms and routines of a hospital stay, she hardly registered the constant interruptions, the constriction of a blood pressure cuff, or the thermometer coaxed between her lips. In most cases, she knew their names, their sounds, and their floral-medicinal smells. Flower arrangements and cheery planters arrived on a fairly regular basis, and stockpiled on every flat surface in the room.

Her mother and brother stopped by from time-to-time, but never the man she most wanted to see. Where was Hank? Why had he abandoned her? His rejection hurt bone-deep. She turned inward, sparing little energy for visitors.

The evening shift nurse had just monitored her vitals and had softly murmured that everything looked good. She should be released soon. Angie managed a vague smile, though in her heart, she had no desire to return to her old life. Hank had given her a glimpse of passion. A life without that passion suddenly seemed to be no life at all. Angie had eased back into a restless sleep when something jarred her awake. Wearily, she opened her eyes, expecting to see the plump face of Nurse Carson. She lifted her head, squinting her eyes. "Is someone there?"

A form, darker than the rest of the room, took shape. A man, she guessed from the broad shoulders, covered in black.

"Hank, is that you?" Had he stepped from her dreams into the room? Instantly, she knew this man wasn't the man of her dreams. A mask hid his face. Only his eyes and twin circles of surrounding pale skin could be seen. She gasped. Her fingers crept toward the call button tethered to the sidebar of the hospital bed.

"Who...who are you?"

"Ssh, go back to sleep." The muffled words sent a chill through her spine. The overhead monitors beeped the accelerated pace of her heartbeat. She pushed the button at her fingertips. The man advanced between the bed and the doorway.

"I don't think you should be here," Angie said, frantically pressing the call button. Wasn't anyone at the nurse's station? "If you leave now, I won't scream. But if you—"

"Relax, Short Stuff. Everything will be much easier if you just relax."

"Raymond?" Uncertainty froze her in place. "What are you doing here?"

She thought she heard a muffled curse. He hesitated for a minute, looked toward the corridor, then quickly removed the ski mask. His black hair tumbled across his forehead, boyish and disheveled. He smiled. "I guess visiting hours are over, huh."

"Yeah, some time ago." She relaxed slightly.

"How did you know it was me?" He moved closer to the side of her bed. She stiffened and edged to the far side of the narrow mattress.

"I recognized your voice, and then when you called me Short Stuff..."

"I suppose you would find my voice familiar." He was so close, she could smell the rubbery latex gloves on his hands. He reached across her to tug at the cord connecting the call button to the wall socket. Gloves, why gloves?

"What else do you remember about me?" He braced his arms on either side of her, as if he planned to kiss her. She looked in his eyes, but it wasn't desire burning there. It was something else, something cold and crazed. A monitor near her bed jumped in erratic peaks. "What else, Miranda?"

"Who is Miranda?" She put her hands on his shoulders to stop him from lowering himself any closer. The pressure pushed her back further into the mattress and pillows.

"Don't play games with me," he whispered. "Do you remember the night we made love?" He slid his hand slowly up the left side of her chest. "Hmmm, you feel hot. Are you burning for me, baby?"

"Raymond, I don't think—"

"Ssh." His hand slipped over her breast and stopped right above the crest. "I can feel your heart beating, Miranda."

"You're scaring me, Raymond. I think you should leave." She squirmed to escape his touch, but only managed to move her legs back to the middle of the bed. He pressed harder on her chest, pinning her to the mattress. She tried to scream. He quickly clamped a hand over her mouth.

"You remember the night you told me you were pregnant, don't you? I had to kill you, don't you see? You didn't leave me much choice." He used his body weight to hold her still while he fumbled in his pocket with his free hand. "You should have told me that you had more lives than a cat, Miranda. I cut your brake lines, and you survived. I tried to shoot you in that warehouse and some idiot takes the bullet instead of you." He pulled out a hypodermic needle and held it upright. "This time it'll be much faster. This time I'll --"

Using all her strength, Angie pulled her knee sharply into his groin. Cursing, he rolled to his side. She kicked him squarely in the belly. She tried to scream for help, but her weak yells couldn't have carried far. He tumbled off the side of the bed, catching the intravenous line and dragging the attached medicine bag and pole down to the floor with a crash. The line ripped painfully from her arm, but she had more freedom. She pulled herself to the opposite side of the bed.

"H-help!" she cried, feeling in the dark for something to throw.

"Don't—" he yelled seconds before a planter aimed at his head crashed on the floor. The door to her room banged open. Raymond turned toward the sound.

"What's going on in here?" Nurse Carson filled the doorway.

Raymond drove into the nurse, forcing her back against the outer wall of the corridor. Angie followed them, her arms filled with another planter. Raymond quickly regained his footing and ran down the corridor. Angie tossed her planter, but it fell short, splattering over the hallway. Angie, out of breath, stumbled over to Nurse Carson. Someone down the hall called for security.

"Are you all right?" She tried to help Nurse Carson to her feet but found that she was the one in need of assistance. Her legs crumbled beneath her.

"Let's get you back to bed," Nurse Carson said, slipping her shoulder under Angie's arm. "Dear me, there hasn't been that kind of excitement here for a long time." With a second nurse's assistance, they managed to get Angie back in bed. Nurse Carson bustled about, re-hooking monitor lines and checking vitals. "Who was that man? Why was he here?"

"I think...I think he wanted to kill me." Angie replied, not sure she completely understood what had just happened.

"Well, he almost did," Nurse Carson said with a frown. "But you showed him, didn't you, sugar?" She flushed out the intravenous line and reattached it. "Yessiree, you sure showed him."

"Miranda," Angie tested the name out loud. "He called me Miranda." More out of habit than thought, her hand reached over and pressed on her chest to feel the pulsing beneath. "Who on earth is Miranda?"

Chapter Twenty-Three

"You're very lucky, young lady." Her cardiologist straightened after examining her chest. "There's some surface bruising where he pressed on your chest, but nothing damaging to the heart itself. It's a good thing the mattress had some give to it."

"It didn't hurt," Angie said with confidence. "Wouldn't it have hurt if he damaged my heart?"

"Not necessarily. When we do the transplant, we connect the arteries and veins, but we can't connect the nerve endings. They never grow back. Consequently, you won't feel pain around the transplanted organ."

"How's everything else, Doctor?" Angela's mother asked.

"Her lungs sound good. It'll take some time to work all the phlegm out, but obviously the infection has been eliminated." He flipped papers on his clipboard and recited blood count levels. "All in all, I want to keep you a bit longer, just to keep everything under observation, and then I'll release you into your mother's care." He smiled his approval.

"Thank you, Doctor," her mother answered for her. Angela buttoned up her fancy bed jacket. Cardiac patients accumulate fancy bed jackets, the way others collect shoes, she supposed.

"Cheer up," the doctor patted her leg, "you've got a new lease on life." Just as the doctor exited, her mother excused herself and followed. Angie expected as much. Out-of-earshot hallway conferences with the doctor were another commodity in a cardiac patient's life.

Stephen burst into the room, clutching a tiny black and white plush puppy. She couldn't help it. The sight of her big hulking brother with a tiny cuddly toy brought a smile to her face.

"Angie, I'm so sorry about Raymond," he said, apology evident in every feature on his face. "I never knew. Believe me, I never would have hired him if—"

"Ssh. I know you had nothing to do with this. How could you have known he would try to hurt me?"

"I brought you this," Stephen offered her the stuffed animal. "Oreo says hi. She misses you."

"At least one of us is out of the hospital." She patted the toy and set it next to her. "How's she doing?"

"Pretty good. She's knocking things right and left with that tail of hers. They shaved her where she took the bullet. She looks pretty pitiful."

"I know the feeling," Angie replied, fingering the bandages on her arm. "The doctor says they might release me in Mom's care soon."

"That's good news." He shifted his weight and glanced toward the open door. "Listen Angie, I really feel bad about all that happened. I mean, I'm the one who said you didn't know how to take care of yourself, and then I send this psycho guy to watch over you and—"

Angie reached over and tugged on his hand. "I know you thought you were doing what was right for me. After all I'm still your kid sister."

"Yeah," he smiled, "but after last night, you've proven you're big enough to take care of yourself without interference by me."

She knew his admission was difficult. Her chest swelled with respect for him, and for herself too. She squeezed his hand in gratitude.

"At least hospital security caught him last night," she said. "We won't have to worry about him coming back to finish the job. What I don't understand, though, is why Raymond wanted to kill me in the first place? Why did he call me Miranda?"

"I can answer that," her mother's gentle voice answered from the doorway. She directed a sad smile toward Angie. "Five years ago, Miranda donated her heart for transplant."

277

"Miranda was my donor?" Angie paused, waiting for her heart to give an extra thump or some other sign in recognition of her identity. However, the monitors continued their steady rhythm. Her mother walked over to the window and pulled aside the curtains. A few lazy snowflakes drifted by the window in an otherwise overcast, depressing sky. Angie let go of her brother's hand. "How do you know?"

"I've been in contact with Miranda's father for many years now," her mother said, straightening the fallen cards on the windowsill.

"You? But you never said anything."

"Yes, I know. I never told you. I didn't want you to be upset." She held up her hand to stop Angie's protest. "Let me finish. In the weeks before your transplant, all those years ago, we didn't know if a donor would be found in time. You were so sick then" She sat on the side of Angie's bed, the shimmer of unshed tears glistened in her eyes. "You were so pale and thin, every breath was a struggle and your lips and skin were almost blue from the lack of oxygen." She took a deep breath and exhaled in a whispery rush. "I thought you were going to die."

"We all did," Stephen added.

"But I didn't die. I'm still here." Angie settled her arm around her mother's huddled shoulders. Tears coursed down her mother's cheeks.

"I know that, dear, I know that." She patted her daughter's hand. "But back then I grieved for you as if you were already in a coffin. Then God gave us a miracle."

Angie retreated from comforting her mother. A cold ribbon of sorrow rippled at the memory that someone had to die so she could live. Her mother always regarded this event as a wonderful miracle. But Angie knew it to be something else.

"I know you don't like to think about the person who died." Her mother swiped her cheeks dry.

"It's not that." Angie shook her head. "I think about the person who died with every heartbeat."

"Miranda. Her name was Miranda," her mother reminded her. "I thought I knew what her parents were going through, having been so close to losing my own daughter. When you didn't write to them, I did. I had to tell them so they would know the joy they had brought my family. One letter led to another."

"You wrote them," Angie exclaimed, feeling betrayed by her mother's actions. Her mother knew she didn't want to know about the donor. It would make the sorrow too real.

Her mother nodded. "They've wanted to meet you for years. Perhaps now…"

"No." Angie pulled back. "I'm not their daughter."

"They know that. But you do have her heart." Her mother smiled warmly. Angie glanced at the beeping heart monitor, then focused her gaze on Stephen.

"Did you know about this?"

He nodded. "I knew Mom had contacted the donors, but I didn't know the girl's name until now."

Angie studied their faces, realizing anew that her transplant affected more than just her, and more than just her family.

"I'll think about meeting them," she promised. "But let me write to them first."

Her mother's smile spread across her face. Angie had to admit to a new lightness of spirit herself. Why had she avoided this subject for so long? Still, another concern nagged at her. "But what does Raymond have to do with Miranda?"

"Miranda was murdered," her mother said. "She was stabbed and left for dead in a pile of snow by the edge of a road. A stranger found her, but it was too late. The cold had slowed her bodily functions enough to allow some of her organs to be harvested. Her killer was never found."

Angie gasped; she could almost picture the scene in her mind. "Raymond said she was pregnant."

Her mother smiled thinly. "If she was, her parents never told me."

"So Raymond was her killer." Somehow, it was all making sense.

"The police are exploring that possibility right now," Stephen said. "They found a gun in Raymond's apartment and they're testing the bullets against the one removed from Pete Burroughs. Meanwhile they're holding Raymond for attempted murder, criminal trespassing, and assault." Stephen shook his head. "You know the guy had the nerve to ask me to post bail." He shook his head. "I hope they put him away for a long, long time."

"What happened to Burroughs and Wilson?" Angie asked.

"Wilson is dead. Shot in the back at the warehouse." Stephen stuck his hands in his pockets. "I was at the police station before I came here. They're thinking Raymond might be tied into that murder as well. They're currently holding Burroughs for fraud and attempted murder. Apparently, your audit threatened their cozy little scheme and you hadn't heeded their warnings."

"Warnings?"

"Burroughs ratted on Wilson big-time. They're the ones that shot Oreo, only the bullet was meant to scare you. Hank said—"

The blood rushed from her head, making her feel faint. She went still, very still, while she focused her full attention on Stephen. "Hank? You saw Hank?"

"Yeah, he was at the police station this morning." He smiled. "He asked about you."

Angie bit her lip, hoping the action would mask her reaction. He was at the police station. He could talk to the police but not to her. A cold lump settled in her ribcage, while the tiny flame of hope that he still cared sputtered out.

Stephen frowned a little. "Actually, I'm surprised he hasn't come by to see you, you being in his employ and everything. After all, if it hadn't been for his company, you wouldn't—"

"That's enough, Stephen." Her mother abruptly stood. "Your sister needs her rest. Why don't you wait for me in the hallway?"

Her brother, properly chastised, leaned over and kissed her cheek, "I'll see you later, sis."

"Raymond...a murderer?" Angie sniffed. "Who would have thought? I never felt comfortable around him, but I never suspected... He sure fooled me." Tears burned in her eyes. She'd been fooled by Hank as well. It had been weeks since she heard from him, not a visit, not a phone call, not even a card.

"Raymond fooled a lot of people. He's a master at deception," Stephen said.

"Yeah, a master." The doctor was wrong about not feeling pain around her heart. She could feel it breaking in two. Now that his problem at Hayden was solved, Hank didn't need her. He had his famous model, after all. Why would he want an invalid?

"You rest now." Her mother patted her hand. "I'll be back later this afternoon. I want to go home and get your room ready."

Angie looked up through blurred vision. Even her old room would be a welcome relief after this world of late night needles and overly familiar probes. Being surrounded by a family that cared was better than being abandoned by a man who didn't.

"Don't worry, dear. It'll only be temporary," her mother said. "Give yourself some time to recuperate before you take on the world."

After placing a quick kiss on the cheek, she slipped out the doorway before Angie comprehended the significance of her mother's words. For the first time, she wasn't insisting that Angela stay at home.

Still, that realization held little comfort now that her world had fallen apart. She curled into a tight little ball, pulling the hospital sheets up high on her shoulders, and let the pillowcases soak up her tears.

Hank hesitated in the hospital corridor outside her room, considering his options behind an extravagant bouquet of dark red roses. He should have called first, inquired as to her recovery. The same thought had entered his mind, at least a thousand times a day since he had left. But each time he reached for the phone he'd stopped. He had too many words, too many emotions to express long-distance over cellular airwaves. Somehow time had gotten away from him. Some things needed be said face-to-face and now that he was about to say them... Maybe it would be best if he just turned tail and ran back the way he had come.

"Nice flowers," a pleasant-faced nurse sniffed at a barely open bud, smiling at the pleasure. "Go on in. After the time she had last night, I'm sure she'll be happy to see some friendly faces." The nurse quickly rapped on the doorjamb before continuing down the hallway.

Hank took a deep breath, stuffed a carefully folded newspaper under his arm and lifted the large bouquet high enough to cover his face. As much as he wanted to see Angie again, he wasn't sure he wanted to see her face when she saw him. He should have called first.

"Max? What did you do, buy out the florist?"

"Max?" His heart plummeted, he lowered the bouquet. "You were expecting Max?"

The joy drained from her face. "I wasn't expecting you."

Okay, he deserved that. Her anger knifed through his gut. Grasping for a chance to recover, he took his bouquet to place on the windowsill. That done, he jammed his hands into his pockets, unsure what else to do with them. For someone comfortable with making quick decisions, he was...indecisive.

He turned back to face her, initially pleased to see healthy color rising in her face. The last time he saw her she was so ghastly pale, now she looked...infuriated.

"Where have you been?" she demanded, each word punctuated by the beep of the monitor. Should he be alarmed at the increasing tempo of the beep or be relieved at her obviously recovered strength? He glanced toward the door, half-expecting a nurse to investigate the monitor readings.

"Up until two weeks ago, I was here," he said, his feet rooted to the spot. One look from her and he'd be at her side, if she'd have him. "I was here day and night, praying for your recovery."

"Praying?" She snickered. "I thought you didn't believe in praying."

"Miracles happen to those who believe in them," he said, the words tightened in his throat making speech difficult. "And I needed a miracle."

"You?" Her lips slowly recovered from their pursed position. Her brows lifted in question like two angel wings. He longed to take her in his arms and kiss her questions away, but he stayed put. He hadn't earned the right.

"I needed you to recover. Dear Lord, I had just found you. I couldn't lose you." His voice trembled and he stepped forward, then checked himself and stepped back.

"I needed a miracle," he rasped.

"Then why did you leave me?" she asked, her voice barely above a whisper.

"I didn't leave until I knew you'd recover," he said. Now that she had provided an opening, he couldn't stop babbling. "Once I knew you were going to be okay, I figured—"

"You knew I'd recover two weeks ago?" She snorted in disbelief. He smiled, how he'd missed that sound. "It would have been nice if you would have told me."

"You told me," he said, daring to take a step closer. "You told me that you wouldn't leave me, that you'd be all right." He managed another step. "It was late at night, you were still in intensive care. You looked straight at me and told me. And I knew, right then and there, that you would recover. I wouldn't have left otherwise"

"I must have been delirious," she said, rolling her eyes. "Still," she looked back at him, "I kind of remember..."

Hank took the last step and sat on the edge of the bed. He took her hands in his. "I needed to take care of a few things, clear the way for us. Believe me," he lifted her hand to his lips, "if I thought you were in any danger, I'd never have left your side."

She started to say something, then stopped and shook her head. "What do you mean, clear the way?"

Hank lifted one of the angel-fine strands of spun gold from her shoulder and soothed it back in place. "You know that my engagement to Elizabeth Everett was a sham?" Angie nodded. "I wanted to make sure once and for all that Elizabeth's father understood that no engagement between his daughter and I was ever going to take place."

"You did that?"

Hank warmed at her slight smile. He kissed the inside of her wrist. "Of course, he fired me on the spot."

"Fired you?" She pushed on his shoulders to make him lift his head. "Owens fired you?"

His smile broadened. That one-arm shove was hardly one of a weakling. There could be no doubt; she was well on her way to a full recovery.

"Oh, he hired me again. Especially after I explained how two of his trusted employees had milked the profits out of the company all these years. But he rehired me at a greatly reduced salary, and without all the perks of a future son-in-law."

"I could live with that," she said, nodding her head.

"I should hope so." Hank saw confusion race across her eyes.

"What about Elizabeth?"

"Elizabeth has successfully completed her drug rehabilitation and is currently engaged to a photographer she dearly loves. I brought you this." He handed her the newspaper, carefully folded to the society section. Elizabeth's new engagement announcement nearly obscured the retraction notice of the earlier false announcement.

Angela smiled and Hank's hopes soared. "Good for her," she said. "And your family?"

"Aaah, my family." He dropped her hands and stood. "I can't say as they were pleased to see that lucrative financial arrangement fall apart, but they're relieved that I won't be tied down by a loveless marriage. I've worked out a payment arrangement with their creditors that will eliminate their debt in a few years. Both my parents are going into counseling and I think, even with my reduced salary, I can manage to help them out on that score." He walked over to the windowsill and glanced at the sun breaking through the overcast day. "The important thing is that they'll be working their way out of their problems." He turned back to her. "You taught me the importance of that."

"I did?"

"Yes, my independent angel, you showed me that depriving someone from making their own decisions is not love, it's manipulation. The best gift I could give Elizabeth and my parents was the freedom to make their own mistakes, and grow from them." Angie smiled and nodded at him. *So far, so good.* He took a deep breath. *Now comes the hard part.*

"And the best gift I can give you is the same freedom. I won't pressure you, or compromise you, any longer." He unsuccessfully tried to swallow the lump in his throat. He looked down at his shoes, so she couldn't read the despair in his eyes. Letting her go was breaking him in two, but if that was what she wanted; she deserved no less.

"Are you saying you don't want me anymore?" Her voice shook. It certainly didn't have the satisfied ring that he expected. He glanced up to see a shimmering in her wide sad eyes.

Before he could voice his denials, a nurse bustled in with a cart of medications.

"Hope I'm not interrupting anything." She beamed a smile at the two of them. "It's time for your afternoon meds, Angela. Can I see your hospital bracelet please?"

Hank waited patiently for the routine identification and pill administration. Angie kept her gaze from his, but seemed to retreat within herself with every tablet and accompanying swallow of water. Finally the nurse left them alone once more.

"I understand." Angie said quietly. She adjusted her bed jacket.

That she checked to ensure her scar was hidden hurt like a fist to the jaw. He remembered a night when she abandoned such precautions. His stomach roiled while his arms hung limp at his sides. He had his answer. She effectively dismissed him.

"You want someone healthy, someone who can give you children," she said quietly.

"No." He covered the few steps to her bed in seconds, desperate to make her understand. "I want you. I've never wanted anything more in my life. But only if..." He sunk down to his knees beside her so they could be on the same level, face-to-face. "I love you, Angel."

He began to pull her into an embrace but she was already there, her arms around his shoulders. Her lips met his with an answering hunger, and he poured all the longing and despair he had felt with her absence in that kiss. Once started, he couldn't stop. He kissed her lips, her neck, her cheek, her lips again. "Marry me, Angie." He pulled back, surprised that the words had leapt on their own accord. Didn't he just promise not to pressure her?

She laughed. "Yes, yes. I'd marry you in a heartbeat."

"You will? You don't want to think about it first? Check with Stephen? With Oreo?" He laughed, taking the plush toy by her side and waving it in the air. The confining hospital room was too small to contain his soaring spirit.

"I don't need to check with anyone," she laughed. "This is my own decision. I want to be with you."

"In that case, I have something else to show you." Hank dropped the plush toy before lifting the folded newspaper from Angela's lap. He unfolded it to full size. On the page opposite the society announcements, a full-page ad with big, bold print proclaimed: Henry Renard begs Angela Blake, Will You Marry Me?

Her jaw dropped. She raised her glance to his.

"I wanted to set the record straight." He shrugged.

They kissed again, this time a more passionate union of souls. The monitor overhead beeped with a strong, healthy pulse and with it, Hank sent a thank you prayer—*I believe in miracles.*

About the Author

To learn more about Donna Richards, please visit www.DonnaMacMeans.com. Send an email to Donna at Donnaweb@columbus.rr.com.

Charlie's day went from bad to worse when she tripped over a dead man on her living room floor.

Deadly Mistakes
© 2006 Denise Belinda McDonald

Charlie Foster's life morphed from shoestore owner and college student to murder suspect in one trip across her living room. Can she clear her name and find out what in the world happened in her apartment before the she's booked for murder one? Or before the real killer gets his hands on her?

Detective Bobby Allen never meant to become his suspect's alibi. Is it his sixth sense that tells him blue-eyed Charlie Foster is the key to unraveling the clues to his 'unofficial' case? Or is it the one night of passion they shared?

Can they ignore the attraction to one another long enough to figure out what the killer's next move is before they both become casualties in an unknown battle?

Available now in ebook and print from Samhain Publishing.

Enjoy the following excerpt from Deadly Mistakes.

"What?" Charlie said, half-scared and half-angry. Her empty hand clenched at her side, her books grew heavy in the other.

"I wanted to ask you a couple of questions about your friend, Charlie," the anonymous stranger declared.

Charlie raised her eyebrows, stunned–speechless. The man grasping her shoulder could overpower her. Six-one, maybe six-two, and roughly guessing she put him just under two hundred pounds, which, in turn, put him at a great height and weight advantage over her slight frame.

"Who wants to know?" She thrust her free hand on her hip.

The tall stranger reached into his jacket. Charlie flinched and considered running again. But instead of a weapon, he produced a brown leather wallet. Inside, a Chicago Police Department badge and ID said Detective Robert M. Allen.

"You're a cop?"

"Yes." He nodded.

"Do you normally follow people around? Sneaking up on them?"

"Well, I…"

"Why *have* you been following me all morning?" She interrupted.

"I have been tailing Brian McMillen."

Charlie wobbled, lightheaded at the name.

The detective deposited his wallet back in his wool sports coat.

As far as Charlie knew, the police had not yet determined the dead man's identity. The media had not ventured a guess on who he was with nothing to go on. The fact the man who stood before her knew his name frightened her.

"I followed him down here from Chicago last week. I lost track and haven't been able to find him. I read someone died in your friend Charlie's apartment. From the description they wrote up in the paper this morning, I put two and two together. I know it has to be him."

"You're investigating *him*? This Brian?" Charlie toyed with the edge of her psychology book. "Is he some kind of criminal?"

"No."

Staring up at him, she waited for him to continue.

"I'm not exactly investigating him, but I have been following him for some time."

"What does any of this have to do with me?" Charlie ran her hand through her hair and replaced it on her hip, shifting her weight to other leg.

"I got Charlie's address from the police report, down at the station. I was watching the apartment when you and he left. I wanted to ask you if he had any kind of relationship with Brian." His dark brown eyes penetrated hers as he waited for an answer.

"But why follow *me*? Not *Charlie*?" She lowered her gaze to the books in her arm.

"I thought you might help me out first. I know the police have grilled him at length and he might not be willing to talk to me."

The detective was right about one thing at least.

"Maybe you could give me a straight answer. Help me get a handle on the situation. Before I go talk to him."

"There is no relationship between Charlie and Brian. They didn't know each other."

"And you're absolutely sure there is no relationship?"

"Positive." She nodded.

"Why?" Detective Allen pushed on.

"Man, what the hell is wrong with everyone." Charlie looked up at the cloudless sky. Turning all her attention back to the newest detective in her life, she continued, wagging her finger in the detective's face. "Look, first you *follow* me around all morning, frankly scaring the crap out of me, then you tell me you want to get a better handle on 'Charlie's' supposed relationship with this dead guy.

"When I do answer your damn question you don't believe me and question my certainty. What the hell is wrong with you?" She didn't wait for him to answer. "Don't bother me if you aren't going to listen. As a matter of fact, don't bother me at all." She turned and walked away.

Detective Allen grabbed Charlie's elbow. "I am just trying to be sure about everything. I apologize for scaring you and apparently annoying you." His voice dripped with sarcasm. "But as you can surely tell this is a sensitive situation. Can you please tell me why you're so sure?"

"Because *I* am Charlie." She placed her hand on her chest. "And I have never met the guy, never seen him before in my life. I have no idea how he wound up on *my* floor," she yelled at him, all her patience lost.

Can Shane convince Jessie he's the only man for her before her stalker attempts to end both their lives?

Fireworks
© *2007 Loribelle Hunt*

Jessalyn Banks is a respected gallery owner in a small coastal Florida town. She isn't looking to make any major changes in her life, but events collide in a way that takes that option away from her. A stalker enters her life, and she has no choice but to notify the town's police chief, Shane Moore.

Shane has been trying to maneuver his way into Jessie's life for a year. Getting added to her Fourth of July planning committee is a brilliant move. Convincing her they belong together is much harder to accomplish. When her mysterious stalker escalates his activities and another woman is badly injured, events spin out of his control. Does Shane have the time to convince Jessie he's the only man for her before the stalker makes his move?

Available now in ebook from Samhain Publishing.

Enjoy the following excerpt from Fireworks.

The bells over the door jingled. Jessalyn Banks didn't look up, didn't acknowledge his presence. Even though she had called him over, she needed a minute to steal herself against his appeal. Her best friend and assistant Nancy came up behind her, her spicy perfume heralding her advance, and leaned over the desk, one hand braced on its edge. Her voice was light and teasing when she whispered in Jessalyn's ear.

"Oh, the sexy police chief showed up. You really get service in this town, huh?"

Jessalyn shot her an evil look and stood. Nancy knew it was a sore point. Plastering a fake smile on her face, she turned to face Shane Moore. For a split second, his expression was unguarded and hot eyes clashed with hers. They seemed to promise long wild nights if she would just give in. *No way, Jessalyn. Get a grip.* He was bossy and arrogant and she didn't like him much, but she couldn't help the way her heart stuttered or the flush that spread up her neck. He crossed his arms over his chest and his gaze was shuttered. "I hear you have a secret admirer."

She snorted. If you could call him that. Jerking her head for him to follow her, she led the way into the small back kitchen. It was filled with roses. Not your garden-variety red or yellow or white roses either. Someone had gone to a great deal of effort to paint these black. She'd checked—there wasn't a florist for ninety miles that sold black roses.

"They were here when you opened the gallery this morning?"

She nodded, anger at the invasion of her space closing her throat.

"Was there are a card?" he asked, a slight tremor in his voice.

"No," she said, her voice sounding gruff to her ears.

He met her gaze and his expression didn't change. She couldn't tell if he was pissed or worried. Knowing how territorial Shane was of "his town" and how seriously he took his job, probably both.

"Anything else going on?"

She shrugged. Was a vague feeling of being watched something going on? Or the rash of hang-ups on her voice mail? Until he asked, she hadn't thought anything of it. She didn't think it meant anything. There was always someone watching her in Banks Crossing and the phone calls... Well, someone obviously had the wrong number. No, she wouldn't give in to paranoia.

Unfortunately, Shane could read her like a book. It was one of his more irritating habits. His eyes narrowed and he took her elbow, leading her back into the hall. Leaning down so they were almost nose-to-nose, he searched her face.

"What else, Jessie?"

Trying to put some distance between them, she stepped away and landed with her back against the wall. She realized her mistake immediately as he pressed closer. For a moment, she was completely distracted. He wore a white polo style shirt with the city logo emblazoned on the pocket, the black of his bulletproof vest visible through the weave. It stretched across wide shoulders and a broad chest her fingers itched to explore. He smelled masculine, aftershave mingled with deodorant and sweat, and was way too close for comfort. Shifting closer, he pressed against her hips and her eyes widened at his erection cradled between her legs.

Her pulse jumped in response and she firmed her resolve. *No no no. Not him.* Why couldn't she respond to another man like this? She shoved at his chest, and he reluctantly stepped back. Breathing a sigh of relief, she glared up at him.

"What else?" he asked roughly.

"Just some hang-up phone calls. Probably the wrong number." She rolled her eyes. "Happens all the time."

He gave her a hard look. "Maybe. What about the caller ID?"

"Private number," she mumbled.

"I'll check into it. Y'all go ahead and clear out for the day. My crime scene guys will come over and see what they can find."

She nodded and turned to find Nancy.

"Jessie?"

She looked over her shoulder, ready to blast him for using the nickname but he wasn't even looking at her.

"What?"

"Get your locks changed tomorrow."

She bit back a sharp retort. *Ya think, Shane? Never would have occurred to me.*

"I will," she answered instead.

"And Jessie?"

Jesus, now what? Throwing her hands in the air, she turned around to face him again. He moved closer and caught her around the waist.

"Be careful. I'll see you tomorrow."

He pushed her out the door before she could ask why or where.

GREAT CHEAP FUN

Discover eBooks!
THE FASTEST WAY TO GET THE HOTTEST NAMES

Get your favorite authors on your favorite reader, long before they're out in print! Ebooks from Samhain go wherever you go, and work with whatever you carry—Palm, PDF, Mobi, and more.

Samhain Publishing

WWW.SAMHAINPUBLISHING.COM

NOV 0 8 2014

CPSIA information can be obtained at www.ICGtesting.com
Printed in the USA
LVOW13s2249210314

378496LV00001B/24/A